DECEPTION

MAGGIE BELVOIR

Matador
9 Priory Business Park,
Wistow Road, Kibworth Beauchamp,
Leicestershire, LE8 0RX
Tel: 0116 279 2299
Email: books@troubador.co.uk
Web: www.troubador.co.uk/matador
Twitter: @matadorbooks

ISBN 978 1789017 366

British Library Cataloguing in Publication Data.
A catalogue record for this book is available from the British Library.

Printed and bound in Great Britain by 4edge Limited
Typeset in 12pt Garamond by Troubador Publishing Ltd, Leicester, UK

Matador is an imprint of Troubador Publishing Ltd

DECEPTION

You know who you are
Thank you for all your love and support

01

SIOBHAN

After what she had just witnessed a sense of doom had permeated every pore of Siobhan's body and she had just wanted to disappear. How she had made it out of the room in front of all those people including the one she had once regarded as the love of her life was beyond her. The simultaneous shattering of the glass clasped in her hand along with vertiginous heels sliding in all directions over the spilled drink hadn't helped the situation. The only assumption people were bound to have made was that she was as pissed as a newt. Hyperventilating and retching consecutively, once in the multistorey car park she had time to ponder the irony of the entire spectacle – for once in her life she had never felt so sober after a night out.

Fumbling for her keys Siobhan finally reached the inner sanctuary of her car, her only source of comfort being that she was now free to curl up into a totally undignified embryonic position. Ripping her glamorous and tight Ghost dress in the process she found herself rocking to and fro on the hard, plastic seats of her utterly impractical Mini. Jolted from the transitory escape she suddenly remembered her parking ticket had not been paid for. Rather than waste the time accruing more expense she unthinkingly stumbled out of her car, narrowly avoiding being hit by a departing vehicle, and staggered across the car park to the ticket machine. Given her current state of mind it was something she almost desired; obliteration from her current situation would be a welcome release.

02

JANE

Jane was the personality in the school playground, the larger than life mother that would talk to anyone. She was the kind of woman everyone wanted to know; there was no hidden agenda with her, what you saw was what you got; she was gregarious, kind and positive. A person with that rare ability of being able to see the positive side to things no matter how dismal. To some this would be an irritating quality, constant euphoria can of course wear thin and begin to grate, for others however, it was contagious and far more uplifting than antidepressants.

When the demise of her marriage became public knowledge, it came not only as a massive shock to all her friends, but also to Jane herself. Of course, she knew that relations with Robert were not as they were. So what if sex had become virtually non-existent and that they led separate lives; this seemed to be the hallmark of everyone's marriage as they hit their forties. It was a case of muddling along with things falling into and at times out of place, along with the passage of time. Companionship and tolerance prevailed over those torrid earlier years of passion and energy. If Robert was fine with it so was she, there were hundreds of other things she did that occupied her time. It felt good attending Relate once a fortnight as it confirmed there was nothing fundamentally wrong with their situation; indeed, both publically acknowledged things could be initiated and worked on. For the time being however, house renovations and Robert's dwindling business were the main priorities. Or so Jane thought.

It came as a complete bolt out of the blue once Jane realised Robert's stance on saving a troubled marriage was not to adopt their counsellor's Five-Step strategy, but to choose instead to take a completely different tack, one that happened to involve a twenty-year-old who went by the name of Tatiana.

Yes, predictable, reliable, boring Robert had not only fallen hook, line and sinker for what he described as being the absolute pillar and love of his life, but he had also chosen to leave Jane and the family with no warning at all after a few days away celebrating his fiftieth birthday in France. The minute Robert left the scene her faithful band of pals (thank God she hadn't abandoned them throughout their married life) were there to totally support her no matter what. If it was trips to the theatre, tray dinners in front of the TV, or just nights of copious glasses of white wine, so be it. The unspoken code of solidarity meant that anything said on these nights stayed within the four walls. What's more, nothing was analysed or brought up unless Jane initiated it.

However, the day she turned up in the playground clad in Lycra along with the prerequisite baseball cap and a pair of shiny new trainers, her friends knew she had finally put things into perspective and was ready to face the world again. Running was going to be the making of a new her; the blubber and cellulite that had become permanent anatomical features were now going to be a thing of the past.

It was therapeutic running regularly with a group of women with a similar mindset and issues even though initially, due to her poor fitness levels, she was unable to say a word. Once she built up her stamina however, there was no turning back. Interestingly, on reaching this stage she did, however, become more aware of the subtle competition between the women – who sweated the most, who was able to hold a consistent conversation whilst running, who had the best gear or looked the most glamorous as they ran, who had the most defined stomach muscles and of course the ultimate question, who indeed was the fittest one of them all? With these preoccupations the ethos of the running group invariably altered and went from 'having-a-laugh-and-a-chat-as-you-jog club' to 'power jogging', before finally culminating in 'The Elite Ladies' Running Society'. When it was suggested they all paid subs to be in the club to control numbers Jane knew it was time to move on.

Dog-walking club sounded low-key and fun; the first thing she had to do however, was to obtain a dog. This had never appealed to her in the past; she had seen friends looking at life after their children left to go to university, exploring the new-found freedom of travelling out of school holidays, taking up hobbies and doing something for themselves at long last. On what appeared to be impulsive, irrational acts, these women came up with inspiring plans to venture into dog breeding convincing themselves it would not only be fun, but at the same time profitable. Of course what followed appeared to be complete enchantment; the tiny, doe-eyed, helpless chocolate-box bundles of fur and cuteness cast their spell and were not sold but remained for the rest of their days in the bosom of their natural family.

Jane's decision was an impulsive one, and the minute Lucy came home enthusing about how her dad and Tatiana had the sweetest pup ever, one that actually fitted into a Chanel handbag (when did she start realising what designers were?), Jane wasted no time whatsoever in contacting a lady she knew who had recently gained a litter of micro sausage dogs. You couldn't get any smaller than this; it really was a perfect handbag dog. What a shame the glamorous breeder hadn't been a little more diligent in tracing the family tree. She certainly wouldn't have marketed him as a micro breed had she known the debatable pedigree and size of one of the grandparents (there was some suggestion a Great Dane may have been involved).

When Tiger was first carried over the threshold he really did embody the term 'cute'. Everything about him was so tiny he was ten times more adorable than any battery-operated toy in the world. His legs were like little toes, far too tiny to walk on, resulting in him being carried absolutely everywhere. He was literally kept in a hamster cage as the metal crate they had intended for him only enhanced his vulnerability and size. Jane could not imagine ever taking him out on a lead as she was sure that the RSPCA would be knocking on her door within minutes. This really was a handbag dog, and it seemed that most of the running he would be doing would be on a hamster's wheel.

Perhaps this explained why Tiger had a constant flow of food to his mouth. The minute he barked or yawned things would be placed on his tongue to enable growth and strength. The novelty was wearing off pretty rapidly in Jane's books as unfortunately numerous snacks meant copious amounts of stinking shit all over the garden and house. Furthermore, she was the only one who did anything to remove it.

It didn't take long for Jane to also realise they had created, or was it down to genes, a bad-tempered, psychologically disturbed family pet that bit at every man or attempted to shag any females' legs that entered over the threshold. He also adopted the same approach to any dog with no regard for breed, age, size or sex (recollections of history repeating itself, some might say). It became totally embarrassing for Jane, but not so for the children who found Tiger's rambunctious behaviour hysterical. At first, she would laugh it off by telling people she was going to rename him Tatiana irrespective of his sex. That fell flat after a while particularly with the dog-walking girls who always looked forward to their morning ramble in the woods where they could switch off completely with like-minded people for an hour or two every week. They had found Jane's initial lamentations about Robert highly amusing; over time, however, the novelty had worn off particularly once they realised there was no variation. It had been bad enough hearing about Tatiana, but now that the dog had been renamed Tatiana all you could hear echoing through the woods was, "Tatiana, come here now"; "Tatiana, stop that"; "Tatiana!"; "Noooo, bad dog, Tatiana", and "Bloody hell, I am so sorry, girls, Tatiana is such a bloody psycho".

It didn't take long for Jane to realise her dog was becoming an object of hate and discord amongst the group. It smacked of playground politics and her child was the target. The first thing she noticed was the solidarity amongst the women. It was almost as if they were forming a literal line of sisterhood supporting their dogs on leads whilst eyeballing and scowling at Tiger whenever the possibility arose. The ostracising was gradual; it began with Jane spotting the ladies with dogs on leads rushing through the school gates glancing furtively over their shoulders. The first few times that Jane caught them up she actually believed the mumbled excuses that they were taking up extra fitness training, etc. With no further ado she also adopted the same routine although at times it was tricky depending on Tiger's mood and whether he would be led or not. The next significant thing that slowly dawned on Jane was how the ladies, once in the heart of the woods, only appeared to release their dogs when Tiger was on his lead.

Deciding to test her observations, true to form the minute she released him there followed a scene beyond the wildest realms of imagination. Every single lady in the group would start shouting hysterically for their dog to heel. Poor Tiger must have thought (if dogs had such thoughts) that he had died and gone to heaven surrounded by all these nubile bitches, only then to be thrust into the depths of hell once the girls were gathered up into their owner's arms into what appeared to be a group breastfeeding exercise. The remainder of the walk continued with the dogs like babes in arms until they reached the car with Jane breathing deeply and choosing to make no comment whatsoever.

The final straw was the following week when one of the dog-walkers gave Jane such a withering look she decided she could no longer hold back. Lashing into a tirade of the foulest expletives she could conjure up, a complete feeling of relief came over her. This moment was, however, very short-lived once she discovered a few minutes later that the poor woman in question had woken up two days before suffering from Bell's palsy, which had left her with an unintentional scowl. Jane decided to bow out at this point, hopefully with dignity, by sending a round-robin email to all the dog-walkers thanking them for their utmost kindness and support, whilst emphasising the fact the time had come for her to move onwards and upwards to concentrate on other projects.

Leaving Tiger to his own devices in the back garden until he appeared to be growing beyond realistic expectations (Was grass really that nutritious? Had Jane discovered a new phenomenon that could be included in regular dog food?), she began to realise something was amiss. Deciding to see the vet for a costly consultation about reasons behind his astonishing growth spurt Jane was devastated to discover that Tiger was going to be a monstrous size. The detailed assessment which merely involved the vet, Jean Christo Jones, lifting Tiger's foot gingerly in the air and uttering the immortal words, "This is a colossal sized foot," resulted in not only an eye-watering bill, but also a lot of hand rubbing on his behalf when mentioning lifelong treatment. Apparently, it was all down to pressure on Tiger's tiny legs which although long were abnormally thin and the accelerated growth around the torso was going to be an issue which would need constant monitoring along with probable surgery. He did not go into the specifics of the surgery needed but suffice to say Jane knew it was going to be a costly exercise.

Jane was left with a couple of moral dilemmas as far as suing the lady that had sold Tiger to her as a micro pet. Her solicitor's advice was, "Forget it", she wouldn't stand a chance in hell, as it had been a cash transaction with no proof of purchase. This was also a very emotive issue as the woman who had sold her the puppy was Lucy's best friend's mother. The thought did cross her mind that she could opt for an eternal sleep injection, but she moved on from this idea pretty rapidly however, knowing that the kids would be left devastated.

There was a brief moment when death seemed inevitable after an unfortunate incident involving Tiger devouring an entire box of Godiva chocolates from under the Christmas tree (collective present from the dog-walking girls that could have been very ironic). Despite being touch and go, Tiger miraculously pulled through all thanks to Christo Jones who, on breaking the news that they were facing a crisis point in Tiger's life, rubbed his hands to such an extreme Jane was tempted to recommend prescriptive cream. News finally filtered down to the waiting room via his nurse (an elderly woman who seriously resembled a poodle), which rendered Jane to tears at the realisation: seizures, rapid heart rate, and a body being pumped with charcoal were definitely going to result in an eye-watering bill. Why the hell in heaven hadn't she taken out pet insurance? It was a double whammy, as she also had to adjust herself psychologically to the fact that Tiger was going to be around for a good while yet.

Wasting no more time on the matter Jane pulled herself together knowing she had no choice financially and mustered up a pretty impressive CV full of totally exaggerated credentials. Thankfully it didn't take long for her to land a part-time job in a family-run law firm, which was totally liberating not only for financial reasons, but also for being able to put the whole playground domestic life to a subordinate level and to concentrate on entirely different things.

Indeed, not long after this newly-found confidence, Jane found herself a toy boy – a male au pair aged twenty-four who hailed from Romania. He was there to walk Tiger three times a day, to entertain the kids and to do any manual jobs that were needed. He was tall, and Byronic with his floppy black curly hair, sun-kissed flawless skin on a chiselled bone structure, with the longest eyelashes she'd ever seen on a human being, encapsulating deep brown eyes full of passion which didn't just end in his irises. It didn't take long to expand his childcare duties to Jane's world. This resulted in a sudden epiphany on her part that there were erogenous areas of her anatomy she had never known existed; areas that weren't just explored by his long, thick, solid penis, but by his equally long, flexible tongue. She certainly had no use for the numerous bottles of lubricating oil that had played a significant part in her sexual past with Robert.

What were also to become history were her hand positions. It was no longer a case of them being contorted into almost a praying position under the duvet; certainly not, they now appeared to have a complete life of their own. She wanted to touch and grasp everything, be it the muscular buttocks, the taut torso, anything – she was a complete willing vamp wanting sex everywhere, anywhere and all the time. Of course there was one limitation which involved two stroppy teenagers also residing in the house who thankfully at that stage were so immersed in their own lives they were oblivious to any existence of a life for her beyond their needs and concerns.

Confiding in various friends resulted in a mixed reaction. Some believed he was a positive force in her life, others, however, were so vitriolic and vociferous in their reactions Jane did wonder from time to time whether they might be wishing they could swap places with her for the life she was leading with her Adonis.

Robert on the other hand was having a much more miserable time finding himself on the receiving end of something he was not accustomed to: loss of control and horror of horrors, rejection. Tatiana really was the embodiment of things that fantasies were made from: a tall, leggy blonde with pneumatic boobs – the girl of his dreams that he honestly believed had genuinely fallen for his charm and charisma. Again, how wrong he was, for as time moved on Tatiana's idea of a life of luxury and glamour worsened. For the first time in her life, Robert's halitosis, weak bladder, love handles, enormous paunch, and worsening flatulence coupled with the fact he fell asleep immediately after two minutes of sex, began to hit home. Imagining she would be revered and adored by a man so grateful for her youth and beauty, she had envisaged a life all about designer shoes, clothes and handbags. Imagine her devastation on discovering this was far from the case and that in reality he was in fact a stingy old git who had plastic bags containing every cheque stub he had written since the 1970s and at his admission, the only designer product he had ever purchased was not for Jane, but a pair of Yves Saint Laurent boxer shorts for himself. Tatiana was well and truly pissed off.

Once the relationship ended Robert decided he had to head home as the rent on his penthouse love-pad had become astronomical and pointless now his girl had gone. It was either his mother's home which she shared with four cats and two budgies or his former family home. Although Jane was left with no choice but to reluctantly agree knowing that financially there was no alternative, she ensured that he put in writing he would be sharing a bunk bed with their son, Jack.

One night whilst Jane was out with the girls and not coming home Robert thought he would seize the opportunity and decamp into the marital bed to catch up on some much needed quality sleep; it wasn't much fun being bunched up into the foetal position on a very narrow bed every night with a jack-in-the-box hanging over the rail shouting, "Wake up, Daddy," every second. How he revelled in the soft Egyptian sheets and the good quality designer duvet made from duck feathers that seemed to contour the body. Once again, he was master of the remote control although he had a shock trying to retrieve it from where it was always housed. In its place was the biggest vibrator he had ever seen, and having inadvertently switched it on he couldn't for the life of him locate the off button. The vibrations caused it to fall to the floor, so upside down whilst trying to retrieve the throbbing rubber stick, he came nose to nose with a drawer that he had never seen before that thankfully housed the dusty remote control. It also contained items of underwear and Robert could not believe his eyes; this really was the thing that fantasies were made of. Forget Tatiana's raunchy, brightly-coloured tacky G-strings, this drawer contained the most beautifully ironed, dainty French knickers along with very sexy suspender belts placed on top of what looked like to him various forms of burlesque underwear. His wife of old would never have looked at this sort of thing, let alone bought it and most importantly worn it. Jane's style was big off-white frumpy knickers with bras that barely served a purpose; she would undress, and her nipples would be poking out of the top of most of them. This get-up in the remote-control drawer really represented classy, seductive and sophisticated stuff. Thank God she had chosen to move away from the thong approach that had been particularly repulsive; shades of an elephant's arse coupled with sumo wrestlers would immediately come to mind when he saw her thundering around the bedroom with what he concluded was not a care in the world. She was obviously changing her image and for a while he felt nostalgic about how things had been when in those heady days they couldn't leave one another alone. Reverie over, Robert finally located the lost vibrator and the off button and lay back on the goose-feather pillows channel-hopping via the remote control, to his heart's content.

It was in the early hours of the morning he got the biggest shock of his life with Jane looming above him looking larger than life in the most seductive outfit he'd ever come across. He didn't even have time to contemplate whether it was rubber or leather, he just recognised that it was extremely raunchy. All he was capable of muttering breathlessly was, "OOOhhhh, baby, for old time's sake, sexy lady, why not?" nudging her in the tummy button at the same time with his erect penis that felt like it was about to burst. Imagine his horror when expletives were the only thing that reached his ears followed rapidly by a whack across his face. "You dirty, worthless bastard, who the hell do you think you are, after the way you've behaved? How dare you! If you don't get out now I will call the police and press charges."

In Robert's defence it wasn't his fault that he had thought Jane had dressed up for him, but it transpired that this corset was a prerequisite for anyone following a tummy tuck and boob job. (Jane had undergone surgery a month earlier.) Her decision to return home that night had been a purely physical one – she needed sex, and nothing was going to stop her. So focused on this intention she had clean forgotten Adonis was away for a couple of nights staying with a mate in London. Assuming the sleeping figure was him and looming over ready to jump into action only to be confronted by a tiny, semi-flaccid member straining into the darkness crying to be stimulated, did she realise with absolute shock and horror that it was not her Adonis, but her ex.

This little incident definitely spurred Jane on to dissolving the marriage as quickly as possible. She was surprised about the pangs of sadness and regret at the demise but knew that reconciliation would be impossible despite Robert's suggestion that they had another stab at it. His main motivation, obviously unbeknown to her, was the financial implications; he had absolutely no idea divorcing was such an exorbitant business.

Jane weighed up the pros and cons – yes, they had a lot of history between them and it certainly hadn't all been hell. It was always a source of humour whenever she recounted the events of their nautically-themed first meeting. Working as a temp in Robert's family business Jane was invited by his father to join them sailing for the weekend. Love at first sight between the two of them it certainly was not. The first thing she thought on spotting Robert looking like a caricature of a sailing enthusiast in his Breton top complete with neck scarf, Bermuda shorts and stripy deck shoes, was, *what an absolute prat.* The raised eyebrows juxtaposed with the way he mentally undressed her with his immortal words, "Those need to come off," addressing her totally inappropriate vertiginous heels, made her want to turn around backwards and run for her life.

As the boat was being manoeuvred out of the harbour Jane made the mistake of offering her services. Robert's father suggested she dropped the fenders over and as she threw each bit of rubber into the sea she recalled thinking to herself how strange it all seemed. Robert suddenly redeemed himself when he jumped into action with what looked like a huge hook and started retrieving them. How was she meant to know that she was supposed to tie the fenders over the sides of the boat? Eternally thankful that no one else had witnessed the scenario, Robert was rewarded with a long snog and a quick fumble at the end of the day on the starboard part of the boat away from prying eyes. The following day it was dinner in London and the rest was history.

For Robert it was love at first sight. Up until Jane he had had two very serious, intense relationships with attractive, but very high-maintenance women. With Jane he had a laugh. She was quirky, wacky and brought out the humorous side of things. She had him in stitches telling him of her life's anecdotes ranging from her sixth-form days when having left a very prim and proper convent boarding school terribly shy and inhibited she was asked to read a Shakespearean soliloquy aloud to a class of thirty, trendy highly competitive sixth-form students. Putting all her emotion and utilising every voice range she could conjure up she launched into an emotional presentation. Unbeknown to her, however, she was incorporating the stage directions into the piece, and not only that, she had also mispronounced 'ass' and had read it as, "Each actor comes onto the stage on his arse."

Another situation was whilst working as a waitress she was chosen to serve an important client. Placing the food in front of the customer a ball of rancid gum she had been chewing fell onto the woman's food. Jane was placed in an invidious position – she either whisked the gum off the woman's plate pretending nothing had happened or she apologised profusely at the same time as acknowledging the situation. Choosing the former she had whisked the plate away whilst at the same time muttering the immortal words, "Oops, sorry about that. Would you like a glass of wine on the house?" Sadly, as she did, the gum once again fell from her mouth, this time onto the table.

When Jane became pregnant, one of her friends who hadn't had children asked what had made her decide to become a mother.

"Because I wanted to see what our baby would look like," was her deadpan response. She later announced when going outside for a cigarette, "I need fresh air, I'm going out to smoke." Whilst these random, throw-away, thoughtless, politically incorrect jibes often offended and ostracised her from others, Robert had found them hysterical and described his life with Jane as never being dull.

Years later, however, this was not the case. Celebrating Robert's fiftieth birthday the entire family and a group of his colleagues, as he had no real friends, had gone on a skiing trip. Despite being in the most amazing location, a place that appeared as though it had been sprinkled with twinkling fairy dust, finished off in a fine layer of marzipan, juxtaposed against electric green spruce forests and turquoise lakes, and set against a deep, clear blue sky with the occasional burst of sunshine, it had no effect. Thankfully for Jane the colleagues were all a laugh. Robert, however, who was in the throes of his seedy affair had come to the realisation his life with Jane was incredibly dull, showing no qualms about where he would much rather be it became glaringly obvious to all as the trip progressed.

The staff in the chalet were delightful and could not have been nicer. They were helpful, warm and energetic. Two girls Sophie and Emily on a gap year, this was their first season and enthusiasm was their catchword. Furthermore, it was contagious. Relieved that they were looking after a family as opposed to their last clients – a group of decadent, uncouth Russians who partied hard every night and assumed that room service meant the early hours of the morning. They were keen to pull out all the stops to please the new group of charming people, all but one exception who happened to be the birthday boy; Robert was at his absolute worst and really did epitomise a grumpy old man. He always fancied himself as a foodie; indeed given his life again he definitely believed he would have found considerable success as a food critic. It appeared that he was on an absolute mission however, to find fault with every meal that was served. Normally pissed by 5pm he could have been eating anything, and indeed one night this was definitely the case when he gorged himself on a handful of potpourri mistaking it for crispy canapés. He then washed it down with a glass of chilled Chablis, but made no disparaging comment at all. Luckily the others were models of discretion masking their guffaws so well that Robert had no idea whatsoever. A little later, however, uncontrollable laughter could no longer be contained when Robert sent the mangetout back saying it was overcooked, and in his words, "Virtually inedible."

The next point of drama was the development of a food allergy he was adamant had started due to something in the cooking. Jane at this stage panicked slightly, wondering whether she should bring up the potpourri and then decided some things were far better left unsaid. True to form the allergy didn't come and go, it got far worse and Robert could only scratch and pick thereby leaving his skin raw, red and infected. It then moved to his scalp and wearing a helmet seemed to exacerbate it even further. He refused to visit a doctor and instead became hell-bent on finding the source. The sheets and duvet had to be washed and changed daily and the mattress was hoovered so vigorously it began to appear threadbare after a few days. Rooms were cleansed constantly. Food preparation had to be done in latex gloves and yet the itching got worse. Luckily the guests were all chilled and barely noticed the obsessional behaviour around them. The only obvious thing was that conversations around the table hardly touched on skiing conditions, adventurous routes and life experiences both avant and après. It was all about the itch, both its source and cause all of which was obviously leading to the birthday boy's displeasure.

Feeling indeed that things were not going anywhere, and that people were not taking him seriously enough, Robert began ranting on about legal action due to poor hygiene. Sophie and Emily were beside themselves with worry and Jane initially stepped in with her sympathetic, caring look assuring them all would be fine. It didn't take long, however, for her to get pissed off with being nice and consequently she made an academic decision that the only way of coping was to drown her sorrows along with everyone else, in copious amounts of Apremont (not Robert's choice) every night.

On returning home there were a lot of relieved people on the plane who had really had enough of Robert's moaning and shenanigans. It was here also that the source of the itch was discovered – it transpired that Robert had a particularly virulent form of nits, and his hair was riddled with them. A writhing mass of live entertainment that had obviously died and thought they were in heaven.

Jane noticed his head as it was bobbing away directly in front of her on the plane, and her initial reaction was to laugh hysterically. Literally doubled over with tears pouring from her eyes all she could do was to point at the scene unfolding in front of her eyes. It was a very busy scene as Robert approaching middle age had decided the higher his hair got the younger he would look resulting in quite an impressive bouffant, obviously now being thoroughly enjoyed by the nits. It transpired that all the people on Jane's row were also highly amused and once Robert realised the source of their humour he was livid.

As soon as the plane began its descent he was on his Blackberry texting the ever-faithful Tatiana, his assistant, who had until a month ago been a twice a week shag on his desk in the office once the cleaners vacated the building. Tatiana, on reading the words *She's a complete bitch, I've had enough*, knew that this was her moment, and wasted no time whatsoever in responding with the immortal words, *Nit annihilation guaranteed within an hour of treatment. I will have it all here, love, miss and need you soooo much.* She rushed off to purchase the correct treatment ensuring that in the process she had not only touched up the roots on her platinum crowning glory, but had also shaved in all the appropriate places. Thank God she had the art of multitasking sorted. At long last behind the wheel of her immaculate car en route to the airport Tatiana was able to take stock of the situation – her impoverished days were over; her boss had finally seen the light. Lucky for her Robert was running extremely late, as retouching her locks had been a damn sight more time-consuming than she had assumed.

Robert had misjudged what pains in the arse his kids were, and instead of rushing out of the airport into the arms of his flawless, blonde, Scandinavian sexpot, he had been detained by immigration. His eldest child thought it would be a laugh hiding money in his sock. 1. Because he wanted to hoodwink the machines that kept buzzing. 2. He wanted to prove his analogy that no matter how suspicious you looked, immigration officers were merely decorative and were present solely as a deterrent. 3. He wanted a free body massage; his mother was always going on about her trips to the spa and this was a free opportunity. Unluckily for him a job's-worth immigration officer who had taken a sneaky forty winks having had a really heavy night on the lash the night before resulting in the worst hangover ever, had heard him divulging his wish to his sister. If job's-worth had known the amount of hassle he was going to have with all the paperwork (it had been so long since his particular area of immigration had experienced any security risks – they usually left it to the sniffer dogs to do all the hard work), he wouldn't have bothered reporting it in the first instance.

For Robert, meanwhile, the situation was becoming intolerable, the itching was unbearable, and he wanted out as soon as possible. The minute he had gone through the ridiculous administrative crap he located his suitcase on the carousel and was gone, no word of warning to Jane and the kids; he couldn't escape quick enough. Spotting his princess across the arrivals' hall he threw himself into her arms. He felt simultaneously sick, bemused and confused at the way she kept embracing his head and kissing it. All he could think about was whether nits spread through the mouth as her tongue, after licking his hair, had then darted around his mouth and throat. Christ, he needed to ensure she rinsed her mouth out before she resorted down below as he really didn't relish the idea of putting nit lotion on his pubic hair. The fundamental thing for him was that he needed to prolong his sexual performance with this babe for as long as possible and not hinder it in any way. Such concerns dissipated pretty rapidly however, once she had pulled over on a layby completely out of the blue and wasted no time in giving him the most sensual blowjob he had ever experienced in his life. Life was certainly turning out to be good; onwards and upwards was all he could surmise as he pulled down the car seat and had a long snooze en route back to Tatiana's bedsit. If only Robert had realised that in time Jane was to become the thing that fantasies were made of and not, ironically, the sexy, willing Tatiana.

03

SIOBHAN

I am not a good socialiser. I feel trapped in the playground with all these people mainly women. I keep pretending to be on my phone. I wish I could just merge into the ground instead of standing out like a sore thumb because I appear to be the only one dressed in jeans and a scruffy old top.

Matthew has just rung in a real state wanting to know where all the numbers of the rugby team's tops are. I give up, that poor boy. Is there nothing I can do correctly? He was yelling at me last week and my mind had switched off from his rant. It was, however, something along the lines of me taking him to some local football club dressed in his older cousin's hand-me-downs.

"I mean, didn't it dawn on you that you don't send a kid off to a football activity dressed in a pair of Tottenham Hotspur shorts and a Chelsea top?"

"I would hardly have done it intentionally; I didn't realise it wasn't the done thing. Don't forget, I had a sister, I don't know the etiquette of football," was my response.

"That's my point; you would think by now you would know. All my friends' mums do. They would never have put their kids in such an awkward situation. You weren't even around for me to tell you what the bastard had said to me."

"I seem to recall I was in the car on the phone to Granny Clarissa who had a problem with her friend Tory."

"Yeah, great, Mum, some guy comes over and informs me I'm a 'fuckin' nob with an identity problem' and you are in the car. It was my first session; you could have stood and waited like my mate's mum would have done."

"Well I'm sorry, Matthew, what more can I say?"

"Yeah, well, you are just weird. You just don't get it. You're not like a normal mum."

"What do you mean by that?"

"Mums should know how to deal with things like that and not make their kids go through these things, that's all."

"Honestly, Matthew, how am I meant to know information like that?"

"Because you're my mum and mums should know things like that."

"Okay, I've got the point. Let's move on now. Let's put this behind us. Just deal with the fact that you've got a different kind of mum, a mum that's a cut apart from your mates' mothers."

"I just want a normal mum, not some weirdo that does weird things. I mean, who cheers when their son scores an own goal for God's sake?"

"Matthew, I didn't know about the rules of the game. I apologised profusely when I did. Why don't you just forget these things and look at the positive things I do for you?"

"Yeah, Mum, I swear it's all you've ever done, it's so weird. Look at the time we went to the golf range. You wouldn't let me talk to my mate Angus because you didn't want to speak to the other mums. So I don't and that is odd. Then you walk past them and say hello which makes me look really lame. Then you're so busy asking me what other boys are there, who their mums are and all that shit and why wasn't I invited, which makes me feel great. Then the next thing you've put the money in with no bucket underneath, and all the balls go everywhere.

My mates and their mums all look over in horror as you're screaming and swearing. And cringe of all cringes your thong is hanging over the top of your jeans. What other mums are like that?"

You try your best for these kids; you want to give them the best possible start in life. You pray that everything will go well for them. Does he really think I did those things deliberately? Does he not realise I was dying inside at every single one of those incidents? Does he have any idea what it takes for me to walk into the playground and to wait for him every day to drive him home?

04

JANE

It was in the playground that I first spotted Siobhan obviously unaware that she was standing in the area reserved for the self-proclaimed '*Yummy Mummies*'. A lone figure who stood out in what appeared to be a random gathering of the animal kingdom, ranging from the goldfish lookalikes with their flattened noses and pursed lips, to startled rabbits caught in headlights all Kohl eyes and facelifts, culminating in pantomime cows with their ridiculously long eyelashes, and big, dazzling white teeth. All variations of a similar generic look, this being frozen smiles etched into ridiculously deeply tanned, smooth skin and trout pouts. Siobhan was the exception; here was someone who had chosen to wear what she felt like wearing not what fashion dictates. What were fine lines and wrinkles in the grand scale of things? Eating healthily and exercising were the only ways to improve things, and she was certainly not going to fork out money for any cosmetic procedures. Face cream and foundation were exorbitant enough.

Engaged in what appeared to be a very intense phone call, the phone suddenly actually rang, and she was able to continue a conversation with a real person at the other end. It took me back to the time I was working in telephone sales. The manager, feeling that I wasn't putting enough aggression into what should have been the point of sale, sat opposite me, pen in hand, assessing my performance. For once I was amazingly assertive, would not take no for an answer and stood my ground. He was extremely impressed. I wonder whether that would have been the case had he been aware that all the phone calls he'd been assessing were actually me having a one-man conversation with my home answering machine?

Siobhan's now genuine phone conversation with what sounded like a disgruntled teenager involving a washing machine and something being ruined was hysterical. I had indeed been down that path many times. It was her teenager's turn to wash the entire school rugby team's match shirts, something that he was not at all happy about, begging her not to dye them pink or to shrink them, as was her usual trademark. Washing them all on a very delicate wash and seeing they were intact and the correct shade of clean grey, she proceeded to place them on a delicate cycle in the tumble drier. Again with a spring in her step she piled them high in a laundry basket ready for her son to return them to school. As luck would have it however, it did not end happily. The sticky residue she had found days later in her tumble drier was not things accumulated over the years, but instead it transpired, every single team number that had once been ironed onto the back of each boy's shirt. What was particularly humiliating for her son was that the mistake was not discovered until minutes before the match began. This it transpires was the background to the phone call just made as she had rung him earlier to explain how the numbers had come off and how she would pay to have them reinstated.

"At least I didn't tumble-dry your scrumcap, darling," was her exasperated reply and at that he put the phone down.

Laughing about our sons, Siobhan and I immediately hit it off. It transpired that we had both been at Cambridge University albeit in different years, but in the same college (mind you, it was the biggest of all the colleges), so probably explained why we didn't know one another. We were from very similar backgrounds it appeared and both of us suffered a complete inferiority complex, intellectually as well as socially, particularly in our first year away from all the familiarity of home. We were able to recall mutual acquaintances; for example a naked cyclist whom we concluded was probably not a student but nevertheless always seemed to be hanging around on the campus. I was normally in the cafe (Siobhan would often frequent here, gorging herself on the apple pie it transpired, so without a doubt we would have passed or stood next to one another). The naked cyclist would make a point of not only disembarking in a totally inappropriate manner from his bike, but horror of horrors, would then stand astride backside facing the café where he would spend an age with no embarrassment whatsoever locking his bike with the most elaborate, complex, time-consuming system that ever existed in the world of bikes and locks. It wouldn't take long for the police to arrive and escort him off the premises. I guess it was one way of staving off hunger pains as there was nothing remotely attractive about a sagging bony old bum being contorted in God knows how many ways. I can't believe it didn't affect Siobhan and that her claim to fame was that throughout the entire first term of college, she consumed one of the legendary apple pies every single day.

There were other things that slowly came back over time to me and one of the most upsetting involved my favourite, inspirational, kind, drop-dead gorgeous lecturer. It transpired he was a prolific paedophile who had abused children as young as nine in a school he had taught in before becoming a lecturer. A seedy mainstream tabloid exposed him but we were all utterly convinced he was innocent and indeed we even held a silent protest on his behalf. We felt it was a complete miscarriage of justice. Imagine the shock when on sitting in the court holding up banners protesting his innocence, it was announced that he had changed his plea to a guilty one and that all he had to say was, "I am so sorry", to his traumatised victims. It was a deeply upsetting time for us all.

The one other sensation was some guy being stalked by an ex-girlfriend in such a disturbing way that he ended up leaving the college.

On light-hearted matters there was a single mother who had grown up in a circus and managed to write the most profound essays ever. They were so phenomenally academic I felt I was listening to a foreign language when our lecturer chose to read one out. Featuring on the local news she talked about how she would revise for her exams in a field. The first of anyone in her family to achieve qualifications, let alone get a first-class honours degree – she was a legend. Coincidentally, Siobhan had heard on the grapevine about me as I was the dim fresher who ended up in casualty on the first night having got a beer bottle stuck on my finger. I'd attempted to smash it but a shard had pierced my finger resulting in the need for stitches. The funny thing was the rumour that reached Siobhan was that a first-year student had attacked a love rival in the union bar. The blood stain supported this theory and it became known as the circle of hate.

The first few years of our friendship were great, rosy and comfortable. We were both in what we thought were pretty secure but dull relationships, our husbands also got on together and we had many laughs. Weekends were spent on the windswept beaches of Norfolk, particularly the beautiful desolate beach at Holkham Bay. Here the kids would take their bikes and tear through the woods suddenly finding themselves on magical beaches dotted with sand dunes, crab-hunting pools, and salt marshes. Oh yes, those long, hazy days of summer whiling the time away crabbing, sailing, swimming and playing cricket on the beach were memorable. Usually they culminated in barbecues with freshly-caught fish from the market followed by roasted marshmallows over a roaring fire and if we were really lucky and if he was in the right mood, Matthew would strum away on his guitar. Copious amounts of wine would ensue at this stage and then the embarrassment of parents dancing would begin. I mean, come on, gyrating to REM and the Eagles was downright lame as our kids kept informing us. Other days we would be more adventurous embarking on strenuous walks along the beach and through woods covered in Corsican pines to Wells or Overy Staithe, finishing up after the exhausting, exhilarating venture with fish and chips in a local pub complete with log fire roaring away.

Over time we ventured beyond Norfolk and went to France staying in one particular place, a huge gite in a dreamy hamlet on the slopes of a mountain overlooking vineyards, lavender fields and olive groves. One month there would be trestle tables on the open terrace groaning with bowls of locally grown cherries, apricots, peaches and nectarines, other months, figs and the juiciest grapes ending in the *piece de resistance* – the elusive truffles that we would all go scavenging for. There was always someone to play or talk with; in short, never a dull moment. We would spend our time running through fields full of lavender, hiding in cornfields, plucking grapes from vines, taking shade if it was too hot under quince trees, or stuffing our faces full of the sweetest ricotta I have ever tasted. We adults would light a fire and sit on burnt amber linen sofas in the main room with its rustic autumnal hues on the walls along with disintegrating brick tiles and exposed beams, drinking heavenly Chateauneuf-du-Pape, accompanied by an enormous array of cheese.

We had an incident one evening when the extensive cheese tray that we had left to breathe outside on a fence separating our house from our neighbour's, suddenly disappeared with a note in French saying, *Merci, mesdames, the cheese was delicious. It was very kind of you to think of us. Kind regards, the Pereux family*. It was fresh egg omelettes with truffle shavings instead for dinner that night.

Skiing then became our next passion. The recession hadn't hit at this stage so money was no object. We still managed to piss people off though… think Christmas Day, communal chalet, lots of people we didn't know, everyone putting their Christmas presents under the tree on Christmas Eve. In comes our group having drunk far too much of the festive spirit and omitting to inform the children that the presents under the Christmas tree were not just for them alone.

Imagine our horror being woken up in the early hours with Lucy holding a bottle of whisky in one hand and a book on good sex in the other. Yes, they had opened every single present under the tree. Problem is who brings glue and sellotape on skiing holidays? Thus resulting in the re-wrapping being pretty ineffectual. The great thing was the other people in the chalet were so miffed at our children's actions we didn't have to deal with any small talk whatsoever.

It was during one of our skiing suppers that Siobhan and I conjured up the idea of organising a college reunion. What a laugh it would be to get together past alumni who had studied at our college over the years. Where had Wizzy, the circus girl, ended up? Did Loretta and Steve's romance continue after college? I wasn't quite as motivated as Siobhan was about meeting old friends; for me it was more about broadening my social network and meeting new people.

This idea took an eternity to organise and everything that could have gone wrong did. My marriage ended as did Siobhan's, though I never really got to the bottom of what went wrong between her and John. I know his redundancy hit him badly and culminated in him moving out into a hotel and literally disconnecting himself completely from the family for a short while. I felt sorry for her, as her support system seemed to consist of just her mother who she said cared more for some adopted sister called Margot, than she did for her. Her father was dead and I believe there was an older sister with whom Siobhan had been close, but she always referred to her in the past tense. It was always on the tip of my tongue to ask her whether her sister was around, as a brother-in-law and nieces and nephews were never mentioned. There was just never the right opportunity to ask her.

With our husbands no longer on the scene I must admit certain aspects of our friendship seemed to change. Siobhan became a lot needier ringing me at least three times a day, which became a bit tiresome. It was bad enough for me having to pick up the pieces around my children after Robert left for Tatiana without having a friend needing twenty-four-hour counselling. At times when she knew it was Robert's turn to have the children she would think nothing at all about turning up unexpectedly, then suggesting dinner. Initially it was fun as we would have a bottle of wine and watch a film and I must admit it was nice to have the company. However, as I seemed to get stronger it was almost as though she was regressing and definitely needed me far more than I needed to see her.

The situation became so annoying that I decided I would say something to her. However, that particular evening she arrived with a list of all the people she had contacted regarding the reunion. Thinking this was her way of moving on I decided not to say anything. There were two main reasons for this; firstly, I genuinely wanted to go ahead with it, and secondly, I felt it would channel the time that Siobhan seemed to be spending wanting to see me and would basically get her off my back.

Initially she really did throw herself into it all and although I still got at least three phone calls a day I almost welcomed them as it was certainly intriguing listening to everyone's news. The only spanner in the works happened about three weeks later when Siobhan rang and all I could hear was hysterical, nonsensical sobbing down the phone. It transpired that the anorexia Patsy, her daughter, had suffered from for many years had been reignited with vengeance. Siobhan was distraught feeling that it was the acrimonious divorce that had been the catalyst. Sadly, Patsy had decided she no longer wanted to live with her mother and was moving in with John who was now in a relationship with some woman who owned a string of dog kennels in the area. All slightly ironic as dogs were always his pet hates.

I was flabbergasted on hearing Siobhan's news; I couldn't for the life of me think why Patsy would want to move out, her mother was always so kind to her. She was foremost in any decisions Siobhan ever seemed to make; on reflection perhaps this was why she wanted to move out. Perhaps Siobhan did have a point; the divorce and events leading up to it had been particularly acrimonious and would without doubt have taken a toll on their kids; God, what an awful situation.

Robert and I, thank God, had eventually managed to work through our issues and were on a more even keel. The main issue had been his getting back and moving in with Tatiana. Bottom line for me was that it kept him off my back but my God he was so smug when I finally ended my relationship (if you could call it that) with the Adonis. The-body-of-a-god thing was flattering initially, but over time I was becoming painfully aware of my sagging waist and boobs. I was also finding the lack of mature conversation highly irritating. Things finally ended when I decided grey matter was more important than highly-toned pecs. You could sense the relief on both our parts when Adonis finally plucked up the courage and announced that he was moving to pastures new. Surprise, surprise, he was starting another job with a lonely divorcee and her kids in the south of France. He had obviously fully researched the families he chose to work for.

Robert had mentioned in passing that he and John were still in contact and often met up for meals with their new partners. I was intrigued. What could an owner of dog kennels who according to the kids resembled an old bulldog with hygiene issues, have in common with Tatiana, the plastic chick obsessed with cleanliness, money, and image? How I would have loved to be a fly on the wall through the dinners. Robert's inevitable reaction to my immediate piss-take was to insist all the meals had been resounding successes and that the ladies hadn't stopped talking.

"To themselves or to each other?" had been my response, which wasn't met with much reaction.

The one thing of interest that Robert, who was normally reticent about discussing other people's lives, did mention was that John had had enough of Siobhan's obsessive disorders. In fact he insisted much to my surprise that the entire family had. This was one of the main reasons, it transpired, for Patsy choosing to move out. Siobhan had the tendency to control and to take over people's lives, it had become intolerable and finally the worms were turning.

05

SIOBHAN

I am an odd type, far too sensitive and worried about upsetting people. I guess that's why I have so few friends. I find it so stressful trying to please and placate. I seem to spend my life putting my foot in it because I am so bloody honest. I've had things in my life that have been unspeakably upsetting and feel I am incapable of being hurt by anyone as a result. If people ask me whether something suits them or not I will tell them so. It may upset them but surely it is better for them to know the truth? At the time, John would constantly tell me it was my honesty that to him was my most endearing quality.

Oh yes, I've dropped a few clangers. I still recall a dull middle-class, middle-aged dinner party where for a change various parents were all extolling the virtues of their children. One really incredibly boring bastard spent at least an hour talking about his children's talents and how amazingly brilliant they were. Wife on the opposite side of the table must have got the wrong impression and concluded I was flirting with the twat, so she rudely interrupted our fascinating one-sided discussion saying, "Darling, darling, do you remember that crazy dinner we went to when that guy, the geneticist, suggested we would be great candidates for gathering data on creating superior beings? God, he was practically salivating over me and asking if he could literally bottle my assets. What the hell is the term called? It's completely slipped my mind."

Looking at her pug-like, bovine, self-satisfied, smug contentment, with her whole body-image thing going on, I just couldn't control myself. "I know the term it's genetic mutation!"

If looks could kill I would have died an instant death. An awkward silence ensued until the boring twat to my left corrected me with the correct terminology.

"It's genetically engineered actually, which makes far more sense, something that I am sure will never affect you," he said glancing up and down at all 5ft of me.

John, my ex, was always used to my tendency to faux pas, indeed in the old days he actually found them amusing. The biggest one was probably the day we went to visit a very important client of his who lived in the naffest house I have ever visited. The curtains were horizontal stripes, the three-piece had vertical stripes in contrasting colours and to complement the scene the floor was covered in faux zebra stripes.

"My God," was all I could manage with my tongue firmly ensconced in my cheek. "What an amazing house, this looks fantastic, I have never seen such colours and patterns in one building let alone in one room." Thinking that he had retorted, "Don't you think it's too Zigi Stamford?" I unknowingly replied, "Ughhh, no, of course it's not, Zigi Stamford has such bad taste he really hasn't got a clue, all his colours clash, he's the tackiest designer around."

John's voice I noted had gone an octave higher as he informed me that Gary had actually said, "Do you think so? It's all thanks to Zigi Stamford." What more could I say? I had just been honest. It was a tense evening and business faltered with that particular client. Nevertheless, once the rejection aspect had passed John dined on that story many a time.

That is me pretty much summed up; professionals would describe it as having no filter. It made no sense to me at the time, I just saw it as misjudging things despite telling the truth. As a kid I was always the one who somehow messed up. How, for example, was I meant to know when working as a sandwich-maker that the work scarves issued were to be tied at the back of the neck? The only scarf I ever knew about was the one my gran wore fastened like Red Riding Hood around her chin. Why would I find the manager's description of me as being a 'joke' amusing? I don't think anyone with an ounce of self-respect would have taken this on the chin. I had made a genuine mistake and didn't expect to be ridiculed for it. Neither did I expect to be fired when I confronted the manager at the front desk that afternoon.

Yes, I should have locked up the post office bike when advised to by fellow workers whilst working on the Christmas post. No, I shouldn't have lost it completely when they all laughed and taunted me with, "We told you so", when the bloody thing had vanished an hour later. If I thought I was being amusing by putting the entire road's post into one individual's letter box nobody else did and again I was asked to leave the premises within the next hour. How diverse could two siblings be? There was me with all my inconsistencies and calamities and then there was Scarlett, the wise and stoic one.

Scarlett, dear Scarlett; I say this with gritted teeth. She was not only kind, thoughtful and incredibly clever, she was also beautiful. Luckily for her she had inherited my father's long, willowy frame with ridiculously endless legs. She also had his blonde shimmering hair that literally looked unrealistically glossy and shiny, the sort of hair that is often replicated in magazines. As if that wasn't enough from the gene pool she also had the most extraordinary eyes thanks to the Irish blood on my mother's side of the family, namely my grandmother who had the exact same opalescent blue shade. From my mother's side she was again lucky to inherit all the positive genes such as her olive skin, photographic mathematical brain and linguistic abilities. I was lucky in that I too had inherited intellect and an aptitude for maths.

Unfortunately though, I had also inherited my father's large conk and crooked teeth. I was a dream case for the local orthodontist who used me for her fieldwork when she was first setting up her practice. Typically I also had my father's massive Welsh rugby-playing calves along with his mother's generous-sized voluminous backside and wide hips, great for bearing children was what I was always told – ironic as I ended up having two sections! Shortsighted and with styes and cold sores I was not the most attractive teenager. Scarlett juxtaposed alongside me definitely created the impression that God was having a laugh. I can tell you from my perspective this was not the case.

In those days, child psychology was not as prevalent as it is now. Dr Spock's handbook was the main source of any explanations parents needed in answer to any deviant or complicated behaviour that manifested itself in their children. I was constantly being compared to Scarlett and it didn't help that my dyslexia hadn't been diagnosed so I really struggled at school. It was always in a hushed voice people would say, "Oh dear, Siobhan is nothing like Scarlett, is she?" Perhaps this is why to this day I don't need people. It was so easy to escape into my own little world where I really did develop a survival strategy of sarcasm and irony. This probably explains why people didn't warm to me although thankfully I was lucky to have a, albeit small, loyal group of friends that really understood me.

I had no feelings of resentment towards Scarlett, far from it. I simply adored her. Whenever we were together we would end up laughing. She made everything fun. There was always a dramatic story behind everything she did, which now seems so ironic. I saved her life once; what a shame I wasn't able to twice. She herself said at the time that she owed her life to me. I was her guardian angel. Why the dramatics? Well, basically whilst hanging out with a group of friends she ate a chocolate-coated nut and as a result suffered an anaphylactic fit completely out of the blue. Her mates were oblivious to the fact that Scarlett had made a mad dash from the room to the bathroom but luckily, I saw her en route as I was leaving to go to college. Looking a ghastly shade of light blue she wavered then collapsed to the floor and had literally stopped breathing. Using my rudimentary first aid skills I had gleaned from a lifesaving course, I gave her the kiss of life whilst instructing one of her mates to call an ambulance immediately. Knowing she hadn't choked on the nut and having watched a recent episode of *Neighbours* I knew it was epinephrine she needed as quickly as possible. Luckily the ambulance arrived in no time. Public awareness about Anaphylactic shocks were rare in those days and it didn't take long for a local newspaper to come out and do an article on her. Typically her photo was spotted by a model scout and before long, my sis was on the cover of magazines with her own agent and a very healthy bank balance which she very kindly left to my disposal too.

The incident affected me in many ways; in hindsight I am sure it was post-traumatic stress disorder. I suffered anxiety; terrified people I loved were going to be harmed I convinced myself that if I wasn't on hand everything was doomed. This also spilled into my life outside the family as I felt making friendships would add more to the burden of responsibility I felt towards people. Such a shame I chose not to confide in my parents, trying instead to deal with it myself.

The one thing that I really did have issues with were Scarlett's friends. They really were bloody awful. Complete sycophants to her face, behind her back they were unbelievable. I can recall at least two occasions involving her so-called friends all bitching and ridiculing her. The looks on their faces when I rose up from the same compartment on the train and just glared at them whilst one of them was in full flow was utterly priceless. Did the job and shut the bitches up. I decided not to repeat the incident to Scarlett – no point whatsoever.

There was only one friend she had that I really did like and that was Margot. We first met her at the school sports day. I had imagined a chic-looking French girl with a beret and matching clothes; my presumption couldn't have been further from the truth, however. With her cropped peroxide hair, ears, eyebrows, nose and tongue piercings she couldn't have looked more extreme, particularly standing alongside Scarlett all wholesome and outdoorsy in her tracksuit and thermal cardigan. My parents and I were definitely taken aback. Never before had we engaged with someone so hip and trendy. The epitome of cool she was a complete one-off, a rebel with a background to match her image. Childhood for Margot and her sister had been spent in and out of foster homes as her parents who were both alcoholics were basically unable to cope. Once her father died of chronic liver failure her mother tried rehab and for a while mother and daughter were reconciled. Margot was eventually allowed to live with her again and for a while things appeared to be improving. The one significant thing that was achieved was her mother's determination to apply for a bursary at a private school having recognised her daughter's prodigious literary talent. The application was successful. The school did not just award her a full bursary but they also gave her full boarding status. It was here she encountered Scarlett, which was to completely change the direction that Margot's life had been heading in.

None of the girls would ever have guessed that only eight months previously this attractive, conventionally dressed, calm, doting mother who walked into the dorm with her wayward-looking daughter had been sleeping rough on the streets black, bruised and completely off her mind. Sadly this would be the last time mother and daughter would put up a united front as literally a month after Margot started school her mother had a spectacular relapse. It was almost as though having realised in her sober moments that the peripatetic moving from one foster home to another was totally destroying her daughter's sanity and life she had finally decided that the mission was now over and there was nothing more to be sober for.

This obviously affected Margot as her behaviour deteriorated once back at school after the summer holidays. I guess with her mother permanently drunk, there were no restrictions or boundaries, and she had been allowed to run wild. Ramina, her very scary social worker, was asked to attend a meeting where she was duly informed that the school was threatening expulsion as Margot's inconsistent attendance, rudeness to staff and general wayward behaviour was no longer acceptable. At this point my parents stepped in arguing not only for her to be given a second chance at the school, but also offering a room in our house.

Intellectually Margot and Scarlett had loads in common, one of their main passions being the history of art. Wandering around art galleries and visiting various exhibitions around England on school trips they got to know one another well and became firm friends. They also had a mutual interest in recording epitaphs on random graves in local churchyards and writing them in a notebook. This activity really concerned the school as knowing Margot's background they suspected there was something very sinister to it all. My parents were duly summoned to the school and it was then they learnt about Margot's background from Ramina.

Bottom line is that with consent from Margot's mother whose other daughter had chosen to stay with her foster family, my parents ended up becoming her guardians and that's how our lives coincided. God, she must have been very pissed off on first entering our house.

There was my comment as she walked in:

"Why are you here? We're about to watch a family film", and wondering why Mum was grimacing at me. I reacted again later when Margot headed over to the sofa, dinner in one hand, remote control in the other.

"That's so unfair, I'm never allowed to have dinner there, Mum, I can't believe you're letting her."

"Yes, I'm afraid Siobhan's right, Margot, that's not what we do at home here. Please come back to the table."

Margot seemed to be hovering and we all sat staring waiting to see what decision she would make. Luckily, she adhered to our rules and joined us at the table. Mum had cooked spaghetti bolognese and it was obviously a new concept to Margot judging from the state of the tablecloth.

"I preferred that to Pot Noodles but they are so much easier to eat. Boil water, pour it and you're away."

"Yes, but there isn't much nutritional benefit to such food, no fresh meat."

Margot retorted with, "Well, there must have been some, somewhere along the way. Chicken and mushroom's my favourite. Are you telling me that's not meat?"

I agreed with Margot and didn't get Mum's argument at the time about flavourings.

Margot eventually announced to us all, "Well, it hasn't been too bad for me all that crap food; look, I'm taller than the lot of you."

Mum, trying to dispel any tension, asked what other food Margot liked when she was living with her mother.

"Well, Mondays were Pot Noodle days, Tuesdays – pizza, Wednesdays – curry night if Zen down the road was feeling generous and dropped us over any leftovers from his takeaway. Thursdays – kebabs – that was my sister's friend who donated those and Fridays it was fish and chips – we got a free portion from the bloke who sold them from the back of his van. Only downside of that was we had to eat it in the bus shelter while Mum was having sex with him in the back once the last portion before ours had gone."

Of all the responses, Mum, who was obviously not paying attention to the conversation, said, "Sweet." It was such an odd reply to Margot's lurid description that the only thing to respond with was a laugh. This certainly dispelled what could have been an awkward moment. Luckily Mum realised her absurd choice of diction, and apologised profusely commenting on how her mind had been on other things. Needless to say there were no more mentions of Margot's mother's sexual life again.

Life certainly wasn't boring, that's something I remember distinctly. Gradually, as we got to know Margot, things got into a pattern. Most weekends they would both arrive home on a Friday night and the weekend would start. However, the days she was collected from school by Ramina to meet with her mother meant that she would be returning in a foul mood and it was better to stay out of her way. Loud music and banging would emanate from her room not normally stopping until the early hours. At times Mum would dare to enter and attempt to placate her but that just resulted in her storming down the stairs where she would proceed to smoke ten cigarettes in one go. Then she would go back upstairs to her bedroom where the loud music and banging would begin again. To this day I feel stressed and anxious whenever I hear Led Zep or Bob Dylan.

How different things were on the occasions Margot was happy, the mood became contagious and we too were filled with euphoria and contentment. She would be buzzing, and so full of life, fun and adventure. Everything was one big laugh. It is not even as though we were doing anything specific, we just acted like kids with no deadlines, no timetables. We would spend hours outside building dens, playing with the dogs, climbing trees, or making dandelion chains. Alternatively we would just lie back on the grass creating theoretical animals from the various cloud configurations. It was times like that we all really enjoyed her company – for Scarlett it was her intellectual equal who was also her best friend. For me it was someone who was a lot more exciting and adventurous in comparison to my lovely, gentle older sister who seemed to be going down the sensible route as the years went by.

My dad – well, as long as his wife and girls were happy he was too. My mother was the same. She not only wanted us to all build meaningful relationships with each other, but she was also very aware of the philanthropic side to it all. Margot was almost a social experiment to her and consequently she wanted to ensure integration into this completely new life was a smooth transition for her.

A real bond was established between the five of us over time and got stronger as time passed and the initial excitement of Margot joining our family wore off. Like all families there were good and bad days, as well as times that were not great. It was all about learning to accept things and to move on with more insight and understanding.

One passion we all shared was a love of travelling and at any given opportunity when we were able to pack our bags and jump into the car, we were gone. Our long weekends and summer holidays were spent youth-hostelling in Cornwall following Daphne du Maurier's stamping ground. We would traipse through fields full of gorse and cowslips surrounded by the rugged, timeless coastline, looking down onto pretty, little fishing ports and sheltered coves. The physically exhausting days would finally culminate in picturesque, isolated hostelries once former meeting places for smugglers, now converted to cosy pubs offering delicious food, complete with a log fire and most importantly a room with a bed.

Sometimes we would choose to travel to Yorkshire, reliving scenes and visiting places featured in the Bronte sisters' novels. What laughs we would have at Margot's expense. There she was looking so incongruous in her hiking gear, moaning on about the amount of walking we were doing, all rosy-cheeked and looking decidedly wholesome, blending into visions of rural bliss with cattle grazing on rolling hills, and apple orchards criss-crossed with streams. She would ruin it all, however, by removing her jacket and stripping to her halter-neck top which accentuated her incredibly pale and scrawny back, which was literally covered in tattoos with somewhat disturbing images that none of us would dare mention. What had been fresh, unadulterated air was now ruined as a waft of smoke from her hand-rolled cigarettes would permeate in and around us. At that juncture with nobody wanting to ruin the moment, we would make our way back to various charming picture-postcard cottages, all whitewashed walls, with low beams, roaring log fires and most important of all, the ubiquitous, home-made mouth-watering food.

The memories of such experiences were invaluable and all of us would return home a little more relaxed and happier than before.

Furthermore, we had also bonded as a family unit. Instead of arguing around the kitchen table or leaving as soon as we had eaten, we started sharing our personal views on such things as life after death and what things were important to us – the list was endless.

Looking back now it is all very cringe-inducing; we obviously imagined ourselves as the British version of *The Waltons*. I can't believe Dad actually put together a flipchart for all to see, of our collective core values – tolerance, reliability and patience. What's more, when he saw demonstrations of the values listed they would be ticked off with the example noted. Scarlett showed kindness and consideration to Mum on the final descent down a rather steep hill coaxing her kindly instead of hurling insults as was normally the case. (It would normally be me telling her to 'Man up' and 'Get a move on, we are all bored and cold'.) I have no idea what people must have thought seeing this anomaly in our house. All I know is I found it bloody embarrassing.

Such values served us in good stead however when Ramina broke the news that Margot's mother was gravely ill. Understandably devastated we knew it would take her a considerable amount of time to come to terms with this news particularly bearing in mind they were estranged from one another. Dad ticked the flipchart in a subtle manner showing that he approved of the patience and understanding Scarlett and I were showing Margot at such a difficult time. Admittedly I did have to curb my tongue at Margot's announcement she wanted to honour her mother's life by taking her on safari. *How could someone who was dead and buried join us?* were my initial thoughts. I then assumed she meant metaphorically. Unlike the Siobhan of old, however, I chose to say nothing and to wait on the reaction of the majority. It transpired her plan was to take her mother's ashes with her. *Great*, were my thoughts, *I will be sitting next to them too. It is going to be bloody weird and disturbing, I can see it now; Margot will be talking to her and expecting us all to do the same.* The thought of my mother carrying out a conversation with an urn full of ashes actually made me want to take myself off and vomit in the flower bed. However, I adhered again to the core values and remained silent on the whole issue.

We left four months later on a trip of a lifetime. The dramas began at the airport before we had even left for Kenya. First our flight got delayed then just before we finally boarded the plane Margot realised Joan (her mother) was no longer with us. *Yes*, I thought to myself, *we know that, Margot, she has sadly died.* What she was saying, however, was that she had misplaced the urn and at that Margot became hysterical. The airline then had the dilemma of either looking for the ashes or taking our luggage off the plane and allowing us to disembark as Margot at this stage was in the full stage of a panic attack. Lots of men with walkie-talkies and fluorescent jackets then boarded the plane and began negotiations on what steps needed to be taken. Luckily the pilot, displaying a huge amount of logic and practical intelligence (thank God since we were going to be in his hands for the next eight hours), decided to ring through and to ask the check-in desk to check in the lounge there. Luckily Joan was located in the toilets on a shelf by the sink. Half an hour later (totally illogical – the person must have walked one step every five minutes as the lounge was seconds away) Margot was reunited with her mother.

Mum's suitcase did not turn up in Kenya which meant we had to stay an extra night at the airport; again core values were shown in that no one made any comment about the inconvenience of it all, and just tolerated the situation. Collectively we all breathed a sigh of relief, however, when it finally arrived the following day. No explanation was given, but hey ho. Annoyingly we had, however, lost out on our overland vehicle; it must have been the smug prats on the seats next to us on the plane. All decked out in their immaculate safari gear they spent the bulk of the journey communicating with one another in Swahili. Mum had struck up a conversation with them and expressed her admiration that they had put in time and effort with a 'tutor' that had been teaching them all collectively. Through learning the language their intentions were to reach out and communicate with the indigenous people. The only problem was that none of the locals could understand a word of what they were trying to say.

The prats had obviously got their revenge by taking our reserved jeep equipped with everything for self-survival in the bush. Consequently by the time we arrived at the car-hire desk the only thing on offer was a rather battered and sad-looking Ford Focus. Instantly I knew the core values were going to be somewhat tricky to maintain bearing in mind I was going to be in the middle of Joan, Margot and Scarlett for the next three weeks. The most annoying bit was having Margot's head and Joan's everything resting in my lap every time Dad drove over potholed roads, ravines and dust tracks which were appearing to be a typical trait for the bulk of the journey.

Through bush, savannah, desert and townships sometimes with journeys lasting at least seven hours it was all (looking back, of course, as there were bad days) such an incredible experience. Managing to cover eight thousand kilometres in total with no one throttling one another was an absolute miracle. Amazingly, upon seeing the prats in their vehicle complete with an enclosed area at the top to look at the animals, we just raised our middle fingers up to them through our back window once we had pulled in front of them. Karma had finally prevailed seeing the considerable amount of dust covering their car and most importantly their pristine safari outfits from head to toe.

There was nothing quite like the safari experience. Margot was adamant she wanted to scatter Joan's ashes amongst a pride of lions. As we drove into the park the first thing that slightly dispelled the sombre mood was Margot's reaction to a warthog that she assumed was a baby rhinoceros. The sights of the bush were awe-inspiring, the variance in colours, the landscape, it was astonishingly beautiful. On the horizon we saw what we assumed were deer. On closer inspection and with lumps in our throats, we realised we were literally in the midst of a pride of lions.

"My mum is here with us right now," announced Margot.

I was about to confirm this fact as she was in the urn on the floor on the back seat, but for once chose to keep my mouth shut.

"I want to scatter her right here. Dad, please can you stop?"

We all sat silently and waited for Margot to issue instructions. I was slightly concerned as the last thing I wanted to do was hold a vigil in the middle of the bush surrounded by lions no matter how spiritual the experience was going to be.

Margot then made some guttural noise and I wondered whether she was overcome with emotion, bearing in mind the terribly sad circumstances of her mother's death coupled with the realisation of finally saying 'goodbye' to her mother. (I couldn't wait for Joan to leave. Her constant presence in the car had made me feel very uncomfortable. I felt I was not only being constantly watched but also judged. Adhering to the core values constantly was definitely wearing thin as was the incessant worrying about the fear of her ashes being scattered on the floor of the car due to my leg banging against the casket.) Nursing the urn with one hand, and raising her free hand in the air, Margot made the noise again and I realised it was actually meant as a sort of drum roll preceding the event.

"Mum, you have had really tough times, I know. But now I hope you will sleep well with heaven above and below you. Here you will have eternal sun. At last you will be sleeping under the stars, surrounded by the animals you always yearned to see. I will always love you.

"Jambo Rus in vrede, Mum – Rest in Peace."

Seconds after Margot's moving eulogy she moved somewhat awkwardly across me to open the car window. I was about to launch into a tirade of respecting personal space when for some inexplicable reason I happened to glance to the right. Luckily Dad also happened to be looking right, and just in the nick of time, thank God. He started revving up the engine big time in a desperate attempt to move us on from what looked like a massive lion literally thundering directly towards us through the bush hell-bent on destruction. It was becoming increasingly evident that we needed to remove ourselves as quickly as possible. Screaming and holding on to one another, the smell of burning rubber was nauseating, as well as unbearable. The car appeared to be well and truly stuck in the sand. Margot, without hesitating, held the urn at the window and threw it onto the terrain near the lions, shouting at the same time "Rest in peace, Mum, I love you." Dad, during the 'scattering', meanwhile was still trying desperately to extricate the car from the heavily sanded area we had found ourselves in. Luckily the massive lion we had spotted earlier coming within inches of our car had deviated on another tangent. It transpired he was in hot pursuit of a young lioness who was just ahead. It was glaringly obvious he wanted to take *their* relationship to a different level. The lioness, however, did not seem quite so keen and was running like hell.

We were still stuck in the sand however, burning rubber continuing to infiltrate the car. With lions still visible but in their own little worlds it was tempting to throw caution to the wind literally, and open the windows. Logic, however, prevailed and we decided it was probably not going to be a very sensible idea. When Dad gave it one most almighty rev the relief in the car was palpable; at last we were on safe terrain and now able to take stock and to think about the sobering events that had just taken place. Margot agreed that her mum had experienced a funeral like no other.

"Which would have been right up her street," Margot added.

Food, of course, played an integral part of the trip. What could be more heavenly (vegetarians obviously not included) than sitting around a campfire roasting whole sides of beef and lamb (and testicles of some random animal we discovered one night) with rice infused with cardamom, cinnamon, star anise, and turmeric spices? Our parents would be enjoying their gin and tonics (particularly Dad who seemed to have a few every night suggesting that they relaxed him and helped him forget the awful trauma he had suffered with the cars, the sand and the lions along with ensuring we adhered to the core values at all times) whilst we sipped warm water with fresh lemon.

It was such fun listening to the sounds of life in the bush and feeling protected at the same time by the simplicity of a roaring fire (the armed guard which we had paid a fortune for, somehow never appeared to be visible). Sometimes we would be up to experience the early-morning landscape. Conjuring up a litany of colour – names that I remembered from the old paintboxes scattered ad hoc on the art tables at school: yellow ochre, burnt sienna, raw umber and salmon pink juxtaposed against what was becoming the norm – a brilliant, blue cloudless sky.

I remember thinking how perfect life was despite the circumstances of the trip, wallowing in a freestanding bath on a wooden platform overlooking a gorge watching hippos and crocodiles with elephants and wildebeest in the far distance. This was the life, what an amazing experience and how lucky we were. Life would be so bloody simple if it was always like this. Everything was so calm and peaceful, so removed from the everyday living with all its silly trivialities that left me feeling constantly anxious and stressed. Perhaps this was the life I should be living, out here on a farm in the middle of nowhere, at one with nature, surrounded by this timeless landscape.

At the same time, however, I was aware this was not reality; it would be such an impossibility to sustain a life like that out here. Surely boredom leading on to that destructive feeling worthlessness would prevail? On the other hand perhaps it could lead me onto a path of creativity. One thing I was certain about I really didn't want it to end.

But to quote a clichéd phrase, sadly all good things come to an end and over time this became apparent. It was a gradual transition for both Margot and me from one life to another and the pivotal moment came with Scarlett's decision to apply to Cambridge University to study medicine. The first my parents heard of her intentions was at Scarlett's parents' evening where they were informed she was an extremely gifted student and should be encouraged to pursue her dream.

"Why didn't you ever mention it before? It was news to us when Mr Grey spoke about it as though we were in the know. I can't believe you kept this to yourself. I mean, what a wonderful, shocking surprise Dad and I had last night."

"Mum, I was as shocked as you were, believe me. I mean, I mentioned it once but in a very blasé way. We were also made to fill in a questionnaire about whether we were thinking about university and what subject to study. I would never in a million years have expected this though."

This opened the floodgates as far as Mum was concerned. Nobody in the family was a doctor; in fact it would be the first time a family member had attended university. To be combining the two was something fantasies are made of. Clarissa was naturally hell-bent on following this through and supporting Scarlett one hundred per cent. Paradoxically I was so proud but at the same time realised that a precedent had been set and anything Margot and I did was going to have to be significant.

Clarissa, with a new goal in her life (Margot having been the previous one), began mustering all her energy and time into supporting Scarlett with anything that could assist her application. This meant therefore that suddenly the time she had to invest in both myself and Margot began to dwindle. It came as a relief initially as up until now she had always been so involved in everything. The main focus had been all about ensuring the smoothest transition for Margot into a new, fulfilling life, but as Margot herself said, at times it was too much. Instead of voluntary work and pursuing new interests, Scarlett's decision couldn't have come at a better time.

Margot decided I needed to be initiated into the world that would have been hers had Mum and Dad not stepped in. Intrigued on one hand but terrified on the other, curiosity got the better of me. I had assumed it would be former friends of her mum's, but the friends Margot meant were amphetamines, weed, cheap cider and casual sex. It took a long time for me to loosen up and become involved, but over time it did become a perverse norm, one done, however, subversively, which was to me where the excitement lay. It was all about avoiding knowledge from others and luckily Clarissa, Ben and Scarlett had no idea. It was a guilty secret both Margot and I shared. Returning from events in the early hours of the morning and not emerging until lunchtime looking like complete wrecks I was shocked that Mum, Dad and Scarlett didn't suspect things were not as they seemed. Did Clarissa honestly believe we had been to the cinema or to 'tame house parties'? If so, I couldn't believe how naive they were.

I guess subconsciously I was willing them to discover our parallel life. However, ignorance prevailed and as a result a growing anger festered away inside me. The drugs I was taking along with Margot's constant audible stream of consciousness did nothing to alleviate my mood positively. The catalyst was in the early hours of the morning having smoked weed I listened to her explaining her life story to some random guy.

"I mean, I am sure I was perfectly happy, I loved my mum and yet they decided I couldn't be happy living the way I was. So what happens? This 'lovely' family take me in. Don't get me wrong, I love them, but what pisses me off is the fact I've been made to feel inferior, I will never be as good as them. I am low-life made good all because of them."

I recall my comments to her as though it was yesterday. "Yes, but, Margot, the way you were living was not acceptable for an animal, that's what Ramina described your mum's place as being. You probably wouldn't have survived beyond a certain age."

"Bollocks, 'course I would have done. I am just pissed off. I mean, one minute Mum can't do enough for me then next thing you know Scarlett gets this whole thing about wanting to be a doctor. And that's it as far as you and I are concerned; Mum's no longer interested."

Since when had my mum become her mum? That is what really hit me. Why was I suddenly in the same category as her? This was bloody crazy. I really was lost for words. There were many more conversations that followed on from this one and the bulk of them were about how Clarissa had abandoned us both. Margot kept switching emotions – one minute it was all about how wrong my parents were, then it was my mother being the whole reason for her existence.

"My mum's the most important thing in my life, that's the bottom line. I am all she has."

I assumed she meant her natural mother but then it suddenly dawned on me this was not the case.

"We have this bond that she doesn't have with you and Scarlett. She knows I have suffered and she has saved me from everything."

There was no logic to what she was saying and I knew she was stoned; I was, however, shocked. Her attitude was beginning to put things into perspective for me and I was beginning to realise she was a scheming manipulator who was only interested if things were going her way. The final nail in the coffin was when she let slip my parents had adopted her.

"Yeah, about two years ago. It wasn't a big deal. Mum just asked if I wanted to be, I said 'Yeah' and that was it I guess."

I was absolutely devastated on hearing her words. Did Scarlett know, I wondered? Why the hell hadn't our parents confided in us? Surely it should have been a joint decision? Why this cloak and dagger act? It just didn't make sense. If Margot had been my friend would my parents have adopted her? I needed to find out whether Scarlett was aware of the situation. If so then I was without a doubt the scapegoat in this sordid, awful affair.

Could I be bothered to confront my parents? At that moment in time not really; I just retreated into myself feeling increasingly resentful towards them all particularly when Scarlett confirmed Margot's adoption, which meant I was the only one kept in the dark. As my inner turmoil increased I began changing my image. Dyeing my naturally mousey hair to black was my first move. I then graduated to very pale foundation, heavy Kohl-rimmed eyeliner and black tops and leggings. Clarissa and Ben voiced their disapproval which I enjoyed as it guaranteed some, albeit temporary, attention.

Armed with the knowledge that Margot was a permanent fixture in our lives her novelty began wearing off. It was all too close for comfort and as a result I began nurturing other friendships. My new crowd, although still druggy and alternative, were different in that they were able to maintain everyday life, including attending college. Margot was following a life that I no longer approved off which wasn't helped when I discovered that she was carrying on with an older, married man. Why the hell would she stoop so low? Was I jealous because she had someone who lavished her with love and attention? Who knows? I just saw it as her being destructive. It was a case of whatever Margot wanted, Margot got. A prime example of this was her becoming part of our family.

The final *coup de grace* in my eyes, but a *piece de resistance* in Margot's was when it became apparent she was with child. Of course, I gathered this through innuendos and an analysis of furtive whispers that appeared to be taking place between both her and Mum. Did she really think I thought she had indigestion as she sat on the sofa with a wasted look on her face, rubbing her abdomen and trying to catch Clarissa's eyes throughout the evening?

Ramina ended up visiting the house on one occasion looking frazzled and concerned. Mum ushered her into the kitchen where I was told in no uncertain terms that I had to leave. Margot was lying on the sofa, one arm across her abdomen, her left eye fixed on me as I left the room, with an extremely smug expression on her face, looking very much like the cat that had succeeded in getting the cream – her master plan had succeeded and all attention was focused on her. Ramina, however, looked decidedly unimpressed as she sat down on the empty chair beside her. All I managed to gauge was that an issue had arisen due to an unplanned pregnancy of a dependant.

Life in the house continued, however neither Mum nor Dad realised that Scarlett and I were totally aware of Margot's predicament, and nor did we want them to. The less attention she had as far as we were concerned the better for all. It was nauseating hearing what came out of her mouth. Scarlett came running to my room telling me of how Margot had whispered, "I can't believe you are going to be a grandma, Mum, I am giving you your first grandchild," to MY mother. We chose to take a passive-aggressive stance ensuring that any time babies were mentioned we switched off the television or expressed our disdain in no uncertain terms.

Thankfully a few weeks later the course of events changed; Scarlett's application was accepted for Cambridge and she was asked to attend an interview (not however at the college of her choice) and two days later the commotion we heard in Margot's bedroom was (we learnt later), a miscarriage. Her words resonated through the house.

"Scarlett doesn't achieve something for the first time in her life and look what happens, I have to take on the stress and now you've lost your grandchild!"

06

MARGOT

The tall Amazonian brunette picked her way through the labyrinth of corridors at the supermarket's main office. It had been another hard day as a buyer and her boss was not at all happy. Two of her suppliers had let her down; she had been relying on a huge consignment of bananas that had ended in disaster. The importing company was unable to honour the shipment as all the bananas were rotten on arrival from Jamaica to the port in England. It didn't help that the managing director of the company was a guy she had been sleeping with. It was also a complete pain as this wasn't the first time it had happened which meant questions and warnings were going to have to be issued. It hardly seemed two minutes ago when she was fending off the press who were hounding her for news on the spider found in a suburban home in Surrey that had hitched a lift with a container full of bananas from the Ivory Coast.

"Like I bloody well need this." She was still reeling from the bizarre handwritten note she'd received from Siobhan through the post via her work. It was a complete unwelcome jolt from the past and brought back memories that were no longer welcome in her life. She had learnt over time to dismiss most things from her past with perhaps one exception, her dearest Clarissa.

Driving home that evening after all the issues she endured during the day, most notably the letter, she felt a surge of relief knowing she was returning to her sanctuary. This to her was a symbol and reminder of all that she had achieved by herself over the years. At times she almost had to pinch herself to believe that this was reality.

Margot had worked bloody hard for this; nothing had been handed to her on a plate, far from it. She thought back to the nightmarish task she'd had to endure in winning over and finally convincing the planning committee. She wouldn't have wished it on her own worst enemy; it had been an utterly exhausting ordeal and one hopefully never to be repeated. How ridiculous that nasty, ordinary little men in dull, boring jobs with their boring brown suits can exert such power. Her contact, the main planning councillor, was definitely elevated to superhero status not through his own personal charm and charisma, but through her networking skills nurtured over the years. Her powers of persuasion resulted in him receiving an infinite amount of social engagements all of which she duly attended as his partner. Alongside this she also threw in a few unofficial liaisons (very tame ones that were over thankfully in minutes; he was very easy to satisfy).

When, however, the official paperwork was finally signed, sealed and delivered she was able to breathe a huge sigh of relief. Not only would she now be able to pull down a substantial part of the structure and rebuild it in the style she wanted but she was also now let off the hook with regard to the numerous social functions. She found herself wondering at the same time how the councillor was going to cope with his significantly depleted social life.

Pushing her remote-control button having driven off the main road onto an undulating windy track she came up to a pair of huge wrought-iron gates that began opening. Before her were hundreds of trees arching from one side of the road towards the other so thickly intertwined they had created a magical illusion of meeting in the middle to form an endless vaulted ceiling. It happened to be one of those lovely elemental evenings when the transition from noon to dusk was beginning to happen with the sun thinking about setting.

Driving through and entering into her enchanted garden she deliberately wound down the window knowing she would be greeted with the pungent, sweet aroma of roses. The ramifications of a fairy-tale story were all around her. Surrounded by a myriad of colours greeting her, glowing with the evening hue, flowers were literally blooming in front of her eyes without effort in the dark green of the yew hedges. Juxtaposed with this were the beautiful tended lawns looking like flawless emerald-green carpets and there, taking centre stage, the absolute jewel in her crown, the thing that she had sweated blood, sweat and tears to attain – her beautiful Queen Anne-style Georgian house. She looked with pride at the front of this majestic building with its central bay of three windows each showing off the hand-woven silk and taffeta curtains she had commissioned from India on her last business trip. *A good choice,* she thought as she observed them from that angle. They had only been hung recently yet looked as though they had been there forever although it had been a lot more complicated than she had first envisaged. Choosing these had been a real labour of love what with getting the exact colour she wanted from the magazine supplement but ultimately, she was glad she had prevailed as they were a perfect match.

Scattered ad hoc, but artfully placed, were heirlooms and antiques she had collected from various fairs all around the world over the years. This time-consuming passion had also been worth it. *Wow*, was all she could think, who would have thought that she would ever in a million years have achieved such an amazing property as well as such an affluent lifestyle like this, bearing in mind where she had been brought up? Antique then either meant things worth nicking or what someone would be described as looking like following on from years of solvent abuse.

What was inside was also of great significance. She knew that when she arrived home he would be there waiting for her, hanging on her every word, a glass of chilled white wine or perhaps a champagne (she couldn't remember what was in the fridge when she had taken the milk out for her coffee that morning) in his hand, followed by a massage.

God, does it get any better than this? Well, it did before that bloody letter from bloody Siobhan.

Her thoughts immediately turned back to her Adonis, her whole body tingling at the thought of his lithe, muscular body. Here she was, a woman in her late forties, with a twenty-nine-year-old as her lover. Luckily, she had the taut body of a woman years younger, there were no complications in her life, and if she wanted to go to the gym so be it, she didn't have to answer to anyone. She had no idea how long they would both be seeing one another and certainly did not want any serious commitment. Monogamy was anathema to her as far as she was concerned. If she had wanted children perhaps she may have had different views on marriage and she knew that sometimes she took her aversion too far. Remembering how she felt on learning from an elated Clarissa through a phone call that Siobhan would be having the first grandchild in the family, she couldn't help thinking to herself, *God, you poor cow, that's the end of your life and it's hardly begun.* Subconsciously she also ruminated on the fact that had things gone to plan she would have had the first grandchild.

Margot's baby was her house; she loved it more than anything. Visualising the state it was in during the early days when she first clapped eyes on her newborn seemed an age away. Back then it was literally a dilapidated wreck of a place totally uncared for and unloved. Pigeons had come through the broken windows and made their nests in the rafters. There were great gaping holes in the ceilings, plaster hanging down, beams exposed; it was a fine example of subsidence and neglect at its most extreme. You could stand underneath the lowest floorboards and look directly up to the attic. Rats and mice had gnawed the skirting boards and cornices. Cobwebs adorned every corner of every wall, beautiful, intricate designs spanning infinite distances throughout the house. It really was a house in decay and on seeing it, despite the potential, she just didn't feel she had the energy or imagination to take it on. It was Clarissa, dear Clarissa, who really had inspired her and given her the vision.

"You will regret it if you don't, believe me. This is a bargain, snap it up now," were Clarissa's wise words as she walked around the estate with Margot.

It really was going for a song as the guy who had inherited it from his great-aunt had envisaged knocking it down and building at least six houses on the land. When permission was refused the only option he had was to get rid of it all, the quicker the better, as maintaining the land was turning out to be a crippling financial burden. Margot's cash offer with no estate agent's fees was a godsend. A few days later she was lady of the disintegrating manor.

How far I've come, when I think back to those grim times when it was Mum and me in bedsits and squats. We never knew where our next meal was coming from. It all depended on whether she was on a bender or not. Good days it was Pot Noodles or takeaway fish and chips, bad days a bag of crisps or stale bread. The foster homes were okay, a bit hit and miss. Food was normally awful and in most of the places there was always a feeling of being an outsider, an interloper in the house particularly if the family had their own kids. My constant fantasy was sitting in front of a fire drinking hot chocolate and playing board games with a family that really wanted me there. Who would have guessed that very thing would happen once I moved in with the O'Brien family? I had dear Scarlett to thank for that; if it hadn't been for my friendship with her along with her compassionate heart none of this would ever have happened. I would have continued at school with no knowledge that beyond my social circle and defunct family there was another world that was almost beyond my wildest fantasies.

Admittedly there were times when Scarlett drove me beyond the point of distraction, almost nuts, because she was so bloody perfect. You could never get really mad with her, however, as she was oblivious to the effect she had on people. It was just this annoying knack she had of literally turning everything to gold. In practical terms, if ever she was in a concert, play or debate you just knew she was going to sail through it and not only that, anyone who saw her in action would come away swearing they had seen a star. Perhaps that is why over time I came to bond with Siobhan. It is a harsh thing to admit but it is almost as though we knew neither of us would ever be able to match up to Scarlett's level. Mutually unmotivated and disinterested in school, we were like peas in a pod. It wasn't about hating the work, it was all the crap around the process, all the petty rules and regulations which were totally superfluous to everything. Siobhan's disruptive behaviour in lessons probably also came from the teachers' constant presumptions and comparisons to Scarlett, which were always detrimental. We bonded because I found her antics amusing whereas the other girls in the class didn't, choosing instead to ostracise us, which therefore strengthened our bond. We were the first to drink alcohol, the first to smoke and in our opinions, we were by a long shot the coolest chicks in the school.

Our friendship, like most close friendships, was not without its issues and we were constantly falling in and out with each other. I would have loved Clarissa to have been my blood mother (not feasible, I know). There's always been a strong bond between us and ultimately, I really believe that Clarissa cares about me the most. Looking back this has to be why Siobhan and I began to fall out. It was a reluctant acceptance on her part that due to all my issues, I was centre stage. Ironic really as deep down I knew it was Siobhan who was suffering, but hey ho, that's what happens in life. It is all about the survival of the fittest.

Looking back to when things started to go sour I recall an incident where tension did manifest in what seemed a comical way. Having sat for biology O level Siobhan remarked on how embarrassing it had been writing penis and testicles as one of the answers. Flummoxed, as biology was one of my best subjects, I asked her in more detail about her answer. It transpired the question 'Name the horny area on the human anatomy' was not what she had been reading about in the soft porn books she devoured, but was, of course, the toenail. Laughing at her expense I brought it up over Sunday lunch with Clarissa, Ben and Scarlett. Siobhan, I could tell, was absolutely livid with me.

A few weeks later, however, she got her own back and I was left feeling gutted. Basically, a family friend looking at a mother and daughter photo shoot that had been taken of Clarissa and Scarlett for a magazine commented on how alike we sisters looked, particularly Scarlett and myself, which really pleased me. I had recently taken a gamble and had dyed my hair from peroxide blonde to a far more natural shade and felt fantastic with my new image. Siobhan, however, immediately interjected saying how bizarre the comparison was bearing in mind her sister and I were nothing alike and why would we be, bearing in mind I was not a relation. God, that hurt. I could see Clarissa, Scarlett and the family friend were stunned into silence. I just had to leave the room. It was a hideous situation and not one I want to dwell on. A few more incidents similar in nature to this idea that I was no relation continued and each time I suffered like hell inside. I'd convinced myself I really was an integral part of the family and Clarissa herself kept reiterating that to me and I really was beginning to believe her.

Things began to change, however, when Scarlett decided to start applying to universities. Every day one prospectus after another would arrive through the post and the two of them would spend ages painstakingly studying them with a fine-toothed comb. Not only that, they then spent virtually every weekend visiting them. Siobhan and I were left with Ben and his inedible cooking. I was barely talking to her so mealtimes were silent and I just wanted to escape as quickly as I could. The great thing was Ben had no idea and he wasn't bothered where we were going or what we were up to. The flipchart with the core moral values became a message chart listing who was out during the week. Even that came to a stop as Siobhan and I were never in.

She was out partying hard with some pretty dodgy people, smoking, taking drugs and basically getting off her head on a regular basis. I was doing the same thing but with a much harder-core group. Our drugs were the real thing. The only problem was my nightmares and paranoia returned big time and Clarissa was no longer available to support me through them. That pissed me off as I felt she wasn't stepping up to the mark, bearing in mind that was in the pledge when they finally adopted me.

Looking back now I realise what a screwed-up fruitcake I was. My main mission in life was bringing Clarissa back into mine; Ben was superfluous, he just came in the package. If it meant self-harming would make her stand up and notice, well, that was the approach I would take and boy, I did some good ones. It alleviated the stress I was under and made me feel a lot more in control. Luckily it didn't take too long for Clarissa to notice; coincidently this coincided with the slowing down of the university applications that had now reached a shortlist.

Showing concern for my self-harming ensured that Clarissa was once again with me at all times. Amazingly, Siobhan was still continuing with her antics undisturbed. Clarissa was not happy however, with the dyed hair and new image, but what could she do? It was easier to turn a blind eye than confront the situation head on, perhaps?

I then got the break I needed. It transpired that my late-night antics and relationship with my fancy man had been brought to her attention (some do-gooder had apparently spotted us snogging in a cinema foyer – of course, we were having sex behind closed doors but they weren't to know). What I didn't get was why I was the focus and not Siobhan and this is what made me realise I was more important to Clarissa.

On the other hand, perhaps I was seen as a real-life case study, part of a social experiment, the practical part of her theoretical social psychology course she had been studying part-time at a local college. As far as she was concerned she had saved me from a predictable fate where I would have probably ended up with at least three children all with different fathers living on benefits and having some form of addiction.

Discovering I was pregnant was one of the best days of my life. Despite the protestations from that bitch Ramina and the rest of the social services team that I should have an abortion, I felt fantastic. The icing on the cake was that Scarlett and Siobhan had no idea about my condition; it was just mine and Clarissa's secret. I may not have been Scarlett with her golden touch but my baby would be the firstborn grandchild. I was touched that Clarissa really did care about my well-being and equilibrium, which is the last thing that would have occurred to my own mother.

Thinking back now, Clarissa may have been a wonderful mother to me and yet closer to home her mothering skills were crap. It must have been bloody difficult for Siobhan, firstly having Scarlett as a sister then having me infiltrating her life; I am sure there would have been no family discussion. One minute I wasn't there; next thing, I've got a bedroom in the house and am calling Clarissa 'Mum' as though it was the most natural thing in the world.

To me all my fantasies were answered the day I entered their family – comfy bed, warm meals, hot chocolate on tap, clean clothes, ready-made entertainment with two sisters and a wonderful, supportive adult who actually cared.

Scarlett was happy as it meant her best friend was with her twenty-four hours a day, Ben probably didn't even notice but was happy Clarissa had a mission and then there was poor, dumpy Siobhan. Perhaps that's why she was forever changing her image; one minute she was blonde, then natural, then an out and out gothic with her dyed black hair, white powdered face, and thick black eyeliner. Her conversations alternated with her different images; sometimes she was happy and normal. In her Goth stage, however, it was all about being on the dark side, which really freaked me out as I assumed it would mean Clarissa's attention would deflect from me onto her.

07

FRANK

God, what a bloody holiday, all about placating the miserable wife and two moody teenagers." They'd gone to Sri Lanka for a family holiday to chill and unwind from all the turmoil of redecorating their home. The wife had claimed it would take at the most a couple of weeks; well, it took a lot longer than that because suddenly little building projects had emerged, things that needed refitting and revamping. Trivial things, he noted, that had not only caused the costs to mount up, but had also taken up a ridiculous amount of time so that it had become akin to living on a building site for some time.

When he had spotted their present destination in the glossy brochure with the all-inclusive meal, sport and alcohol programme, as well as an infinity pool and rooms directly on the beach, they all agreed it was an offer that could not possibly be ignored and by the end of the day he had booked the holiday for them all. From the minute Frank arrived at the hotel he made his way down to the pool where he collapsed on a sunlounger deciding to set the precedent there and then, reading his sports magazines (even his own family were confused at the subject matter bearing in mind the only sport he seemed to participate in was lifting beer or wine adeptly to his mouth). With his tight swimming trunks and pale, flabby body he was not far off resembling a huge beached whale. The mirrored glasses he had discovered in the back of his cupboard were just what he needed. Trendy and cool they also enabled him to ogle young (preferably over the age of twenty-one – younger ones were far too complicated), firm-buttocked ladies in their bikinis, all creeds and colours, whilst giving the impression to his family he was actually engrossed in his stimulating reading material. The sporting magazines had been next to *Playmate of the Month* magazine which he had been on the verge of buying before the wife scuppered his plans and he had to choose the neighbouring magazine. He was now grateful this had happened as at least he had a socially acceptable stage prop which enabled him to look discreet when staring.

Things were not bad at all. The only fly in the ointment as the holiday wore on was the fact Frank had to set his alarm clock at some unearthly hour every morning in order to ensure prime position on the sunbeds in between the bar and the toilets, directly near the pool. This surety of positioning entailed placing all his worldly possessions, i.e. his out-of-date suntan lotion, sunglasses, swimming trunks, and towels on the chosen sunloungers. Imagine his horror on the fourth day of his routine on returning from breakfast to discover his belongings had not only been discarded to the ground, but lying like a fellow beached whale on his reserved sunlounger was a big fat European enjoying the novelty of stretching his right hand with plastic cup attached directly to the beer barrel whenever it took his fancy.

Understandably incensed, Frank took no time in duly informing the European that he had broken a law, which came under the misuse of non-personal possessions. The European immediately sprang into action with no embarrassment at his hefty buttocks wobbling in his thong, a wobble that increased as his voice reached a shrill crescendo. "*Ya*, we are in Sri Lanka, we are not in Britain. *Ya*, it is not British law all over the world. This law does not exist here. I can lie on this bed whenever I vant. You have no rights to it. I will call the management if you don't remove yourself from my space."

For once Frank had nothing more to say on the matter and was relegated to a lone lounger by the pool with no shade resulting in a very burnt body.

Perhaps using the out-of-date suntan lotion was not such a great idea after all, were his only thoughts as he sat down to dinner that night feeling very uncomfortably hot and self-conscious as his face had turned a vivid shade of scarlet.

The following morning when he came down to bag his beds he noticed that the moron (he could only guess it would have been the European), had put really personal items on all four of the sunbeds usually reserved by Frank: dirty underwear for starters along with a nasty looking snack that looked somewhat like a fossilised piece of dog shit. Frank decided that although he had the stomach figuratively he could not stomach the idea metaphorically of removing it. The same lone seat with no sun shade was his only option again, however, he was able to console himself at that point; it was not the end of the world as this too was in very close proximity, if anything a tad closer, to the bar. His innovative strategy for ordering drinks had taken a different stance; this time it was a case of raising his thumb and eyebrow in the air, to which an attractive, busty local girl would run over and fill his cup to the brim. The poor girl had been misinformed and had wrongly assumed Frank was filthy rich, hoping for a generous tip at the end of his sojourn. She couldn't have been further from reality. With her willingness to please, Frank was able to keep an ever-flowing plastic glass consisting of rum and Coke from 11am until 1pm which meant by lunchtime his wife and teenagers who had been at the spa all morning spending a fortune on various treatments, arrived to find a very pissed, even more sunburnt but jovial Frank.

Next thing on the agenda was his pre-order of fresh curried lobster along with a plate of steaming mussels, jasmine rice, and poppadums with fresh mango chutney, all to be washed down with a bottle of Chablis. Thinking ahead he had ensured this was on ice from 11am as the Riesling the day before had been like mulled wine. After the delicious meal and having collapsed on to a choice of any sunlounger (at this stage people had moved on), Frank bitterly regretted tempting fate with his spontaneous statement to his family, "Well, folks, this is the life. You can't get much better than this, can you? Are we in paradise or are we not?"

Judging from the looks on their faces he immediately regretted his statement as he sensed they were not on the same vibe as him.

"Frankie, love." The minute Jackie addressed him in this way he knew she was dissatisfied about something. "We are so bored, we've got cabin fever. We need to get away from the hotel, love. We want to see some local life, some indigenous people perhaps or animals."

"Yeah, Dad, there's nothing to do and me and Jess are bored. You're all right cos all you seem to want to do is eat, drink and sleep."

Frank looked at his kids' faces looking at him as though he was the pantomime villain. It broke his heart the way they spoke to him these days. There was not one bit of respect or love anymore. Jess had always been his little princess. She used to adore him then overnight it seemed she had turned into this ungrateful, aggressive teenager who really felt that his purpose in surviving was to keep her happy.

He found himself thinking of all those hockey and netball matches he had attended because she wanted him there. Then there had been all those Saturday nights as she got older and was out carousing on the town discovering boys and booze with good old Dad at her beck and call ready to collect her at any hour she decided she wanted to come home. He really was the centre of her universe then but now she barely noticed him and when she did she was so bloody rude. Likewise his son as a toddler had various food allergies and Frank had spent hours concocting meals that were safe but tasty for him. There was also the time he bought Sam's first favourite football team's kit complete with signed boots. Frank had been to every football and rugby match his son had ever played in no matter what the weather. The only time there had been a major dispute was the year he was acting physio for the team. How was he to know Jackie had misspelt his new role which was emblazoned on the back of his tracksuit jacket? Running onto the pitch for the cup final, perhaps he wouldn't have whooped and cartwheeled quite as much had he known the letters actually read 'Psycho'.

Now, years later the bloody little twat was barely talking to him and in the rare times he did it was though he was a piece of shit. The two of them probably had absolutely no recollection whatsoever of these special events and Frank really did wonder what it had all been for.

At that precise moment in time, however, he had to think of a response to their statement and found himself feeling really riled and pissed off. He stipulated that they were bang out of order as far as he was concerned, as they knew the score – this holiday was purely on a rest and recuperation level, nothing more. He then concentrated on the subject of domestic appliances mentioning that they were calling the kettle black bearing in mind the only thing the two of them did at home was to sit on their backsides, night and day, in front of computer screens barely acknowledging people, just venturing downstairs for nutritional sustenance. Surely that was cabin fever at the worst extreme? At least here they could sit in the sunlight with fresh air circulating around and within them. Why couldn't they read books if they felt they were missing out on the cerebral high their computers provided them with? If they wanted to meet people why didn't they go to the teenage beach barbecue or the speed-dating dinners that were laid on for lonely hearts some evenings a week in the hotel?

"It's bloody different, Dad, we are on holiday; give us a break, will you? You aren't only pissing me off, you're pissing Jess off, you're pissing Mum off, you're pissing everyone else off around the pool and another thing, you're permanently pissed and it's bloody embarrassing."

At that Frank decided to take the easy option and to let them book a trip. He wasn't very impressed when they informed him they would be having an early morning call at 5am.

"Where the heck are we going?"

His wife replied, "The other end of the island, love. We are going on safari and it's a dead cert we will see tigers and monkeys and maybe some elephants."

Christ, of all things he would much rather have embarked on a fishing trip to the coastal village of Unawata and learnt to fish using a traditional Sri Lankan method where the local fishermen appearing like hungry storks would drive massive stilts into the seabed, dropping their lines into the water from there. One of the hotel guests was raving about the experience and had caught a humongous fish, which had saved having to spend another small fortune on the hotel meal that night. At least, he thought to himself, he could put towels out on all the sunloungers to piss the European off.

As luck would have it there was only one other family that had also signed up for the trip and of course it had to be none other than the European and his family. Frank, on seeing the size and states of the daughters and wife, could only thank God he hadn't touched the underwear that fated morning.

The journey was not pleasant; it was all eight of them plus the driver and a guide virtually sitting on top of one another in a small non-air-conditioned van.

The picnic in the boot smelt as though it was congealing by the minute and Frank wondered what it consisted of, as there was a strong smell of garlic sausage, which in unison with the collective body odour emanating from the other family, was plain and simply bloody offensive. For once Frank was silent, lost for words and doing his absolute best to keep the increasing nausea at bay. There were various theories as to why the van driver felt that he had to drive at such suicidal speeds to reach the park – perhaps it was the atrocious smell in the van spurring him on or a need to arrive before breakfast in order to eat it in a picturesque café that would have a panoramic view of the journey they were about to embark on. Another theory was a need to clock off early or perhaps he did genuinely hope he would die from his breakneck speed. The bottom line was that in this mad haste it was impossible to really take in the scenes unfolding through the van windows: majestic, craggy mountains juxtaposed with lush, fertile rice paddy fields with a backdrop of a sapphire blue sky. Or to see the indigenous people going about their daily routines on rickshaws or by foot, chatting and occupied, completely oblivious to a van full of stinking foreigners trying to take random photos of any local they saw.

The mad haste also exacerbated the onset of violent vomiting on behalf of one of the European daughters, who was sitting virtually on top of Frank due to the driver negotiating a tight corner again at breakneck speed at that precise moment in time. Fortuitously she managed to catch what Frank concluded must have been a mammoth cooked breakfast that morning (it must have been special room service as the buffet breakfast had consisted of croissants and nothing more), in her hands. As there were no bags or tissues on standby, Frank, feeling somewhat paternal over the poor suffering girl did for one minute think about offering his sunhat as a means of collecting the vomit. Luckily, however, the gods must have been on his side as at that precise moment the van came to a halt having arrived at their destination.

Surprisingly Frank felt unable to stomach the lavish picnic prepared by the hotel; particularly painful was the knowledge that he had paid for it as an extra. How much nicer it would have been had he stayed at the hotel, that lovely reserved table strategically placed for viewing young ladies in bikinis. The restaurant staff were currently bending over backwards to serve him particularly now they thought he was a real-life lord (his tongue had become a little lapse after too much Chablis and when questioned he had revealed that he knew the Queen). Surely it was his prerogative; this bragging was a meretricious way of convincing himself all was fine in this new life he was now adhering to.

Joking aside, whenever Jackie and the kids were with him, however, he had to cough profusely ensuring they didn't discover his newly discovered title. What with their builders' bums, tattoos and numerous piercings coupled with their unionist loyalties, lord would not have gone down well. *Yes, how much nicer today could have been,* he thought to himself as he saw the European family setting off by foot complete with binoculars, thick walking socks, heavy-duty hiking boots and matching beige khaki trousers and jackets. They stood out like sore thumbs much more suited for the bloody savannah as they approached the lush, dense rainforest. Frank was hoping there would be a canopy for the entire rainforest as he had inadvertently left his suncat on the festering vomit in the car. Feeling the sun beating down furiously on his bald patch he knew this was going to be the worst day of the holiday.

What a bloody disaster the entire excursion was from beginning to end. The unbearable heat, coupled with the fact that he was extremely unfit with a gut that had expanded daily since the start of the holiday, made it extremely unpleasant. The difficult uphill terrain that got his heart pumping furiously panicked Frank into thinking he was on the verge of a fatal heart attack. Never before had he craved so much for water over booze. Typically, however, he had failed to pack any. The hand of fortune beckoned however, and he knew by this simple act from the European girl that they would be platonic friends – fancy her, he certainly did not. Bravely overcoming the rancid smell of recent vomit mixed with garlic sausage there was no stopping him guzzling down as much as his throat could take; it was one hundred per cent up there with the Chablis on ice, back in civilisation.

Finally collapsing on the ground with sunburn, because he was positive it was, imagine his horror on discovering the soft mass was in fact thousands of ants hard at work constructing their accommodation. The dancing on one spot continued for a full minute creating a catch-22 predicament whereby he was yet again hot, exhausted and extremely dehydrated. Sadly he had consumed her entire bottle of water so nothing more could be done.

This had been a disaster; he had gone full circle and had devastatingly reverted back to the stressed, physical wreck he had been before the start of the holiday. To top it all the only animals they had spotted were wild dogs, cats, and a couple of rats but the thing that really got Jackie going to the point that she was screaming and gesticulating was when she saw a squirrel with two babies. This act completely flummoxed Frank as he dutifully reminded her she had a makeshift guillotine at home that beheaded squirrels on an hourly basis. Why the hell in heaven was she going all soft and emotional just because she had seen a Sri Lankan squirrel with two babies?

Bloody great; three days left of the holiday and what had he done today? He had risen at an unearthly hour, nearly died of a coronary, had an arse covered in ant stings, drunk second-hand vomit, but had been given the rare opportunity to view Sri Lankan vermin in a rainforest. Voicing aloud his dissatisfaction he said, "We can't even have a decent meal in the hotel tonight as we'll be too bloody late." The only response he got was mumblings from Jackie and the kids about how it would do his gut good to have a rest what with him wandering round looking as though he was pregnant with triplets.

When the Europeans started laughing at this Frank was very tempted to knock the man out with the binoculars hanging around his neck particularly when he caught Jackie raising her eyes to the heavens at his hugely clichéd response of, "We won the war so watch yourself." Frank instead took himself off towards the bus whilst the others exchanged pleasantries around the picnic table. *The sooner I get home the better. I can't be doing with this anymore. God, there was a time when women literally threw themselves at me. My old bag of a wife has bloody well crossed the line this time, bloody nerve with her jowly face, dry fanny and bloody huge ego. When I think of what I could have had; if I had just gone into the sunset with some of those young female police officers, the possibilities are endless,* he thought to himself.

Mind you, on the other hand, it could have all gone belly-up. He considered his mate Roger; all full of it when they had met down the local for a pint, it transpired he had met, shagged and spoken to (all in that order) a good-looking, uncomplicated bird and what's more got on really well with her. Frank could recall almost word for word his announcement. "I've met this girl, she's really fit, she's great and the amazing thing is she's got a career that she loves. She can't have children and luckily doesn't want them. She loves sailing, skiing, and travelling, she loves the idea of my retirement and we are going to just travel the world, no ties. She can work freelance, it will be fantastic." A year on they were married with a child with another on the way, and she was no longer working – that had been terminated days after Frank's drink with him. Subsequently came the confession; it transpired she actually hated skiing, sailing, travelling and now she had her two children, sex for pleasure. Ironically, his ex-wife was leading the life he had hoped for and was currently in Goa having enrolled on a yoga retreat for a month.

Perhaps Jackie wasn't as bad as all that; maybe he should make more of an effort. Frank, his irritation having subsided a little now he had reminisced about his friend, began putting things into perspective, thinking outside the box in which he liked to think. Perhaps, after all, his family was right. Yes, he had put on a little and it wasn't making him feel good. He could feel his waistband digging into his gut and had also been overcome with terror that he was facing a heart attack when climbing the steep terrain on the trip in the bright sunlight. Perhaps this was a warning that he needed to take stock and calm down. His whole life when he was gagging on the garlic sausage-flavoured water, seemed to go before his eyes.

Right, he thought, *when I get back it's going to be a new me*, and vowed there and then he was going on a drastic health kick and was going to sort himself out once and for all. Perhaps he and Jackie could make things work again? Mind you, there had been so much water under the bridge, not that Jackie had a clue, or maybe she did and wasn't bothered. There must be so many marriages like this where boredom sets in; you dabble here and there but also continue on as a couple as though nothing untoward has happened.

Admittedly she had been amazingly supportive through the crisis time at work and she had done all she could to try and pull him out of his deep depression, but the bottom line was, however, deep down he simply didn't fancy her anymore. She had become old, frumpy and bloody boring. He felt he definitely had the advantage over her. He may have his gut but he had aged better, the grey made him look more distinguished and the lines around his face conveyed the fact that he laughed a lot. One thing he did know, although he hadn't been able to put it into practice for a long time, was that he definitely had the stamina of a young man. *That's if my heart doesn't conk out,* he added almost as an afterthought.

Yes, coming to the end of the holiday he felt wistful now at the thought of lost opportunities he had hoped would happen between him and the kids. He thought they would be fully bonded returning with a much closer relationship than they had when they started off on the holiday. Suppers and reminiscing, playing board games, none of these had happened. In the full two weeks it had been pretty grim, actually. *Lazy arseholes, the lot of them.*

Thank God for the booze, that had been the lifesaver. He and Jackie were definitely getting on better however, even resorting to a couple of fondles under the bed covers which made a change. So what if she still kept her nightdress and bed socks on no matter what the weather? His main motive was to hopefully move on from strictly hands to something a lot more satisfying; his only preoccupation was the amount of time it was going to take.

Arriving home his fanciful intentions of really working on his relationship with Jackie were soon dispelled the instant they arrived at the front door of their 'home sweet home'. Placing the key in the lock the rancid smell hit him full on. The entire house smelt like a massive sewer and on further inspection it came to light there had been a huge flood during their absence.

It didn't take Jackie long to recall her movements prior to their holiday departure, and it transpired that the quick bath she was running had continued running for two weeks as she had become distracted searching for passports and checking her make-up. It made sense to jump into the taxi which had arrived twenty minutes early, "Just in case there were traffic hold-ups". The extent of the damage throughout the house was irreparable, the entire top-floor ceiling had caved in, and it was a disaster. What really got Frank's goat was that he had forked out an absolute fortune only months before to have the entire place decorated and designed by some trendy (useless in his eyes) company in London that went by the name of Zigi Stamford. For Christ's sake, who would call a company by such a name? He had his bloody father to thank for that expense; his final message to her on his deathbed was, "Whatever happens when you move to your new house get a designer in. Frank has absolutely no idea and you aren't much better." Frank found these comments highly insulting; his house was the height of cutting-edge fashion and what was impressive was that they had designed it together. Based on Van Gogh's *Sunflowers*, they replicated the bright yellow walls and green painted woodwork throughout the house and had the inspired idea of coupling it with horizontal and vertical stripes which gave a geometric Mondrian effect – all the rage then. It looked good and Frank couldn't believe a few years later, as part of the road to forgiveness, he would allow Jackie to redesign the house. It was now full of neon lights, kaleidoscopic décor and psychedelic wallpaper and certainly no longer felt like the cosy, colourful home it had once been. The invoice from Zigi was eyewatering, daylight robbery, which had now literally gone down the drain.

The next stop for Frank was to collect the real loves of his life, Sugar and Spice, their two cocker spaniels, from the kennels. He also liked to use this time to have a good old flirt with the gorgeous Indian-looking girl who was in the admin section behind the reception desk in the entrance hall.

En route he reflected on how this idea was a far better option than leaving his babies with the mother-in-law. For a start he would have had to pop in there to collect them and much as the idea would have been to pop in and out as quickly as possible this would not be the reality. Forced into a corner of the room he would literally be interrogated and eyeballed, halitosis and saliva being thrown in his direction at the same time as being asked about the state of his marriage and whether he had treated Jackie as a princess on holiday. Jackie also avoided going, as her mother would spend the entire time telling her to ditch Frank and find herself a, "Young lover who will want to please you in every way."

More importantly he knew from past experience that on the rare occasions his babies had stayed there they had been relegated to the room in the basement. The love of his mother-in-law's life, her Persian cat, an overweight lump of fur that lived on smoked salmon and sat in its own shit on the best chair in the sitting room, ruled the house and hated Sugar and Spice. During their stay at the kennels Frank had decided to treat his pooches to a full day at the pamper parlour which entailed various beauty treatments culminating in a wash, cut and blow-dry, and excitement building he couldn't wait to see how they looked. The contented smile on his face didn't last long as he suddenly recalled their current situation. *Shit, we really have no choice; we're going to have to move in with Mother-in-law for the foreseeable future until all the mess has been cleared up*. Jesus, what a bloody nightmare it was; just what he needed. She was a complete pain in the arse. The only redeeming thing she did well (shame Jackie hadn't inherited this gene) was cooking. Sitting down to a meal made by her was an almost orgasmic experience in complete contrast to the crap that Jackie served up on a daily basis. It would, however, put a hold on any hanky-panky with Jackie as she regarded any expression of intimacy in the family home as a violation of her childhood.

For a transitory moment Frank wondered about moving his babies into Mother-in-law's; after all, they would have had what equated to a luxury five-star holiday at the kennels so he would feel guiltless. He and Jackie could stay in a hotel; that way he could master the art of moving away from the hands and bed socks to the real McCoy. Then again, he hadn't progressed much on the holiday so it was perhaps a case of too much wishful thinking on his part. He also recalled the psychotic state his babies were left in when they last stayed at Mother-in-law's; they were so traumatised he had to engage the services of an eye-wateringly expensive dog psychiatrist who concluded that they both had an extreme, pathological terror towards bundles of blue/grey fur. This was analysed through their reactions to images; it was apparently all in the bark. Mother-in-law did not, as predicted, respond well to the conclusive report. Her cat was the most loving and affectionate of all animals and she was adamant there was no way on earth Lima would have terrorised the girls. According to her friend (lover? Ugh, he needed to move on quick; the very thought of that), expert (bull-shitter), vet (God knows how that happened), Mr Jean Christo Jones (stud), the dogs were far too indulged and just needed to 'man up'. She was not at all amused when Frank announced he never thought his mother-in-law would be the type canvassing for dogs to be allowed sex reassignment surgery. "Frank, where on earth does that come into it? I said nothing of the sort."

"You told me they had to man up."

"Frank, when I said man up, I meant behave like men."

There had been an incident many years before when the children were young and had a pet rabbit that Mother-in-law was looking after for the weekend. It transpired that one of her old cronies was over having a cup of tea and nursing Snowy when she discovered a huge lump under its leg. Wasting no time, Stud the vet, who was probably ensconced in her bedroom, created an instant appointment. Mother-in-law and mate supposedly arrived at the surgery (was it Mother-in-law's house?) where Snowy was rushed in for a physical examination only to be told by Stud that the lump was actually the bloody testicle. It didn't end there as this so-called excursion resulted in a hefty invoice addressed to Frank entitled 'Vet's Professional Services'. (He wasn't a detective for nothing and it really did beat him up when, on closer inspection, he recognised the spidery writing on the envelope deducing that Jackie's mother also appeared to be doubling up as Stud's PA.) Frank had no choice but to pay, nearly breaking his heart in the process particularly when Snowy had to be put down at more expense having developed some mystery illness two weeks later. He did try ringing the surgery asking if the lethal injection could come under the same invoice as the gender discovery. The answer was a definite no.

Stud made one more final attempt to extort money from Frank during a much longed for holiday whilst Mother-in-law was pet-sitting. It was Hammy the Hamster (Jess's beloved pet), who had developed what appeared to be glaucoma. Again it was one of her old nursing cronies who discovered it. Instead of coming downstairs in his silk patterned dressing gown and admitting to all and sundry they were in a relationship, Stud went through the back entrance and legged it across the lawn to his car planning to dress in the surgery. Metaphorically rubbing his hands together at the knowledge he would be making some money from professional services on the hamster he failed to notice a rogue rock on the front lawn. Sadly, he concussed himself and did himself no favours lying in his morning glory, dressing gown opened to reveal his tiny, shrivelled manhood. If this wasn't enough his dentures had also shot out of his mouth and were lying beside him. He had no strength to close his dressing gown, or put his teeth in, let alone pull himself up to face the blue-rinsed entourage watching the entire scene in abject horror. Mother-in-law was mortified. Firstly, because of what he was exposing, and secondly, it was obvious he had been staying in her house and thus her friends would know she was sexually active particularly because it was a one-bedroomed double-bed house. She spent most of her time holding up the pedestal to dear Jackie's dad and saying no man would ever violate her body after her one love. Thirdly, and this was the most significant, she was truly mortified because she thought his teeth were his own.

Hammy, who had never been out in daylight, traversed the entire front lawn whilst all this drama was taking place and once found was rushed off to an out-of-hours vet's practice. At this stage the eye was firmly closed and exhaustion with the long walk had set in. After a ridiculously short inspection the vet ascertained that Hammy was suffering from exhaustion (no rocket science there) and most significantly the glaucoma was none other than stray sugar globules that had found their way to the hamster's eye (lady holding Hammy must have helped herself to a spoonful of sugar for her tea, inadvertently misjudging the eye for her cup).

It was easy money for the vet and with one sweep of the eye with a moist tissue the offending mess was removed and the hefty bill for such efficient service was handed over within minutes. Frank concluded that it was far more lucrative to be a vet than a premier league footballer in this day and age, all that money to be earned and no restrictions on eating and drinking. What more could anyone ask for in a job?

On arrival at the aesthetically pleasing dog kennels he found himself wondering how much it must have cost to bribe a planning officer to erect the huge glass building bang, smack in the middle of what Frank thought was green belt. The wrought-iron gates were an example of art at its finest, and on closer inspection it became apparent that there were hundreds of dog images carved in 3D adorned on every single bit of space. The gates at the back were a fine replication, the only difference was they opened out onto a public footpath that took up, in the process, a huge chunk of land. Surely ramblers and members of the general public had lodged numerous complaints over what was daylight land-grabbing? Frank would give anything to know the name of the planning officer that let this one 'slip' through.

Why hadn't he got a job working with dogs? The amount of money he had spent on dog psychiatrist fees, dietician's fees, as well as a bark analysis coach would have been enough to buy a house in Spain. Bloody annoying thing was, knowing what he knew now, he would never have commissioned any of them. Why did he listen to his bloody mother-in-law in the first place? All a dog needs is love, attention and food, and you've got a happy pet.

Whilst the girls were jumping up and licking him Frank got a glimpse of the gorgeous young lady on reception, a big smile plastered on that stunning face. He had the distinct feeling she was fantasising that she was one of his dogs climbing astride him licking him all over. Okay, the smile on those beautiful cupid-bow lips wavered slightly when he reciprocated the doggy licking on both his babies but it didn't take long for the dreamy look on her face to reappear. He praised himself inwardly on his facial dexterity, as he was able to combine licking with a smile aimed directly towards her despite the fact that at this stage his back was facing the reception.

A while later, as he was filling in the details and paying the bills as well as negotiating a further indefinite stay for his girls, he contemplated asking her whether she fancied a drink. Literally on the verge of asking, the phone, which hitherto had not made a sound, started ringing. Judging by her response it was not an unknown customer but someone she was obviously intimate with.

"Hi, babe, no, can't talk, had a last-minute booking, guy who is a serious dog lover and I mean serious." (What the hell that meant was beyond Frank's imagination.) "Yeah, I will be there in a sec, okay, kiss kiss."

He decided to loiter for a while just to check out her marital situation and whether she may be in a dead-end relationship with no future (quite frankly the intonation in her voice when addressing him was far more positive and passionate compared to the way she addressed the person on the other end of the phone). On the pretext of needing to phone his insurers to validate who was responsible for paying the cost of the dog home Frank was able to legitimately loiter.

Frank was thankfully sitting down when he got what could probably be described as the biggest shock of his entire life. Jesus, the sight that greeted his eyes was one of the last things he would ever have imagined. A real blast from the past coming back to haunt him was all he could think. This old bag had wrecked everything for him; she was the absolute catalyst of all the crap he had suffered all those years ago. For one rotten moment he wondered if they were lesbians. On closer inspection, however, there was no mistaking it, they were definitely mother and daughter. How the hell she could have created such a beauty was beyond him, the girl's father must have been one good-looking dude.

This woman was literally the complete bitch from hell that had cost him his job, honour, dignity and success all those years ago. He had been so near to solving everything until she threw her bloody spanner in the works basically fucking up absolutely everything he had set up. He had indeed, good reasons to inveigh against the bad luck which pursued him and yet there was nothing he could do to redeem himself, which meant he was left with no choice but to leave the force.

Seeing no recognition on her face Frank knew he had to remove himself as quickly as possible. He was going to have to rebook his beauties in by phone later. Wasting no time at all he paid the bill, threw the girls into the crate at the back of his car, put his head on the steering wheel and yelled in absolute anger and frustration, "Jesus Christ, I cannot believe it was her, she literally, single-handedly fucked everything up for me. There aren't enough words for me to inveigh how angry I am right now!"

Up until then she had been his inferior, a little minion, a mere social worker who had treated him with the utmost respect. He was so her superior, her boss, whatever he said went; that's how it was when you were in the upper echelons of the police force; it was as simple as that. Those days he had an incredibly efficient team all of whom would sit down in meetings hanging onto his every word; the majority of them would literally transcribe every word he uttered as though recording them for posterity. He had always meant to ask for the papers, which would have come in handy for his memoirs. Sadly his departure had been a sudden one and he had never been given the chance.

Those really were the glory days; he had never had to fantasise about cups of tea, they would just appear on the hour, every hour, followed by coffee and cake in the afternoon. He was the expert, the one everyone came to when they needed information and advice. He was the detective chief superintendent and woe betide anyone who crossed his path. Girls then really were at his disposal. God, thinking back he wondered how he got away with what he did?

Frank's daily routine in those days would begin at the gym followed by a session at the station reviewing various matters. Once he had his tea and morning snack he liked to escape from the station and it looked good because he was out there with his fellow, albeit lower ranking, officers, on the cutting edge. The ulterior motive for this was really because he got the pick of which girls he wanted to accompany him in the patrol car and was a guaranteed way of getting to know them. It was normally routine work followed by a long lunch. The girls would drive, which was good because he could enjoy a bottle on expenses. If he struck lucky and there was a frisson with the body language being right, as long as there were no urgent interruptions on the police radio then the sessions would end with a couple of hours at a local hotel with a fumble and if really lucky, a quick shag. If time was of the essence he had managed sex in the police car although that was not ideal as there was always a philanthropic nosey member of the public sniffing around ready to report what looked like abandoned police cars on wasteland. That was until they looked a little closer and wondered whether it really was a heaving hairy arse rising up through the heavy condensation forming on the windows or whether it was in fact a strange trick of the light.

Luckily nothing was reported. Frank felt constantly justified there, he was virtually married to his work, the hours he and his colleagues put in were next to nothing. Okay, he had certain perks such as the best accommodation when managing training courses, good wine, delicious lunches complete with lavish cheeseboard and the sort of desserts which up until then had been the thing fantasies were made of. It was all totally above board; the good old British taxpayer could rest assured their police force were upstanding, stalwart men and women who had pledged to serve their country, and by God they did.

"Jesus wept; I still cannot believe I went and got involved, it doesn't bear thinking about," he quietly said to himself.

It made him want to physically retch and filled him with shame for he had broken the one law of the police force that has been in circulation since the days of Robert Peel, i.e. never to have relations with anyone under the radar of the police or legal system. He had engaged in sexual relations with one Margot Ville who whilst not being a minor, as had been the original charge, was nevertheless seen as someone who was highly vulnerable. Not only was she seeing a social worker due to drug and alcohol abuse within her family, she had also been cautioned numerous times for shoplifting and hell raising – what a bloody idiot he had been. If that wasn't enough, she had also been a friend of the deceased. Why had he thought he would never be rumbled? Why had he not just asked to come off the case?

Looking back it sickened him to think that he thought he was invincible and immune from any repercussions, though he couldn't deny that what they had was good – she was something else, a complete vamp, up for anything. Any red-blooded man would have felt the same. But that was the problem; he hadn't looked at the situation logically and it hadn't crossed his mind to think about the repercussions of his actions. On top of that she seemed, despite her issues, a real survivor and tough with it, so why did he need to end things if it wasn't hurting anyone?

The day he was summoned to the police station and was shown

photographic evidence of him snogging Margot, was one he would never forget. One hand on her backside and one down her front left him for once in his life, utterly speechless. He was equally mortified about how enormous his backside appeared in the photos – that was going to have to go. Shocked on being told he was being charged with sexual relations involving a minor there was some respite on discovering Margot was actually eighteen at the time of the photo. He was advised, however, that due to the sensitive nature of the situation there was no other option but for him to stand down and leave the force immediately. What a devastating blow for a man at the pinnacle of his success. He had thrown it all away for wild sex with a girl who resembled a bloody stick insect. The day he had to remove his badge and clear his desk was absolutely devastating and he had felt totally dehumanised.

No longer with a driver at his disposal he had to resort to his silent electric car that had been dumped in the police station's car park. Trying to reverse out he had no choice but to beep his horn at a gaggle of gossiping policemen who hadn't clocked his car backing out. His three-point turn turning into a rather laborious, time-consuming, five-point manoeuvre was highly embarrassing and he wondered what they were muttering under their breath as he finally pulled out and left the scene. His next concern was how and what he was going to say to Jackie. Being the detective chief superintendent's wife was the whole core of her existence and she was going to be one very pissed-off lady.

Frank, to his complete astonishment, however, arriving home an hour later, managed to convince Jackie that it was Margot who had thrown herself at him and although he reciprocated, it was a clear-cut case of diminished responsibility on his side. He confessed how his mental state had not been great of late and as a result he had been seeing a counsellor at work who had then passed on his confession about Margot. His depression was news to Jackie (and Frank – it was something he had conjured up in the car after his three-point-turn saga). Jackie, although very upset and angry, decided she would adhere to her marriage vows.

"I married you for life and that is what I am going to stick with. It's going to take many years to forgive you and I need you to know that. The other thing is if I want a cup of tea over sex in my bed at night you are going to have to deal with it, particularly under the circumstances. You are not to make me feel guilty about this issue. Have I got my point straight, Frank?"

"Yep, you have my absolute word. I will not nag you, all right, babe? We can make this work, I one hundred per cent want it to. If I decide I want something I will get it. (He was thinking about Margot and all the other girls at the very moment he unveiled his answer to Jackie.) And I want to save our marriage."

08

JACKIE

It's mad, really; one minute I am thinking about all the things I hate about Frankie and the next I'm thinking about his good points. Holidays definitely bring out the worst in him or maybe it's because we are together 24/7 and there is no escape. The noise he makes when he eats, drinks and shits is unbearable. The only harmonious time for the kids and me is when he collapses pissed and bloated, on various sunbeds, looking like a beached whale, in the height of the midday sun only to wake like a bear with a sore head suffering from extreme sunburn. It's a bit of respite again for us when he overeats at lunchtime and then has to stagger to a sunbed in the shade to sleep for the rest of the afternoon. That's if he's not arguing with the Germans, Russians and fellow Brits about sunbed reservations. It happens every time we go on holiday and drives me nuts.

Don't get me wrong, I love being away; nothing better than to just leave everything behind. It's just too much of Frank drives me nuts. I mean, I can't even escape to the pool. I bloody hate them after all that black scum you get on the sides. I haven't been in one since a lifeguard informed us it was body fat and natural. Frank has got his uses, mind; for a start, you never know what weirdos are around you. There's always this stuff in the news about foreigners being taken ransom, or made to join dodgy religious sects. Frank thinks I'm mad but I'm not. *The Daily Mail* and *Sun* are always running articles on these things. That's why it's good he accompanies me as he would never in a million years get into those situations. He wasn't in the police force for nothing. He is also good with the money situation. I haven't got a clue how to convert currency and all that and I absolutely hate bartering.

When we're home there's that whole sex thing that leaves me cold. I tell you, most people want it when they're on holiday, but not my Frank; I get let off the hook then. It's when we are home; all that heavy breathing lark. I know what he's after every time we get into bed. I tell you, I prefer a cup of tea over that any day. I'm normal, my friends feel exactly the same way. Fine when we were young and our bodies were of a type to do it. Now it really isn't my thing. I mean, I'm not having any more babies, God forbid, I'm in my sixties. But joking apart, what is the pleasure in doing it at our age?

He drives me mad now he's not working. It really is hell on earth. Me and my mates used to meet in the morning at each other's houses. I would make brunch, light the candles, put a bit of Tom Jones on and they would arrive and we would spend the day chatting, doing each other's nails and just catching up. These were friends I had known forever, my gang of girls, and I love them to bits. The only spanner in the works was when Frank lost his job and was suddenly constantly at home. I had to review things.

He drove me nuts and when I say nuts I mean nuts. That bloody football would be on all day. The kitchen stank of bacon and eggs and the amount of grease he managed to spill, it was everywhere. My lovely house felt like a bloody transit café. Then the cigarettes; what an absolute nightmare! It transpires he was a chain-smoker at work and couldn't kick the habit at home. He wasn't even smoking in the garden and I swear by the end of the week our walls had turned yellow. The overflowing ashtrays and the way he walked around the house in sweat pants with his massive torso looking like he was pregnant with triplets, drove me mad. His dirty clothes were just chucked on the floor and it was like having a bloody great demented teenager in the house.

My poor friends found it depressing too as there would be no embarrassment with all that farting and burping going on. The day he left a smell like something I've never smelt before, in the toilet with a bloody great turd jammed in it whilst my friends were there was the most mortifying moment of my life. I could literally have killed him. The turd was so bloody solid I broke the bloody toilet brush trying to remove it. From that moment onwards I vowed I could never invite my friends to the house again.

I mean, it was all okay when he was working, he was out of my hair. Don't get me wrong, he is like part of the furniture and a huge part of my life. We've been together since we were sixteen and to be honest I wouldn't know how to cope paying the bills and the like as he does all that sort of stuff. Sometimes I suppose I think it would be nice to have some 'oomph' in our lives – it's all a bit bloody boring. I don't mean having an affair or anything like that – blimey, one man in my life is enough and as for Frank, I know he would never have an affair. He's a good, loyal man like that. He has very high morals, that's half his problem. What a laugh; thinking about it I reckon if a gorgeous lady tried to seduce him, first he would wonder what her problem was then if the penny dropped I'm telling you he would run a mile. A womaniser? No, not my Frank.

Sometimes I wish he would just spruce things up a bit between him and me as in going out for nice dinners and the like. At least when he was working we had a routine. The house always looked lovely and depending on his shifts we often sat down to dinner together. I always had candles and flowers on the table and made an effort, not that Frank would have noticed, but bottom line it always made me feel good about myself.

I still haven't really got to the bottom of what went wrong at work with that girl, all I know is it was him being his kind self. He has got a ridiculously soft heart and you can't have that when you are in the police force particularly when you are a senior officer. It's put me off any intimacy for the time being and he knows he's got to deal with that. We are going to be living at Mum's whilst renovations on the house are taking place anyway and the last thing I will let him do is go anywhere near me. It is just not right especially bearing in mind the room we stay in when we are there is the room I grew up in. I am hoping when we move back in now Zigi has sorted the house that things will be a lot better. I feel I now have the upper hand as far as Frank and I are concerned. Things are changing whether he likes it or not.

09

HASSAN FAMILY

Imagine the shock that now reverberated through her as she drove home after collecting Zuleikha, when the penny finally dropped and she recalled who he was – Frank DuPont. Horrified at the knowledge that she had not only afforded him a second glimpse as she saw him chatting to Zuleikha (she had clocked that he was rather attractive, a sort of thinking woman's man – a slightly offbeat version of both George Clooney and Al Pacino) but also that he was flirting outrageously with her daughter. Deciding to divulge nothing Ramina chose to internalise the incident and just hoped to God he was at the kennels as a one-off and that would be the end of the matter. Memories of a past best forgotten was all she could think.

Ramina had been seventeen when she met her husband, it was an arranged marriage, and she therefore had no say in the events leading up to it. Her parents had divulged four main facts about her husband-to-be: he was intelligent, liberated, handsome and most importantly to her family, from the same caste. The only conditions he had insisted on were that his future wife was to take pride in her appearance at all times, and to enjoy cooking. Both facts seemed pretty innocuous to Ramina resulting in her entering into the match without any further questioning. If she had had the foresight to read between the lines and to look at things from a more mature perspective then she may have interpreted these stipulations as evidence that he wanted a vacuous dogsbody whose whole meaning of existence was to please and to placate him. It would have been an extremely apt analogy had hindsight been a good thing; however, blinded by naivety, ignorance, his good looks and glib, seemingly mild manner, she had been completely taken in.

Initially acquiescing to his many whims it was not long thereafter that the abuse and violence started. Unaccustomed to such terrifying outbursts and with no one to confide in, she felt guilty and blamed herself for being an ineffective wife. Ramina was also completely taken in by his grovelling and self-loathing that subsequently followed the violence. The only time she felt safe was during her pregnancies, which followed in rapid succession. When they discovered after a routine scan she was expecting a boy, his 'Mini man', Tariq's behaviour towards her was exemplary and could not be faulted in any way. After this second pregnancy, however, Ramina knew that she would never wish to be pregnant again. In theory she desperately wanted to leave him; in practice, however, she feared it would be an impossibility unless she was prepared to lose custody of her children. It didn't help her case that with each pregnancy Ramina had suffered acute postnatal depression to the point that after the birth of her second child she was admitted to a psychiatric hospital, a fact that Tariq never let her forget. At the time, totally oblivious to her condition, the psychotic feelings she had towards her children left her feeling bewildered and confused. Why did she hate and want to maim them despite loving them so much? It took an insurmountable amount of courage on her behalf when she finally took herself to casualty with Kasim insisting the staff took him away from her before she did him some real damage. Her emotional state at this stage was so desperate, and was further exacerbated when asked her husband's contact details, that the hospital staff felt the safest place for her was to be put on suicide watch at a local psychiatric hospital. After three days she was released and reassured by doctors that it was a chemical imbalance and was something that happened to a lot of women.

Ramina felt a great deal better at such support for her condition particularly when she learnt that her GP had herself suffered from it. If only the GP had been aware that along with this Ramina was also having to deal with frequent beatings, no money, no friends and complete mental torture (on hugging or kissing the children she would suddenly become aware of Tariq's presence in the corner, head to one side, a contrived look of concern on his face subtly reminding her she was nothing more than an unstable mother), she would indeed have really put her hand out to help. Ramina was, however, too proud to reveal the reality.

The one occasion she decided to confide in her parents about her desperate situation, apologising simultaneously for the huge amount of money the wedding had cost, it was a hugely cathartic experience, as well as a pivotal moment in her life. She was convinced that they would do their utmost in supporting her and the children, as well as wasting no time in extricating them from the unbearable situation. Ramina could not have been further from the truth. Her mother merely raised her eyes to the heavens and her father shook his head slowly. The bottom line they both emphasised was about not losing face; no one else would want her, and she would be a tainted woman. Divorce was unheard of in the family; it was a case of her dealing with what she had been given, full stop. They all had to keep up appearances no matter how dire the circumstances were, concluding that this situation was all down to them for failing their child. By treating Ramina as a princess her feelings of self-worth had obviously escalated to levels that were ridiculously high hence her inability to cope if things were not going her way. She had failed; it was she and she alone in their eyes who, having fallen foul of all that she had promised to give prior to the marriage, must now deal with it. Her independence, defiance and obvious mental instability were what had caused her so-called 'intolerable situation'.

They emphasised the part she needed to play for herself and their grandchildren which was to make it a 'tolerable situation' as quickly as possible. They also stressed the uncomfortable situation she was creating amongst the social strata in their community. Tariq's father was a renowned businessman and it would have been the end of all social events for them if the marriage were to officially end.

That was it, life continued and Ramina just had to deal with her situation; no money, no social life, no interests, and a virtual prisoner in her own home. The only times of light relief and harmony which even the children seemed to sense, were when the front door slammed and Tariq left for work. On his return, however, the tension would mount again. Firing question after question at her he would tick off the things he had asked her to do, from his list. The long, gnarled finger would then run its way over the various work surfaces and picture frames checking for dust. Ramina would sit on tenterhooks cursing herself for feeling so pathetic and utterly controlled by such a monster in a bid to stop him touching her in front of the children.

Dinner was the next incredibly tense situation. If the meal was not to his liking he would literally hurl it across the room in disgust. How easy at times like this it would be to put the three of them out of their misery. A case of sleeping tablets and painkillers in a cup of hot chocolate and all this would end. It would be a painless and rapid escape. Then again, she also knew damn well how precious life was and why give him the victory? It was her duty and quest to rise above all this and to actually facilitate a way out.

Likening herself to an actress acting out a role in this unbelievably depressing life, Ramina tried desperately to portray all was fine in her relationship with Tariq. She even succeeded in convincing her parents things were improving which meant financial handouts which were immediately stored away ready for when they would escape. At times this facade was difficult as despite trying to hide the reality it was becoming increasingly obvious that both Zuleikha and Kasim were extremely tense and on edge whenever their father was present.

Whispering to one another they would physically cower whenever he stood near them. What amazed Ramina was that he never questioned the fact that on the rare times he did try and converse with them they were both tongue-tied and literally lost for words.

Ramina decided to try and befriend some people at school, allies perhaps that she could ultimately confide in. Her first port of call was to join the active school PTA surprising herself completely by volunteering her services after the first meeting, for an auction offering to provide an amazing gourmet Indian meal made by her from scratch. Tariq for once offered a positive reaction to this; being the networker he was he hoped it may lead on to further contacts for him. He did wonder whether it should be him rather than Ramina showing up to the committee meetings as her pronounced accent did not really do him (or her for that matter) any justice at all. Lapping up the whole dapper, upper crust, jovial, quintessentially British effect, the type in other words who was more English than the English, in his three-piece suit complete with bow tie, different coloured handkerchiefs changed daily in his front pocket and polished brogues, Tariq had often ruminated on what he had been thinking of by marrying a pleb from Pakistan who had never been to England before. Determined to convince people of his fabricated Etonian roots Tariq persevered (the tie he had purchased at a car boot sale had been an amazing find). How awkward when asked by a genuine Old Etonian which house he was affiliated to.

Ramina had to control the urge to burst into hysterical laughter at seeing Tariq in such an embarrassing situation. The pompous Etonian would no doubt have choked on his salmon roulade had he known the old chap certainly wasn't a genuine 'old chap' and instead hailed from one of the roughest comprehensive schools in London where to his credit he had excelled without the help of any networking and nepotism in the city.

Tariq also created the illusion that his parents were members of the Pakistani elite, a complete fabrication she knew as his father was a teacher in an inner-city school. He was the sort of teacher who inspired the majority of his students, an absolute legend. At the same time he was a self-deprecating, modest and warm man who was happiest when up to his eyeballs in history books. Ramina had always had a lot of time for him and had been tempted to seek his help but weighing up the odds and the fact that he was totally dominated by his wife she decided not to. Her mother-in-law could not have been more different. Underneath her disturbingly beautiful face, one that emanated kindness and serenity, there lurked a complete and utter bitch.

Ramina had hoped this one-off cooking venture would serve two purposes, the first that perhaps it would help her at best meet more people and if lucky make a friend or two. The second reason was that it might aid Tariq in his quest to branch out in his networking strategy therefore making more business contacts. It was for this reason that Ramina hoped he would relax the budget on her monthly allowance, which was an absolute pittance, and certainly not in line with the overall salary he earned. His money was his and he could spend it on what he wanted to, hence his wardrobe full of designer suits and shirts, which rarely seemed to be worn. No wife of his was going to be going out to work he told her when Ramina mentioned a job at the school as a teaching assistant. The only thing he did allow her to do was to take in people's ironing or darning but things had recently gone quiet so it became an unreliable outlet.

Despite her protestations and attempts at persuasion for more money due to the increased volume and quality of food in order to create the right impression, Tariq was adamant there would be no increase and it would simply be a case of making do. The mince she used was therefore cheaper than the other cuts of meat but once she had added the numerous amounts of fresh ginger, chilli, cumin seeds, cardamom pods and coriander it smelt good and her guilt was somewhat allayed. She hoped the bid would come from a drunken city trader who wouldn't know too much about the calibre of the meat in the dish and therefore wouldn't complain about the amount of money he had spent in the bidding process. As luck would have it for once someone was on her side or so she thought and a drunken city trader showing off publically that he was worth a lot of money, bid £650 for the meal. The PTA was delighted but Ramina, however, was horrified – the pressure really was on. With her budget she literally worked through the night trying to conjure up dishes of variety and volume but on an obvious shoestring.

The following day she personally delivered them to the trader's house. It didn't take long for her to realise that things were not going to be straightforward as she parked the car directly outside the house in the driveway of a massive mock-Georgian house with approximately five Chelsea tractors parked within view of the road. A woman in a bright red tracksuit came out yelling at her to move her car as she already had a cleaner and if that wasn't the case didn't buy tack from random sellers newly out of prison. Ramina had no time to open her mouth because the woman then spotted the Tupperware containers and twigged what the delivery was. In a slow, hesitant voice as though talking to an idiot, she told Ramina to move her car from where it was, to the tradesman's entrance. This was a few metres away but Ramina noted her beaten-up car was now no longer visible from the road.

Once she had struggled into the house it took four trips with no help whatsoever from the woman who looked strangely similar to the rubberneckers sitting around the breakfast bar in full make-up and high heels sipping on their lattes and smoking. Ramina had been instructed to place the various Tupperware boxes onto the table, and yet again in her life she felt utterly humiliated. The women did not have a good word to say about anything. They didn't notice the home-baked chapattis or taftan bread, nor the delicate flavour of the lentils infused with fresh coriander. The spiced rice mixed with the slow roasted lamb, a delicacy mixed with dried fruit, nuts, cloves, saffron and cardamom, was missed.

Bright red tracksuited woman's first comment was that the koftay with masala sauce dish not only looked like mashed up McDonald's but also smelt like a dog's dinner. She then announced in a loud whisper to everyone, "Nigel is such a twat buying off a Paki when we could 'ave walked one minute away from our local curry restaurant and they don't give it ya in bloody Tupperware containers."

In the best English voice she could muster Ramina asked for the Tupperware back, as it was not included in the deal. Trying very hard to suppress her laughter at their reaction to her voice it didn't take long for this to turn to tears and humiliation as in a bid to return the Tupperware the woman dished the food container by container into a black bin liner, a look of defiance on her face as she did so. Had they known how many hours it had taken for her, Zuleikha and Kasim to concoct each of those containers: the chaat, the chana masala then the lovely desserts, the Peshawari ice cream, gulab jamun, the barfi, the ras malei, they would have understood how badly she wanted to rub their faces in it there and then. These women had no idea how lucky they were, able to sit and chat and drink coffee with no black cloud hanging over them. They did not have to watch and be aware of everything they said or did, knowing it could explode over them or the children, usually for absolutely no specific reason whatsoever.

As she drove home she knew that her idea of branching out to meet people at school had been a futile one. She had served her purpose, raised the money from the auction and that was it. There was, however, one possibility. A kind woman had mentioned a group of the PTA was going out for dinner and drinks and maybe a club one Saturday night. Ramina managed to convince Tariq it would lead to more jobs for her, and as a result he agreed to babysit.

Meeting for drinks in the lobby of the hotel before going through for dinner, Ramina sipping on tap water began worrying about the bill being split evenly as many of the women were choosing to drink alcohol. Luckily for her, however, just as people were paying she was able to make her excuses and waited in the toilets. Her plan was to order a starter at dinner and to leave earlier using babysitting as the problem. That way she could leave an exact amount of cash.

Re-entering the room, everyone was seated. One woman sat with a space between her and another woman; as Ramina was the last one in she had no option but to take the seat. It just seemed odd that the woman hadn't moved up. Her name was Jenna Taylor, and within a matter of minutes Ramina knew her life story. It transpired she was half English and half Pakistani, and she had taught herself Urdu. Her childhood had been a bizarre one. Her Pakistani mother spoke very little English and her father's Urdu was virtually non-existent.

"How my parents met is totally beyond me." One thing she did know was that neither of her parents' respective families had ever forgiven their offspring for marrying out. Jenna had therefore, apart from her mother's friends, never been exposed to the Pakistani part of her life. Likewise she knew very little about her father's life except that as both a child and now as an adult the local pub was more like his home. Her parents had very little in common; her mother loved ornaments, her father hated them; her mother loved sitcoms, her father hated them. Her mother loved the sun, her father hated it. In fact, as her father would often quote, "The only thing we've got in common is that we both hate each other."

"I was lucky I had my mother's love and she made me feel I could be anyone, and do anything. I felt for her as she was powerless. She literally had no standing in the community. My father kept her a virtual prisoner in the home and he knew there was nothing she could do. He's an absolute bastard. I am also sure he knew damn well what he was doing when naming me, but I've had the last laugh; I have kept my name and whenever I'm in the house visiting my mother I always make a point of embracing my girlfriend and our daughter in front of him, and repeating over and over again 'I love Jenna Taylor'." At this stage Ramina was completely lost in the conversation until Jenna pointed out to her the use of a synonym in the word 'genitalia'. That was the first time Ramina had ever laughed and produced tears at the same time. It was virtually impossible to control her laughter until she arrived home to an irate monther-in-law who immediately berated her about shirking parental responsibility by going out alone for what was the first time in her life.

The fun evening made Ramina forget the awful events of the lunch that day. It had been such a breath of fresh air meeting Jenna and it was interesting to see what an amazingly strong and independent woman she had become despite her dysfunctional family life. There was, however, one difference and this was that Jenna's father was not violent. With Tariq it was the not knowing when or how he was going to strike her, and the tension in the house was permanently palpable.

Ramina made a decision a few days later. She realised it was imperative that she left the toxic relationship before things escalated out of control and ended up becoming intolerable and dangerous for both herself and her two children. One evening, Tariq (who was out in the garden clad in yellow marigolds thereby avoiding the smell of nicotine on his fingers) suddenly remembered he had left some naan bread in the oven. It was a pretty painful experience when momentarily forgetting he was not wearing oven gloves he plunged his hand into the oven to rescue the bread and was covered in boiling melted rubber. Ramina could not of course betray any amusement over this scene and instead acted as the dutiful wife fussing over and driving him directly to casualty where he was advised to stay overnight. She hadn't slept so well in years. His hand injury also meant he was unable to raise his hand to strike her so for a few months she was left untouched. The medication controlling the pain also had very beneficial effects, knocking him out cold every evening thereby enabling Ramina to enjoy some very welcome evenings spent at her own leisure.

The second incident that really was the straw that broke the camel's back was a few months later when he had to go on his first business trip overseas to the States. Throwing her his list of items he wanted packed, Ramina did enjoy a wicked fantasy of Tariq's face in reaction to him opening his case in the States only to discover that all she had packed was her underwear and a pair of staggering high heels. Leaving extremely early on Monday morning he was in a foul mood on Sunday night knowing he would be unable to indulge in his daily selfish (there was only one bathroom and combined toilet in the house) activity of lying in the bath until the others had left for school.

To assert his control he insisted on everyone going to bed early that night, as he wanted to enjoy breakfast with his family at 4.30 the following morning prior to him leaving to go to the airport. In all the years she had been with him Tariq never took breakfast. True to his word he took great pleasure in waking everyone, and the false euphoria on his part at breakfast was nauseating as they sat down to coffee and croissants. Tariq again outlined how it was only fair they were all up too as it would have been unfair if they had all been lying in, bearing in mind the only reason he worked was to support his family. Ramina at this stage was praying repeatedly willing time to pass quickly so the house was rid of him.

At 5am the taxi arrived to escort him to the airport. The mood changed dramatically once he realised he was no longer going to be controlling the situation at home. It was all about what lazy arses they were and how it was all right for some who could just bugger off back to bed when he was having to endure the stress of negotiating a deal on behalf of his company and to agree it as soon as possible before the competitors got wind of it and offered a more competitive price. As the taxi pulled off Ramina felt liberated and did indeed go back to bed.

A few hours later with the children dispatched to school, she set off on a little job she had been doing over the past week delivering leaflets. It was one of her fellow workers who realised a ringing sound was coming from her pocket and her heart sank when she realised it was Tariq's phone. He had obviously inadvertently mistaken her black padded jacket for his.

"You stupid fucking bitch," was all she could hear on the other end of the phone working out in an instant it was Tariq calling from the airport with no shame at all. "You cunt, you piece of shit, I am coming home and I swear I am going to kill you, I've had enough of you once and for all."

It transpired the journey to the airport had been a very stressful one as the driver had to deal with innumerable delays due to the end of the bank holiday weekend and various accidents en route. By the time he arrived, Tariq, who hated being late, only just made the check-in desk. He practised a look he had perfected during the many hours of lying in the bath – it was a lopsided smile to which he worked in conjunction with a brow raise – lo and behold it must have worked because she smiled at him and let him straight through.

It was all going so well until he reached passport control and the guy there accused Tariq of 'Having a laugh'. He was then confronted with a photo of Ramina in her passport having the mother of all bad hair days. The next discovery was the fact that the phone was not in his coat either and that through no fault of his own he had inadvertently taken Ramina's coat instead of his. Of course it was all her fault.

"Why do you have a black coat?"

She was the first to buy one was all she could answer.

"Why do you have your passport in your coat?"

She carried it with her at all times; this was a legacy left over from her parents, she replied.

Tariq shouted at how she should pat herself on the back, she had lost the business for him and his company. He demanded that she brought his passport to him and then he would take another flight once it had arrived. The good news was he wasn't coming home that night.

Those significant events spurred Ramina on and were the catalyst for the most important decision of her life. Procrastination was going to become a thing of the past for her. This was it, they were leaving.

Aware that time was of the essence Ramina lost no time in grabbing household essentials and throwing them into a case. Luckily, for the last month or so, she had been carrying around the address of a local refuge.

Collecting the children from school Ramina explained a little of what she was doing. The strange thing was they asked very few questions and almost seemed relieved. Once inside the refuge with the compassion she was shown by the staff Ramina had a complete meltdown letting the tears flow freely for the first time in a very long time. Later on that evening she had been given all the advice and support in taking out an injunction on Tariq, decreeing if he found them that he was not to come within a specific amount of feet before them.

Ramina, as a result of such positive action, had never felt so at one with herself and the world as she did then.

Understandably the refuge was not an aesthetically pleasing place by any stretch of the imagination. It was shabby as well as dirty with a real institutional feel to it, but these things really didn't matter to Ramina and the children as it was becoming first and foremost like a home to them where they felt safe and free from all the violence and mood swings they had hitherto been subjected to. Likewise a lot of the people staying there were not the types Ramina would have chosen as soulmates. However, the fact that their common ground had involved escape from their perpetrators, a bond invariably formed amongst the women and children alike.

Unfortunately for Ramina there was a peripatetic slant to this new life and they had to move refuge a number of times (the hardest move being the first one), once it became apparent that Tariq was trying to track them down. Zuleikha and Kasim were terrified one morning when his car started tailing them as they were walking back to the refuge. He didn't speak to them, but just shadowed them throughout the journey intermittently revving his engine and hurling insults whenever the tinted passenger window opened. This would then happen on a daily basis both morning and in the afternoons and there was nothing that could be done about it. When Ramina, after the second day, started accompanying them it took on a much more sinister perspective with Tariq mounting the pavement as they walked. Despite contacting the police there didn't seem to be much that could be done and they were just advised to adopt different routes or to take either a bus, which didn't actually cover the route to the school, or to take a taxi, which with no income Ramina could certainly not afford. It was such a bittersweet twist to life in the refuge as within its confines she felt safe in the knowledge that Tariq would never be able to enter it, but outside, however, she had never felt so intimidated and scared.

Knowing it was only a matter of time before things really escalated (after all, this was a man whose whole meaning of existence, i.e. control over his family, had been whisked away from him and he wasn't going to let it go without fighting for it), Ramina made the decision to move to a completely different county and what's more to change their identities once there. As a result they went very far north which meant huge changes, but complete anonymity. The three of them found the entire experience of walking around town completely liberating it was such an amazing feeling of new-found freedom. Ramina was also aware of the psychological effect the children must have suffered, part of which was manifested in Kasim's reaction to a black hearse that happened to be driving behind the three of them just as they were walking to the local leisure centre. Ramina was convinced he was having a convulsion when he suddenly started hyperventilating and became completely hysterical. It was only when he pointed to the hearse that she ascertained what the catalyst had been for this apparent meltdown.

The support and subsequent help that the local social services centre offered them was second to none. Likewise, the social worker allocated to them was painstakingly efficient – she did anything that needed sorting in the blink of an eye. A child psychologist was immediately put into place; the school was notified and it seemed that anything that could be done to help their situation was done with no obstacles in the way.

The day Ramina collected the keys to their council home was one of the happiest days of their lives. Pinching herself as she moved from room to room knowing that here they had complete freedom never again to suffer the constant threat of what they had endured with Tariq, she completely broke down. Crying for what her life had become, and how lonely and terrified she had been, but simultaneously acknowledging the love and concern that they had been shown since their public plight, she realised that their future, although uncertain, was so much more positive. It was all extremely cathartic and once she had wiped her nose she felt equipped to face life again. She was going to start living again, get some qualifications, and get a job. Life was good; it was no longer the case of happiness being the absence of misery. It was for living and she fully intended to take everything that came her way.

True to her word once the children were properly ensconced into their respective schools Ramina decided to enrol on a social worker's qualification as she wanted to give back what had been given to her and knew it would be the right thing for her to do. Having been on the other side she knew a lot of the humiliation and loss of dignity people have to endure. People whose lives had hit rock bottom, they were the ones Ramina wanted to support. Any spare time she had she used in setting up groups – one was for women who had experienced domestic violence. It was a support network and she actively encouraged women to come out and talk about atrocities and to advise them that this was not their destiny and there was a way out. Ramina also decided to set up groups for mothers and toddlers having known the isolation of what she had suffered when trapped at home with her pre-school children knowing how lonely and soul-destroying it was.

Qualifying as a social worker Ramina did not take long to create a name for herself and was seen as being an excellent social worker with the perfect amount of empathy and patience for her charges. Admittedly at times she found it mentally exhausting and depressing but on a positive note there was also a great deal of enlightenment, reconciliation and happy endings which she would not have swapped for anything. When, however, a job opportunity involving heading up a department working with troubled teenagers came up internally, Ramina felt it was an opportunity she could not refuse. It meant relocation and obviously the concern was whether Zuleikha and Kasim were happy to leave their friends and their respective schools. Luckily, they were excited at the prospect of moving south to Canterbury in Kent and embraced the project wholeheartedly. The three of them were delighted when the letter offering her a relocation package and a start date arrived in the post a few days later. Leaving the only county they had ever really known, Ramina was surprised at their different reactions to the move. Kasim took to it all like a duck to water. Zuleikha, however, had very manic moments where she was convinced her father had managed to trace her and would be abducting her at any moment to force her into marriage. In time, however, she came to realise this was not going to happen, her father had moved on and she was safe.

After a few weeks Kasim was fully ensconced in the football team at school whilst Zuleikha had secured herself a job at a local kennels that was looking forward to a major reconstruction and expansion project. It was here that she also fell, much to her mother's chagrin, madly and deeply in love. Ramina loved her new job; it was challenging but enjoyable and one of the main reasons for this was the team she worked with. They were not only colleagues but also enjoyed social activities collectively. This was a great novelty for Ramina as up until then she rarely went out. Life was indeed great for the trio.

The city they were now living in had so much happening and culturally was pretty diverse with affluence in certain areas and abject poverty, although small scale, in others. Ramina saw children from many different social strata. Some parents were in denial and chose to turn a blind eye to their children's antics. Others were fully aware of various issues but felt helpless and overwhelmed by the situation. This was where Ramina stepped in and in the process won a lot of respect from those she helped. She held no prejudice or presumptions about anyone. Her motto was to take people on face value and to judge no one. It was no doubt because of her discreet, trusting manner that people confided in her. When a significant bit of news filtered through from a reliable contact she took the unusual action of intervening. News spread like wildfire in this city and it was advised to nip things in the bud as soon as possible. Furthermore, the authorities really couldn't afford to have this particular piece of news tarnishing their reputation.

The hitherto mentioned perpetrator had been spotted canoodling with a very young girl in the foyer of a hotel. The photographic evidence suggested to Ramina that they were perhaps a lot more involved than first surmised. This situation carried a double whammy as the DCS was not only involved with a girl in the social services system, it also transpired that she was related to the local girl who had died visiting a friend one weekend. It didn't help the situation one iota when Ramina read that Frank DuPont, the DCS with a phenomenal reputation and great experience, was heading up the enquiry from all angles and would be reviewing the situation in a few weeks' time once all the evidence had been collated.

Finding herself in a very delicate situation Ramina genuinely had no one's advice to go on. Her heart was telling her to ignore the situation and to dismiss the photos as something trivial and unimportant in the whole scale of things. So what if they were seeing one another; perhaps it had done Margot good feeling desired and loved. On the other hand the girl was under Ramina's care. She may have been over eighteen, but had only become an adult in recent months and according to this letter with the accompanying photographs the relationship had been going on for at least three years. This meant that she was under the consenting age and that he had effectively broken the law a year before, and was on paper a sex offender and in an inappropriate relationship with a young, vulnerable minor. The fact that she was now eighteen and over the consenting age made no difference in the eyes of the law. Margot was someone who struck Ramina as being totally in control and yet professionally she knew this was the paradoxical aspect of children in care – many of them underneath the bravado were emotional wrecks. Margot's case alone spoke volumes, her mother and father having died in a homeless hostel raging alcoholics, both with chronic liver failure had completely failed her. The one saving grace for her had been the wonderful family who had effectively taken her in as their own. Ramina knew they would be devastated at the photographic evidence as she was effectively in their care at the time. Did Frank not for one moment think of the consequences and repercussions not only for Margot, but also for all the helpers and carers (Ramina included) that were responsible for her welfare? It was all about him, an older, sexually needy man preying on a young girl's vulnerability and yet it had been continuing for three years which showed it was not a spur of the moment thing.

Ramina felt extremely uncomfortable about the entire situation. Up until the incident her dealings with him had always been very positive. Okay, he was known to be a ladies' man but he was also fair and good at what he did. She was in a catch-22 position but knew there was only one line of action she could take. With no hesitation and based on the evidence of the photographs, Ramina contacted the relevant authorities informing them of Detective Chief Superintendent Frank DuPont's inappropriate behaviour and gross misconduct. She did feel some slight guilt when she learnt that he had stepped down immediately due to bad health but more fool him for being so unprofessional.

10

MARGOT

When Clarissa some years later after one of our weekly phone calls, mentioned me coming to lunch and meeting Siobhan, the kids and Tory I was very reticent. Clarissa's persuasive powers were, however, so effective that is where I found myself driving to a few weeks later. It all came around far too quickly and as I walked up the drive to their house it evoked countless memories. It felt like yesterday that Scarlett had opened the old wooden front door to this quintessential enchanted cottage, all low, ancient wooden beams and various nooks and crannies. In Clarissa's inimitable way the table was set with all that lovely mismatched Poole crockery collected over the years with the patched tablecloth that had been passed through the generations and looked exactly the same. The table was laden with everything needed for afternoon tea just like the *Famous Five* books we used to read. Clarissa had really pushed the boat out and prepared things in her usual, inimitable style. There was freshly baked bread with lavender honey, smoked salmon and watercress sandwiches, chicken sandwiches with nutmeg and tarragon, and then my favourite, plain old hard-boiled eggs with cress and mayonnaise. Additionally there was a panoply of sweet goodies ranging from scones with fresh strawberry jam, raspberry cream sponge cake, chocolate éclairs and finally, her signature dish, the rhubarb and ginger trifle. She had a roaring fire going just for me, knowing how I could sit staring at the flames for hours on end.

I thought back to when I had first entered this room all those years ago not knowing what had hit me. I recalled how I had never seen anything quite like it before. This was the house where I first sat down to dinner around a table with napkins rather than either walking around or, at best, sitting on a beaten-up, smelly sofa in front of the television. This was where I wore proper pyjamas that Clarissa had warmed up on the Aga rather than going to bed in what I had worn during the day or would be wearing the following day. My bedroom was so cosy with a low, sloping ceiling and again lots of wooden beams. The eiderdown was a patchwork-quilt affair made up from all the scraps of the children's clothes over the years. It was here that I first ate spaghetti bolognese, first tasted fresh lemons, melons, pineapple and mango. It was here I had the best lead up to Christmas ever. Clarissa would go through the entire process of making sloe gin and Christmas cake. A great deal of time and effort would also go into glazing and baking the home-raised ham which she would soak in ale with juniper berries eight weeks before. Subsequently as we got older it was spicy mulled wine and mince pies with pastry that really did melt in the mouth. Then it was the team effort involved in the dressing of the Christmas tree along with creating various Christmas decorations and wrapping presents to place under the Christmas tree. It really was a truly magical experience.

It felt so strange seeing Siobhan again. In the interim she had aged; got fatter, frumpier and moodier than ever. The tweeds, wellies and headscarf were still in vogue, albeit a lot more threadbare than before. We hugged and once the social niceties were over there was not a lot more to say. For two people whose lives had been so intrinsically linked this was all rather sad. Patsy was stick-thin and very morose; it took a real effort to engage her in the simplest of conversations. Matthew was sweet but rather a pathetic creature, shy and lost-looking. Tory, Clarissa's friend, wouldn't stop fussing over everything and everyone. I could see it was going to be a fun afternoon.

Luckily the day passed on the whole without too many mishaps or tactless comments on my part. John was alluded to once or twice but reading between the lines there was not a lot of communication with him now he had moved on and forged a new relationship. Most difficult of all was adjusting to Scarlett's absence in the house; when we were there it was always the three of us and it felt so empty and unnatural without her.

I hadn't ventured upstairs; the memories were too raw. Clarissa had left her bedroom untouched and I could not bear to immerse myself in the memories. It wasn't very sacred however, as Patsy and Matthew kept disappearing upstairs and coming down with memorabilia, keen to learn more about this fragmented family that they knew so little about. That magazine photo that had caused me so much pain resurfaced and it was a job to hold back the tears. All the familiar feelings flooded back to me when Siobhan started burbling on about how like two peas in a pod Patsy and Scarlett were. How dare she? This was a complete red rag to a bull job to me. It was a desecration of all that was pure and lovely in Scarlett. How dare Siobhan compare her spotty, thin, moody daughter to my lovely sister? I knew then the day had come to a close and I needed to extricate myself as soon as possible. Luckily, however, Siobhan had chosen to return home that day.

Once she had left the scene I ruminated on how strange it was not having Ben's presence in the house. A broken man after the event he seemed to literally just fade away, subsequently dying not long afterwards of a particularly virulent form of lung cancer. His funeral was the first time I had seen Clarissa in a long time. Siobhan had been unable to attend as she had been in hospital undergoing a procedure. Clarissa didn't elaborate but it must have been serious. It was almost like old times, the two of us reunited despite the constant fussing of her best friend, Tory, who was incredibly intrusive. It was as though Tory was the bereaved spouse not Clarissa. Indeed the manner with which she plonked herself at the top table as though receiving guests could have been amusing had it not been under such sad circumstances.

What a relief later on that evening when Tory, having consumed vast quantities of wine, collapsed and fell asleep. Finally it was time to catch up with Clarissa as well as learn more about Ben. I had never really thought of him as a person with a life. When growing up he was just a part of the furniture in my eyes. I really had barely seen him over the years and realised how little I knew of him. We didn't discuss Scarlett at all but touched on Siobhan and her life. It was apparent she was very much a middle-class, angst-ridden mother with numerous hang-ups, constantly marching into her kids' schools with issues on the calibre of the various teachers that needed to be reviewed and addressed on a regular basis. Her mode of parenting, she would constantly reiterate to Clarissa, was one of the children leading the relationship. She would adhere and listen to what they wanted, not the other way round. Her approach she was certain would produce well-rounded, happy, content and self-confident children.

We had a good giggle when Clarissa recounted Siobhan's reaction to Patsy playing the part of a tree in the school production. Choosing to ignore her daughter's thoughts on the matter Siobhan, having requested an urgent meeting with the drama teacher, had the shock of her life on being informed Patsy had in fact volunteered to be a tree as she really didn't want to suffer the anxiety of learning lines and facing a room full of people.

Clarissa also touched on the demise of Siobhan's relationship with John, how it had all gone from being childhood mates to falling in love whilst at camp in America, to a very destructive relationship that was based on mistrust and hate. Things had started manifesting themselves years before when Patsy was a toddler. Instead of listening to his advice on tips for getting her to speak (his mother had been a well-known speech therapist, for God's sake), Siobhan chose to listen to a friend for advice. The friend was adamant the dummy was not an obstacle in her daughter's inability to verbally express; indeed, it was necessary she kept it as it was a comforter. "I am listening to what our child wants, John." John did not agree at all and insisted his views were not antiquated; they were based on professional studies. The dummy was inhibiting her ability to express herself; it was as simple as that.

"For God's sake, Siobhan, she sounds like one of John Wayne's sidekicks now she's learnt to talk with the dummy in her mouth." This continued until Patsy was five. John felt powerless until finally losing it completely and throwing every single dummy Patsy possessed into a public bin miles away from home. This was a violation in Siobhan's eyes and sadly she took the situation too far by issuing an injunction out on him which resulted in the two of them separating for a year. Ironically Patsy's speech improved by leaps and bounds but Siobhan just didn't get it. Despite reconciling eventually, Clarissa was convinced this unreasonable behaviour on Siobhan's part had created a rift that would never heal.

Clarissa also touched on the obsessive friendships Siobhan would become entangled in. Starting off on what appeared to be very positive vibes the relationships would invariably regress into very destructive situations. Perhaps this was why the children were so badly behaved; it was the constant lack of family time and having to interact with others on what seemed like an everyday basis. John had confided in Clarissa that Siobhan's latest friendship with Jane would end in tears and it would be sad for all concerned as the two families had a genuine respect for one another. Clarissa was at her wits' end; was what happened to Scarlett the root cause of Siobhan's inability to maintain relationships? She reminded me about how awful she was towards me before I made the decision to leave the family and to go it alone. "That is something I will never forgive her for. You were my daughter and she drove you away. That year I lost two daughters and Siobhan just didn't get it."

So what was Clarissa's next plan? Well, once John had informed her he was leaving Siobhan she knew that there needed to be someone stable enough to support the children should the need arise. John had always provided this, but with him leaving the home Clarissa was very concerned things were going to regress. "The children need an auntie like you; you have so much you could give them in terms of fun, morals, and lessons in life. Please think of some way to build bridges between them. I am at my wits' end and so want some good to come out of what is becoming such an awful situation." How, after all that Clarissa had done for me in my life, could I possibly not lift up an olive branch and build bridges with Siobhan?

Giving her time to recover from some crisis that Clarissa never got to the bottom of, a few months later I took the plunge and invited Siobhan and the two kids on an all-expenses trip to New York courtesy of my air miles. I had penned a long letter to her apologising for the past, pointing out that I had lacked sensitivity throughout the time I moved in with her and the rest of the family all those years ago. I talked about the insensitivity of teenagers and how at the time it was all about me. I apologised for leaving the home after Scarlett's death and not saying goodbye and basically stated that I wanted to turn over a new leaf in the book and to start again. A few weeks later she sent a reply and accepted my kind invitation.

Meeting them at the airport I was completely dosed up with beta-blockers and any drugs I could get my hands on to combat my anxiety. What was I letting myself in for? We gave one another a strained hug and that was it really, not much conversation, and the next thing I knew we were off to the city that never sleeps.

Sadly and perhaps inevitably the entire trip was a bloody nightmare from beginning to end. Patsy was so rude, ungrateful and demanding. She hated walking, she hated the museums and she really hated Siobhan's running commentary of happy times she had experienced with the Californian guy she met on the summer camp.

The descriptions of wild sex and Californian Coolers were totally inappropriate images in front of the children but what was even more interesting to me was her choice of words after the lurid descriptions.

"That, of course, was before I met your dad, who back then gave me a reason to live."

I was intrigued as I had no idea what she was harping on about. I didn't ask, however, as God knows where the conversation would have gone.

We saw the youth hostel she'd stayed in on her own whilst waiting for good old faithful John to join her all those years ago. "That was where we had our loving cocktail, right here in the Hard Rock Café at that table over there." Who did? Her and John, or her and the American guy? What the hell in heaven was a 'loving cocktail'? Goodness knows, but following on from there we found ourselves in some dead-end road called Jay Street where she insisted, despite the owner's protestations to the contrary, that he was the proprietor of the grubby little café she had visited every day for two weeks alone, all those years ago.

The boat trip we took later that evening which included a champagne dinner (one of my many surprises), passing by the Statue of Liberty and into downtown Manhattan taking in the most spectacular views of that iconic, amazingly vibrant skyline as we traversed the sparkling East River, was no more special to her than seeing a burger bar in one of the side streets, so unenthusiastic was her response.

It wasn't very surprising that Patsy spent most of the trip in a complete mood. At times, however, she really didn't help herself. Some poor pregnant woman on the subway asked if she could have a seat as she had a baby in her tummy. Patsy immediately stood up, thank God, but not before she had informed the poor woman the baby was not actually in her tummy, it was in her uterus. Neither did she smile when the lady totally ignored the correction complimenting Patsy instead on her, 'wonderful British accent'.

There was no denying the fact that she was obnoxious; I was, however, almost beginning to understand why. With a mother like Siobhan it was enough to drive anyone to the depths of depression. As for poor Matthew I really felt my heart go out to him. Totally undemanding he just got on with things and made no comment at all. I had no idea whether he was happy, sad, stimulated or bored. The only time I heard a request which fell on deaf ears was asking to visit the toy shop F. A. O. Schwarz. I regret not speaking out and insisting we did, but somehow it just didn't seem appropriate and I kept my mouth shut.

The day before our return home Siobhan seemed more receptive to things, so we walked in Central Park and then took a horse and cart around the periphery; it was so nice to see the three of them smiling for once. I wrecked it all, however, when we ended up in a wine bar and I made a comment about how complete it would be if dear Scarlett were with us. It was shocking; I not only realised how grief-stricken we still were, but it was obvious how badly it still affected her. Judging from the looks on Patsy's and Matthew's faces I also felt that they knew very little if anything about Scarlett's existence, despite the fact they had taken a bulk of her things from the family home only weeks before when we were all together. Sadly things from there hit rock bottom. Boarding the plane Siobhan put her headphones on, ordered champagne virtually on tap, switched on her film and that was it, not a word more was uttered. Matthew and Patsy fought for what seemed the entire flight, and at one stage the two of them were lashing out at one another. Adamant that I was no longer going to endure the looks of hatred from fellow passengers I nudged Siobhan telling her to control her children. Her retort to this was, "It's all right for some, think about me with this going on 24/7 at home. You haven't got kids, and obviously never will, so you really don't have a clue. Please just leave me alone." I honestly thought she was joking. Suffice to say the minute we touched down on British soil I abruptly collected my bags from the baggage hall and stormed out. As I did so I caught a glimpse of Siobhan who looked ghastly, clutching her head and stomach.

After that I heard nothing from Siobhan, not even a thank you from either her or the children for the trip. I know Clarissa was horrified at this fact and had tried broaching it with her to no avail. It had also been her thoughtless, heartless words that had stayed with me. I would of course never understand or ever have a clue as to what it was like having children because as she said I was unable to sustain a pregnancy. Not that I wanted to. My God, no way, definitely not the path I would choose to go down. To me they were primeval beings who sapped their mother's life away. All that time spent protecting their vulnerability and helplessness, for what purpose? No, they were complete anathema to me. What did piss me off, however, was the fact that I had no control over my infertility. It was something I could not decide for myself.

It was therefore very ironic when a few months after my return from New York I dismissed my constant morning nausea as being stress-induced. The ordeal with Siobhan and children I felt had taken its toll and was manifesting itself through my condition. I didn't stop to think about the fact that since arriving home I had been shagging my toy boy furiously with no birth control as per usual. Nor did it occur to me that I could be pregnant having missed a period, putting it down instead to stress and too many alcohol-fuelled late nights. The alarm bells really started, however, when I noticed my usual ironing-board stomach with muscles in the right places, developing a fleshy undulation to it. This was devastating to me as my body really was my temple. Again I chose to ignore it and put the weight gain down to a rapid succession of long and heavy business lunches. It was only after missing a second period and seeing the dark blue line appearing on the pregnancy test at the local doctor's who recommended it, that I realised my subconscious fears were correct.

What really shocked me was my reaction to it all and to my chagrin it was not horror, far from it. I felt instead sheer, unadulterated joy, ecstasy, and euphoria all rolled into one. How I longed to stand on the rooftop of my house to sing, dance and announce my news. I could have done so easily as there was not another house for miles. The reality, however, was that I had no one to confide in apart from Clarissa perhaps. Bearing in mind, however, how spectacularly wrong my last pregnancy went I almost felt I would be tempting fate, so decided to divulge nothing. Adamant also that I did not want to be a victim of pernicious, spurious gossip over speculation as to who the father was, knowing that the gossips at work would have a field day trying to work out the paternal element in my pregnancy, I decided to keep the secret close to my heart.

It would indeed be a complex web for workmates bearing in mind some of the close relationships I had with both men on the main board and my suppliers. Others would, I'm sure, even conclude that it was a sperm donor's as I was obviously in a relationship with a female bearing in mind Carlos had never been seen in public. That was another thing; I had also made the decision that Carlos would not be playing a role in my pregnancy. As far as I was concerned he had carried out his role unintentionally on both his part and my part. This was going to be my baby and my responsibility. I loved Carlos for what he was – a young, good-looking, energetic and impressionable guy. The entire ethos of our relationship was fun with no attachments or commitment.

Physically I could already envisage my baby. It was going to be a girl with amber eyes and olive skin and she would be called Saffron Clarissa. The dating scans I had a few weeks later actually confirmed it was more likely to be a girl although not definite. I felt overwhelmed on seeing this little thing turning somersaults in the amniotic fluid; it was hard to believe this was all happening to me. Here I was, in my late forties, having previously loathed the idea of pregnancy or babies, experiencing the most fulfilling emotion I had ever felt in my entire life.

As luck would have it, of course, and devastatingly for me, it was over virtually as soon as it had all begun. Ironically, I was in a supermarket having rushed in to buy some bits and bobs to placate my bizarre cravings. This time I really fancied blueberries coated in sugar mixed with fresh pineapple with a dollop of Greek yoghurt and honey drizzled on the top. Whilst standing in the queue wondering whether I should also throw some fresh egg meringue into my concoction, I noticed a woman looking over in horror and pointing at what I thought were my nether regions.

What the hell is that stupid woman looking and gesticulating at me in horror for? I wondered whilst simultaneously glancing down and seeing that the pineapple had pierced the sugar causing it to cascade at a rate of knots through the wire trolley. The carton of blueberries, raspberries and wild strawberries combined had also come open and they too were pouring out. I had unwittingly stepped on many of them and consequently a terrific mess of congealed fruit in various forms of red had formed around my feet.

A cashier called the janitor on the loudspeaker system and a moody, stocky blonde lady arrived with a dirty mop and a scowl. It didn't take long for the two of us to recognise one another. As luck would have it she happened to be the old bag that was directly responsible for ensuring that the area around the fresh fruit that I was purchasing on behalf of this particular supermarket chain from suppliers and growers all over the world was kept to the highest standards of cleanliness. This had not, however, been the case. Following a spot check on my part with two trainees from my purchasing team, it came to my attention that grime and dust had not only collected on the actual metal displays holding the fruit, but were also worryingly visible on the surrounding area. Even more disturbing was the fact that quite evidently the containers of old fruit had not been cleaned out properly prior to refilling them with fresh fruit and as a result there were mouldy, hard bits of peach and apple pulp etched on the sides of the displays. To top all of this any rotten fruit in the latest shipment instead of being removed had been left to rot and disintegrate with hundreds of flies living off the benefits. It was soul-destroying bearing in mind all the blood, sweat and tears I had undergone in ensuring the various produce arriving at the supermarket was not only at the most competitive price possible, but was also of the best quality and calibre. Looking at this mountain of apples and peaches it could not have been further off the mark and I was left horrified at the effect this could have on sales. My confrontation with the manager then led to her calling the woman standing in front of me now to explain where things had gone wrong. Stuttering and trying to find excuses for her inabilities I wasted no time in informing her that she was useless and inept. I demanded that she was given a written warning and, on her return, it was essential she had the correct training to ensure that this would never occur again.

So here we were again and I could see a glimmer of recognition on her face along with an inability to work out where she actually knew me from. Half-heartedly cleaning up around me and making a huge deal of it I knew I would be reporting her to my contacts as soon as I left the premises. Obviously the so-called in-house rigorous training was completely ineffectual and a review needed to be held as soon as possible.

As I was standing there waiting to pay for the produce I was aware of an ominous, vaguely familiar, slight nagging pain in my side. Brushing it aside whilst I packed my shopping into plastic bags I decided to visit the ladies' before heading into work. As soon as I started urinating I knew all my fantasies were over. The blood did not show any sign of stopping; it was terrifying and I felt powerless. Should I scream out? Should I try and ring Carlos? Perhaps if medical aid came now they would be able to save my baby. There was no signal in the cubicle and my hands were almost incapable of manipulating the keyboard and the numbers were blurred due to the tears pouring from my eyes. I was left with no choice but to start shouting. I had the door ajar and a poor woman who was trying to change her baby's nappy became aware of my distress. Promising help she disappeared with her baby looking at me as though I had well and truly lost it, which indeed I had. Still no one came and I surmised the woman with baby had obviously left the store and had failed to inform anyone. The next person to enter happened to be a member of staff who ran off to notify a first aider. The young, pimply-faced youth who then poked his head tentatively around the door looked horrified at the state I was in and immediately asked if I was having trouble breathing.

"Of course I am not having trouble bloody well breathing. I wouldn't be talking to you, would I? I am having a miscarriage. Get an ambulance as quickly as possible. You might want to clean up in here too before someone thinks a murder has taken place."

His only response was, "Shit!" and again I was left on my own.

When I heard the door opening and the sound of water swishing to the rhythmic contortions of a mop being used, my heart sank. Before I could lock the door, the janitor's face appeared at the crack, and upon seeing the look almost of triumph on her face I knew she now recognised who I was. Thankfully the demented woman had no time to make a comment as the ambulance staff arrived. They were so kind. I passed out from the toilet cubicle to the waiting ambulance which was probably just as well as it would have without doubt been an utterly humiliating experience. The paramedic in the ambulance who seemed like the kindest, most sympathetic man I have ever encountered managed to calm me down through his information that the bleeding did not necessarily mean a miscarriage; it may just be a cyst or something similar.

On arrival at the hospital however, once I had witnessed the expression on the sonographer's face along with her action in calling a colleague into the scanning room, I knew my fears were confirmed. The only thing that was visible they informed me was an empty embryonic sack and that an evacuation had occurred. Bottom line was my gorgeous little baby was dead, gone, never to be. Why me, why was I so unlucky? I had already had three miscarriages. This was all so incredibly unfair.

Three days later I was discharged from hospital. I had informed friends and colleagues at work that there had been a family crisis which necessitated my presence thereby taking official absence of work, and told Carlos that my business trip to France had been longer than anticipated. On the Monday morning true to my word I was back at my desk ready to start work again. No one obviously had an inkling of what emotional and physical trauma I had gone through. Siobhan's hurtful words came back to haunt me. How right she was. I would never know what it would be like being a mother. I was barren; end of story. I would never experience the sensation of holding a newborn in my arms, feeling that instant bond and unconditional love that exists between a mother and her baby.

On my better days I would surmise that adoption was always an option. Not being a blood relation to Clarissa had never affected our relationship; to the contrary in fact as I had often felt she was closer to me than Siobhan.

Returning to work I did instigate one significant change and that was to delegate responsibility for the supermarket where the drama had taken place to one of the former trainees who had a good idea of my expectations on the fruit display. I knew that I would not have the mental capacity to ever set foot in that building again and that if I ever so much as locked eyes with the demented cleaner again I would go into absolute meltdown and God only knows what I would have been capable of.

Nothing significant changed in my relationship with Carlos, the only difference was that I cried myself to sleep most nights. This had without a doubt, after darling Scarlett, been the most traumatic event I had ever experienced.

11

JANE

I have been to hell and back and I still can't believe what has happened to me over the last year. Things had been ticking along nicely, I had a job that was bringing in a reasonable income and I was getting on with my children. Robert and I were on an even keel; we had sorted out all our financial issues and were now only civil to one another. I had even warmed to Tatiana who over time appeared less like the gold-digger I had supposed and was emerging as not only a good sort for Robert but also a good stepmother. Ahhh, what a thought for the kids.

Tiger was becoming a delight to have around despite his obscene size and bizarre features. I had Adonis to thank for this as he had not only taught him to defecate in one corner of the garden but he had also taught him to deal with the psychotic symptoms that had haunted him endlessly in the earlier days, through old-fashioned affection and grooming, something that had certainly not been my approach.

Siobhan likewise seemed to be back on the straight and narrow, was dealing with her marital breakdown and appeared to be on a complete roll organising the university reunion. It was amazing how names long forgotten kept cropping up all over the place.

It is crazy how things can completely change in a split second; one minute you are living your life taking everything for granted and not really analysing anything then bang, everything changes. Those daily routines and simple pleasures dissipate and all you are left with is the need to survive and to rise above everything in order to continue. It happened on a Wednesday evening after my art history class whilst Siobhan and I were chatting over a glass of wine and some nuts and olives. Inadvertently I managed to drop a nut down my front and in the process of retrieving it my hand brushed past what I thought was an olive stuck down my cleavage. On further investigation however, I realised that this was not the case and that it was a lump. I became hysterical. I was convinced I was going to die there and then. How long had it been there for? I just knew it was cancerous. Siobhan tried to console me but I could tell she was really concerned and all I can recall her saying is, "It can't be anything sinister, it's bound to be a cyst. Don't worry, my friend had a very similar thing and it was benign. It's normally the ones that are hard and virtually embedded in the breast that are the sinister ones. You would have noticed this before. Please don't worry."

All I could think to myself was, *I can't remember the last time I checked my breasts for ominous lumps and no man has been there for a while so it could have been there and just grown over time with me none the wiser.*

The following day I went to see my GP who looked concerned and immediately referred me. The long and short of it is I had a scan and grade 3 breast cancer which had spread into the lymph nodes was diagnosed. Totally devastating news but I knew I had to be strong and to fight it.

My family was incredibly supportive. Robert, Tatiana, and Siobhan were amazing as were the children. I really had so much done for me. The kids and Tiger moved in with Robert which made my life so much easier as that way I could follow my agenda which meant if I chose to stay in bed all day it affected no one. The effects of the chemo were variable – some days I could barely lift my head, other days I had boundless amounts of energy. Sometimes depression would infiltrate every part of me particularly when my hair started coming out in handfuls, other times I felt incredibly euphoric. The day I removed my bandages and saw the results of the mastectomy it all really hit home. It was of course the irony of it all as the last time I looked like this I had gone through a tummy tuck and a boob job.

I did see a very different perspective to Siobhan during my incarceration and privately I was a little disturbed by the intensity of her support. Without bothering to consult me she managed to move in. Whilst initially I felt that she was a godsend, what with the cleaning and sorting the children and dog out, after a while it became too overwhelming and actually very intrusive. My subtle hints that I was feeling on the road to recovery seemed to wash off her completely. I convinced Robert to take the children and dog so that she would realise I no longer needed her help. Finally when I heard her explaining to my cleaner that she was subletting her house in order to nurse me I made the decision there and then that things had to change.

Before long I did actually manage to pull myself together and to deal with my loss. It wasn't easy and believe me I had many days when I would lie in bed at night feeling where my breasts had once been and wondering whether I should go for reconstruction or not. I would then philosophise and feel that these war wounds showed I was a survivor; they were a constant reminder to me to enjoy my life, to seize every opportunity and to never look back. I was a fighter and cancer was not going to beat me.

In time I did become reconciled and was glad I had opted for what I did. With this *joie de vivre* it was me who months down the line with reinvigorated energy brought up the reunion with Siobhan. She looked slightly surprised that this was still on my agenda but went with it with renewed enthusiasm which was a relief as we needed something like this to break the ice. Things had admittedly been slightly difficult after a particularly stressful day for me when I really needed to be alone and yet, not taking the hint, Siobhan was cooking dinner with the radio blasting away at an extremely high decibel.

Making my way down from the bedroom feeling an emotional wreck, my choice of words was not the best when I ordered her to, "Piss off out of my life, I have had enough of you. Can't you get the goddamn hint?" Luckily, she did and what's more she really did seem to understand my outburst and could not have been nicer to me after she moved out. Then it was more on my terms instead of hers and what's more I could control it as I still think, given her way, she would have been going out with me daily.

It was Siobhan who came wig shopping with me and what a laugh we had trying out different colours and lengths of hair that fantasies are made of. I bought a silky brown number at Siobhan's insistence but didn't enjoy wearing it as it was itchy and uncomfortable. Instead I made the decision to go native and although short, I grew to like the colour that had come through which was not grey, as I had assumed it would be, but a light brown colour. What was incredibly odd was the fact that it was curly bearing in mind my hair had always been so ramrod straight.

I was amazed at the number of people who were keen to attend the reunion; the funny thing was I recognised very few of the names. This I thought would make it more interesting as only recently I felt my social life needed a bit of a boost. Being single was not ideal having mainly socialised with married couples before this. Siobhan and I also came to a tacit understanding as I just did not want our friendship to reach the level of intensity that it had during my recuperation. She would always be a friend I could rely on but it was certainly coming to a stage in my life where I felt I needed to branch out. Perhaps the reunion would provide the very thing I was looking for.

I came up with a great idea to break the ice and to provide a cheesy exercise for the alumni which was to bring a photo of themselves, preferably as they were at matriculation, in exchange for a glass of champagne or drink of their choice. The photos would then be placed on a cork board for everyone to see and alongside these would be instant images of how they looked now all under flashing neon lights reading, 'Before and After'. The winner would obviously be the one who recognised the most people.

One of the alumni from Trinity College who it turned out ran the local *Cambridge Evening News*, concluded he would run an entire feature about the reunion as in those days, things on this sort of grand scale, particularly involving people in the public eye, especially a couple of politicians with colourful pasts, were few and far between. Concluding it would be the sort of feature that would interest all ages he decided to run it in three different magazines all owned by the newspaper for the duration of three months on each one. He would send a journalist along to take photographs which would be given to the features editor to create a montage which would be depicted on the magazine cover with an in-depth feature on the then and now.

When the day of the reunion finally came around I hadn't felt quite so excited in ages. It wasn't only the culmination of so much organisation, it really had been an emotional journey for me as well, revisiting my youth, reminiscing about all those people I'd met when I was that naive, idealistic undergraduate who had the world at my feet but simultaneously had no idea whatsoever about anything. It scared me to think how much time had passed and what I had been through with my divorce and my battle to survive cancer. It had certainly been a journey and I was ready to face the memories of my youth. I recalled everything so vividly almost as though it was yesterday.

I was surprised when Siobhan did not turn up early to meet the photographer and the journalist and to ensure that the menu and number of guests tallied. Then again, I also recalled her slightly lacklustre attitude to the entire thing a week before when she commented that she thought I was blowing it way out of all proportion.

"This time next week it will all be over," were her helpful words.

So what, I thought, *that's why I am going to go all out to bloody well enjoy myself, it's been a long time and I plan to get my money's and memory's worth.*

God, it was all so bloody amusing; everything seemed to have worked in reverse. The men who had been decidedly unattractive, too geeky and boyish, were now the good-looking ones and the ones who in their youth had been drop-dead gorgeous were now fat old men with sizeable paunches. For the women it was a similar story and I was amazed how women who had suffered trauma had it so etched on their faces. One woman I spoke to had lost her entire family in a car crash twenty years previously. The grief she felt was so raw and it was her eyes, the windows of her soul, that really did betray the extent of the grief she had suffered. This, however, she felt was going to be reconciling her past and present. "Now," she said, "I have to finally gather the strength to look to the future and I'm feeling positive."

At these words I could feel my eyes welling up and felt I had to excuse myself to look at the board before I became an emotional wreck. I was aware that was the last thing I needed to do as I hadn't worn my waterproof mascara. Staring at the display my eyes scanned the photos and coincidentally I caught a glimpse of her face. Suddenly the penny dropped and I was gobsmacked. Oh my, she was the girl on campus everyone wanted to be – gregarious, fun-loving, beautiful Mary Hold; no wonder her name rang a bell when she mentioned it. Never in a million years would I have recognised her. The matching name to photo competition suddenly seemed a lot harder than I had anticipated it would be, but nevertheless it was pleasing to see people involving themselves wholeheartedly in the task.

All in all the evening was great fun with both men and women enjoying non-stop conversation and laughter about the good old days. For some it was a genuine interest in meeting people from their youth, for others it was perhaps for various reasons laying down their demons.

One particular lady by the name of Louisa would have vouched for that. Her time as a student had sadly been terrible as she had been suicidal throughout. Coming back for this evening she felt had served as a cathartic experience.

Others saw it as a perfect place to network and others like me just revelled in the entire evening. I hadn't enjoyed myself like that in ages and really hadn't wanted it to end. It was fascinating meeting so many diverse personalities. The well-known actor spent his entire time throwing his voice and looking around ensuring that everyone recognised him as being well-known, but sadly for him no one seemed to.

The minor member of some European royal family spent his entire time standing on the periphery observing everyone with a slightly sanctimonious look on his face.

Johnny, the guy who was always pissed, was letching, just as I recall he did at college, with a glazed look on his face nursing his pint and rubbing his crotch. I wondered what he had done over the years but decided to give communication with him a miss.

Wizzy looked disturbingly youthful but it transpired to my relief it was her daughter who had come in her place as she was running a hedge-fund business in New York and was far too busy to attend. My daughter would have had forty fits had I attempted to send her in my place making small talk and networking at a rate of knots, as this girl appeared to be demonstrating.

There was, however, one memorable exception regarding the evening and that was Siobhan; her behaviour was simply bizarre and totally inexplicable. It was towards the end of the evening and everyone was a little tipsy whether through alcohol or the whole adrenaline rush. I was ensconced in conversation with Clara, the student who, no matter what the weather, always sported a beret and when asked why would always make us guess, the most popular assumption being that she was French to which she would give an enigmatic smile but never answered the question. It transpired she had a bald patch on her crown and the beret was an ideal prop for masking it and simultaneously creating an image for her. It came as no surprise that she was a fashion editor on a mainstream magazine.

I was aware of a chap who had obviously fraternised with Clara whilst at college and I had a feeling from the body language that they were an item. I definitely didn't recognise him but felt a frisson as he spoke; he was extremely attractive. His ebony, very black skin was his most striking feature; I had never seen a middle-aged man with such flawless, unlined skin. He was without a doubt the youngest looking person there. His hair was the only giveaway, dark, but with a scattering of grey thereby giving him a professional air. As if that wasn't enough his voice – my God, his voice – it was deep, guttural and husky and could be summed up in two words: utterly seductive. He had only been at Cambridge for a year and alluded to some sort of hassle that caused him to transfer to an American university. He was fascinating; he also had a social conscience and was involved in setting up educational facilities for children in Africa. Alongside that he was a clinical director of a huge teaching hospital in London and managed to find time for the theatre, travelling and touch rugby for the over fifties. *I wonder when he fits his wife and children in?* were my thoughts, but they were not mentioned so I was none the wiser. He himself had grown up in Tower Hamlets, the son of immigrants who had come over with nothing, seeking political asylum from war-torn Somalia. Amazingly he had worked himself through the system and despite a lot of prejudice along the way had fulfilled his dream of securing a full grant to Cambridge to study medicine. He had been the first one in his family to attend an educational facility ever and his family was so proud of him. It had obviously been a heart-wrenching and very painful decision for him when he decided to leave, but he made it very obvious it wasn't up for discussion. He had a wicked, dry sense of humour and quite frankly I could have stood alongside him all evening listening to those dulcet tones and looking into his almond eyes.

However, as I began to launch into a synopsis of my life in answer to his question, I became aware that a commotion involving the sound of glass shattering was taking place on the other side of the room. Catching a glimpse of a bright yellow dress I realised it was Siobhan and things were not looking good. Reluctantly and in mid-flow I had to take my leave of this extraordinary man and his bloody lucky partner and race over to ensure the broken glass was being removed and ascertain what her problem was. Siobhan was hyperventilating as I approached and looked ghastly; she must have squeezed the glass and broken it in the process as her fingers were bleeding. "Siobhan, what has happened? What's wrong? Please tell me, can I help?"

Eyes glazed she just turned on me in response and shouted, "Piss off," directly into my ear and with that staggered out of the room.

It was such odd, bizarre behaviour I couldn't for the life of me imagine what had happened to cause such a reaction. Having spotted her earlier in conversation with Angus I sauntered over to see whether he might have said something to deeply offend her. He had no idea – they had been having a laugh trying to match faces to names on the montage and talking about nothing of any real significance when suddenly she had upped and left with no warning.

At a loss with what action I should take and whether to go after my friend and be supportive or to rejoin the buzzing party, I concluded I had only one option and that was to do the latter. After all, it was the social event of the year. I would ring Siobhan first thing the following day but for the moment I wanted to continue where I had left off and that was to continue my conversation with the gorgeous Ragi. So many people, however, intercepted my route towards him that I ended up barely moving. That aside I ended up having a great night rekindling and making new friendships and it was a shame it sped by so quickly.

It didn't take long for me to realise that something really had gone wrong between Siobhan and me and the sad thing was that I had no idea what that problem was. She didn't answer any of my phone calls and after a while it became very obvious that she was trying to avoid me completely. I caught a glimpse of her driving near the train station in the car and she looked shocking. Pale, hair unwashed, eyes bloodshot and dark-rimmed, I beeped, she looked and then looked away. There was nothing more I could do; somewhere along the line

I had upset her. I had no idea how or why but I had definitely got the message. From now on I would stay away.

I had heard Patsy's anorexia had come back with a vengeance and wondered whether this may be why but surely with John no longer there I would be the ideal person to turn to for emotional support. Perhaps the reunion had sparked something; I really had no idea. Perhaps it was a wake-up call to her regarding mortality and the passing of time. All I could do was surmise and speculate and feel sad that I had lost such a good friend.

12

SIOBHAN

I am absolutely devastated; nothing makes sense anymore. I just don't know what to do. I want to curl up into a ball and just shut myself off from everything. Why? What? Who? I just don't know where to begin. Why would she masquerade as me? When did she take my cardigan? Why did she choose to wear it? What the hell was she doing there? Had Scarlett arranged to meet her there? Why didn't any of us know? Why didn't she tell us she was with her on the day? What the hell! Did they both share the food? If so it just didn't make sense; she knew about the allergies. Was she involved in the death? Who do I turn to? What the hell do I do? Will anyone believe me? I may be incriminated; even I assumed it was me. I can't believe the photo caught my eye, there were so many of them in a frame in a montage. Scarlett just happened to be looking up in the background; her face was literally looking directly at the camera as the flash went off. There were a series of photos all of Scarlett in the background drinking what looked like cocktails with a packet of Silk Cut on the table. Those were the last ever photos taken of Scarlett. This is a nightmare; I am in absolute shock. I don't know who to turn to or what the hell to do.

13

MARGOT

The letter from Siobhan after all this time was definitely odd; perhaps, however, she wanted to make amends. I sent one back acknowledging the fact that I could make the proposed Sunday lunch at Clarissa's. It was going to be strange as I literally had not set eyes on her since our last disastrous trip. I decided it wasn't worth waiting for the perfect moment. I would take the moment and make it perfect myself and would arrive in my own time. I said two o'clock was a suitable time. I had to psyche myself up and decreed that no matter what shit she would insist had been thrown at us in our lives, I was an example of someone that was not going to let it have left an impact on my life. I wasn't going to be led by anything she said. My attitude was that whatever mistakes we had made there was no point looking back. The only option was to move onwards and upwards with optimism and hope. We can't change the past but we can bloody well improvise big time on the future. I likened it to dancing, in that no matter what social functions I attended, despite the music stopping, I was always up there giving it everything. It didn't matter that as per usual the host had to remind me the party was over; I was there to dance, dance, dance.

14

JANE

I was still reeling from Siobhan's phone call – it had been a long time and really was out of the blue. Sounding nervous and breathless it had obviously taken a lot to dial my number and to face whatever demons she had come up against. "I feel I owe you an explanation," were the only words that I could decipher.

We arranged to rendezvous at San Lorenzo's. Gosh, the last time I had eaten there I had been sitting next to Princess Diana who was there with William and Harry. It was so exciting seeing such an iconic figure, I remember my girlfriend and I spent the entire time just staring at the interactions on their table and barely speaking to one another. I had a feeling my lunch with Siobhan was going to be very different.

Ordering a bottle of Chianti, along with stuffed olives, sun-dried tomatoes and salted almonds, I sat back and revelled in the fact it was one of those lovely, rare balmy evenings that are few and far between in England. A lone saxophonist playing a wonderful heart-rending rendition of 'Fly Me to the Moon', completed the setting. I just hoped and prayed whatever Siobhan's issue it was something that would be easily rectified. Mystified, I couldn't for the life of me think what I may have done to upset her. Perhaps it was nothing to do with me and was a culmination of all her pent-up feelings about Patsy. Or perhaps the whole thing with John and his new partner had hit home. The main thing was that the ice was going to be broken between the two of them and the two could resume communication.

I had to compose myself upon seeing Siobhan entering the restaurant as she looked absolutely dreadful.

15

CLARISSA

Siobhan had rung her mother earlier that day. Clarissa had been trying to attack an area of unruly weeds. It had taken days of procrastination and she was now ready. The constant ringing of the house phone implied it was an emergency so she was left with no other option; it had to be answered. On hearing Siobhan's usual, anxious voice her heart sank as she knew it was going to be a high-maintenance running monologue on Siobhan's side and goodness only knew how Clarissa was going to extricate herself from the situation.

There was always one problem after another. Poor Siobhan – the whole marital breakdown had affected her and the children, badly. Particularly worrying was the fact that Patsy's eating disorder had once again reared its ugly head, having got to a very tense situation at one stage when her blood pressure got so low she was admitted to intensive care. It didn't help that her best friend had been carted off with her boyfriend once the exams were over, to a hotel in Turkey, all expenses paid, by her mother whose reckoning was that they could spend the summer shagging in order to rid themselves of any sexual frustration and urges and be ready to knuckle down and start studying for the all-important A levels in September.

Patsy, whose self-esteem was at an all-time low at this time, chose to hang out with another friend. Whilst the two of them were shopping a model scout approached them and started telling her friend how beautiful she was and what an amazing model she would make. Handing over his card the friend left the shop full of euphoria and dreams of endless possibilities. Patsy, however, left feeling like the Hunchback of Notre-Dame and it was after this event she took to her room and had rarely left it. The downward spiral led to her spending a very scary stint in intensive care with her blood pressure plummeting to an all-time low.

If only darling Ben was still alive. He had been the most amazingly supportive husband and the love of her life. It was so sad that all their plans to take off and to do the things they were unable to do when the girls were younger were swept away with the illness that killed him within a month. The fact that they had tried ignoring the increasing breathlessness pretending all was well and that there was nothing underlying, made her feel so guilty. Then again, after the scans, the lung cancer had spread at such an alarming rate any invasive treatment would probably not have worked and at least he had had the summer with the family.

Siobhan had never really offered any emotional support. It was all about how she felt with her father passing away and how she had missed out on a lot of his love and support because of what had happened. Margot, dear Margot, had really tried and it had been very sweet of her to take the time to come up and help her with all the financial matters and putting things in order. Clarissa knew it was ridiculous, but she had been of the old school where women very much left things of a financial nature to their men. Consequently she had no idea how to pay the mortgage let alone a bill. Luckily Margot stepped in and helped sort everything. Clarissa knew Siobhan was not at all happy and felt that Margot, despite their closeness, had overstepped the mark and was being far too intrusive in family matters.

"Hello, darling." Clarissa's voice sounded a little high and not genuine enough. "How are you?"

Siobhan instantly replied, "Horrific. Things are awful. I need to come and see you, something awful has happened."

"Darling, please, tell me what has happened. Can I help in any way? Is it one of the children? What's happened?"

Siobhan sounded as though she had taken something and started rambling. "I haven't, I'm just so scared of her, she freaks me out, she's always there. Patsy's having problems again, I just feel so alone and frightened. I need you to come and support me, Mum. It's okay for you as you've got no dependants at home, please come and support me. Please, Mum, I need you; there is no one else I can turn to. I met Jane last week, but I just couldn't bring myself to tell her what's happened. I've decided I need to deal with it, but I need you there, Mum, I really do. I've contacted Margot and have asked her for the truth so I need you here, too."

Reaching into her innermost self although it was pretty futile, Clarissa decided that she had to follow her heart and visit Siobhan. It was going to be gruelling and mentally exhausting. Also, knowing what Siobhan was like it was probably going to be a big drama over nothing. Putting these grievances aside Clarissa managed to placate Siobhan and told her she would come the following day.

Putting the phone back on the receiver seemed to take all her energy. It was incredible to think that only half an hour before, she had woken up that morning inspired and full of enthusiasm at the prospect of sorting out her garden. Now, however, she felt utterly drained and guilty about the negative thoughts she was having. Sitting down on the step, gardening spade in hand, she began regretting the decision to visit Siobhan. She needed people around her that were positive and looking forward. Siobhan was her daughter, she knew, but she was also a wife, a mother and a person in her own right. Surely it was up to her to sort things out and not always rely on Clarissa? Mind you, she had very few friends and that was no doubt why she had called her mother.

It didn't help that Clarissa's own social life was beginning to dissolve. Devastating as it was after Ben died, a lot of her friends were around to fill the void and she was often out and about going on various excursions and weekends away, theatre and supper trips as well as brunch and lunch. There had also been a lot more interaction with the grandchildren who simply adored her in those days. Clarissa was their special granny and really loved that whole squidgy toddler stage, priceless moments when for example Patsy, making numerous attempts to ask for a sausage sandwich, finally relented asking instead for a 'piggy sandwich'.

Another time Siobhan had rung asking if Clarissa could have Patsy for the day, their nanny having cancelled at the last minute. A rushed changeover ensued at a local supermarket with Clarissa deciding to do a quick shop before heading home. Plonking Patsy into the trolley she rushed from aisle to aisle shopping furiously. En route she was aware of a lot of looks being thrown in her direction and thinking it was because Patsy was singing at the top of her voice Clarissa didn't think too much of it. It wasn't until she got to the checkout and the lady there made some comment that she looked at Patsy who had virtually the whole of Siobhan's underwear drawer draped around her neck: thongs, bikinis, suspender belts, girdles, the lot. Clarissa was absolutely mortified. Looking back now she could barely contain her laughter.

Oh, there have been some laughs. Another memorable incident was Matthew's response having been given a coin. "Oh, Grandma, that's really kind of you, I would really like a credit card though if you've got one," with not a smidgen of irony on his face. One incident that would be forever etched in her memory, one that really summed up the absolute absurdity of life, was when Siobhan was summoned to the school 'as soon as possible' to resolve an incident involving Patsy. Clarissa happened to be staying and the two of them drove straight to the school. Ushered into a classroom with the headmistress waiting for them they were handed Patsy's work. It transpired the children had been asked to list synonyms depicting north, south, east and west.

Patsy had written 'Naughty Eskimos Suck Willies'. The issue and reason the teachers had asked Siobhan to come in were that Eskimos were totally politically incorrect and could we please inform Patsy that they were known as Inuits as she was begging to differ on the controversy surrounding the word 'Eskimo'. There was no mention whatsoever about the disturbing content used in her synopsis of the cardinal directions. Once ensconced in their car Clarissa could not control her laughter, wetting herself in the process.

As time progressed Clarissa definitely felt that she was becoming distanced from her grandchildren and becoming a peripheral embarrassment to their lives. Half the time she couldn't deduce what they were trying to say to her what with the constant usage of 'like', 'don't get me wrong', 'sick', and 'wicked'. Their constant reference to her being 'in the Dark Ages' at her reaction to their jeans being worn under their backsides or huge trainers with laces undone whilst they walked, was all getting rather trying.

At least, however, Margot was accepted as the iconic legend in the family. Clarissa was grateful for that fact. She had been elevated to lofty heights once the children learnt she not only liked The Who, Bowie, Costello and The Smiths, but had also seen them live. Margot had also smoked dope and openly discussed it. Siobhan, however, had decided to say nothing at all about her former habits.

When they spotted the enormous tattoo that ran down her entire back that was it, she really was the 'coolest aunt ever'. This was not something she was wildly proud of having had it etched on her back after a drunken spree holidaying in Thailand with a bunch of mates years ago . She could still recall her horror the next day, vaguely remembering suffering pain from a needle in her drugged state and it was only when she glanced in the mirror and faced a particularly aggressive-looking tiger that it all came back to her. The tattoo artist must have felt he had died and gone to heaven as it had cost all her savings.

Clarissa chuckled to herself recalling Margot trying her utmost to hide the tattoo not only from her niece and nephew, but also more importantly from her disapproving sister and brother-in-law. The shrieks of delight when it was spotted by the children as Margot removed her T-shirt to dive into the sea in her swimming costume really were quite priceless. They had such fun that holiday and Auntie Margot was definitely the centre of attention choosing to sleep on the deck with the children, diving off the boat with them whenever they pleaded with her to do so, and preparing lovely fresh salads with everything and anything tossed into them, all bought by the children with Margot at the authentic market stalls on the various islands they moored at. Clarissa had been tentative about accepting the invitation as the last holiday they had taken en masse was with Ben. It was lovely for her to see Siobhan and Margot interacting like the good old days, obviously not as they were with Scarlett's absence, but nevertheless it was still lovely to see.

What a shame, thought Clarissa, *that things seemed to take a nosedive after Siobhan and John split up. It could have gone so well. Margot had definitely pulled out all the stops to support Siobhan, but somehow things didn't work out. I had been so hoping the two sisters would bond again, but sadly it wasn't to be.* Clarissa could still picture Siobhan accusing Margot behind her back of almost gloating over it all. *Far from it,* Clarissa sighed, still heavily in thought.

The trip to New York seemed to have really tipped the balance. Clarissa had no idea about what had occurred, but knew that the two of them had become estranged ever since. Clarissa was only just coming to the guilty acceptance that she privately enjoyed meeting up with Margot far more than her own daughter. Margot's upbeat manner left her feeling so much more euphoric after their get-togethers where they would discuss everything from their favourite books to meals, politics and now the house renovations which Clarissa found incredibly exciting and enjoyed advising on, having done a similar thing years before. The topics were endless. Wondering how John could have coped with Siobhan after all those years and surmising why he hadn't left earlier, Clarissa attempted to dismiss such thoughts as quickly as they came.

16

ZULEIKHA

Frank DuPont is a complete and utter freak, not only physically with that bloody moustache that shows all the remnants of the meals he has eaten, but also that foul, creepy look he adopts at the reception desk acting like he's undressing me with his eyes. I felt like throwing up a few weeks ago when he just stood there, hairy chest exposed, medallion around his neck, kissing his little rat dogs whilst watching me with one eye as though I too could be part of the *ménage*. I literally felt completely violated. As if that wasn't enough he then started burbling on about his holiday in Sri Lanka and insinuated that if I was up for it perhaps I could join him next time. Like hell, I was utterly gobsmacked he had the nerve to suggest it.

That, however, fades into insignificance bearing in mind his recent behaviour. Luckily, Alice and John were on hand to witness his appalling reaction when I refused to hand over my mother's personal details. I still can't believe what came out of his foul mouth.

17

CLARISSA

Clarissa knew she was fortuitous regarding her good health. Her main niggles were arthritic fingers and a shoulder that flared up from time to time which although painful was nothing compared to many of her friends, some of whom had terrible health problems. As long as she was able to continue cooking and gardening, she had Delia and Alan Titchmarsh to thank, despite feeling that she was far more innovative than them both. There was nothing more satisfying than growing and nurturing vegetables and then using them to concoct various home-made delights. Her pastry whether it was short or flaky would literally melt in the mouth and was the root of many people's fantasies when they were invited to the O'Briens' house for supper.

Clarissa knew that the day she relied on meals on wheels, no matter how good they were, would be the day she had resigned herself to old age and invalidity; hopefully that was a long way off. Genetically, for her things weren't looking too bad; her maternal grandmother had written a bestselling book at ninety years of age and her paternal grandmother was still doing the gardening at ninety-six.

The thing that she most dreaded was losing her mind and developing dementia as she had seen how utterly frustrating it was first hand. Her dear friend Tory Church was now ensconced in a thoroughly depressing institution for people with varying degrees of dementia. It was state run and as a result appeared to have very little financial investment from the government. Dirty, depressing and totally uninspiring the patients all looked like extras from *One flew Over the Cuckoo's Nest.* The staff were no better, appearing totally away with the fairies but in a more macabre manner, in that they were both disconnected as well as uncaring. All except one, who went by the name of Fifi l'Amour and the day she started working there was the day Tory moved in. A transsexual domestic she was wonderful; it was her appearance that threw one initially as she would doll herself up in retro sixties chic along with a massive beehive which made her look about seven foot tall. Her height combined with the false eyelashes made her look like an archetypal drag queen and the fact that she wore a pinny accentuated this. For some of the old biddies in the home, however, her image created a lot of confusion as they had no idea Fifi, whose family were clueless about his alter ego, was indeed a man whose real name was Barry John Williams. Poor Tory would constantly refer to the fact that although they were best friends she felt Fifi l'Amour was somewhat masculine with the hairiest legs and biggest hands she had ever seen on a lady. Clarissa did attempt to explain the whole gender issue, but in doing so realised Tory was becoming more distressed and confused.

Fifi l'Amour was a godsend to the patients although admittedly they may have been slightly confused by her appearance and initially slightly intimidated, but it was only a matter of time however, until most patients in the home realised what a good, kind, intuitive person she was. It transpired, as Clarissa discovered over her numerous cups of tea after work hours, that Fifi l'Amour's mother had suffered from Alzheimer's hence explaining the empathy that she showed to people such as Tory in a way that only people who have had first-hand knowledge can. Nothing was ever an inconvenience or irritation and her forte was to treat everyone as individuals. Without a doubt she certainly managed to bring out the best in people.

Clarissa particularly loved the light-hearted moments with Fifi l'Amour when she would waltz into a room, pinny around her waist, headscarf around her neck, mop in hand simulating a microphone, belting out Elvis Presley's 'I Did it My Way', then moving straight into, 'I'm All Shook Up' in B minor which really hit home to some unsuspecting ladies as to how manly her voice sounded. Tory at this stage would be in her own little world dancing with an imaginary partner around the room, a glazed look of unadulterated happiness on her face.

It was times like this that Clarissa reminisced on their lives before and how things had regressed. They had immediately clicked having encountered one another on the army wives' circuit. Both Ben and Tory's husband, Mark, were majors in the same battalion and were unaware that they lived opposite one another on the same road that housed all the officers' quarters. Tory's reputation as a totally irresponsible officer's wife preceded her before Clarissa actually encountered her. Rumour had it that the colonel of the regiment and his wife who were hosting the dinner party made the fatal mistake of asking Tory what she did before becoming an officer's wife.

"I was a prostitute," Tory replied.

The table went silent and people lived off this story for months to follow. Clarissa heard the account at some deathly dull coffee morning and couldn't wait to meet this unsavoury woman who had caused such a stir. It didn't take long as they encountered one another at an officers' curry night a week later. Tory was wearing a colourful sari with a large expanse of flabby midriff showing. If you looked close enough you could see a piercing on the belly button, she had henna tattoos all over her hands and feet as well as heavy black eyeliner around her eyes. The most marked thing about her appearance was the fact that she was not only dancing whilst everyone was sitting cross-legged on the floor, but in her right hand she was balancing a pint of beer and sipping it as she danced. There was no doubt about it, she was having the time of her life. Judging by the spectators' faces, however, her behaviour was not socially acceptable and definitely not expected from an officer's wife. Clarissa knew instantly that she had at long last found a soulmate and a woman after her own heart, and it was no surprise therefore that they immediately clicked and to coin a phrase, never looked back. They were delighted when they discovered their two houses were on the same road in army quarters. What's more, their children were of similar ages, which made it even easier.

Thus began a long, enduring friendship, which really did take them through some amazing, but also terribly distressing times. Due to the peripatetic life in the army they were not always living in the same countries, counties, towns and villages, but nevertheless both women were avid letter writers and were able to keep in touch regularly. Things became a little more disconnected once Ben decided to go back to college and to retrain as a teacher eventually finding the dream job teaching physics at a sixth-form college in Harlow which necessitated what was seen as a final move for all the family. Both women, however, stayed in touch and would meet for various excursions in London for a couple of days a year.

Ten years later when both Ben and Mark coincidentally died within six months of one another, the two women sought solace and great comfort in one another's company. Mark had been the first to die and Tory had been inconsolable at this stage. Clarissa gave her a great deal of support and time in reciprocation for all the time Tory spent comforting and supporting her over the dreadful events following on from Scarlett's disappearance.

When Ben, however, was diagnosed with terminal cancer, Clarissa was absolutely devastated and inconsolable. It had all come as such an immense shock to everyone and for Clarissa her entire world felt like it had fallen apart. If it hadn't been for Tory, Clarissa knew that she would definitely have gone under. In what seemed a matter of hours her world had been completely shattered with her rock and whole meaning of existence now cruelly taken away. For Tory, who was herself mourning, it served as a cathartic experience as she now had to compartmentalise her grief over Mark and focus instead on Clarissa and her great loss.

It didn't help that Siobhan was ringing her mother every day burdening her with various issues regarding her anorexic daughter, monosyllabic husband and an operation it was imperative she underwent, which would be taking place over the time scheduled for her father's funeral. If Siobhan felt that Clarissa was not empathising with her in the way she expected her to it would result in her ordering her mother to spend time with the "spoilt, adopted bitch who nobody had asked to come into their lives". Poor Clarissa was at her wits' end. Tory was there literally as a shoulder to cry on to support, listen and help her.

A few weeks after the funeral Clarissa made the decision to clear the house of all the memorabilia that had collected over the years. This was a huge step for her particularly bearing in mind that not only were Ben's belongings scattered throughout the house, but also Scarlett's room had remained untouched for twenty-eight years from the day of her disappearance. Entering the room itself took a huge amount of emotional strength on Clarissa's part; in fact, it took four attempts to cross the threshold. Margot as always was thankfully on hand, but Siobhan was no support whatsoever choosing to ring at least four times a day accusing her mother of violating her sister's memory.

Once in the room Clarissa's grief was heartbreaking; it must have unearthed a floodgate of emotions bearing in mind she had not set foot in the room since the night Scarlett went missing. The room was regularly cleaned by the cleaner but everything was untouched. It was a complete time warp from the 1980s.

A Pierrot theme very much in vogue with girls aged eighteen back then was evident throughout the room in the guise of a duvet cover, lampshade, curtains and a rug on the floor. There were posters of Abba, the Bee Gees, Blondie, and Ultravox with an individual poster of Midge Ure alongside Adam Ant. She had also cut out various moving lyrics from *Smash Hits* magazines and pasted them around the room.

Clarissa stood crying and looking in detail at the modelling agency portfolio of her beautiful daughter that had been left on the bookshelf. Cuddly animals collected over the years in a huge pile covering the entire bed along with her polka-dotted pyjamas neatly folded on the top of her pillow were a poignant reminder of how she was planning to come home that night. On the table was a huge pile of revision notes as well as interview notes for Cambridge with a discarded coffee cup complete with a faint outline of lipstick alongside. Photos of the family on their various trips had been made into a montage with air bubbles coming out of mouths written in Scarlett's hand some of which were very amusing. Again Clarissa stood there studying each photo tears streaming down her face. Pulling herself together and turning away only to be facing a home-made painting of a Pierrot as the backdrop with 'Dream what you want to dream, go where you want to go, be what you want to be. Because you only have one life and one chance to do all the things you want to do. Good luck in your exams and your interview at Cambridge. You can do it. Love you lots, Sibby' (Scarlett's nickname for Siobhan), transcribed onto the Pierrot's image. Clarissa, on reading this, completely broke down again and felt she could no longer continue with the task in hand.

It was Tory who was there for her; dear Tory took her hand and told her it was time for Clarissa to move on. Sitting and vegetating was getting her nowhere, she had to look to the future now. There was no reason not to; after all, she was healthy, had money and most importantly had a family that loved and supported her. It was as though Tory had switched on a light, turned the key and unlocked the future. Literally there and then Clarissa began to clear Scarlett's room. It was far from easy and took many failed attempts. However, once she started she found that she could cope and that she was finally facing up to the fact that her dearest daughter was dead.

Clarissa then took the next decisive step, which was to invite Siobhan and the children to have whatever they wanted from the room. To Siobhan this was a pleasing sign that she was still recognised as the real daughter and given first choice over Margot. Clarissa bristled at her acknowledgement of this, confiding to Tory how she found it totally unnecessary and vulgar. Whilst being fully supportive over how Clarissa was feeling Tory also felt at the same time very sympathetic towards Siobhan. Without a doubt it was Margot who seemed to have taken Scarlett's place and poor Siobhan remained on the periphery of everything. Then again Tory knew that Margot was definitely much more in tune with Clarissa and that all Siobhan really had was her mother's unconditional love to fall back on.

A few months on from sorting the house, Clarissa had moved onto a much healthier state of mind. Of course her loss was still felt on a daily basis but now she had the ability to put things into perspective. Tory, by reintroducing a variety of interests that Clarissa had let slip over the years, succeeded in giving her far more focus and reason to continue with life. The gardening and cooking started again as did bridge and cards. Tory booked them into learning Italian at a local college in the evenings once a week, which then diversified into another two nights taking Italian art history. The two of them then decided to qualify as tour guides and were a regular spectacle, particularly in the summer, on board the tour buses in Cambridge. With their microphones and clipboards they built quite a reputation for themselves, these two blue-stockinged ladies in their mid-sixties with cut-glass English accents, pointing out various buildings whilst simultaneously throwing in one or two naughty facts from time to time. Their reputation grew quite a following particularly when a travel programme featuring Cambridge came across them and decided they should play a pivotal role in the filming.

The proprietor of the Pickerel Inn on Magdalene Street was delighted when these two naughty ladies mentioned that it was not only the oldest pub in Cambridge, but was once a brothel and an opium den and with an ongoing reputation. Just as a garden tree in Newnham became elevated to lofty heights after Tory's comment that Rupert Brooke frequently urinated under it. Looking back now Clarissa recognised what a wonderful friend Tory had been. It wasn't difficult to grow nostalgic at those halcyon days long gone especially when thinking about the twilight world that Tory now existed in.

The dementia seemed to hit like a sudden bolt out of the blue and it was around Christmas a year before that Clarissa first noticed it. Tory was due to make her regular visit as she always had done to stay en route back from her daughter's house. They had confirmed it months before and Clarissa had not seen the need to reconfirm it. The only problem was the huge number of voice messages that Clarissa kept receiving on her house phone meant that there must be a problem. Constantly trying to get hold of her, Tory kept either dropping the phone or acknowledging Clarissa at the other end, but staying silent. When Clarissa finally had a breakthrough Tory started harping on about random events that made absolutely no sense to Clarissa whatsoever. Lucidity finally set in at the end of Tory's monologue when she acknowledged she would indeed be coming to stay at the end of that week and was really looking forward to it. They agreed to meet in the usual place to the right of the station by the geranium window pots at midday. Tory just rang off with no pleasantries and Clarissa smiled as she could hear the clamorous grandchildren in the background. It sounded to Clarissa as though Tory could do with a good old relax once she arrived.

Knowing Tory's irritation with unpunctual people Clarissa set off with lots of time to spare. She had brought *The Times* with her and became so engrossed in a particular feature that she lost all sense of time and realised it was quarter of an hour over the designated time for the train to arrive. Assuming the train was late Clarissa left it a few more minutes before finding a ticket officer and discovering the whereabouts of Tory's train. To her horror she was informed it had arrived half an hour before and had been on time. Clarissa was left in a complete dilemma; an hour had passed since Tory's train had come in so the only other thing that made sense was for her to drive home and hope that Tory may have taken a taxi there. Sadly this was not the case; five hours later the police knocked at the door with a muddy, wet Tory who looked as though she had had a fight with a haystack. She had literally been found in a dazed and confused state on a farmer's private land. When she had announced to the farmer that she was Worzel Gummidge's sister it didn't quite correlate particularly due to her twinset, pearl necklace and recently set hair. The fact that she had unpacked her suitcase alongside the haystack set alarm bells ringing and they realised she was not joking but was in fact dazed, confused and in obvious need of support by the local constabulary. The farmer felt puzzled, but vaguely pleased with the knowledge that after his call to emergency services not just one, but two ambulances, a fire engine and a victim support team arrived. Perhaps they were making up for the time he had last rung them having found, chased and fired warning shots at a traveller trespassing on his land. The traveller had then had the nerve to report him and he had wasted twenty-four hours of valuable harvesting land time in a cell where he was unceremoniously released the following day without charge.

Imagine his horror when the incident unit started to question Worzel's sister as to what her name was, where she was going and whether the farmer had attempted to hurt her in any way. On hearing "Tory Church, The Spinney and No," the farmer was relieved she was now cooperating and was able to give her name, destination and reveal that he was certainly not harming her. Thank God the scum (that went by the name of policemen) would be leaving his land promptly. Imagine the poor farmer's horror, however, when some wise arse from victim support suggested she was saying, "Torturing me with a spinney". At this statement all eyes were on him – what a bastard – as well as being a traveller-torturer he was also a granny-basher. As luck would have it in those parts one of the firemen knew of Clarissa's house, The Spinney, having collected some of Ben's belongings that Clarissa had kindly donated to the local hospice, resulting in the farmer being given a last-minute reprieve. Tory was then stuffed unceremoniously into a police car along with her suitcase that had been repacked with half the haystack and arrived on Clarissa's doorstep six hours behind schedule.

Clarissa found it shocking that Tory barely offered an explanation for her lateness acting as though it had been a matter of minutes not virtually an entire day, which had rendered Clarissa housebound and inevitably very irritated. When she questioned Tory on what might have gone wrong Tory who had done this journey dozens of time before nonchalantly mentioned how she decided to disembark four stops before the official stop because she thought the countryside looked pretty. All Clarissa could recall was the fact that it was the industrial area of the city and was renowned for being a complete blot on the landscape. Mentioning this to Tory had as much effect as water on a duck's back; she was adamant she had enjoyed her country walk but was sorry she had been a little later than planned. She hadn't used the station pay phone as she felt there was no need to; Clarissa was after all in the car so could have sat in there listening to the radio. Plus it couldn't have been that wildly inconvenient for her bearing in mind it wasn't as though she was running a multinational company or doing anything of great importance. *Fair enough* thought Clarissa but there was still no rhyme or reason as to why Tory decided to disembark from the train when she did?

It took an enormous amount of self-control on Clarissa's part to maintain her cool. What she really wanted to do was to let rip at her friend and to admonish her not only for being so thoughtless putting her through unnecessary worry, but also for being so dismissive about it. In her inimitable way, however, Clarissa was able to turn it into light-hearted banter saying, "Now you've mastered the art of traipsing around the countryside in brogues and a suitcase under some pretext of keeping away from conventional living, perhaps we could now think about getting tattoos as well as piercings, dying our hair and wearing outrageously flamboyant clothes as we're no longer at a stage in our lives where we have to adhere to timetables and conventions?" At this stage Tory did a double take and wondered whether Clarissa was being facetious and whether she had annoyed her in any way.

Joking aside, as Tory's stay wore on Clarissa began to notice more and more worrying things about Tory. It wasn't just the little things such as finding the kettle and a toilet roll and other such oddities on a daily basis in the fridge, it was also discovering half-eaten meals in the most bizarre places ranging from above the television, to under the bed, and in a wardrobe.

On another occasion Clarissa went to fill the kettle with water only to discover it was full of orange juice. Mealtimes began to resemble the food scrambles Clarissa would have with the grandchildren when they were younger. Tory barely knew how to use a knife and fork and if she did it would be used inappropriately such as when eating soup or cereal. On the rare occasions she sat for dinner Clarissa soon realised, although lucid, Tory seemed unable to maintain a normal conversation tending to begin a story then losing the thread halfway through and on doing so would get up and wander around the room opening drawers and muttering to herself.

After a couple of days cocooned in the house Clarissa wondered whether it may help giving Tory a breath of fresh air so decided they should go on an excursion to the local garden centre. Tory was adamant she wanted to buy some bedding plants although Clarissa wondered where she would be planting them bearing in mind she lived in a third-floor flat and what's more for as long as they had been friends Tory had loathed gardening. Clarissa wanted to purchase a garden gnome for Margot's Capability Brown garden feeling that it needed a light-hearted perspective to it. They had both agreed to rendezvous in the café and whoever arrived first was to buy the scones and tea. It didn't take Clarissa long to locate the most hideous gnome she could find. It was then a case of ordering their afternoon tea and waiting for Tory to arrive. An hour later having consumed two pots of tea and a coffee Clarissa became increasingly concerned about the whereabouts of Tory. Clarissa, whose pelvic floors and bladder were now totally ineffective, decided she would shoot to the ladies then arrange to have Tory's name announced on the loudspeaker system. As luck would have it Tory happened to be coming out of the toilets as Clarissa was rushing in. She thought she was going to wet herself there and then as Tory had grabbed her in a passionate bear hug saying how amazing after all this time they should bump into one another and what a complete coincidence it was. Extricating herself after a significant struggle, Clarissa leaned against the toilet door breathing deeply and trying to calm her racing heart, so troubled was she by Tory's reaction.

When she located Tory at the table moments later tucking into her scone and jam as well as stone-cold tea, Clarissa became even more dismayed at Tory's incredulous reaction. "I can't believe you knew to order me this; how did you know I was going to be here? This is truly incredible."

At this stage Clarissa was so overwhelmed she really didn't know whether to laugh or cry over what had become Tory's obvious rapid cognitive decline. Clarissa wondered whether Siobhan, and Patsy would notice the situation with Tory, but luckily, they didn't. Perhaps it was the general euphoria of Christmas and everything that goes with it that predominated or perhaps they were oblivious to Tory's presence being so immersed in their own lives. Alternatively Clarissa wondered whether Tory may have been left feeling exhausted from all her exploits of the previous days and that once sitting in front of the Christmas entertainment on television may have some sort of meltdown with just enough energy to eat and watch TV. Interestingly enough she was also pretty lucid when mealtimes came around choosing for once to remain seated at the table throughout.

The only oddity that became a source of amusement to everyone was on retiring to bed every night normally before everyone else,

Tory would insist on having her goodnight dance with her beau, Jim, who happened to be a battery-operated gyrating reindeer who would suggestively twist his hips and sing, "Well, hello, it's Christmas". She appeared to have a fixation with him ever since the day they connected in the front seat of the car en route to collecting Matthew from school. Clarissa had come across Jim the Reindeer on their disastrous trip to the garden centre and, left with no time to return home with their purchases, Clarissa's plan had been to collect Matthew (who was coming to spend the evening with them) en route from school. Tory was left holding the reindeer on her knee as Clarissa parked. Standing in the playground she marvelled at the eclectic groups of women and became fixated with one lady trying desperately to balance on one spot in heels, wondering why the woman was adopting this strange position. Clarissa glanced down only to see an enormous bunion and realised the woman was trying to massage the pain with her other foot still in the high heel. Poor thing, why hadn't anyone advised her those high heels exacerbated such conditions?

Another glamorous group of women came to join the existing one laughing hysterically. Clarissa was intrigued to discover the cause and edged towards them ready to eavesdrop. It didn't take long to deduce it was some kind of sex scandal that had taken place. It was only when she heard the words "old dear making love to a reindeer in the front of a car", that Clarissa's heart sank and she wondered what depths of depravity poor Tory had sunk to. Rushing out she was relieved to see that Tory still had her clothes on but could see why the woman had jumped to lurid imaginative presumptions. It transpired the 'on' button had been inadvertently activated and poor Tory was unable to switch all six foot of a plastic reindeer gyrating on top of her in the restricted space of the passenger seat area in the car, off. Rushing over to the car door and desperately searching for the 'off' button all Clarissa could think about was how Tory would be feeling after such a mortifying, perhaps painful experience. She was immensely relieved and amused when Tory, finally coming up for air once the reindeer was deactivated, announced to everyone including a highly embarrassed Matthew who was surrounded by his schoolmates, "My God, I haven't felt that sort of sensation since my Mark died."

This was more like the witty old Tory of long ago that she had really come to miss, was all Clarissa, in between her hysterical laughter, could think.

A few days later once Siobhan and her family had gone Clarissa was again reminded of how Tory's mental state had regressed. The two of them were heading to a communal bin located near the supermarket where Clarissa was planning to offload rubbish that had been collected over the Christmas period. The offensive smell of the remains of the festering turkey was her primary concern particularly once she had observed due to the onslaught of particularly mild weather, hundreds of maggots that had infiltrated the entire contents of the dustbin and were beginning their journey outside onto the path directly beside her porch. It had got to the stage where she dreaded opening her bins as the maggots appeared to be multiplying on a daily basis. She loaded it all single-handedly whilst Tory sat in the car applying lipstick to what should have been her lips, but ended up largely on her teeth, Clarissa observed. Car loaded, Clarissa with Tory holding her nose and looking at her oddly as though the smell was emanating from her, drove to the supermarket with the direct intention of parking alongside the bin and being as discreet as possible bearing in mind it was specifically for benign rubbish consumed on site by shoppers and not for heavy-duty carcasses covered in stinking maggots. The entire operation was going to be slightly problematic in the fact that Clarissa's car was not a particularly discreet colour being bright yellow with a personalised number plate 'Clar 1'. This was a legacy left over from Ben who decided a distinctive colour and number plate would be the only way forward in solving the ongoing problem of a lost car in the car park whenever Clarissa did a supermarket shop.

Hauling the bin bag out of the car with Tory impassive and

stationary in the passenger seat, the contents proved too heavy for the bin liner resulting in all the debris spewing everywhere. The turkey carcass was discernible as were the rotting Brussels sprouts and other such delights with writhing maggots appearing from all directions making the most of their heavenly treat. Attempting to clear up, the carcass literally started to disintegrate in her hands. Objective bystanders who witnessed this entire scene may have thought that the unkempt but rather aristocratic older lady had obviously hit hard times. This assumption would not have been helped either by the fact that Clarissa was having a particularly bad hair day or by the threadbare tracksuit she had thrown on knowing it was going to be a messy business.

As luck would have it these were the very thoughts of the ladies from her old book club, who on seeing the car, suddenly realised it was none other than Clarissa. *She had got her comeuppance,* were the unchristian thoughts that immediately came to some of the ladies' minds. It hadn't gone down at all well a few months before when Clarissa had announced at the last book club meeting that she was leaving as Mills and Boon along with the other historical romantic novelists the majority of the group favoured, were not her forte. Her request about wanting to read more challenging contemporary fiction authors who wrote about morally sensitive issues had been met with blank, uncomfortable faces and she knew this would never happen. The women now physically formed a scrum-like configuration as they passed the bins, sad but also slightly gratified that one of their kind had stooped as low as this. Once inside the safe environment of the supermarket café they discussed what could possibly have gone wrong. One lady standing on a chair whilst attempting to get a bird's-eye view of Clarissa's antics alarmed many shoppers who could see the flimsy chair was highly unsuitable for this rather stout lady's girth. Some of the ladies were convinced Clarissa's downfall had been caused by the questionable literature she had suggested they all read. Others suggested that perhaps she had lost all her savings through dubious means. All concluded that she had certainly hit bad times. It was then back to business and a discussion of the present book, a sentimental, historical fiction set during the French Revolution.

Clarissa meanwhile had indeed noticed the ladies from book club – just her luck! She ruminated on what explanations the ladies would have concocted. If only she had the nerve to have licked the turkey or to have held up a bone and bitten it in front of them. Tory would certainly have been game a few years back. God only knows what little act she would have performed – rancid turkey remains combined with politically correct old bags, Tory would have had a field day.

Turning to her friend, Clarissa wondered what she would have made of it having had a bird's-eye view from the car's side and rear mirrors. No explanation was needed. Tory, looking very pale and horrified, responded with, "Why were you eating food from the dustbins? Are you hungry? Poor, poor dear."

By the time Clarissa reached home, she had come to the painful conclusion that Tory was going to need not only an official diagnosis, but a damn sight more support than she was currently getting. Her little face had looked so confused and shocked at Clarissa's antics. Her dear, dear friend was becoming a shadow of her former self and the most important thing now was to make the decline as comfortable as possible.

The following day Tory didn't rise until midday. Clarissa, knocking gently on her door whilst holding a cup of tea for her, noted how serene in sleep she looked compared to her usual maniac facial contortions, which would range dramatically and with no warning from angst to complete bewilderment. No longer able to keep her emotions in check, Clarissa finally broke down crying, as she had never done before. It was all such a sad, bloody awful ending to such a wonderful life that Tory had had. The battered old suitcase placed beside her bed was another poignant reminder of her regression. In the old days it had only been the best and most glamorous accessories along with all her matching designer clothes. Where had they all disappeared to? Clarissa suspected it may have been the aggressive landlady who Tory mentioned had practically battered her when she announced she had mislaid her front door key four times in a week.

Clarissa was sure about one thing – Tory would not be making the journey home by train and that she would never be living alone again.

Social services were an absolute nightmare to get through to; it took virtually the entire morning to speak to the relevant department. Luckily, however, when Clarissa did, their advice was surprisingly second to none. Fortuitously Clarissa managed to secure a place for Tory in a home for the elderly near to her house; somewhere had literally come up days before.

It was here that Fifi l'Amour entered into the ladies' lives particularly Tory's. This larger than life character offered a complete lifeline to her and had become her absolute rock. Through thick and thin Fifi never left Tory's side.

Emerging from her reverie at the sound of the phone's persistent ringing penetrating the silence, Clarissa heard herself declare, "Yes, thank God for Fifi l'Amour." Mounting the stairs in the opposite direction to where the phone was ringing as she had already guessed it was the persistent Siobhan, Clarissa went to pack her suitcase. Knowing it was going to be a very trying next few days with her daughter, Clarissa prayed that she would keep her mouth shut in order to avoid a huge humdinger with Siobhan that she felt was brewing. It really couldn't have been a more inconvenient time, this trip, as it meant she had to cancel her appointment with the incredibly elusive but brilliant eye surgeon who had agreed to see her after months of being on a very long waiting list. Her vision was deteriorating rapidly leaving her slightly concerned about whether she would be able to decipher the maps, different counties and towns let alone the various roads and motorways in between both her and Siobhan's house.

18

FIFI L'AMOUR

I started the day dear old Tory Church was admitted to Cell Block H, poor darling. I immediately felt a kinship with her. She looked so dazed and confused, a little old lady version of Paddington Bear as she walked down the corridor with her friend and her battered old suitcase. She reminded me so much of my poor old mum, bless her; she had been even more confused when I told her I'd changed my name for good. In some ways I was going to spare her the shock but decided that if it hadn't been for all the love and support she had given me over the years I would never have had the nerve to do what I eventually did. I was so happy and content with my new identity I really felt it was important she knew my secret before, God forbid, she died or was so far gone she would not have the brain matter to deal with it.

Up until I came out it had all been a pretty shitty life for me. I spent my entire childhood in denial and it didn't help that I had a macho Welsh rugby-playing fanatic for a father who the minute I was born thrust a rugby ball in my hands. He and I couldn't have been more different physically. For a start he was short, squat, thick-necked, with huge muscly calves; my poor sister, Lorraine, was blessed with these too. As for me, I was tall, gazelle-like and basically very girlie. I loathed getting dirty and above all I hated rugby.

The day my father happened to be watching a match with me playing was the day he witnessed me wearing my new rugby boots. I had a wet tissue in my pocket and every time I went near any dirt that tissue would be out cleaning the boots. He reckoned on that occasion I missed at least three tries and then thankfully had the insight to realise I was never going to be that rugby-playing son he had always dreamt of having.

Even my name conjured up macho associations: Barry John Williams – that again couldn't have been further from who I was. Thankfully, Dad at this stage chose not to persevere with his prodigy and it wasn't long after that he moved on to promoting women's rugby in the community. Thankfully this was right up Lorraine's street, the main source of enthusiasm being the fact that Dad had two lads from the first team training the girls alongside him and according to Lorraine they were complete eye candy. She played for a number of years but two things put a stop to it eventually. The first was my grandfather telling her what lovely big shoulders she had. The second was her first serious boyfriend. Whilst looking in the mirror at the two of them in shorts on a rare summer's day she realised that her calves and shoulders were actually bigger than his. As luck would have it they finished not long after her rugby days were over and she ended up marrying Rhys, one of the lads from the football team. She had trained with him and luckily for him his calves and shoulders were twice the size of hers so there was no issue. By that time, however, she had moved on and was working alongside my dad training up female rugby stars of the future.

My gender dysmorphia had been brewing for many years, I think. Even at the age of five I was happy dressing up as a mermaid or a princess. Back then people took photos, laughed and almost encouraged me. When I hit nine years of age, however, people did not seem so amused and I came to realise that cross-dressing, unless you were in a play, was not the done thing so would have to be undertaken subversively. Every Saturday afternoon would be a field day for me in my sister's room as I knew I had a window of opportunity for exactly three hours knowing both my father and her were out at rugby training. And what a field day it was; I literally had the pick of her wardrobe: the frilly rah-rah skirts, the shoes, the handbags – oooh, it was orgasmic. The one thing, however, that would piss me off about her was the way she threw all her dirty clothes back in the wardrobe. At times it was gruesome. Being the type of person I am I would ensure her room was immaculate when I left.

A few years later I moved onto Mum's room. Dad always used to call her the closet queen and admittedly the day I discovered my mother's wardrobe I really thought I had died and gone to heaven. Bored out of my mind with revising for Geography O level, all oxbow lakes and glaciers, I went for a nose around the house. Entering Mother's bedroom with all her clothes strewn everywhere sent me into an apoplectic fit; I hadn't realised she had so many designer clothes. No wonder Dad spent night and day at work. When I reached her shoe wardrobe having the shoe fetish I had set me off yet again and I literally spent all day trying different pairs on with different outfits: Chanel kitten heels in black and white, Yves Saint Laurent stilettos in blue. I can still recall the range and diversity and the sheer unadulterated pleasure of being in seventh heaven secure also in the knowledge that no one would be popping home due to their various work commitments.

Following on from this day my fire had been lit, there really was no stopping me and unfortunately the entire study leave I had was taken up by solo modelling at home. As each day passed I became more daring until by the end of the first week I was watching television and eating lunch in all my finery. My main concerns were no longer Chaucer, fractions and equations to name a few, instead I became completely obsessed about the fact that Mum's underwear felt too intimate and quite frankly weird to put on. Lorraine's were grey, dirty and totally unsexy and what I wanted was my very own lacy pants and padded bra as all these lovely outfits I was trying on just didn't feel right in my huge, baggy Y-fronts.

Unsurprisingly I did not do at all well in my exams and deciding academia was not for me got a job training on a YOP scheme at a local hairdressers. When I received my first pay packet I blew the entire thing on a hairpiece and the most amazing matching pants and bra I had ever seen in my life. I wore and washed them every day and it felt good having them on. I would amuse myself imagining how various people would react if they knew what I had on underneath my innocuous jeans.

Joking apart the sad thing for me was that I really had no one to confide in. I was tempted to tell my mum on so many occasions but just couldn't find the words. I knew it was weird; we certainly didn't know anyone like me, but then again who knows what goes on behind closed doors. There were comedians of course that cross-dressed, however, whenever Kenny Everett came on, for example, Mum would pull a face and say what seedy smut it was. These were things that happened to other people, not to the likes of us. I think she would have been horrified. As for my dad, he would have thrown me out on the streets the minute he knew.

My mates would have been no more understanding. I knew that by their reactions to Boy George and the vitriolic displays of emotions he would invoke when we all sat around watching *Top of the Pops*. If only they had known that sitting amongst them nursing his pint and clad in his dirty jeans, was their mate with the pinkest frilliest pair of teeny lace pants and matching bra to match, promising himself that his next purchase would be some decent make-up having seen Boy George's perfect skin as portrayed on the television.

God, it was hard growing up in inner city Birmingham with this constant turmoil inside me. I didn't relate to the guys and yet I fancied them and because I hung around with the girls most people thought I was some kind of lady-killer. Of course I didn't fancy any of them, I was just on much more of a level with them. I envied my best friend, Jessie, but I also knew I really wanted to be her. That was the bottom line. I hated my body; it had been the worst trauma of my life going through puberty realising I really was turning into a man. It hadn't been so bad when I was younger as my voice didn't break, my penis didn't grow and I was fresh-faced with no need to shave for what seemed years after my friends. I even harboured a fantasy that perhaps it was never going to happen and that my penis was going to drop off and my whole thing about turning into a female would happen. I prayed every night and promised God I would do anything. Just as I started getting used to the idea my world crashed around me and I realised nature was taking its course.

Not long after this, my dad died of a sudden heart attack at work and although devastating for my sister and me it was of course far worse for Mum. Dad had been her world, he had waited on her hand and foot and worshipped the ground she walked on. Utterly bereft, the thing that would really cut right through me was when she kept reiterating I was now the man of the family and it was up to me to look after the family. God, talk about pressure. I didn't to my chagrin even have a job; the hairdressing apprenticeship hadn't been my thing at all.

I tried to make it on the burlesque circuit having been inspired by Leigh Bowery. There was nothing like his Taboo Club, it was the most amazing place, a fantastic combination of wild decadence and crazy people. Gaining entry before I ended up working there was a cabaret in itself. On the door Mark Valtier would hold a big hand-mirror to us the punters and would ask, "Would you let you in?"

I recall one guy who turned up once in a plaster-of-Paris wig, a string skirt and a pair of clogs; luckily, he was allowed in. I loved it; all that drama and being the centre of attention was right up my street. The fact that I could do it as a woman was the absolute icing on the cake; that way I knew I would be able to indulge my inner passion without feeling any recriminations. I was even able to tell Mum who predictably put her nose in the air and said it would be much nicer if I did it in a smart suit. Once, however, I had convinced her that my way was far more lucrative and ensured a regular stream of work she got on with it and even advised me on my wardrobe.

As time went on and with fewer demands on her social scene now Dad was dead (the only thing I ever remember her doing was bingo club every Tuesday night and out dancing with Sheila and Kevin at the local event held once a year), she even let me loose in her wardrobe. Mind you, the shoes sadly never fitted and she wasn't keen on my idea of making them into slingbacks. It was great to be wearing some of those iconic things from my youth now in legitimate circumstances and with Mum's blessing rather than creeping furtively around the house in them. Poor Mum, as time wore on she would often ask me about partners. I was still confused as I had relationships with various men but didn't see myself as gay. I was a woman; I wanted the sex organs of a woman so that ultimately, I could have sex as a heterosexual woman with a man. The sex I had with men at that moment in time was not what I really wanted and yet the sex with a woman was not what I desired either because I wanted to be the woman. It was only when dear old Jessie mentioned that she had had enough of ignoring the elephant in the room and put the question to me that I realised I had to make a decision.

"Do you think you enjoy the whole burlesque thing where you are wearing all the women's gear and not in my opinion sending yourself up, but consciously making an effort to look good because you want to be a woman?"

Oh my God, when she said that to me all I could do was hug her and cry; finally someone had got me and I was so happy it was my best friend. What's more, in her down-to-earth, pragmatic way she suggested I got rid of my bouffant as it was too dated and clichéd and that I pulled myself together and instead of leading a double life made it the norm. Drawing on her knowledge as a medical student she asked me if I was aware that there was an operation, albeit a complicated one, which could be covered by the National Health that would enable me to have an operation and become a proper woman.

Mum started changing when she was in her early sixties. It was nothing really significant, just little things she started doing that were out of character. For a start she kept referring to my name as 'Barr' and then a few seconds later 'y'. She had never shortened my name as in her opinion she had given me the name and that was the name she had chosen. This odd pronunciation happened all the time. It was so odd and what was even odder was that she didn't seem to notice. One evening for example, she asked me, "Draw the thing that keeps daylight out." She looked confused when I said, "Do you mean the curtains?"

Her sister came to stay with her grandchildren, twins, a boy and a girl aged ten. Mum kept asking if they were identical and just didn't seem able to understand that different sexes could not be identical. On another occasion, one of her friends who had made an impromptu visit, popped over and mentioned the lovely smell of vanilla permeating through the house (Mum had lit a scented candle). Next thing her friend knew she was screaming at the top of her voice for me to come down immediately. I was in the shower and immediately thought an intruder must have entered or that someone was having a heart attack so rushed downstairs immediately only to be informed by Mum that Connie had smelt a gorilla in the house. I didn't know whether to laugh or cry at such a reaction.

She would go off on shopping trips returning with nothing and just seemed confused. I would frequently answer the doorbell to her being escorted home by the police. The first time it happened I was convinced they were coming to arrest me because I had been spotted out and about during the day dressed as a woman. Mum was beginning to make it a habit arriving at various destinations only to forget where she was. The police would then be alerted and would accompany her home.

It was amazing how she often forgot her name and yet always remembered her address and postcode. What was really worrying were these were routes she could have walked blindfolded having lived there all her life. It was becoming very hard for both of us and I realised she could no longer ever be left alone.

The final straw was one night when Lorraine and her husband, Rhys, were staying she tried to climb into their bed wanting a cuddle and was hysterical when they wouldn't.

My life subsequently became that of a carer for her to the point that I ended up sleeping outside her bedroom on a makeshift bed knowing I could not take any risks with her. Capable of doing anything it was akin to looking after a toddler but in an old woman's guise. Over time the entire thing was soul-destroying. My lovely mum had regressed to an almost animalistic state.

When the end finally came it was a relief, perhaps not to Mum as she was in her own little world, but knowing how feisty and independent she had been this would have been the worst-case scenario for her had she known. It was almost a relief for me that Mum never knew me as Fifi. I just don't think in hindsight she would have got it.

Don't ask me why I decided to go and work as a domestic slave in a home for the elderly. I guess a lot of it was because I felt I had an understanding of what a cruel disease dementia was and wanted to put what I had learnt from Mum into practice. Plus it was the only job I had experience of. I also made the most important decision of my life thanks to my guardian angel and constant fount of inspiration, Jessie. I was no longer going to be known as Barry; it was Fifi l'Amour forever. Lorraine and Rhys were more horrified about my name than my decision to become a woman which really made me laugh. I was expected to undergo a transitional period for a couple of years and if that all went according to plan my fantasies were going to become reality and as Jessie confirmed, the NHS would support me all the way. Life at long last was certainly looking up.

19

TORY

The nights seem so much longer than ever before; I wake up then it's time for bed again. I seem to spend a lot of time in bed. I hate sleeping; I am the party girl, the one who is always the last to go to sleep. Here, however, they are always putting me to bed. It is so annoying. The other night I got dressed into my party dress, my lovely sparkly one; the nice man-lady, Danny La Rue, let me put it on. Normally the other people here say I have to wear a tracksuit and a nappy. We had a dance together in the corridor. He doesn't dance like my Mark (or is it Reg?) did, but it was lovely wearing my dress. I know I looked fantastic. Everyone else was staring at me; I bet they wonder why I am here. Danny was called to do something so I carried on dancing down the corridor on my own. This horrible lady grabbed my arm and asked me what I was doing. She said Fifi was no longer on her shift and she was the boss and I had to go back to my room to have breakfast. What do I care that Fifi is not on her shift? Who is she? I had a rabbit called Fifi; there's no rabbit here. I informed the nasty lady I wanted dinner not breakfast and she told me to shut up and to go and take my nightdress off and to put my tracksuit on and not to argue with her. When I told her it was my dancing dress she started laughing at me. I decided to leave this horrible prison, but when I reached the door it was locked and the ladies in the office wouldn't give me the code to get out. Another elderly lady told me I would never be able to leave. I told her I had to as I had to feed my dog. No one would listen to me so I started shouting then they took me to my room and lifted me back into my bed. They said they would make me a nice cup of tea. I didn't want tea, I wanted champagne and they told me to shut up.

Everyone here is so old and boring. I am so much younger than they are. I like bell-ringing though, that's fun and the men like it when I dance to the chimes. One lady's very rude though and turns the television up so loudly you can't hear any of the bells chiming. Whenever I tell her to turn it down she starts crying saying she is going to report me. I tell her, "It's my house, I make the decisions, and I didn't say you could stay here." Then again, it can't be my house as I can't drink champagne or leave when I want to. I wonder whose guest I am. Whenever I ask the people in uniform they laugh at me. Danny La Rue is kind, she says l am her guest and I can do whatever I like. I found out her name is Fifi; that's who Fifi is, not my rabbit.

Fifi Danny La Rue will not let me drink champagne though. All they do here is bring you juice in a plastic cup with a straw, and tea. I hate tea. That's another thing in this place, they are always talking about the weather.

"Oh, it's sunny today, it's raining, it's too sunny, it's windy, it's raining, mind it's always raining."

When it snows the whole home stops. They wouldn't let me go out and feel it on my face saying I would die of the cold; so what if I did? I don't care; no one else would care either. Why would they, or should they? I don't need to be told what the weather is like, I can just look out of my window. I'm not blind. Who cares the only time I see the weather is through the window? When I saw the night all lit up in different colours the other night I asked the woman in blue overalls (no idea who she is, she is either a guest or works here) if I could go out and dance. She just laughed and asked me if I wanted a cuppa. When I said I only drank champagne she laughed even more and told me to go to bed. They keep giving me pills too. I can't swallow them, they are too big and I don't know why I have to take them. I think they are trying to poison me with them. I put them under my bed; no one ever cleans under there so they are never noticed. There are a lot of them under there now.

A kind lady visits me quite a lot. Her name is Clarissa. She is very nice. I remember her from somewhere. I think she was my cleaner. She smiles at me and sits on my bed asking me if I remember things and keeps talking about people I have never heard of. I wonder why she doesn't clean under my bed; maybe I should ask her. I am not sure whether she cleans my room now I am here. Sometimes she brings me food. I can't remember the name of the things she brings, but she says I like them. They have lots of pips in them, which get stuck in my throat. By the time I have spat them out there is not a lot of fruit left, but it's very nice of her.

Fifi-Danny and Clarissa are the two kindest people I know. I think they both work here or maybe they live here and I work here, I don't really remember. Sometimes I feel as if I am in a dream. I just don't like being put to bed all the time and wish I could have champagne instead of tea.

20

SIOBHAN

Siobhan felt physically ill; what the hell was she doing? She was acting like a chicken with no head. Why the hell did she ring her mother? What was she thinking of? It had all been such a nightmare what with spotting Ragi at the reunion. Luckily, he didn't seem to have clocked her otherwise that would have been really bloody awkward. She had had no idea he was coming, she hadn't seen anything on the guest list and the situation could have been horrendous had she not spotted him first. Fortuitously he looked totally engrossed with the woman that had always worn the hat at college. Funny how after all this time she was still wearing it. Judging from the body language between the two of them Siobhan suspected they were in a relationship. How she would have loved to have marched over and demanded to know what the hell he was thinking of, disappearing the way he did with no warning, no forwarding address, and no way of tracing him whatsoever.

Even to this day his behaviour had been inexplicably bizarre; one minute they were enjoying a pretty passionate relationship at Cambridge with him spending his entire time telling her how wonderful she was, and lucky he was. The next thing he was gone, a non-person. It didn't take long for people to forget him, but for her Ragi had been the best thing that had happened in a long time. He had been instrumental in her image change. Okay, it took a while to cope with her new name, but luckily anything that did not add up at the time was totally overlooked by him in his bid to cope with life at Cambridge. It certainly made her life a lot easier.

Moving into his room was an excellent idea as it meant she was never left alone with awful thoughts. He was always there to support her; he was her absolute rock. If she cried he was there, likewise when she was happy he was always at her side. It had been fantastic. She had devoted herself to him and they did everything together. A lot of girls on campus appeared to want to take advantage of his kindness and the fact that he was such a good-looking guy but luckily, she soon scared them off.

By the end of that first year his English was so much better all thanks to her. Then he had suddenly left, completely out of the blue with no explanation. He hadn't even collected his stuff. One of the porters accompanied by some weird, intense older lady took everything. That had been embarrassing as she had cooked dinner and he was late so hearing him outside the room she had lost her rag only to open the door and to be confronted by these two. The woman had given her a form about counselling; God knows what that was all about. Bottom line was that they couldn't tell her about Ragi's whereabouts and that was it really. She had been devastated at the time and had put it down to some sinister happening on the part of his family. They were obsessed with him and it was a case of a letter a day from his mother.

Siobhan wondered if Jane might have been chatting to him. Good luck to the woman in the hat if Jane got her clutches into him. He would be her type – mysterious and different to the usual brand of city slickers she went with. Siobhan's memories of him were of immense gentleness and serenity. Mind you, he obviously had commitment issues too. Jane would not be able to cope with that, she knew for a fact.

Time for him had obviously been good; there was no denying that in the brief peripheral glimpse she had of him he was no longer the gangly, skinny, hauntingly beautiful, but awkward eighteen-year-old that she had known. He had grown into it all and was now a bloody gorgeous, sophisticated, albeit slightly weathered (which made him even more attractive), middle-aged man. She had without a doubt been his first love. One thing she knew for sure and that was that he had been a virgin before he met her.

Across the room as she was heading for the exit she spotted a guy she had named Prat-Angus at college. He was a postgraduate student who made it quite clear he was. A sanctimonious party-pooper and misery he was not very well liked at all. Even now in his brown slacks, knitted jumper and trainers with a superior air to the project in hand he looked no different. He had obviously taken the suggestion of bringing an old photograph as an undergraduate one step further as he was stapling up what looked like a montage of the day he visited Cambridge as a baby, then with the school, then with his French-exchange student and had even posted photographs of the day he attended his interview along with the celebration afterwards with all his extended family in Browns. This was all presented alongside an arrow pointing downwards saying 'Before'. The sad thing was there were three sets of photos as it was only on his third attempt he finally got a place.

Having forgotten her photograph along with wanting to avoid the *Cambridge Evening News* photographer who was standing by the exit ready to take an up-to-date photo and brief synopsis of the present lives of each alumni, Siobhan decided she would make her way over and look at the montage and escape the minute the photographer turned his back hoping desperately at the same time that Ragi would not see or accost her in the process. Finally making it out of the room near to collapsing point, hyperventilating and sweating she knew she had to exit the room before she fell.

Once home she still couldn't believe how she had felt and the memories of everything which came flooding back were so vivid. She needed to see her mother; she needed people around her that she felt close to; there was, however, no one else that she could turn to. Her loss now seemed insurmountable. Who could she see for advice and support? Ringing John and telling him he had to move the kids to his place for a while as she felt dreadful, she very nearly let everything out at his words.

"Are you okay?"

She was on the brink of telling him, but the mood immediately changed at his words.

"It's just that I am taking Alice out for dinner tonight and it will be a pain having the kids there as I've got a hotel booked. Can I pick them up tomorrow?"

She agreed to that, but the moment had gone. Putting down the phone she spent the rest of the day crying. She decided she would call Clarissa later on in the week and drive down to see her when the kids were home. At least for a while she could grieve as much as she wanted without being accountable to anyone whilst they were gone.

21

JANE

I feel no more enlightened than before. Poor, dear Siobhan, I barely got a word out of her during our lunch together. She is terribly upset about Patsy and Matthew choosing to live with John and Alice. I think her father's death has affected her more than she ever expected. And perhaps it is all about losing control of things right now in her life. Looking back she was such an inspiration in the early days and definitely inspired me. It was all about moving onwards and upwards no matter what had been thrown at her. The Siobhan now is a shadow of the person then and it has left me feeling very sad.

At the same time I also feel she was holding back and not being totally straightforward with me. We didn't get to the bottom of the reunion, and whenever I alluded to it she steered the conversation away and I realised it was going to be a pointless gesture on my part.

22

RAMINA

Oh my, what a bolt from the blue, Frank DuPont asking Zuleikha for my phone number – what a nerve: apparently, he had to talk to me urgently. Thankfully she didn't and conferred with me beforehand. I was amazed that he had recognised me after all those years. He certainly didn't show any recognition when I spotted him in reception. Apparently, he was waving some magazine article at her urging me to get hold of a copy saying it would interest me. She had no idea what the magazine was which wasn't much help. Anyway, I sent back a curt message via her saying that if he had anything of interest he was to go to the relevant authorities particularly if it was a police matter. I would not be making any comment on anything despite being retired that could discredit me or bring the social services department into disrepute. Honestly, the man was an absolute sleaze ball; if it hadn't been for one of the team seeing him canoodling with a young girl under social service care and then realising how closely connected she was to the missing girl, we'd have had real problems. It really did beggar belief. How the hell he wangled an early retirement and not a dishonourable discharge had been another mind-boggling insight. Racial discrimination without a doubt – if he had been Asian or black that would have been it.

It was all the deception that went on. He had obviously got the girl to lie as when questioned about where she had been the night

Scarlett O'Brien went missing there had been some cock and bull story about being at a boyfriend's house, his name and address conveniently having slipped her mind. Eventually, of course, she had to come clean once I and the team confronted her about her connection with Frank and how important and integral to the case it was that she told the truth. It transpired that the filthy bastard had ensconced her in his house whilst his wife and children were visiting relatives for a few days in the West Country.

Predictably Frank was not happy with the reception he got when Zuleikha reported back with my response at his request to contact him. For an ex-detective chief superintendent apparently his choice of language was more on a par with a hardened criminal; it also became a personal rant involving wholly unwholesome and inappropriate comments not only about me, but also about Zuleikha in the kennels' main reception. *Mashalla*, I was not too worried as I knew her friend, Boris, was on hand had things got out of control. He really has been a godsend, he is such a good friend to her, but nevertheless.

That is something I would never in a million years have envisaged myself as saying. Indeed up until the age of eighteen I was terrified my dearest Zuleikha would fall in love just as I did with someone wholly inappropriate and that history would once again repeat itself. When Tariq managed to track her down through Interpol just after her sixteenth birthday I was convinced he was going to steer her on the path that my parents mapped out for me, brainwashing her that an arranged marriage was imperative. I had not realised, however, what a strong, independent young lady I had raised. Perhaps it was because of the constant moving and reinventing us for fear of discovery that she had matured. She was also able to handle her father and made it clear to him that she was no pushover, she was not compliant as I had been and that if they met it would be on her terms and her terms alone. What I would have given to have seen his face on first meeting his long-lost daughter; the piercings through her nose, eyebrow, lip, tummy and top of the ear must have thrown him along with the blonde hair and heavy make-up.

She reported back that the only time his face looked very uncomfortable was when she mentioned staying the night at various boys' houses, clubbing and alcohol. Whilst part of me could not condone this behaviour, another part of me felt proud that she had the self-esteem and self-confidence to assert her identity. She was so unlike me at that age; no one, not even her father, was ever going to intimidate her.

Funny how my nerves did get the better of me when Zuleikha mentioned her plans to attend a wedding in Pakistan with her father. This was it, I convinced myself, she would definitely be abducted and forced into marriage. Laughing hysterically at my reaction she assured me this would certainly not be the case.

"No man would want me, I'm far too bossy. Don't worry, even Dad knows that. I would never be forced into anything, Mum, for God's sake."

When Boris and I came in person to meet her at the airport after her three-week trip away I could honestly say I have never been so relieved in my entire life.

23

FRANK

Jesus, as if things could get any more complicated. I tried to get hold of Ramina so I could run everything past her. It all started off as a totally boring, run-of-the-mill day in the life of Frank DuPont. There I am supping my coffee in some generic coffee place on my own. With no nubile girls to smile and banter with I turn to a local magazine; not a lot going on in there. Loads of bloody interior design columns and at some stage that dick *Zigi Stamford* is staring out at me. Moving on rapidly I hit the back of the magazine with all the social engagements that have occurred over the last month.

There was an article on a Cambridge University reunion showing all these students reuniting years later. The photos before and after were interesting. It was one, however, that really caught my eye and left me cold. It was without a doubt Siobhan exactly as I remember her all those years ago. The date and time correlated exactly with all the sordid events. I was absolutely gobsmacked; suddenly everything had fallen into place and it was shocking.

I cannot believe bloody Ramina's daughter's reaction when I tried to get her mum's contact details. I mean, she is a good-looking girl, don't get me wrong, but I had got the message she had a fellow so why would I have pursued something that I knew was not going to go anywhere? All I wanted was to run ruddy things through with

Ramina, nothing sinister in that. Ah well, I've had to go it alone. I wasn't Detective Chief Superintendent Frank DuPont for nothing.

I still can't believe I remembered the O'Briens' home phone number. Bloody amazing; half the time I barely know mine, let alone the mother-in-law's, and yet theirs was as clear as day set in my brain. What was great on top of that was that Clarissa answered it immediately. It was then I realised the severity of my discovery.

24

CLARISSA

Just as I was preparing my things for Siobhan's I had the strangest phone call of my life and I am devastated as it has brought back everything. Of course Scarlett infiltrates my everyday life; not a single day goes by when I don't think of her. Thinking back to the day she was born when the midwife handed our darling little bundle over to us, I can still recall the love, gratitude, euphoria and relief that we felt that nine months of worry were over. Even now these feelings are still too intense to explain. Watching her open her eyes for the first time and looking straight into our eyes is something I will never forget. Then there was this crazy, inexplicable situation years later and the thought of her leaving the world totally alone with no one there to hold her as some evil bastard took the gift of life away from her. Whose evil eyes full of hatred and anger did she look into as she left this world? Why couldn't I have been with her as a proper mother protecting her when she most needed it? Why didn't I bloody well go with her for her interview like most mothers would have done? Why was I so preoccupied with my own little world of trivia and unimportance and above all why couldn't it have been me? The recriminations just go on and on and never stop. Poor Ben never got over it. He seemed to slip into a complete decline and I never once saw him smile after dear Scarlett was taken from our lives. Nothing was ever the same for him. I knew I had to carry on for Siobhan's sake and of course Margot, but things were never the same.

Looking back it had all been so wonderful. The night before her interview Scarlett was the only one at home, the other two having cleared off to various parties with friends. Both were being particularly argumentative and obnoxious at the time and I recall feeling relieved they were not at home. Ben suggested we went to a French bistro down the road. I recall the evening so clearly. It was a lovely, clear, balmy night, one of those few and far between in England and we opted to eat outside. Adding to the authenticity of it all a chap was playing the sax.

Scarlett ordered our food as neither Ben nor I for that matter could read the extensive menu in faint candlelight outside. Reading aloud wasn't much help either as the live jazz band drowned out her words. The wonderful steaming bowl of mussels that we shared with melt-in-the-mouth brioche, could not have been better. Similarly the steak that came with dauphinoise potatoes was cooked to perfection, as was the Châteauneuf-du-Pape, which complemented the meal perfectly. It was a delightful evening and like most things that are enjoyable passed far too quickly. If only we'd known that each moment would be of so much significance and importance to us. The last sip of wine, the last flick of her hair, the last burst of laughter; all these things became so important to us in the days, weeks, months and years that followed. Scarlett was her usual sparkly-eyed, humorous self, alluding to how nervous she was, but at the same time really looking forward to it. We had a laugh about Margot and Siobhan and what they had been up to. Ben then did a mock interview with her and I recall saying I would eat my Brussels sprouts at Christmas if she didn't get the place. We talked about her various friends and what they were doing. What her plans were for the summer. She mentioned how she was really keen on taking off with the family to somewhere quiet and hot with a swimming pool. Ben promised he would look up availability in Provence, perhaps Apt, Goult, Gordes or Bonnieux. And that was it;

the final happy memory of my darling daughter looking so beautiful. I believed she was on the brink of a very significant moment in her life. If only I had known it was to be the night before her death.

The following day she was up at the crack of dawn looking nervous and pale, barely able to digest the cup of jasmine tea and toast with apricot jam. I had left a *Good Luck* card for her on the table, but she failed to see it and it was never opened. To this day it makes me cry as being slightly inhibited when it came to expressing emotions I had really opened up in her card expressing not only our deep love for her, but also our pride at everything she had achieved and done in her life. We would, no matter what, always be the proudest parents in the world.

In the car driving her to the station we didn't talk much. She was breathing deeply trying to calm her nerves. Once there we hugged and she promised to ring after the interview and then that was it. One backward glimpse from her as I pulled off with an irate taxi driver beeping impatiently behind me. I recall people taking second glances and staring at this beautiful, tall, serene girl on the platform with a smile that literally lit up the room and thinking, *that's my daughter.* Then that was it, that was the last time unbeknown to me that I was ever going to see her alive. The next time would be in a police mortuary all bruised and swollen and unrecognisable. I can feel my eyes welling up and again that dreadful feeling that can only be described as a broken heart which in spite of everything continues to function.

It was just a normal day for me, all the usual things. I cooked pancakes for what had become a late brunch. Siobhan and Margot joined us and it was pleasant, but with very little dialogue. I listened to the play of the day on Radio Four. I did a supermarket shop wondering who would be coming for dinner that night as Margot and Siobhan were erratic when it came to mealtimes and I remember making a mental note that I must start proper mealtimes again as things were becoming too fragmented and inconsistent. Darling Scarlett rang as promised after her interview. In true style she mentioned how challenging but thought-provoking her interview was and how amazing it felt being interviewed by people who had written various books that she had actually studied. She loved the college and the town and was planning to wander around before catching the train home. We agreed she would ring later on that evening to let me know her plans as there was also a possibility she may be meeting a friend in London. If that was the case she would stay with her and come back the following day. The pips then ran out on the phone and we were unable to say goodbye. I then spent the rest of the day carrying out various chores. I also had a deadline for a magazine article that had to be finished and before I knew it Ben was home and we were eating dinner.

None of the girls was home for dinner and I recall making the mental note again that I would start being a lot stricter. I was surprised that reliable Scarlett hadn't rung to tell me of her plans but just surmised that she had obviously met up with her friend and was naturally preoccupied. Margot and Siobhan were not in my good books and I resolved that from now on they were to let me know exactly where they were and who they were with. It was all getting very tricky this whole teenage thing where they assumed they could come and go with no parental interaction. I really felt I was losing control. Ben pointed that out over dinner saying he could not believe that I had allowed Siobhan to not only wear the heavy Goth look she had adopted of late but also that I had let her dye her hair black. He looked at me blankly when I replied I was literally faced with no choice.

I remembered waking in the early hours of the morning, my heart pounding for no particular reason. Ben was spreadeagled on the bed dead to the world and snoring loudly. Unable to go back to sleep I sat on the terrace drinking tea and listening to the dawn chorus feeling very relaxed and at peace. Little did I know that I would probably never enjoy that state of equilibrium at any other stage in my life again.

A while later I returned to bed. I marvelled at the wonders of tea as it had completely knocked me out for the count and it was late morning when I woke feeling refreshed and sated. Ben had left for work at his usual time and I decided to prepare pancakes again for breakfast. Margot was the first to arrive home looking remarkably chirpy and cheerful. Slightly disappointed as she had been hoping to bombard Scarlett with a full analysis of the interview, she found obvious comfort however in demolishing the entire plate of steaming pancakes washed down with copious cups of coffee.

Siobhan suddenly appeared at this point looking awful with her bloodshot eyes, spotty, blotchy skin and a desperately bad hair day. I remember feeling tempted to take a photo to show her how she was abusing herself with these bloody drugs she was obviously taking but denying she was. Half-heartedly eating a piece of toast she sat down for a few minutes reluctantly answering my questions about where Scarlett must have spent the previous night. None of us were worried it was more intrigue at this stage. I did recall Siobhan saying she would ring Scarlett's friend Felicity once she had showered.

Things carried on as normal and I didn't give Scarlett another thought as I had chores to do as well as another magazine deadline that had to be finished by 1pm. I needed to go to the supermarket but had decided I would wait until Scarlett rang from the train station. That way it would only be one journey. I had said to Margot and Siobhan that I wanted all of us to have dinner that evening which amazingly they both agreed to with no ado. Scarlett could choose what was on the menu. I knew she'd enjoy pottering around the supermarket deciding on different concoctions for everyone to eat.

I put the champagne in the fridge and decided to give the kitchen a good clean whilst waiting. At around six o'clock that evening just as my heart had begun racing after Siobhan had come in announcing that Scarlett had not turned up as expected at Felicity's the night before, the doorbell went. Immediately assuming it was Scarlett who had perhaps got a taxi from the station, I felt instantly relieved not stopping to think, but rushing to the door to greet my baby. You can imagine my reaction when on opening it I was confronted by two very young policemen on my doorstep. The only thing I recall after this was answering my name and confirming Ben was home and then hearing a loud, primeval, terrifying scream that resounded around the room. I later discovered it had been me as I felt myself falling to the ground.

Under sedation hours, rather than what felt like days, later, I found myself sitting with a counsellor. Ben, Margot and Siobhan were in the sitting room. It was then that I learnt about the dreadful turn of events. My beautiful angel's body had been discovered floating head down on the River Cam, the main river in Cambridge, in the early hours of Thursday morning by a man out jogging. At the time the police had suggested it was either an accident or suicide. They could give us no further details until a post-mortem had taken place on behalf of the coroner. We all knew there was no way on earth it would be suicide and yet if accidental why on earth would she have been wandering in such a lonely place unless she was completely disorientated? Things just did not add up.

It's amazing how you hear this devastating news that your child is dead. She is no more, even to the point that she loses her identity and people in authority start talking about her no longer as a person, but as a body. The post-mortem report came out and it read: *The body* (not Scarlett) *shows an 'empty heart' attributed to reduced venous return from vasodilation and redistribution of the intravascular volume from the central to the peripheral compartment. Laryngeal edema, eosinophilia in the lungs. The heart and tissues show evidence of myocardial hypoperfusion*. The autopsy also noted that water had entered the air passages along with the inspired air. Within the air passages there was evidence water had merged with the sticky secretions but I have no idea what they were. There was then a description about air going in and out of the windpipe along with respiratory efforts with water getting churned up in the windpipe along with the sticky seretions. The secretions then decrease the surface tension of water, much like soap does, with the result that a lot of foam is generated. The foam located on the body apparently proved that she was alive when she fell in. The synopsis of the report showed she must have had an anaphylactic shock, fallen into the river and drowned. Was she with someone and if so why didn't they raise the alarm? Why didn't they attempt to rescue her? Did they push her in as she was having the anaphylactic shock? What made her eat the food when she knew she had an allergy to it? If she was there alone why did she end up there if she had arranged to meet Felicity for dinner in London? Nothing added up. The police were on the case and had promised they would do all they could to assist us.

The main thing was no one could bring her back and that was all we wanted. It's the trivial things in life that hit home; people don't stop laughing, birds don't stop flying, dogs don't stop barking, and time ticks by utterly regardless of this monumental loss that has stopped everything for us. And yet we still eat, drink and sleep, but it is an unconscious act. No pleasure goes into it whatsoever; it's just a means to an end, fuel to persevere, no more than that. We were all like an automaton in our private grief. Margot was a dramatic wreck. Siobhan had withdrawn into herself completely just rocking, breaking down and staring into space and poor, dear Ben; the anguish etched on his face was heartbreaking.

As time wore on events began to hit home and led to yet more anguish; it was the lack of any evidence that was frustrating. The final inquest stated that the most likely cause of death was an anaphylactic fit that had caused her to fall in and drown. Initially we were filled with positive vibes, as the police were under the command of Frank DuPont, the detective chief superintendent who was assigned to our case; he was a wonderful man. He was one of the most understanding people I had ever encountered in my life. The fact that the first thing he did on meeting us was to just reach out and hug all of us in turn, then to offer tea, said it all. Everything about him was full of empathy and sincerity. We really felt our pain was his. He gave us so much comfort and support I had to keep pinching myself that Scarlett was dead as he really was the sort of guy we would have been friends with under normal circumstances. He did not, however, give us false hope; honesty was his main motivation he told us, not realising how ironic he was being. He, like us, was convinced that Scarlett had died under suspicious circumstances and his pledge to us was come hell or high water he was going to prove it.

When the news broke, however, about the relationship between Margot and Frank, I still to this day have no idea how that passed me by; it was another unbelievably devastating blow. It was the betrayal of trust that was so difficult to handle from both sides. I didn't have an issue with the relationship and although Frank denied it I could see how he might have become embroiled in it as, knowing Margot, once she had channelled her feelings onto someone it would be impossible to ignore them. Frank was such a soft touch, caring to the point of stupidity. Had she been all out to get him he probably wouldn't have wanted to hurt her feelings and self-esteem by rejecting her. What I didn't get was why they didn't come clean right from the outset. Surely, they would have realised questions would have been asked bearing in mind the incident they were both linked with and the fact that he was the officer in charge? I just knew that all the time invested with him and his team, ranging from retracing the events leading up to her disappearance, holding press conferences and appealing to the public for any possible sightings of her, all appeared fruitless as nothing came out of them and no breakthrough emerged. When he was taken off the case everything seemed to slip and the momentum was lost. I know that Frank felt he had failed us. We met him for lunch months afterwards and he broke down confessing how terrible he felt at letting us down. Years later at my darling Ben's funeral, Frank, giving me words of comfort at my loss, again reiterated how not a day went by when he didn't think about how he had let us down.

Indeed, not long after his departure a new tragedy occurred involving the murder of a prostitute in another town and that appeared to be it as far as Scarlett's case was concerned. The new team basically called a press conference to which we were invited where they stipulated that the case was self-explanatory: Scarlett's death had been a terrible accident with no suspicious circumstances. Knowing that we were going to have to face the prospect of closure, Margot and Siobhan made the decision to visit the area where my baby's body had been discovered. Ben and I both decided we could not face it. The only comfort I got on their return was that it was a beautiful natural area full of wild flowers with floating lilies on a pond to the right and the river on the left. Siobhan described it as a natural haven, the sort of place Scarlett would have loved.

That is why, when I answered the phone call just before heading to Siobhan's and learning the caller was Frank, I was at a complete loss for words. He said he had some extremely important news for me with certain questions that were going to have to be asked. Taking into account, however, the humiliation he had suffered at the hands of the police force it was all obviously extremely confidential at this moment in time. I really didn't know whether I wanted any epiphanies or revelations, but concluded that perhaps he could see me, Margot and Siobhan together as it was obviously a situation that involved us all. Without conferring with Siobhan but assuming it would be fine with her, I suggested he joined us for lunch from around one o'clock at Siobhan's house the following week.

25

MARGOT

What a bloody nightmare! I feel like I have survived a part in *Who's Afraid of Virginia Woolf?* There we were sitting at a dysfunctional lunch just like old times with Siobhan muttering throughout the entire duration of the meal into what appeared to be a never-ending glass of wine, the main priority appearing to be more about intoxication over enjoyment. Throughout she kept up a running monologue about some bloody photo and of how I needed to keep my head above water as it could really land me in a professional pickle. It was nonsensical and basically very bizarre. Clarissa, on the other hand, just kept bursting into tears mentioning to me that Siobhan had been talking about Scarlett non-stop since she had arrived, reactivating all the long-repressed emotions. Seeing Clarissa's anguished face then got me going and the three of us were just sitting there looking like the three witches from *Macbeth*, red swollen faces with mascara smudged in all directions. Clarissa then let slip that Frank DuPont was arriving any minute. I was gobsmacked; that was a blast from the past. My first ever shag. No doubt the minute I saw him I would regret everything; he seemed old at the time and that was years ago.

The events that followed next were truly unbelievable. The doorbell rang and Siobhan, off her head, lurched over and opened the door to none other than old man Frank DuPont. God, he looked awful, bless him. He obviously didn't want to waste time on niceties and wanted to get down to business. I sensed he still fancied me rotten after all those years judging by the way, despite all the high drama, his eyes focused on my breasts for far too long. At the sight of the battered brown leather suitcase and the old-fashioned tape recorder he hauled out I realised it was something very serious. The next thing I knew he pulled out an innocuous magazine, thrust the tape recorder under Siobhan's nose and asked her to identify the people in the photo. She immediately lurched over to Clarissa mumbling about the fact that being her mother she should know it wasn't her alongside Scarlett and that she would never forgive her if she got it wrong. It was at this precise moment I was able to glimpse the photo and it rendered me absolutely speechless. I heard myself gasping as Frank moved the tape recorder to Clarissa and posed the same question to her.

"It's darling Scarlett. Look at her. She looks so happy and look at you, Siobhan; it's not such a good photo of you. Is this what you were saying you wanted me to see? I see why you thought it was Margot. Your hair looks similar, and there's that awful luminous green cardigan you always wore. Where did you find this photo, Frank? Where were you, darling?"

As she glanced down at the magazine article and ascertained the date and year her face literally turned a deathly shade of white and the primeval scream that came from her was a sound I would never want to hear repeated. The next thing I knew she was out cold on the floor. There then followed a bizarre tussle between Frank and me both rushing around like chickens with no heads trying heart massage and the kiss of life knowing that there were no vital signs whatsoever.

Siobhan meanwhile had appeared to have lost the plot completely. She was just rocking on the spot muttering to herself appearing oblivious to everything. Both Frank and I spent ages trying to locate the landline. I sat beside Clarissa when we finally made contact with the emergency services and the floodgates opened. This person had been my whole existence, her love and kindness had supported me through everything and I absolutely adored her and that was it, life extinguished in a matter of seconds. I put my coat over her and said a private prayer. Frank meanwhile was on the phone to the police. Two officers were on their way to talk to Siobhan in greater detail. He was adamant she should be taken to a psychiatric unit, as her fragile mental state was unquestionable.

Screeching to a stop outside the house the paramedics arrived to certify Clarissa's death. Siobhan at this stage appeared to register what had occurred and became uncontrollable, hitting out at the people around Clarissa and screaming her name. She then turned on me, shouting obscenities whilst foaming from her mouth. A member of the team then sedated her and she too was taken off in an ambulance. It was then even more surreal as Frank and I found ourselves in her kitchen surrounded by the chaos of lunch. I felt extremely awkward with him as we stood in silence taking in the dramatic events that had occurred. What really struck me was the fact that I was not feeling grief-stricken; it was more a case of extreme shock that had numbed everything. Frank tried to take me in his arms; I have no idea why, and I made my feelings very evident. I recollect him attempting some sort of apology for taking advantage of my youth and naivety. Following on from that he dropped the bomb. Having gone through the dramatic events with Clarissa's death I had completely forgotten about the photograph depicted in an article on a reunion at Cambridge University showing Scarlett and the back of Siobhan sitting down in a restaurant together. They were part of the background scenery. I was just amazed that Frank had noticed it. He mentioned it was the date that had jumped out at him, as it appeared the chap in the foreground had also been at an interview that day and had celebrated it all with a family meal. What could this possibly mean? Why hadn't Siobhan admitted to being in Cambridge that day? Did this mean that she was linked to Scarlett's death? Her own beloved sister? It all seemed such a crazy situation.

The fact that Frank had Clarissa's confirmation that it was Siobhan sitting alongside Scarlett as well as my positive identification of her meant it was reliable evidence that could prove crucial to proving that Siobhan had played a major part in the sequence of events and that at last questions would finally be answered. Frank was adamant that Siobhan wanted to convince Clarissa it was me not her in the photo but had planned to do it once I was away from the house ensuring then that she could convince her. Her main gamble had been that because I was not flesh and blood Clarissa would definitely take the side of her daughter no matter what, thereby letting her off the hook and leaving me in the lurch. She knew also that time was of the essence as circulation of the magazine was infiltrating everywhere.

I felt absolutely devastated. Okay, we may have had our differences but to try and frame me was beyond everything. It was bad enough coming to terms with the fact that after all that time Siobhan had been carrying this heinous secret with her. How she could have looked into the eyes of both her mother and father knowing the truth chilled me to the core. Siobhan must have realised that time was catching up with her and that she was no longer able to ignore it.

26

FRANK

Jesus wept; I can't believe what took place, all bloody unbelievable. I still can't believe Clarissa. Christ, I couldn't say anything to her before she had identified the photo; the look of horror on her face when realisation set in. She of course recognised Siobhan immediately. I guess Siobhan thought motherly love and loyalty would come into it. Of course, she couldn't have been more wrong. Poor Clarissa, it must have been simply horrific discovering such a terrible fact. In the cold light of day I'm thinking about what a bastard I've been, launching this on her so unexpectedly. It's almost as though I was so caught up in my discovery that I didn't for one moment think of the repercussions for her. Jesus, Siobhan was obviously panicking, quickly covering her tracks and attempting to convince her mother that it was none other than Margot who had intercepted Scarlett after her interview. I wonder how she managed to get her to eat the food she was allergic to. Makes you wonder what she was planning on doing, inviting Margot and Clarissa to the house. Strange how she'd farmed the kids out; it just doesn't bear thinking about. The fact she's psychotic shows what she's capable of, but the good thing is she's been sectioned so at least no one's in danger.

Some friend of Siobhan's, Jane, with the sexiest voice I've heard in a long time, one of those twenty-a-day gravelly numbers, contacted me mentioning how depressed Siobhan had been over the weeks. It transpired that Jane was now dating some ex-boyfriend of Siobhan's who recently confirmed that when they were at university she had a pseudonym. What news to me, why would she have changed her name to go to university? What the hell had she done in her life to take such a radical stance? It makes you wonder what else she may have done. I must say I always thought she sounded a little odd from Margot's accounts. She was definitely the black sheep, I know that much. If only I had followed up her alibi more thoroughly at the time instead of relying on teenage assurances she was at a party. I can't believe Ben confirmed it. Mind you, why wouldn't he? I wonder if she was planning on doing away with Margot that day otherwise why would she have invited her over after all those years completely out of the blue? If it wasn't under such horrific circumstances this entire thing could appear absolutely farcical: the murderer sitting at the table in a psychotic state salivating and rubbing her hands pissed out of her head. It was like a scene from a fairy tale. There was Margot, the ugly sister, wondering what the hell was going on. Scarlett – Cinderella – is already annihilated and then mother drops dead after identifying the frumpy, quiet, needy one as the murderer. Had Clarissa realised she had nailed the perpetrator in the guise of her own daughter? That must have been her final conscious thought. Thank God he had had the hindsight to bring along the tape recorder.

It was certainly not a case of all in a day's work. This was my swansong and it had taken years to nail - no thanks to the old team. I would be ensuring noone else would get recognition for this. Frank DuPont was making a comeback. I was back in the game. It still beggared belief that Siobhan would have been capable of harming her sister. How could she have kept it a secret for so many years? Why had the finger of suspicion never been angled towards her? Okay, she had not been the most charming young person but; she was like any other moody, non-communicative, spotty, past teenage stage but still not grown up; young adult.

When I had encountered Siobhan all those years ago she had gone through huge emotional uphearal which could explain her actions and inexplicable behaviour at the time. Neither Ben, Clarissa nor Margot had a clue where she'd gone. Half the time she would just leave the house for days on end with no explanation. Seeing her now it didn't take an expert to ascertain that she was a nutter judging from her psychological state replicated in the manner with which she kept rocking and rubbing her hands together almost as though all those years of repressing this secret had finally caught up with her. I don't even think she had twigged that her mother was dead. That was another shock-fatal heart attack of the aorta. The post-mortem showed it had literally split in two, almost as though she had a broken heart.

I am no longer *persona non grata* in the force and I am so glad that I've managed to redeem myself, not that it's going to make any difference. I won't exactly get reinstated, not that I would want to be anyway. I just always had a hunch about Siobhan and it was right. Why the hell didn't I just come out with them there and then rather than waiting for my indiscretions to come to the forefront giving me no choice but to leave the case? There was no way I could let Margot lose her alibi to save my reputation, I would never have forgiven myself. It's just so bloody strange how things come around in the end. This thing that has been my last obsession, that golden ticket I always felt eluded me, suddenly appeared on a plate all these years later when I least expected it.

I am seriously rolling. Now I am a reinvigorated man I can do anything, I feel invincible again. I was interviewed on a local radio station and felt so inspired I mentioned a book I'm planning to write on the entire case and also mentioned I'm in the process of setting up a private detective agency. I may ask Ramina to be my partner. Ha, ha, like hell, fat lot of good she's done anyone if you ask me. Funny thing is years ago the wife and friends commented on how I looked like Magnum the American detective. They are not that far from the truth and once I've got the old Grecian 2000 out I will look even more like him.

27

JANE

My God, is all I can say. Who would have guessed all this? It's like something out of a murder mystery story. I am engaged in the most passionate love affair of my life, things are progressing so well with Ragi. How crazy that now at my age I find my soulmate, the love of my life. Ironically, it's all thanks to Siobhan. If it hadn't been for her I would never have had the idea of the reunion. One question I would love to ask her though is, why? Why did she want to go through with it bearing in mind all that went on when she was there? Had she convinced herself she was the normal one and all that stalking was nothing unusual? I really can't answer it, as I have absolutely no idea what the hell she was thinking of.

I didn't even think twice about Frank's intrusive questions over the phone asking me if Siobhan had seemed depressed. What's more, I had no idea that my response would be the pivotal reason as to why Frank wasted no time in contacting Clarissa convinced that Siobhan's next action would be to annihilate Margot before too many questions were asked. Events followed as they did and the first I knew about the situation was when I read about it in the national and local papers. It was unbelievable; a complete bolt out of the blue. Things like this just didn't happen in small towns such as ours. I just couldn't believe that Siobhan had eluded everyone for so long. The fact that she had become such a close friend of mine was simply devastating. I shudder when I think of all the wonderful times we had as families over the years. The mind boggles; all along she has been a cold-blooded murderer and yet on holiday she was the one who was totally unable to reel in a fish for fear of harming it.

Bottom line was she had single-handedly killed her own sister; what sort of monster would offer her sister food knowing she was allergic to it, and then as if that wasn't enough, push her into a river leaving her to drown in agony? What's bloody weird is that throughout our friendship Scarlett's name was never mentioned, not even by John or the kids. There were no photos of her, nothing at all. It was only Margot and when her name came up it didn't take long to realise there was not a lot of love lost between her and Siobhan.

It's funny looking back now but our friendship wasn't actually a close one. Yes, we holidayed together but there were always things going on. Looking back on meaningful conversations I realise now there was literally nothing said of any significance. She appeared to have had a very peripatetic childhood with lots of travelling around and that was about it. Why didn't I stop and think about how bloody odd it was that I never once met any of her old friends or knew anything about her childhood? Looking back now I realise that we had no one in common during our time at college bearing in mind we were there at the same time. Why had she wanted the reunion? It was all her idea; bearing in mind how insular she must have been it all seemed so bizarre. What was she thinking of?

Another bloody odd, inexplicable thing was why the hell did she attend an institution her dead sister had been aiming for all her life? I will never ever forget that shocking moment when sitting over breakfast and reading the article about Siobhan, Ragi, looking over my shoulder, screamed, "Christ, that's not Siobhan O'Brien, that's my bloody stalker, the girl who made my life hell; Trudi Masters. She is a complete utter nutter, a psycho."

28

SIOBHAN

I've got nothing to say or think on the matter, all I know is I have lost all that's dearest to me: my mother, my sister, my friend and now my freedom. What is there to do? I am tired of fighting. I feel exhausted and powerless. It is all so surreal; a living nightmare. That evening I spotted Ragi was the catalyst to everything; nothing has been the same since. In fact, being really honest, it's really from the time Margot bloody Ville arrived that everything in my life went really wrong. I would never have fallen out with Scarlett and everything would have been fine. Yet the psychiatrist who is assessing me said that she thinks I am incapable of feeling love for anyone or anything. Theoretically I can see her reasoning bearing in mind I have confessed to her how I have never felt really loved. I've spent all my life wishing I was more beautiful, cleverer, and funnier. I was nothing compared to Scarlett, I really did live in her shadow. Everyone who met her seemed to consider me the afterthought, an afterbirth, the complete disappointment. I hated her for it. Yes, I hated her so much. The number of times I fantasised about her death. When she did die it was amazing how Mum transferred how she was feeling to me, burbling on and likening it to a missing limb. Hardly; we were not in reality that close. I mean, we were as close as most sisters are, of course; I loved her. I was also insanely jealous and insecure. Who wouldn't be, having a sister like her? I would, however, never in a million years have wanted her dead, let alone have killed her myself.

I still can't believe what happened to Mum. It was absolutely unbelievable really, the sort of thing you read about in books or watch in films. I can picture her now so vividly, looking at that horrific photo, saying what she said then simultaneously keeling over in what I assumed was a faint. But it wasn't. Far from it. Then the next thing I know she is turning blue and is obviously dead. All the while that twat, Frank, the randy seducer of young girls, is there with his archaic tape recorder recording me despite the fact I'm trying to resuscitate my poor mother. I have no idea what Margot was doing at the time; probably cheerleading in the background, choreographing her victory dance.

Bottom line is Mum betrayed me. Surely, no matter what, you fight your own flesh and blood's cause? It is unconditional love and should surely take precedence over everything. I cannot believe her betrayal; I was banking on the fact that she would back me up. How utterly wrong I was.

Jane sent me a letter of condolence and also horror at the fact I was Ragi's stalker; what the hell did that mean? I was his first and only love. Stalk him! Far from it, we had a loving, strong relationship. He really loved me and was constantly stroking my hair, telling me how I was his life. I have never seen anyone look the way he looked at me; I knew I was the centre of his world. He was also mine. We were soulmates, two lost souls who discovered one another and I really thought we were going to be together forever.

I changed my name at college as I wanted to reinvent myself; I wanted to move away mentally and physically from all that had gone on with Scarlett. Why did I apply to Cambridge? I guess I wanted to replicate everything she had set out to achieve. I wanted my parents to be as proud of me as they were of her. Bottom line was quite frankly they were so devastated by her death they barely noticed my incredible achievement at gaining a place as an academic scholar, despite all the vicissitudes that I had incurred. It was as though I was only there because of the groundwork Scarlett had prepared for me and nothing more.

Things that followed on from Scarlett were obviously never the same, her passing created a huge void for us all and we were broken people. I may have managed to move on but my parents were left utterly bereft and disinterested. It was almost as though I ceased to exist which made the loss even more painful. I effectively lost three of my loved ones when Scarlett died. Of course no one gave it a moment's thought.

I realise how little I knew my mother and I still can't believe she let me down over Margot. What a desperate situation. At least I was able to attend her funeral; it was all a blur as I was completely drugged to the eyeballs and resented being escorted by two nurses.

It felt so bloody awful arriving at our family home and crossing the lawn to the woods where, as kids, we had built dens. Those were the days when it was just Scarlett and me before the bitch came on the scene. We had no cares in the world then. Who would have thought it would all come to this? Mother was buried in what had been her fruit and vegetable patch, her complete pride and joy. I remember furtively collecting succulent strawberries one summer and eating every single one of them blaming the birds for pilfering them and then feeling terribly guilty that everyone except Dad, who gave me a knowing wink, believed me.

Mum's funeral was held on a beautiful day. The birds were twittering away and had it not been for the sombre people dressed in black it could have been a civilised garden party in a lovely English garden. God, if only, if only things hadn't turned out like this. It really is a living nightmare.

Patsy did a very moving reading about her grandma and what a huge influence she had been in her life and Scarlett inevitably got a mention. There was no way John would let a ceremony such as this take place without her name being alluded to. It all seemed bloody ridiculous to me as no matter how much I loved and knew Scarlett my kids didn't know anything about her.

I, of course, was not referred to at all. Inevitably everyone looked terribly shocked when I stood up on a chair and expressed my love for both my sister and my mother likening myself to Hamlet, even quoting parts of the soliloquy that I felt were definitely relevant to the situation in hand. At these words the 'witch bitches' restraining me had the nerve to try and remove me. Luckily my assurances that I would conform and not cause a scene placated them and I was able to stay, much to the chagrin I noted of both Margot and John. It was their joint eyebrow raise and eyeball roll that made me wonder whether they were actually shagging one another. I concluded, however, that it was more a joint disdainful regard for me that had perhaps united them.

Looking around at the people there I realised how depleted my mother's social circle had become. Obviously, there was family there but what had happened to all those ladies she had lunched and had coffee with years ago? Where were all the numerous couples that would come for dinner? Surely they couldn't all be dead?

Coincidently at that very moment I spotted Tory, bless her, in a red evening dress of all things, swaying all over the place with a very odd-looking woman; I swear it was a man dressed as a woman looking after her. Tory had the most outlandish make-up on and she could barely move in her sharp, spikey heels which made her legs look ridiculously thin to the point of emaciation. Furthermore, the cigarette she was smoking spent most of its time outside her mouth dropping ash on the floor as though it had gone out of fashion. All in all it was not a pretty sight and judging from the completely vacant rabbit in the headlight expression on her face I felt it would not be of any value to either of us in wasting the time introducing myself and reminding her of what life had been like for her in the past.

I don't really remember much more. I couldn't look Margot in the eye. How could she have done this? What sort of monster was lurking within her? I felt absolute hatred, but also totally and utterly lonely, unloved and powerless. I recall questioning John about the nature of his relationship with Margot then being aware of some hairy, scruffy woman at his side whom he introduced as his new partner, Alice. For someone who runs a chain of lucrative dog kennels and dog pampering she looked pretty dog-like herself, but with kind eyes. As for John, he looked no better. Blimey, how he has changed from that guitar-playing, skinny beatnik to the middle-aged paunchy, moody, lazy man he has grown into.

29

MARGOT

This is the saddest time of my life. Everything I have done and achieved has faded into insignificance with Clarissa's passing. She was my everything; she saved me. I cannot believe she is no more. The funeral is all a blur. I recall seeing Siobhan flanked by two very masculine women; she looked ghastly. Her mental state is obviously extremely fragile as she kept shouting out and pointing her finger at me. It was mortifying. I knew I had to stay, it was the least I could do for Clarissa.

30

SIOBHAN

Being cooped up in this godforsaken place, all I do is think. My brain does not switch off and it is exhausting. Seeing John at Mum's funeral has really been dominating my thoughts. Even then when we were teenagers it was all about Scarlett. He was part of our home-mate gang, basically a bunch of kids who lived locally; we were not at the same school however, which made it more exciting when we met up. It wasn't rocket science to work out that John amongst most of the boys in the gang had a thing about Scarlett. They would literally just sit there staring, willing her to speak or smile at them. Bless, I don't think she had any idea they existed and it didn't help that they were a couple of years younger, had no dress sense, diabolical haircuts and snotty noses. I remember being really pissed off when on learning we were sisters he asked what had gone wrong. The slap across his face took him by complete surprise, I must say.

That was literally the story of my life back then; Scarlett this, Scarlett that. Everything I did was second best. I had to be stoical and take it like a man. To all intents and purposes I maintained my facade, but how I hurt inside. Looking back now I feel really bitter and am without a doubt terribly scarred by it all. I have zero self-confidence and just feel a failure all the time. I have no friends, nothing to live for. I have admitted to my psychiatrist that I definitely have a problem differentiating reality and fantasy. Scarlett has become this complete representation of everything that is perfect. Was she really? I can't answer this.

I know that her death affected people in the most profound way; people walked around in a stunned state. Strangers would come up to us in the street sympathising with our loss. My father became a shadow of himself and the gang virtually broke up and disbanded such was the grief at her death. It really was mass hysteria. I hated the attention. Margot, however, really seemed to revel in it and this pissed me off big time as she so wasn't immediate family.

John sent me a lovely card about my loss empathising with me knowing how close we were as sisters. He was the only person who thought about how I must have felt through everything and it meant a lot to me even though I sensed that deep down he wished it had been me not her.

Time passed and John and I saw very little of one another in the interim. I went off to Cambridge and he went to Edinburgh. There would be the odd snatches of drunken conversation at various parties, but all very inconsistent and far between. It was in the autumn of 1985 that, encountering one another at a party over a few drinks, we thought it would be a great idea to apply jointly to an American summer camp with the prospect of travelling around America for a few months afterwards. It was on a totally platonic basis. There was not an iota of romance between us, we were literally just good buddies.

That summer, as planned, we found ourselves working on the same summer camp in North Carolina as counsellors. It was all very exciting as well as shocking arriving at a Jewish American camp; the children were the offspring of some extremely wealthy people. I had never been exposed so intimately to other religions so it was fascinating celebrating the Shabbat on Fridays, lighting the candles and eating the bread. We celebrated Passover with many of the children's parents joining us. What was also moving was listening to guest speakers sharing their experiences of living in the ghettos and concentration camps. It was all very sobering.

In contrast to this I have never in my life seen so many fancy cars being driven by chauffeurs. It was unbelievable; the obnoxious children pouring from the cars were even more unbelievable. The emotions on reuniting after a year back at summer camp for many of these children were surprisingly moving although there were a lot of contrived hysterics. You could see for some children these friendships they had made were genuine and everlasting.

There were a couple of partners on the staff who proved love could occur at camp for they had met once a year and over time had fallen in love, married and were now reliving camp as staff with their children attending as they once did.

Camp brought out the best and worst of people. Often it would begin on a bizarre note as noted in the trunks that preceded the children's arrival that we as counsellors were expected to unpack for them. How parents allowed such unsuitable items as computers, high heels, jewellery piled high in ornate boxes, make-up and curling tongs at the tender age of up to fourteen, seemed ludicrous bearing in mind the emphasis on the whole experience was being away from all mod cons and being at one with nature. The trunks of children aged four or five and coming for the entire summer whilst the parents were away in Europe having quality time together were full of things that obviously alleviated the parents' guilt for leaving them for so long: sweets, cookies, carbonated drinks; the pile was endless. Invariably placed on the top of all the lavish indulgences was a list of all the allergies each child had alongside the name and number of their personal psychiatrist and what issues the children had. Most of them appeared to have anxiety at separation from their parents. I initially thought this was an attempt at irony on behalf of the parents but was soon reprimanded by the head counsellor and told to ensure I was diligent at spotting any child experiencing anxiety. Needless to say she was not at all impressed after the first night when I showed her my list of all the children who were finding it hard to settle aged four who wanted to be tucked into bed, with the television on, by their parents.

The list remained the same for the entire camp; the good news was that in some cases the psychiatrist was able to conduct a telephone consultation with the traumatised child as they ascertained it would be more traumatic for the child to hear their parents' voices on the phone. Psychiatric experiences aside it was all a wonderful episode in my life and we definitely exploited our Britishness pretending we had no idea what restrooms, trash cans or sneakers were. Seeing the looks on their faces when we feigned confusion was priceless. John and I were lucky as these kids were on the whole hyperactive and opinionated and listened to no one in authority apart from us because we were different. Likewise the little ones just wanted to be carried around by us at all times. The only time they became vaguely freaked was when one of them saw my armpit hair. They were absolutely appalled and until I shaved it off I was for a while seen in a different light.

Whilst there I had a very pleasant surprise in the guise of a man. He was the quintessential Californian guy with his huge biceps, tanned skin, and long, endless legs. Ruggedly handsome and with an extremely chilled manner, all the girls on the camp staff and campers alike were in love with him. I had certainly noticed him, but knew he was way beyond my expectations. Imagine the shock when the message reached me that he fancied me. After Ragi, this was one of the most exciting moments of my life. I could not believe it. I was so chuffed I just wanted to dance with joy. John just raised his eyes to the ceiling and commented that he hoped it wouldn't end in tears.

"Don't worry, I'm far too strong for that," was my reply.

The following day Pat was working out under a tree near to the entrance of the dining hall. He called out to me, "It may look odd, but this is what all the regular guys like me do on Venice Beach." It made no sense to me at all but I laughed and continued walking. Next thing

I knew Pat Marks, yes, Pat Marks, the resident camp heart-throb was walking by my side. What's more, he then called me by my name, well, 'See-oh-bahan', which I found hysterical. He didn't find it as amusing as I did, but just commented on why it was spelt in such a ridiculous manner. He was even more flummoxed by the pronunciation of my grandmother's name, Niamh. Bearing in mind his family was Irish I ridiculed his ignorance. After this little interlude the gorgeous hunk asked me to join him for a ride on his motorbike to watch the sun come down with a Californian Cooler or two. I could barely contain myself. It was an amazing feeling walking into the communal dining room feeling all eyes upon me. I knew I was the most envied girl on the camp and I was revelling in it. At long last it was my turn to feel wanted. When I walked into the dinner hall I knew everyone was looking at me with envy.

We met at around eight o'clock just outside camp. I had showered and felt bloody marvellous. Pat was leaning against his motorbike, his tanned skin glowing in the evening hue. What a hulk standing there in his cut-off T-shirt and worn out Levis. I just wanted to be taken by him then and there. With adrenaline racing, we charged off on his motorbike with me holding on for dear life. The sexual tension could be cut with a knife as we turned corners and I felt my body pressing into his.

We stopped at the top of a grassy hill giving us a panoramic view of the surrounding area. It was a beautiful, balmy evening so we lay down on a rug and just chatted for what seemed like hours. He was irresistible. Now and then he would hold my hand and I would literally feel electricity charging through my body. I was in a wonderful dream, living the fantasy. It didn't matter that all we had to hand were tortilla chips and chilli sauce, washed down with Californian Coolers. I was in heaven. When we finally kissed I wanted his lips to remain on mine forever. With Ragi it had all been about experimentation and awkward, inexperienced moves. Pat obviously knew how to 'woo' a girl and I was hooked. The movies didn't lie, after all; I had fallen, deeply and madly in love. That was it. We spent our first night under the stars just kissing and looking up to the night sky. Nothing more happened and it didn't need to. The air started to get colder and we agreed it was time to head back to reality. I could not contain my excitement on the ride back laughing to myself maniacally as he revved the engine. Once back in the cabin my camp workmates were up waiting for the low-down. I was riding high. What a feeling.

The following day Pat came up and whispered in my ear asking if I was up for another picnic and bike ride. I knew we were going to have sex that night and I could barely contain myself. The last man I had slept with was Ragi and that seemed an age away.

Pat collected me earlier this time. It was another beautiful, balmy evening, and he took us to a beautiful spot covered in wild flowers and butterflies. For some reason I could smell coconut and it is a smell that has resonated with me ever since. (I am guessing it was the suntan lotion I had borrowed from a friend before leaving.) The sensual kissing began and then he moved further down with his hands and tongue; it was like hundreds of butterflies exploring my body. Had I really seen them earlier or was it all part of the fantasy I was experiencing then and there? I felt disconnected from the person lying there and wondered where the moaning was coming from, before realising it was me filled with desire. I could barely answer when he had the grace to ask if he could enter me. Nibbling on his earlobe desperately, he got the message. Within no time there he was, my Californian god, looking down on me with love and desire. His penis arched up and he tentatively entered me whilst at the same time massaging my hair then kissing me gently on my mouth and breasts. I felt like a goddess. The thought of this ending was a devastating thought. I wanted it to last forever.

We met one another on four more occasions and things were more mind-blowing on each occasion. Pat seriously had no flaws; to me he was an embodiment of perfection in both body and mind. John, however, was not at all convinced and actually started pissing me off with his constant reiterations that it was 'all going to end in tears'. Deep down maybe I knew, but hey, I was living for the present and as far as I was concerned it was the happiest chapter so far of my life.

Inevitably things were beginning to wind up, starting with the culmination of team wars and announcements of the overall team that had come first, along with individual certificates for all the campers. Then it was a big campfire singing session and it was there that I shed my first tear at the thought of separation from Pat. He held my hand and reassured me that 'we were going to be together forever' and I believed him.

Reality finally set in when all the coaches and parents arrived at camp to extricate the campers. The mass hysteria from the boys and girls, counsellors and staff reflected the turmoil I was feeling inwardly. I began feeling very sad and very anxious knowing my little bubble was bursting.

What was really beginning to bother me was Pat's lack of initiative. I tentatively drew up plans with John on places we wanted to visit. Not once did Pat suggest I travelled with him immediately afterwards. Far from it. The night before, whilst lying in his arms, he said, "It's so weird to think this time tomorrow we will be apart. I can't imagine it, it is going to be hell."

My immediate response to this was logical. "Pat, I can come to California, meet your folks, meet your friends, I can't wait to see Gary. And we can go from there. I have no ties in England, the world's my oyster. We can just stay together forever."

His response to this was not what I wanted to hear. "Hell no, that won't be happening, Sibby, I have college. My folks would go crazy if I ditched my studies." I tried to convince him that would not be the case, but he was adamant it was not fair on me to just wait around. "Plus you have John to think of. I want you to make the most of this great country, babe, get a real feel for it if this is where you're gonna be. What if you hate it? Imagine the responsibility I would feel if you gave up everything to come to me."

I fell for his words hook, line and sinker. His last words to me were, "Babe, remember I love you." We wouldn't be seeing one another for another two months before our rendezvous in New York. Devastated at the thought of random travelling across the States I consulted John.

"I can't believe you, get your life sorted, Siobhan. The guy's a phoney, can't you see it? To him you are just a summer romance, end of story. I doubt he'll make it to New York. I doubt you'll ever hear from him again. You're history. I'm sorry to break it like this, but you need to hear the truth from someone. He is taking the piss. Why give up an amazing opportunity to travel this country to do what? Sit and cry over a guy who led you on a song and dance? Man up. Just get that rucksack on your back and come travelling with us."

I knew then I was not going to be joining them. My mission was to travel to California and to surprise Pat. I had no address for him, the only thing I knew was that he would cycle on the boardwalk every morning and work out in a communal area near Venice Beach. It was up to me. I didn't care about seeing the rest of America, all I knew was I wanted to be with the love of my life and nothing was going to stop me.

John and I hugged goodbye and agreed we would keep in touch. It was going to be hard as neither of us knew the outcome of our travels. We finally decided to either physically meet or to send a phone message to the YMCA on Times Square. And that was it. He went east and I went blindly south-west. It was pretty gruelling travelling on Greyhound buses particularly stopping off at the various seedy stations. I felt very ill-equipped both emotionally and physically. I spoke to no one and no one spoke to me. That was until I was woken up in the early hours of the morning with a really creepy, smelly, unshaven guy sitting next to me rubbing his nether region and my thigh at the same time. It opened the floodgates and I started sobbing my heart out. Luckily, a couple my age whom I had noticed boarding the bus earlier, immediately jumped to my defence and told the guy in no uncertain terms what an absolute pervert and twat he was. The bus was stopped and the man was ordered to disembark.

Arriving in California I spent the first night in an amazing youth hostel in the centre of Los Angeles. Neon lights flashing, massive billboards advertising pizza and Coke, action wherever you looked, the constant noise of police sirens, this really was something else. Some people were randomly dancing, others choosing to skateboard, or run on the boardwalk. Everywhere you looked someone was engaged in an activity. Then there were the amazing ice cream parlours selling an array of the most delicious concoctions of flavours that I did not know existed. Besides that, these places were also full to the brim with gorgeous guys, all toned pecs and golden suntans, holding hands. I just didn't get why Pat had been so reluctant for me to see such amazing sights and sounds. In his words, "Man this was my scene, my kinda place".

The next morning I set off for Venice Beach full of trepidation and slightly nervous. What was I doing? What if he didn't want to see me? What if John was right and that this was just a summer romance? I had no preconceptions about what to expect. The first thing that threw me were the throngs of people blocking the promenade. How was I ever going to spot Pat in this mass of people all working out, milling around, dancing? The noise was crazy, a cacophony of boom boxes all playing different tunes and contrasting vibes. It was beautiful people preening themselves whilst looking each other up and down. I felt decidedly out of place in my linen sundress and sandals.

Walkman plugged into my ears playing 'Hotel California' because firstly I wanted to set the scene and secondly it was Pat's tune, I wandered along the boardwalk looking for him. It was like looking for a needle in a haystack and I felt I was never going to spot him. Relaxing in an outside café eating frozen yogurt, something entirely new for me, and just soaking up the atmosphere I began to realise how impetuous I'd been. I was never going to spot him; I had no address, nothing. The only thing I could recall was a mention of him living in Venice and working out on Muscle Beach.

It was on my second day in Santa Monica I had the shock of my life. I was sitting in an outside café reading or should I say glancing over the top of my magazine people-watching when suddenly I spotted him jogging on the beach in front of me wearing his unmistakable Lakers cap. I just wanted to run into his arms there and then. He stopped to chat to a friend who had just finished working out and I wondered if it was Gary, his best friend from home.

A few minutes later, after watching them kissing and holding hands as they walked off, the reality hit. Whenever Pat talked about California, he would constantly reminisce about Gary in conjunction with the scenery. Now our conversations prior to leaving came back to me in slow motion; this was why I wasn't invited back. Why had he done this? What had he been trying to prove? I knew I would never discover the truth. Within an hour I was at the Greyhound bus terminal ready to take the bus to New York.

Once on the bus, some aged guy sat down next to me and asked where I was from, something that I regretted immediately as he spent the next hour telling me how Great Britain was no longer an empire and was just a tiny dot in the middle of nowhere. Did I care? Was I patriotic? I didn't give a damn, I just wanted to curl up and die.

On arriving in New York I felt totally destroyed. I just curled up on my bed in the hostel and literally cried for four days. I had no energy and felt an absolute wreck. It was the hostel's owner who suggested I rang the camp and got the contact details of the American guy John was travelling with. Miraculously John was contacted and being the thoughtful, compassionate person he was, he arrived to comfort me as soon as he heard I was in New York. I didn't tell him the truth, I just mentioned how I realised Pat was not the one for me after all. "No surprises there," was his only comment. "Thought he was a prat from day one."

Within a matter of weeks John and I became an item. I am not sure how it happened, but it wasn't too emotionally painful. I guess I was grateful I had someone. My self-esteem was at such a low ebb; John made me feel good and secure. When we returned to England three months later and I discovered I was pregnant it seemed the most natural thing in the world for John and me to get married.

The marriage took place in a registry office. My parents and Margot attended along with a handful of ageing relations. Dad thought we were crazy; Mum was worried that John was doing it for the wrong reasons and that he was fixated on Scarlett and never me. Second best again; thanks was all I could say. When I reached the first trimester we announced the news to all and sundry. Patsy had white blonde hair as a baby and the first thing both John and my parents announced was that she was a little Scarlett. The first thing I noticed when she was born was she looked just like my Californian surfer.

John was a great dad and couldn't do enough for his baby. Did he ever suspect? I honestly don't think he did. So consumed by love for her it would have been the last thing on his mind. I, meanwhile, really resented when both him and Clarissa held her. I just wanted to be cocooned in my own little world apart from everyone. Pat may have been eliminated from my life but Patsy was here to stay no matter what.

It was ironic as I very nearly did lose her to a horrible illness. It began as an innocent throw-away comment; I could see that Patsy's body was changing with the onslaught of puberty. For Matthew, my son, gaining weight was never going to be an issue. Without a doubt he had his father's ridiculously slim physique. Patsy, however, had a completely different body shape. She was lucky in that she was tall and athletic, but unfortunately like me she had a slow metabolism and therefore put on weight easily.

I decided to tone down our Friday family nights in when we would gorge ourselves on pizza, fries, popcorn and chocolate. I decided it was going to be fish, salad and fruit instead. Needless to say this did not go down well with the rest of the family. Patsy was outraged. Unfortunately my response to her was not meant to have been quite so blunt.

"Out of all of us you are the one that should be heeding my advice, as you have put on loads of weight recently." The minute I uttered these words I just wanted to take them back. John was outraged at how cruel I had been. There was nothing I could do to placate her that night. She was devastated. I was in tears. Poor Matthew sat there looking perplexed and wondering why it had all escalated into a massive drama. He didn't look any more enlightened at my words.

"People should never comment on a female's body."

"But, Mum, you just have."

"I know, that's why I am telling you, don't you ever. I so regret what I said. It was totally and utterly thoughtless."

The following day thankfully Patsy appeared to have got over the drama and I was able to breathe a huge sigh of relief. She also seemed to have taken my point on board and started eating far more sensibly. Not only that, she started taking up sports, and lying on the sofa doing nothing had become a thing of the past. Now she was either playing tennis, swimming or working out at the gym. Furthermore, all the food she ate was healthy stuff. It may have cost more but in my eyes it was worth it. Everyone commented on how well she looked and I must say they were totally right.

It wasn't until the start of the September term that things took on a different perspective when the school nurse rang and informed me that they had noticed Patsy's huge weight loss over the summer holidays.

"It's fine," I replied. "It's all under control, I am perfectly aware of what's going on."

"So I take it," she replied, "you are okay with the fact that you are paying for school meals and your daughter is either missing them or letting her friends share hers?" That, I must admit, came as a surprise to me and I promised I would discuss it with Patsy on her return from school. When I confronted Patsy she claimed she ate fruit and what's more she was eating a normal, healthy meal in the evenings with us. Nothing to worry about I surmised and life continued as normal.

Patsy was still exercise mad, but looked great and happy which was the main thing. She also began to get seriously into cooking and it really seemed to become her passion. Spending hours concocting the most amazing things I was amazed at her self-control; how did she manage not to wolf them down? Inexplicably, however, there would just about be time to look, admire and taste but seconds later, however, they would disappear. Matthew was obviously making the most of the wonderful culinary offerings.

Things unexpectedly then took a turn for the worse beginning with John's comment that someone had been vomiting in the night. No one mentioned it the next morning and it was soon forgotten. However, it was only when my mother who was staying for the week noted that she heard someone being sick in the night that the matter was raised again. Recalling John's comments from a month before it suddenly dawned on me that Patsy obviously had a problem. I decided not to confront, but instead to observe her at supper. It became very obvious she was not relishing the food but seemed more intent on consuming as much as possible. Water was also consumed at regular intervals in unison with the intake of food. It was all very perplexing. Eavesdropping outside the toilet she was using, the unmistakable noise of vomiting confirmed that my precious daughter had an eating problem. I was at my wits' end about how to go about tackling the issue.

Bulimia then was not something that was universally acknowledged so I had no knowledge of this terrible, controlling illness. Should I confront her with my discovery? I had no idea it was terrifying. It was twofold; at school she was eating next to nothing then once in the sanctity of home self-deprivation was replaced by a lack of control where she would eat and drink everything and anything within her reach, culminating in self-loathing and in rapid succession expelling everything from her body before it was properly digested.

Patsy meanwhile was becoming moody, introspective and secretive. When she wasn't storming up to her bedroom or ranting and raving around the house she was either in the kitchen stuffing her face, in the toilet or exercising like crazy. It was exhausting to watch. She would cycle ten miles to school, rush home, and then go straight to the gym. Whenever I tried to confront the issue I was told to take a chill pill and relax.

My shopping for the week would be depleted every couple of days. Patsy physically didn't look as she had done over the summer; she was far too thin, her skin was spotty, her hair lank, greasy and sparse. Every time I tried to confront her she would yell and tell me to shut up. I noticed scars over her arms and asked her where they had come from, but again she sent me to Coventry and I felt dreadful. She was literally deteriorating in front of my eyes and I had no idea what to do. I felt so alone and frustrated. It didn't help that around this time John declared he was having relationship issues and wasn't sure whether he loved me or not. Clarissa kept urging me to seek advice from a child counsellor, but perhaps she should have practised what she was preaching – it would certainly have helped me growing up. I chose not to follow her advice on principle. As luck would have it the school nurse rang me again and said that Patsy had collapsed at school. We rushed her to hospital and she was assessed as being extremely dehydrated and also way underweight.

For a while social services stepped in and I rang Clarissa knowing the experience she had dealing with them over Margot. She thought I was being patronising so put the phone down on me. I lost it a bit after this phone call and I could tell social services felt that they needed to hang around to gauge more about my life. Nothing came of it and basically Patsy was moved over to an eating disorders clinic. It was hell; sometimes she would be sweet and lovely and other times she would be positively demonic and evil.

The clinic sent reports to me the contents of which, like her moods, were often erratic: one day she would eat when given food, and would be nice for once to the escort taking her to the toilet, as she had to be with someone wherever she went. Other days, however, she would insist on drinking copious amounts of water, along with things in her pockets, thereby ensuring at the weighing in time her weight had reached her target for the week.

This was the pattern of things with Patsy in the clinic and during this time my husband left, my friends slipped away, my mother washed her hands of us and then Matthew stabbed me in the back with his decision to live with his dad. Despite the fact that I was Patsy's main visitor when she was in the clinic bringing in anything she requested at any time, when she was finally released six months later I was devastated that it was John the clinic contacted at her behest and what's more, he collected her and she begged to be allowed to stay with him. What could I do? I came extremely close to telling her the truth about her paternity but something kicked in and I chose not to. I didn't want to be responsible for destroying two lives knowing they would both be devastated.

Things were particularly bad for me at this time so I started drinking; it was all I had to look forward to in the evenings. The first bottle was fine, it was when I finished the second everything went black and I would find myself in various parts of the house having fallen asleep on the floor. The next morning I would wake up feeling ghastly, and looking in the mirror was such an ordeal. My eyes were puffy, lines accentuated around my eyes. I normally had a splitting headache, dry lips and felt extremely dehydrated. I would vow not to touch a drop again and yet by six o'clock I would open another bottle. On bin days I could barely drag the bin to the collection point outside my house due to the numerous bottles I had single-handedly consumed. I knew I needed to seek help, but quite frankly oblivion was all I wanted.

31

PATSY

Oh my God, I can't believe this is happening to me. I can't believe my gran who may have driven me crazy and was a dictatorial old bag that disapproved of everything I did is dead. It's so shocking. Then Mum in prison convicted of killing Auntie Scarlett. Mind you, I wouldn't have wanted her as a sister, she sounded like a real prima donna. Matthew's a pain in the arse, but at least he's no competition. I dread the thought that everyone is going to be staring at me at college whispering about what my mum has done. I don't know how I am going to cope with it.

We had a girl at school whose dad had come into her best friend's room, sat on her bed with a joint and showed her his penis. They then had some sort of sad fumble and he ended up getting convicted for attempting to rape a minor. Poor Rachel having to come into school knowing what her dad was! Looking back now we were mean as we took the piss out of her and bullied her. It must have been horrendous for her and yet we had no idea what she must have gone through. I was always quite jealous as I had a major crush on him. The minute I saw him anywhere near the communal garages by our houses I would immediately rush out, nonchalantly chewing gum, leaning against the wall ensuring my boobs were strategically placed at a vertical level ready for our encounter. That had no effect so I decided to take it further by asking directly if I could join him in his commute to London one morning as no trains were running at that time. The gullible fool fell for it and the following morning there I was flirting outrageously with him in the passenger seat. I made it obvious that I wanted him to book a hotel room and that he had a green light to ravage me in any way possible, but he certainly failed to oblige. Instead he asked me questions about school, work and my choice of universities in the future, in between constant chain-smoking. I felt gutted. When he dropped me off in front of Eros in Piccadilly Circus, dead on eight o'clock, I had given up the will to live. I had limited financial resources, nothing was open and it was pouring with rain. I just wanted to curl up into a ball and sleep for a week.

Everything had seemed so much more positive weeks before when I had spotted him from my bedroom window just staring up at mine from the armchair in his sitting room. I knew the configuration of the room having spent time with Rachel drinking Babycham a few months earlier. In between eating, throwing up and exercising I would just stare at him all night. At times he would obviously get up, walk around, or leave the room, but for most of the time he was ensconced in one place, staring up at my room.

On my return from the disastrous trip to London, the following night I decided to try to entice him for the last time. Music up full volume in my bedroom to create the vibe, I had a fluorescent towel draped around my body. If anything was going to get him going this would. But no, he was obviously still interested as his head was facing directly at me and in the opposite direction to the television. It was just the passive, unresponsive way he was sitting there. Grabbing some binoculars from downstairs in Dad's study I just wanted to die when I realised what I'd been flirting and staring at for the past six months – a light bulb of all things. It may seem funny now but I took it really badly and my health plummeted, I collapsed at school and ended up being admitted to a bloody mental unit.

Mum was so bad at supporting me, unlike Alice who just seemed to get it and appeared to anticipate the vibe I was in and behave accordingly. Mum, however, was utterly clueless, standing and staring at me with this crazy, anguished look on her face as she twisted strands of her hair at anything I tried to tell her. Did she think that helped? She is mad and really has no idea. When I think of poor Matt with all her antics with his matches and sports coaching I'm amazed he is so chilled and normal.

I remember the time he got into cycling, poor, poor boy. Mum had spotted a group of men dressed in Lycra with their bikes meeting on a regular basis near a public phone box on the corner of a road. She decided to approach them with a view to Matt joining them as he loved cycling and needed a father figure in his life. Cringe of all cringes, did she really say that, or is that a figment of my imagination? Well, she could have said that to them. Anyway, they acquiesced and the next thing Matt went off on a jaunt with them, dressed at Mum's insistence in Dad's Lycra cast-offs. All I can recall is his pissed-off face when he arrived home shouting, "Never again, don't you dare do that to me again, Mum. It was awful."

It transpired that the only cycling being done was from one public phone box to another. In total the men covered ten phone boxes. The format was to arrive at a certain phone box then one of the ten men would get off and make a phone call confirming they had arrived and then it would be on to the next one and another man would get off and make the call. The final phone box was near a transit café where they would have a fry-up and review the bike ride. It transpired these men were literally passionate about phone boxes and each week the cycle ride would be based around phone boxes in the United Kingdom.

"Soooo lame," were Matt's words. "Then when they weren't talking about phone boxes they were on about train and bird-spotting and postage stamps, no word of a lie. At least I didn't see anyone I knew."

Mum's got this knack of humiliating you no matter what. She's also paranoid to the point of ridicule thinking everyone on the earth hates her, so much so that when someone makes an effort, actually not even that, when someone is civil to her, she gets completely obsessed with them to the detriment of all her family.

Dad is so much more chilled and easier to talk to. I still can't believe she would murder someone but I knew she could fly off the handle. Look at my sixteenth birthday party where after one hell of a lot of persuasion on my part she finally let me hold a party with both sexes. I wanted them to go out, Dad agreed it would be for the best, but Mum insisted they stayed so I looked like a complete idiot. Luckily people know what she's like so no one commented. Anyway, she was standing at the door vetting people as they came in saying she hoped they had nothing dodgy in their rucksacks. She checked Zac's, the coolest guy in the year, and even opened his bottle of water convinced it was vodka. Apparently, it was, but ha ha, she missed it. Anyway, the party was controlled and could have been better had she and Dad gone out, but it was okay until Mark Austin threw up. Girls were screaming because he looked like something out of The *Exorcist* sitting in a chair covered in spaghetti. So what does Mum do? She gets the goddamn hoover out and starts hoovering up all the vomit like a medusa. I just wanted to die. Then she announced "I hope your willy doesn't get caught up at the end, that will be really embarrassing." Nobody laughed. I was crying inside and I could see everyone standing around thinking *What a bloody nutter, thank God she's not my mum.*

With Mum in prison and Granny dropping dead I feel like I'm living in this surreal world detached from reality and that at some stage I will be returning back down to Earth. I am in no fit state for my exams; I've literally done no work. I asked if I might get some extra marks for extenuating circumstances, but it transpires it's a case of three per cent per exam if you're ill and five per cent if someone close to you dies. When I asked for eight per cent as I was suffering from both, the special needs woman looked at me as though I was mad. I know I am not going to do well, as I haven't put the work in. My mother hasn't supplied me, like some of my friends, with a tutor for every subject they are studying as well as an exam adviser who shows them how to work certain questions. (How am I meant to compete against that, for God's sake?) I've had to do it alone, albeit being at college, and it makes me sick. Even extra-curricular things like Matt's sports, he's never had an individual coaching session in his life and yet a lot of his mates have their own personal coaches, for goodness' sake. It's hardly as though any of them will play for the county let alone tennis at Wimbledon or Premier League football. I mean, a lot of his mates' dads have ended up being coaches for the team ensuring their sons get to play in matches. It must be bloody humiliating for them when they finally realise they are the same if not worse than the rest of the team.

I will never forget one of the mothers bragging to my mother at a school concert that her daughter was being taught by one of the world's most successful guitarists and it wasn't Eric Clapton as my mother immediately piped up. It was some classical guitarist I had never heard of. Bottom line though and something the dumb-arsed mother missed was that this teacher was obviously not very good as her daughter, aged fifteen, had not progressed beyond her second grade. These mothers were always so much more ambitious for their kids than my mum was and I was jealous as maybe if she had been I would have been excellent with my natural talent. Her stock phrase has always been, "Do whatever makes you happy." Fat lot of good her degree from Cambridge did her, I must say.

Maybe I will just drop out and wing it. Look at Dad's brother, Tim; I mean, he is dyslexic and earned a fortune teaching English in Thailand. He then worked as a singer in a nightclub in Indonesia, had a following and made a record and a load of cash and yet he's tone-deaf. Finally, he worked as a photographer and again built up a reputation as a brilliant one despite a pronounced squint and massive issues with his sight generally, even though he never wore his glasses apparently. Mind you, he ruined it all in the end by marrying a Thai prostitute with whom he had two kids. She stopped her work but they carried on living a pretty peripatetic life, moving countries every couple of years. He then got busted trying to smuggle drugs into Indonesia, was incarcerated and has lost everything. I must say, though, his wife is lovely. Her reputation preceded her so we were expecting a real cow. Far from it, she really is very sweet and considerate. Who knows if Tim will ever be let out? Actually, I just realised there is no point in this pep talk as he is an appalling role model and a walking example of why I should be working harder.

I moved back to Dad's as soon as I came out of my unit. I knew it would be an absolute nightmare with Mum. I mean, for God's sake, she was in relationships and having sex at seventeen. I know that because Auntie Margot told me she was also a Goth with dyed black hair and earrings all over the place. They both went through a real wild stage together going to parties, doing drugs; the works. And yet she's so controlling over me. There was the time she discovered I was on the pill after my sixteenth birthday having found them in the bathroom. The bitch flushed them down the toilet even though I had told her they weren't mine.

That's the problem – I can't talk to her about anything. I confide far more in Auntie Margot who's so much more on my wavelength. I know she despised me after our trip to New York all those years ago and, yeah, I was pretty obnoxious. I just found it disgusting the way Mum got all sentimental about some American prat she had a love affair with in a summer camp years before. *Spare me this* was all I kept thinking, but no, we had to literally follow all the sights that they had planned to visit but for some crazy reason didn't which made it even more boring. I know without a doubt she was obviously shagging the American left, right and centre. So bloody hypocritical.

It reminds me of Marina, a girl in my friendship group that I loathe and despise. She is so bloody 'holier than thou'. She was the bitch who had the nerve to ask me why I was abusing my body, announcing with her nose way up in the air as she said it (one of those awful snub ones where you can spot all the bogeys and hair up there), "My body is my temple". I was aghast and very nearly started listing the number of boys I knew she had given blowjobs to and had had sex with, but thought I would just add it to the growing list of things I despised about her; other things, like how at the age of eleven she was adamant she was going to be studying history at St Edmund's College, Oxford, for God's sake! She really is one of those sanctimonious types that should be put down. Another thing I'll never forget is her announcement in an American literature class at school, "I don't like the way the Americans put 'and' in front of every sentence. They are ignorant and badly educated." Hello, this is Steinbeck and Fitzgerald we are discussing. Get a life, girl. What's more, you may say 'Restrooms' is not a logical word to use; well then, what the hell is the point of the word 'Toilet'?

I need to speak to Auntie Margot to find out more about why my mum did it. I always thought she adored Scarlett; she always used to harp on about the three of them being so close. It all seems so surreal. Why did she choose to do it so subversively and to have lived with this guilt all these years down the line only to be discovered through a photograph? It seems so odd that she was the one who saved Scarlett's life when she had the near-death reaction to the nuts in the first place. Maybe it was some love match. Maybe she knew Dad fancied Scarlett and thought if she was off the scene he would love her. Then again, that makes no sense as she only realised she loved Dad after she was separated from him at the American summer camp.

32

JOHN

Scarlett was the pin-up girl in our school. She was a few years above me and considered an ice maiden but my God she was gorgeous, the sort of look that teenage fantasies consist of; with her luscious locks, shimmering and blonde, tanned legs up to her armpits, and her blue sparkling eyes with so much life and laughter she was perfection personified. Seeing her gliding around town with that amazing ethereal aura about her, she really was the embodiment of all schoolboy fantasies that guaranteed, after seeing her, a series of successful, endless wanks once in the cosy confines of home.

Christ, looking back it really was all about how a girl looked and whether I could get laid. Nothing else came into it, which is slightly ironic bearing in mind that I'm a human rights lawyer working specifically against the exploitation of women. If only I knew then what I know now I certainly wouldn't have spent my whole time fantasising and maybe learnt more about the Industrial Revolution.

I'm aghast at all the revelations emerging about Siobhan. Absolutely shocking, it is all so devastating. I like to think I'm an astute judge of character and am still finding it hard to reconcile myself with the fact that my ex-wife is up for murdering her sister. It just doesn't add up. It's just not in her make-up. Yes, she is an absolute pain in the backside and seems to be getting worse as she gets older but cold-blooded murderer? No, absolutely no way. Stalking, yes, I can believe that. How she managed to keep up the pretence at university is beyond me. In some ways I understand why she did it, wanting to start afresh after the awful event that had taken over their lives. The thing about her is once she sets her mind on something there is no stopping her.

Look at her determination at camp, pulling out all the stops no matter what it took to ensure I arrived back in New York because she had decided I was the one for her. I was a gullible geek even then but recall feeling so relieved that at last she had seen the light. I can see how Patsy has got that determination, but sadly it has gone into a negative mode and manifested itself in this horrific eating disorder that I just can't understand. The psychologists describe it as food being a way of semaphoring out her anxiety. I understand that, but then I just don't get why she can't just pull herself together and put things into perspective. Her life is no different to anyone else's. We divorced, that may have been upsetting for her. Was it acrimonious and violent? Not at all. I feel Siobhan and I handled it in the most civil way possible. Matthew has no issues, it hasn't affected him. At times I feel like dumping her in the middle of an African village so she can see how people use food as a means to stay alive and work, not to slowly, bloody well kill themselves.

Thank God Matthew seems to be heading on a straight path, fingers crossed. That's the thing about life; one minute you can be heading one way, then completely out of the blue something like this occurs, which is without a doubt going to irrevocably change our lives forever.

33

MARGOT

Phew, what a nightmare. What a fiasco – hopefully it has all come to an end now. I still can't believe the photo, what a complete shock. What a bolt from the blue. Funny how things turn out. I haven't visited Siobhan since things kicked off. I really don't think I ever will. She can rot in hell as far as I am concerned. God, she must absolutely hate me and the fact that she tried to nail me is unbelievable. Frank is convinced I was next on her list of people she wanted to annihilate.

Apparently, some of her friends have been suggesting she may have deliberately made their children ill. *The Daily News* ran an article about two girls who whenever they stayed at her house returned with dreadful sickness bugs. They were in the first teams for everything whereas Patsy wasn't. It also turns out she stalked some guy at Cambridge making his life so stressful he ended up leaving. I can't believe she changed her name; what was all that about? What a complete, bloody nutter.

Here I am bobbing around in a beautiful translucent turquoise sea, sun shining, juxtaposed with a beautiful white sandy beach evoking for some bizarre reason an image of clotted cream, and the beauty of it all is that there are so few people on the beach. If you want company you can saunter up to the bar and drink a sundowner whilst watching the most sensational Indian Ocean sunset. You know you're somewhere exotic when you hear the melodious tones of the muezzin's call to prayer. Sometimes you hear the whir of a seaplane coming in and you wonder who's infiltrating what feels like your private island.

Like all social situations there will be those that are here to network and after only a few hours these people act like they are lifelong friends and bosom buddies. I've actually seen a woman handing out her personal details to so-called friends she has made on what looks like an authentic scrap of paper. The details weren't as spontaneous, however, as she had wanted people to believe; I spotted at least thirty of them in her beach bag. Why would people bother?

I love it here as I watch and am entertained, but I speak and acknowledge no one. People have tried, but as some sad middle-aged git discovered I am not game for small talk. I joined the traditional island barbecue not for the communal aspect and to be stuck with flabby, boring, city bastards; no, I came purely for the food. Basically a pit is dug in the sand with hot rocks at the bottom. They then wrap raw lamb in Fujian taro leaves and lower it in before the sand is piled on top. It is then left to cook for a few hours and the result is the most incredibly tender meat with a smoky taste. Everyone then sits around eating the meat with pitta bread around a campfire with limited light which is just as well as the meat is so succulent the juice gets everywhere.

There are other guests who are more like me who stick together and have absolutely nothing to do with anyone else; they are in their twilight worlds, normally honeymooners, who just want to shag, chill and sun themselves all day or they may be families who stick together because they socialise too much at home and now want to totally unwind, not speaking to anyone outside their unit.

I am in the Maldives and it is utterly heavenly. Even here, however, dramas have taken place. The resort manager is a youngish, suave, good-looking Italian with the requisite hairy chest, and an impressive six-pack. He also has 'I am God's gift to women and I have affairs' embedded on his forehead. Well, in reality he hasn't, but he should have. I watch him every night as I sip on my cocktails, adopting his most ingratiating smile as he approaches various tables in turn ready to work his small talk and charm. He obviously realises I have the measure of him as he warily skirts around my table with no eye contact whatsoever. I have had so many of these guys; they are ruthless with no backbone whatsoever. I, however, could eat him for breakfast.

Carlos was going to accompany me but at the last minute I decided I wanted to take stock of things and spend some time alone. He wasn't happy but when you spend your life free-loading off someone he realised he had no choice. Of course, it hasn't taken me long to find a sweet local. This one is in his late twenties, naive, doesn't speak too much which suits me and most importantly is bloody good in bed. I literally nod my head and that is it, straight back to the room. He makes me feel what it's like to be a woman and then back out to the sun and cocktails. Heavenly. Would I want to be anywhere else right now? Certainly not. I'm just hoping he doesn't think this is going to gain him free access to life in England as that certainly won't be happening. What goes on here will stay here as far as I'm concerned.

Maurizio, the hotel manager, aka God's gift to all women, doesn't want to stay here particularly when he thinks the island he is managing is about to be devastated by a tsunami. No, he favours illicit travel, taking hotel boats out in the dead of night ensuring his family and any valuable articles are also packed up carefully.

Sounding the alarm in the middle of the night, a few days ago, he assured everyone that whilst their safety was paramount they were forbidden to take boats out to escape the tsunami that could be heading to the island, as morally there were not enough to accommodate all the guests. The only option for all was to remain in the main bar with lifejackets on and to hope for the best. In other words, if one was to hit the island we were buggered as there was certainly no higher ground to escape to.

Ralph is a seasoned traveller who has been to the Maldives a number of times. He is one of those smug know-it-alls who thinks he knows everything there is to know about indigenous people all over the world. (However, he didn't get my comment when I said there were very few on our island.) In response to my suggestion that the majority of staff were Indian and Filipino, he not only contested my observation, but also informed me I was very wrong. Not wanting to assure him I had inside knowledge I decided to concede and let him think his observations were correct.

"Surely it makes sense to arrange an evacuation now; there is a cruise liner just beyond the reef. It won't take long to run the boats to it in relays. Perhaps the liner itself will also oblige and run some boats in to help with the evacuation." Everyone including me applauded after Ralph's words and agreed it was the most logical thing to do. Maurizio, however, dispelled this suggestion saying they had already contacted the cruise liner and they were not prepared to give authorisation for an entire island of people to board their boat.

"Ladies and gentlemen, we have no option I am afraid but to ride the storm out."

No one laughed at Maurizio's choice of words despite the fact he was looking up obviously expecting a reaction.

"Please be patient, we are all in the same boat (again, no one laughed). There is a free bar (that caused a reaction) and food on tap. Please just order whatever you want at the bar. I am very sorry, please stay calm and patient. Your safety and well-being are paramount to my life at present. God willing we will survive this and tomorrow our lives in paradise will continue."

The next day, however, my holiday lover told me of Maurizio's escapade in the night. It transpired that minutes after addressing his people he rushed off to the only flash brown leather speedboat belonging to the hotel and sped off with his wife and children to that cruise liner moored at sea.

At breakfast two days later having caught his eye Maurizio sauntered over to me.

"Ah, good morning, Miss Ville I trust all is well and that you are enjoying yourself in paradise?"

I couldn't stop myself. "All wonderful, thank you. Your staff certainly know how to look after their guests. I'm surprised you didn't suggest the staff on the cruise liner do a swap with your staff here. I bet you discovered your staff are so much more efficient in comparison."

The look on his face was utterly priceless.

"Miss Ville of this I would have no knowledge, however I would imagine it would be impossible to find better staff than we have here. They are naturally the best."

I haven't seen much of him on the island since the 'event' but what a wonderful treat it was to receive a bottle of the best champagne, beautifully chilled, ready and waiting on my table every night when I arrived for dinner with a handwritten note saying *With best wishes – Yours sincerely, The Kura Island Management Team.*

What bliss, just lounging around on a sunbed on the perfect white sand beach then cooling off in the clear, crystal, turquoise water. It has got me thinking about all the events that have taken place throughout my life. Everything seems so surreal and unbelievable it is like tripping. It is as though I am coming in and out of reality; I am a bystander up high looking down on someone else then realising it is actually me.

At the end of the day it is all about people believing too much in themselves. Look at Maurizio; despite getting rumbled he's convinced he's the best asset the company has. That may be the case, but in his desperate bid to save his skin he let his clients down. Look at Frank; he's convinced he's the best detective in the world. Not true, Frankie. If he hadn't been so intent on shagging me senseless and actually taken stock of the situation afterwards instead of acting like a headless chicken, he would have taken more control of the paperwork and realised that I was not actually at his house on that fateful day, 16 November, which meant that I did not actually have an alibi after all.

My main objective in the lead up to the events was ensuring Siobhan was out of my hair and off her head. That was easy to plan, I just waved a huge wad of cash at my mate, Dogsbreath, and he ensured her drink at the party she was attending gave her the big start she needed for an all-out psychedelic experience, where she would have mind-blowing hallucinations believing that life was fucking wonderful. She would wake up the next day, however, to paranoia, fear, insecurity, exhaustion and not only a complete inability to get herself to the train station to arrive home in time, but also with a completely unreliable alibi.

Sweet, unsuspecting, nauseatingly irritating Scarlett, meanwhile, had absolutely no idea about my plan to surprise her in Cambridge. I took the train from Kings Cross, arrived in the morning where I spent most of my time milling around charity shops. I came across a great place, Mill Road, with loads of eclectic shops so I was really in my element. One antique flea-stall shop so reminded me of my nan's front room I wanted to throw up at the depressing memories it evoked and yet I loved the *objets d'art* in there. I remember feeling tempted to buy an amber ring in one place, but decided against it as amber is meant to be unlucky.

I knew Scarlett had her interview at 1.50pm at Trinity College. She had promised to ring Mum and Dad. Despite me not being their flesh and blood I always addressed them in this way; in fact, it was only when Scarlett referred to them by their Christian names when talking to me about them that I would get the message, i.e. no matter how hard I tried I would never be completely part of the family.

Siobhan didn't have an issue at all; maybe that's why she was never a threat to me. Her main fault was her presence and that was it. Anyway, I knew Scarlett had promised to phone home as soon as the interview was over, and knowing what a diligent and conscientious creep she was, I decided to loiter near a public phone box in anticipation, where I would then jump out and shout, "Hi-de-hi," to her. Like clockwork she finally approached at 2.55pm. She had a smile on her face, which represented the fact that all had gone according to plan for her. She rang and again as I spied through the telephone box and saw her gesticulations I knew that for Scarlett it meant that she not only thought the interview had gone well, she had probably enjoyed it. I jumped out from behind the telephone box as she sauntered past me. I surprised her because I was all in Goth gear; in fact, she thought it was Siobhan at first glance. She quizzed me as to why I was dressed up as I was and I said I would as a dare from Siobhan. She was amazed that I'd been allowed to borrow her precious lime-green cardigan.

"Oh my, you must be in her good books," and we laughed. Anyway, the great thing was Scarlett was pleased to see me; so far, so good. "Mum and Dad didn't let on to me that you were coming." Again I laughed.

Scarlett was impressed that I'd brought a picnic; she didn't know it was one with a difference. I suggested we walked to a nice secluded place on the River Cam that I had been to and knew was very picturesque. We walked along Trinity Street past all the beautifully preserved historic buildings and cobbled lanes, including Senate House, known, Scarlett informed me, as the place where degrees are conferred on students. Apparently, the poor sods have their exam results listed on special boards placed along the south wall of the building at the end of their exams in May and June. This is also where if all goes well the students receive their graduate of the University of Cambridge certificate all done in Latin.

"So you might be there with Mum and Dad watching me with that bit of paper if all goes well," to which we both smiled.

We then sauntered along King's Parade where a South American group were playing instruments and singing to salsa music; a group of foreign students were dancing seductively to the rhythm. One couple was totally engrossed in each other's bodies completely oblivious to everything around them. I wondered at that moment how many secrets people were harbouring under the guise of normality. How many serial killers or murderers or perverts had I sat next to on a bus, for example, or shared a lift with, or simply walked past in the streets? Who knows? One man in a suit watching the dancers was absent-mindedly picking his nose and eating it. God, if he did that so publicly what the hell did he get up to behind closed doors?

All I kept thinking to myself was imagine if these people around me knew that Scarlett's life was going to be extinguished by the end of today. No longer a person with a soul, just an anonymous body. How will I feel? I've been informed it will be akin to an amazing trip, a massive adrenaline rush and you're left feeling utterly invincible. However, conjectures on this subject are many and varied. I guess each experience is unique to the person in control. Looking at her then and there out of the corner of my eye, all I could think was, this bloody irritating human being who is so smug and happy in her own skin, really needs to be taken out and sorted as soon as possible.

We stopped off at the Copper Kettle known to serve the most amazing fry-ups after the May Ball where from the sounds of it no one ever bothered sleeping and stayed up all night. The place was full of people; there was such a buzz about it not only there, but also the surrounding area. It was nothing like my memories. Mind you, in those days I had not yet crossed paths with the O'Briens and instead I was up visiting my sister in her foster home. An average house, in an average street, were my first thoughts until we walked through the house. The garden was nice enough but it was the lake beyond that which really blew the mind away. I mean, there we were in the middle of suburbia (okay, picturesque suburbia) in the middle of Cambridge and fuck, seeing this you would think we were in the middle of the country. It was unbelievable, an absolute paradise, a utopian vision of nature in its purest form. I felt like crying it was so peaceful and heavenly. I didn't want to leave; I certainly didn't want to face up to all the crap in the outside world. Ultimately, I had no choice as the twats my sister was living with decided I was a negative influence on her. The last straw was when they found the two of us pissed out of our heads, smoking weed and lying on a boat playing loud music.

I had considered setting up the picnic with Scarlett around the lake, but decided it was too public what with all the houses backing onto it, plus it was further from the train station and logistically I wasn't sure where the deepest part was. Whilst ruminating on this dilemma I couldn't really deduce what Scarlett was burbling on about as it was a complete monologue about the bloody events of the day. Apparently, the lecturers who had interviewed her were amazing, the college interior was beautiful and of course all the prospective students who were also there for interviews were in her words, "Amazingly brilliant, lovely people who totally deserved to receive offers to study there."

Blah blah blah was all I could think. *Can't you shut up for one bloody minute?* Of course the last thing I could do was upset her so instead I had to disguise my irritation with a totally sycophantic smile and intermittent nodding ensuring that she assumed I was listening and hanging on to every word that she uttered.

For one glorious moment silence did ensue and I was able to take stock and relax a little, but not for long however, as the next thing I knew she started banging on about Cambridge's bloody history, of how Samuel Pepys had walked the very streets we were walking on. *And?* was all I could think, but of course not say. Scarlett then mentioned Cripp discovering DNA in some pub called The Eagle. I felt physically ill when she mentioned that and did ask some questions, as I was genuinely interested. That was why I had ensured I'd packed four pairs of latex disposable gloves.

We then arrived at Browns deciding to have a celebratory drink at my suggestion although I hadn't realised how busy it was going to be. It transpired from our irritatingly indiscreet (knowing that day was his final one) waiter that most of the restaurant had been taken over by a guy who had just had an interview at one of the most prestigious colleges at Cambridge. Turned out that his entire bloody family, friends, as well as rent-a-crowd had turned up. They were not only loud, uncouth and irritating but were also incredibly rude and obnoxious snapping their fingers every second and virtually drinking the restaurant dry. It took bloody ages to get a drinks order in.

The annoying waiter also divulged to us that it was a pretty foregone conclusion that the guy was going to be following in his family's footsteps to the college of his choice. The waiter also provided us with info that pointed to the fact these guys were dodgy; they were obviously running some illicit operation. How the waiter had deduced this was questionable, but I guess that the presence of three blacked-out Bentleys outside the restaurant complete with menacing-looking, chain-smoking bodyguards with earpieces was a lot to go by. *God help the admissions tutor and director of studies if he fails to get in,* was all I could think about. Not without reason, however, the waiter didn't hesitate to extrapolate on this subject insisting that this scenario had in fact already been discussed by the patriarch over lunch. It had been decided that if the worst scenario were to happen then a huge donation to the college would have to happen. Preferably before the offer letters got sent out. Scarlett was adamant this would never happen. *Naive bitch* was all I could think.

It wasn't just the sound levels in the restaurant that were infuriating; it was also the constant flash from the cameras, which did not appear to stop. My guess is that every single person there had an individual photo with the twat in question. They didn't just stay in the corner either; no, they had to take centre stage in the restaurant so that every time Scarlett looked up the flash would blind her eyes. Luckily, by the time I had decided to go and have a word with the complete twats (she was doing my head in saying her eyes were blurry) it had all stopped so I could sit back down and relax.

Scarlett and I had a cocktail and chatted about the usual mundane crap then I suggested we headed off for the special picnic which she was pretty keen to do. "I'm starving," were her last words. *All the better to kill you with*, were my thoughts and for the umpteenth time that day I laughed out loud.

We decided to walk across the common towards Grantchester by Fen Causeway. I was beginning to get pissed off carrying the picnic, but wanted to reach the specific area that I had earmarked as it was nice and secluded and I thought of it as my special place. I knew I had to really get my adrenaline going so as we walked I began to think of all the reasons I hated Scarlett so much. There was that constant analogy for a start about Beauty and the Beast, an old one that really pissed me off. Siobhan had been tarred with the same description and ironically laughed it off, but I found it grossly humiliating and would never forget the humiliation I felt when some git referred to it at a club. I therefore saw it as a mission on Siobhan's behalf as much as mine to rid the world of Beauty and annihilate the pain and anguish she had caused me throughout my life. I was sick of constantly being made to feel inferior and inadequate by her. I knew from the minute I met Clarissa and Ben I was destined to be part of the family and I also know deep down they would have been much happier with just me as their daughter. It is this unspoken connection that can't be put into words, but is something the three of us were obviously aware of. Without Scarlett it would be a perfect situation as she'd always been the one who had demanded ninety-nine per cent of my parents' time. Siobhan had always let her get on with it, whereas for me it had escalated into something that I was no longer able to tolerate.

I couldn't believe that yet again she had started prattling on about Cambridge, again describing it in her words as a, "paradoxical place, so much permanence regarding history and yet so much transience at the same time." We cut across the common towards the river and for a while it was almost enjoyable. We reverted back to childhood pursuits, sitting on swings seeing who could go the highest, and playing the who's fastest at naming countries beginning with a letter from the entire alphabet game.

From here we cut through the back of Newnham Park walking past a couple of disused toilets with birds resting on the green galvanised iron roof near to an abandoned tennis court surrounded by glossy weeds. It was here a mournful bird presaged rain. The contingency plan would be to seek shelter in the toilets should this happen. A few metres along we pushed our way through the briars, nettles and tussocks of dead grass reaching the impenetrable, overgrown bank of the River Cam, and just to the right we reached a narrow pathway made of stones. We crossed it and came across a clearing where wispy strands of pale grass shimmered as the wind sighed gently through.

"This is magical, Margot, how on earth did you know this place existed?"

"My sister and I used to hang out here whenever I went to stay with her. This was our den," I replied.

Scarlett would have no idea what this place meant to me. I was still reeling from the fact that I had actually found it.

So began the next part of my plan.

"So, Scarlett, I've prepared a tasting picnic. I'm going to blindfold you and test you on food we've eaten throughout our lives so far. You've got to guess and tell me what it is, and what memories it evokes. I will give you a clue, every dish has a significance."

"Wow, Margot, I can't believe you've prepared all this. What a wonderful idea. This is a day I will never forget."

I opened a bottle of champagne, gave a gushing tribute to what an amazing person she was and how she deserved everything she had achieved and that I had no doubt whatsoever she would be accepted into Cambridge. I ensured that throughout my nauseating words, I was topping her glass up and that she was drinking far more than me. The next stage was the delivery of the food. The first concoction was cold spaghetti bolognese, the first meal I had at the bitch's house where she actually apologised to everyone because I had no idea how to eat it. Naturally she guessed straight away and true to form felt no compunction on her part commenting on the mess I caused trying to eat it. Did she have any idea of how humiliated I felt during the meal?

The next thing was bara brith. We ate loads of this in Wales when we embarked on a mixed-year trekking trip with the school. We had a few reminiscences on this and then we moved on. The roast beef-flavoured Monster Munch crisps she immediately guessed correctly; these would always be the number one priority when friends came for sleepovers. Next, a drink that needed, I emphasised, to be downed in one like the old days. Yes, good old Babycham, our regular New Year's Eve tipple before we hit the hard stuff. Next it was Oreo cookies dipped in milk – these were normally eaten the morning after the night before when we were feeling dire. The wine was opened at this stage; with a forty per cent alcohol content I could see it began working a treat. Scarlett's words were beginning to slur and she was not quite as adept at guessing the samples. Biltong was meant to bring back memories of Africa but she failed to recall them. Next it was mangosteens from Indonesia and passion fruit from our trip to Mauritius. I could tell the novelty of the game was wearing off and at this stage long shadows started to creep in. The sun moved slightly, casting shafts of streaky light through the creepers surrounding us. A shower of tiny yellow confetti leaves rained down from a nearby tree. I felt this was symbolic and decided to push on and produce the *piéce de résistance*, before she announced she had had enough and was ready to leave.

Dipping a good tablespoon into her poison - peanut butter. I added some jam thereby ensuring the severity of what she had ingested was not an immediate realisation. Pretending the spoon was a plane I asked "Who does this sound like, Scarlett; 'I'm coming into land, open your mouth, darling'?"

Scarlett immediately responded, "Mummy, of course, force-feeding us night and day. Wow, this tastes good."

Her final words on Earth were, "Oh, my God, Margot, shit, quick, I need my zapper now; it's in my bag, first pocket on the left. Quick. Oh shit, shit. I can't breathe. Help me!"

I then lunged forward, deliberately avoiding her eyes and with my hands inside latex gloves, mustered all the strength I could and pushed her into the river at what I knew was the deepest point. Every time I heard her hands lunging to the sides of the riverbank I pushed them away. I rushed to pack everything, careful not to leave anything behind whilst at the same time listening out before eventually running off when the splashing ceased, replaced by an eerie silence. I then retraced our footsteps back to the deserted toilets where I was able to remove some of the make-up and dumped the wipes, latex gloves and remnants of the picnic in an overflowing bin near to the entrance of the park. I then ran like hell in areas where it wouldn't look out of place, or adopted a brisk walk to reach the train station.

The train was on time. Once I had boarded it all I could do was sit back and smile to myself. It looked like I had just carried out the perfect crime. I changed trains at Kings Cross and caught the underground to where Frank lived. When I finally located his house I spotted the wellington boot on his porch that housed his front door key. It was at this stage that the adrenaline started racing in my body. What if Jackie and the kids hadn't gone away after all? What the hell was I going to say? I decided it would have to be a case of a mistaken address. Luckily enough no one answered and once I had checked for nosey neighbours I was then able to open the front door and slightly relax.

God, it felt bloody weird being in his house for the first time. I kept imagining someone would jump out. They didn't, however, and I was able to take a bath, have a mooch around the house, and then waited to shag Frank senseless. I could imagine him rushing home knowing that he had me, his little (ha, I'm taller than him) princess waiting in his bed, naked and willing for the entire night. Bet that bed saw more action that night than it had done in the entire twenty-five years they've been married. I ensured it would be a night he would never forget and pulled out all the stops possible.

When I arrived home the next day Dad had left for work, and Mum was listening to the radio in the kitchen and seemed remarkably chilled. Pancakes were on tap with steaming, hot, fresh coffee. Just what the doctor ordered. I stuffed those down and felt marvellous. I was obviously very tense at Frank's house worrying I may have left something incriminating at the scene or that miraculously Scarlett had recovered and made it home. Luckily the coffee dissipated my anxiety and I felt as normal as I could bearing in mind the circumstances.

Siobhan sloped in at some stage and looked absolutely wrecked. Dogsbreath had obviously organised a night she would never remember. What a star he was. Barking some inaudible words at Mum, she staggered up the stairs and demanded nobody disturb her as she 'had the hangover from hell'.

"That's told us," was Mum's comment and we both laughed.

Mum then disappeared into the study as she had a deadline on an article she was submitting to a magazine to work on. I decided to have a bath and relax. At one o'clock Mum came out of the study and asked if Scarlett had returned. I knew she was on edge as her voice was an octave higher than usual and her hands kept touching her face and hair. At this stage Siobhan had managed to make it downstairs and Mum asked her if she would ring Felicity to see if Siobhan was still there or had left. In the meantime, Mum and I started writing out a shopping list as we were going to have a nice family meal that night celebrating the fact that Scarlett's interview was over and done with.

The tension in the room was palpable and could literally be cut with a knife when Siobhan came into the kitchen and said, "Scarlett didn't stay with Felicity last night; she was meant to but didn't turn up. Felicity assumed she came straight home to us."

I saw the blood literally drain from Mum's face but still she was trying to remain brave and resolute.

"Ah, she's obviously gone to stay with another friend and on her way home now. It's fine, I can collect her from the station en route and she can come with us to do the shopping. It is her right to choose what we eat tonight as it's her interview we are celebrating."

All I could think was, *this is the very reason I wanted that bitch out of the way. She literally clouds everything because it always comes down to her, no matter what. Well, Mum, she ain't gonna be coming. Hopefully she is face down in the water, as dead as a dodo. If not, then great, I am a dead woman walking.*

At some stage during the evening Clarissa's bravado began to waver. Siobhan rang Dad and suggested he came home as Mum was clearly upset. In the meantime she rang all Scarlett's friends hoping that someone may know of her whereabouts. Nobody however did.

"Perhaps she met someone at the interview and went to stay with them?" I volunteered.

"Yes, but if that was the case she would definitely have rung us to inform us of her plans. I have a horrible feeling; I have had it since the early hours of this morning. It felt like a premonition and I am feeling so sick. This is so out of character. We need to ring the police and report her missing."

This didn't happen as whilst we were in the kitchen at around 6pm deliberating about whether or not to ring the police the doorbell rang and Mum rushed out shouting as she went, "Thank you, God, thank you. Scarlett's obviously got a lift home."

It was then we heard a terrible, primeval scream and a thud. Mum was lying on the floor in a heap. The front door was open but through the glass screen between that and the outside world we could see the unmistakable silhouettes of two police officers standing on our doorstep. They were bearing news that would change the O'Brien family's lives forever.

Inevitably, when the devastating news finally reached us that Scarlett's body had been found in the Cam and that it did not appear to be suspicious, I felt proud of myself for masterminding such an event. The look on Clarissa's and Ben's faces was priceless. They were utterly bereft, of course, but I knew time would heal and that inevitably it would be to me that they would turn for all the things they looked to in a daughter. Obviously, Siobhan too, but I knew I would be the one who would deliver and live up to all the expectations which hitherto had been Scarlett's domain. I was going to do it – I knew I would at long last be regarded as the golden child. What I had not banked on, however, was the fact that both Clarissa and Ben would be so emotionally caught up in Scarlett's death they would as a result have absolutely no interest in me or Siobhan whatsoever. What a complete waste of time and energy on my part.

Invariably, over time, however, I have come to realise that Scarlett's removal has brought me closer to Clarissa. I was ecstatic when she identified Siobhan as being me in the photograph. What a betrayal, what an achievement on my part. I really believed that from then on with Siobhan locked away Clarissa and I would be able to walk off into the sunset together. How wrong I was. It was meant to be us against the rest of the world; we were one. We were a united force; but what happens then? Unbelievably she drops dead at my feet. It was devastating. The most upsetting thing that has ever happened in my life. I have never cared about anyone as much as I cared about her.

When I was asked about my alibi I thought it would be fun to put the cat amongst the pigeons so I acted all coy and said I couldn't say. It wasn't until the police officers really pushed me that I asked to speak to Frank; I hadn't seen him since the night of Scarlett's death. If all went according to plan I knew he was going to back up my statement of where I had been. I knew I had nothing to worry about there. Of course, I hadn't bargained on battleaxe sociopath, my social worker, Ramina, of all people, seeing me snogging Frank. I can't believe she did as my peripheral vision is usually phenomenal and always active. I really must have slipped up on that occasion. Seeing us together was when the shit really hit the fan and he ended up leaving the force. For once I felt bad as I knew being in the police force was his life. Silly git shouldn't have been so unprofessional, on the other hand, basically shagging a ward of the court; really, he had it coming to him. It was quite fortuitous in the end as Frank was beginning to bug me. He had now served his purpose and it was time for me to move onwards and upwards.

Siobhan and I bobbed along in the aftermath of it all rarely talking about Scarlett. I couldn't believe how utterly crap the forensic scientist was, decreeing it was accidental death. Jesus, why would she have fed herself peanut butter, for God's sake, knowing she stood the risk of dying from merely touching a goddamn peanut? I ask you! I mean, it was great for me, but honestly what are half these guys on, is all I can say. Why would she have gone to such a secluded area too? It just didn't add up.

Clarissa and Ben seemed perplexed, dazed, and confused, basically the works, initially insisting it must have been murder but on the other hand knowing that that was not a realistic option. How would the murderer know she had a dangerous allergy? How would he or she have forced her to eat something that as far as she was concerned represented poison that would kill her? The only people who may have taken such action would have been me and Siobhan. Our alibis, however, were watertight. Dogsbreath and others were able to confirm Siobhan had attended an all-night party and Frank knew that I was at his house at 10.00am where I spent the day chilling and left the following morning at 8am.

34

ZULEIKHA

Watching the news that night and seeing Frank DuPont being hailed as a hero having discovered that Scarlett O'Brien, whose death had been recorded as accidental, had in fact been murdered by her own sister, was a shocker. Sibling rivalry taken to the extreme. I know Mum was indirectly involved, but I hadn't asked too many questions as quite frankly I am so not interested. Frank is an ignorant twat and a rude one at that and I still can't believe his insults towards my mother. I mean, why tell me he couldn't believe I was so pretty with a mother that looked like a dog? Did he really think I would turn around and say, "Frank, all is forgiven, of course you can have my mum's personal details, I am chilled about the way you are haranguing me for her details. I totally get it."

Thank God Boris was on site to throw him off the premises. If I hadn't been a dog lover and working in a kennels nothing would have stopped me torturing Sugar and Spice in revenge against Frank. The two of them are so their owner; it's amazing how dogs come to resemble their owners. All I can say is Frank's are so him what with their constant yapping, shifty, sideways glances and perpetual cocking of their legs. Quite frankly (funny that), there is not a great deal of disparity between them and their owner apart from the fact they probably have more sex appeal.

Good old Boris, he has always been there when I've needed him most. He has just literally popped up out of nowhere and been there as a huge support. Let's face it, I probably would never have acquiesced to my father's request for a meeting. It had been a huge bone of contention between me and Mum who wanted me to have no contact with him. If Boris hadn't acted as a go-between calming the waters between us and convincing her that it had to happen, who knows how things may have ended up between us. Thankfully she listened and cried hearing about Vladimir and realised I had to forge something between Dad and me. Otherwise I don't think I could have lived with myself.

This seemed to be the crux of our relationship; Boris is always there to support me. It was strange to think of life before meeting him and yet I most definitely had one – in Ibiza at that. Both Candida and I had found work through an agency working in a club promoting the facilities; it was an ideal job for students as all accommodation and drinks were included. Our hours were from three o'clock until the early hours where we were then encouraged to get involved in the club scene selling and serving as much alcohol as possible.

Whilst there we got friendly with a group of boys. The days would be spent meeting at the girls' accommodation where we would all hang out chatting and larking around before work. Both Candida and I unusually for girls working in such an environment, made it perfectly clear whilst we enjoyed the guys' offer of companionship we weren't at all interested in any sexual relationship whatsoever. Initially this was fine and the six of us had fun. One night, however, having consumed copious amounts of Sangria things were getting out of hand and then we knew the newly formed friendship was in peril as it became very evident the boys wanted more than we were prepared to give. There was an underlying feeling of aggression and the light-hearted humour that we had always enjoyed together began to definitely move to a new dimension. We knew we had to stop the unspoken gesticulations and body language that we had always used to tease them, before the shit hit the fan. It had in fact become so much of an issue we knew we would be leaving Ibiza the following day.

True to our word twenty-four hours later we were literally on a plane heading back to England having enjoyed our time, but bloody pleased to be returning home. A few days later, having collected my holiday photographs, I recall sitting down in the reception area of work and flicking through my holiday snaps. I had clocked the new guy gorgeous Boris – how could I miss him with that mop of long blonde hair and all his trendy piercings? – but just dissed him as I assumed he had a girl or was gay and if neither of those, that he was far too cool and trendy for the likes of me.

I remember roaring my head off at memories confronting me of our time away. What a laugh it had been. I almost felt a slight pang of guilt that things didn't develop with any of the guys as we had all been such a close-knit group with our shared experiences in Ibiza. That was, however, until I came to the final batch of photos.

There they were, those boys, all bending over showing their bare arses and at first, I didn't clock the nature of the photos. When I saw my fluorescent pink toothbrush up the arsehole of Nick, the one that was definitely keenest on me, I felt sick; in fact, I literally vomited there and then. It was an absolute violation. I know for a fact that toothbrush had been in my mouth a number of times after the event recorded on my camera.

Lovely Boris ran to my rescue and got me mouth rinse. Okay, I discovered later it is for dogs, but I felt cleansed after gargling with it and the main thing was he just held me and told me everything would be fine. I wouldn't have caught anything and in his eyes, I was the most beautiful girl he had ever met. A cup of tea followed on from that and over time we have got closer and closer, as in we chat a lot at work. I haven't actually asked him if he is seeing anyone and he hasn't asked me. We never see each other at the weekends or after work during the week; it is strictly business. Who knows what will happen?

I do know that totally unlike the former me sometimes I can't wait for the weekends to be over.

I am also adament that, if I ever get into a relationship, and don't get me wrong I've had my fair share of partners, it won't be anything like the one Mum had with Dad. I want to be in a relationship with someone who regards me as an equal. I know a lot of that stems from a generation gap and that things are so different for women now. I just cannot believe that Mum accepted it was the norm at the beginning of her marriage to Dad. She hasn't confided in me at all about where it all went wrong between them, but I know having spoken with my brother and with flashbacks I have had from time to time it was not good. In fact, it was terrible. There was violence, but I think I have blocked a lot of it out. We suffered, the three of us. All that peripatetic living in different hostels, they are my worst memories. Some of the women's stories will remain with me forever.

When Dad contacted us out of the blue I know it was really difficult for Mum to deal with. She had made a life away from him. When the divorce finally went through it was incredibly acrimonious and Mum had suffered reliving many of the awful memories she had. Thank God for Jen Taylor who was an amazing support to her. Initially I had no interest whatsoever in rekindling anything with Dad, but I guess putting things into perspective I realised I had nothing to lose. He is part of who I am so I decided perhaps it would be good as then it would give me more understanding about myself.

The first thing that struck me when my brother and I met my dad at Jen's house (she was the impartial observer, just in case) was the similarity between me and Dad. That's where my height and nose and the dimple on my chin came from. It was such a surreal experience. He appeared calm and understanding and it was difficult to gauge whether it was an act or whether it was genuine. From time to time, however, things came out that indicated his views on women had not changed at all. His second wife, Indira, was definitely expected to be in the home and to look after him, but then he intonated that was what she wanted to do. Perhaps Mum and he had such a volatile relationship because they both wanted different things and his behaviour to her was a one-off. Who knows?

Fortuitously it didn't take long for Dad to realise that if he wanted a relationship with this modern, westernised Pakistani daughter of his he was going to have to let her lead the life that she had chosen for herself, step back and for once in his life let her control the situation. It was difficult, but he really was left with no choice. With Kasim, my brother, it was not so much of an issue. Of course, Dad abhorred the fact that his son drank alcohol in copious amounts and did not pray enough but at the back of his mind however, he knew that Kasim, who was pretty similar to how he'd been in his youth, would ultimately marry a good Pakistani girl just as he had done. What's more, Allah willing, it would be a match with a daughter of one of the many influential families in Pakistan whose friendships Dad had managed to nurture all thanks to Indira and her influential contacts in Pakistan.

There was no way this was happening to me and after our first few meetings I told Dad about Boris; he didn't need to know others had preceded him. Mum was amazed that he accepted things no questions asked. I then felt things were definitely looking up and going in the right direction. That was until Dad asked me to accompany him to a distant relation's wedding in Pakistan. Mum was convinced he was going to abduct me and force me into an arranged marriage where I would never be seen again. Boris sided with Mum and I was left in a dilemma. Part of me was terrified about going but another side of me was completely intrigued. After all, being Pakistani was part of my roots and I wanted to discover more about my heritage.

The next thing I know I was finally on a plane flying to Pakistan with Dad. Boris and Mum had come to wave me off; honestly, you'd have thought I was leaving to go to a war zone the way the two of them were carrying on. I think seeing Boris with all his piercings slightly threw Dad. Well, if he was planning anything off the planned agenda for me he had another thing coming. Never underestimate a girl who's cleaned her teeth with a literal arsehole – great I can laugh about it now.

There was nowhere like Lahore; wow, it was crazy and the strange thing is I felt a connection. It was crazily frenetic; people, animals, rickshaws, street vendors. Wherever you looked there was some form of action taking place. Juxtaposed with this were the numerous mosques representing calm, stability and beauty. Many of them appeared to be covered in tiles made from mother-of-pearl which coupled with sunshine created a surreal sublayer of glistening beauty which was both hypnotic and mesmerising to those who glimpsed them. For me, however, the allure existed in the street bazaars with the eclectic colourful clothing that I couldn't wait to barter on as well as sampling the wonderful array of delicious smelling street food with all those wonderful-tasting curries and the cornucopia of candied fruits, fresh fruit, herbs and spices bursting with vitality.

Our first destination was the home of Dad's niece; this was going to be interesting and suddenly I felt very nervous. As I walked in the room I could feel all eyes on me. I must have looked pretty scary with all my piercings – the Boris effect – and my butterfly tattoo visible to all on my shoulder. At least I had covered up until I stepped foot inside the house. I could see Dad was mortified, but this was me, warts and all, and they would just have to accept me for who I was. Speaking to me in Urdu it soon became obvious my grasp of the language was pretty minimal so they switched to English. Most of the girls were around my age. They were all sitting together and were fascinated by me; I could literally feel their eyes watching my every move. Could I dare to reach out and ask one of the motley-looking crew of unshaven men on the other side of the room for a beer and a fag? Logic, however, prevailed and I stayed in my seat sipping tea in a very demure, quintessentially British manner, complete with my little finger at right angles to the rest of my hand.

My long-distant relations seemed lovely and nothing like the inhibited, terrified women I was expecting them to be. Far from it and where were the burkas? They all had this amazing glossy black hair, they were wearing make-up and had stylish, colourful outfits on, exposing their shoulders; nothing like what I had been led to believe. There was constant chatter, laughing and music which made it difficult for me to infiltrate any meaningful conversation, but it was a great place, however, to observe and note. *Where were are all the repressed women,* was all I could think to myself.

When I finally relented and decided I needed a beer, some dirty old man started stroking his beard and looking me up and down and kept reiterating the word '*baji*'. Smiling demurely I chose to say nothing. It was only after he started following me around that a girl came over, said something and he finally moved away. She informed me it was 'piss off' in Urdu. Ayesha, as she introduced herself, was my dad's second cousin's daughter, she was in her twenties and became my mentor throughout the rest of my time in Pakistan.

Ayesha revealed a whole new world I had never imagined existed.

Yes, there were many restrictions on women and I was exposed to an entirely new world of sexism and expectations of women that I had no idea actually existed. She herself said her father had never thought anything about '*Chamaat*', which was, it transpired, an expression applied to women which meant a light beating. Jesus Christ, it was unbelievable. At the same time, however, although it was something that truly reviled me it gave me more insight into what my father had expected when first married to my mother. Particularly in the fact that according to Ayesha and the rest of her cousins (and mine, I am guessing), a lot of the families that had chosen to leave Pakistan and to make new lives in England actually adhered to a far stricter lifestyle, both for themselves and their offspring, there than they may have done had they not chosen to leave Lahore.

The girls were shocked that I had already been in three sexual relationships and a one-night stand; they were also shocked to hear I smoked dope on a regular basis and always drank far too much on a Friday night. They were amazed my father accepted this despite the fact I mentioned he didn't have a choice. They couldn't believe I had also decided I didn't want to go to university and had chosen to go straight to work instead. I made my views on marriage known and mentioned that whilst I would probably be happy to have children with Boris one day, the likelihood of me marrying him would be a very slim one.

I mentioned Vladimir and the fact that he had been gay and that sadly he had committed suicide and the girls asked if that was a regular thing in England with Pakistani girls who had chosen to pursue relationships with Western guys over fellow Muslims that their parents had assumed they would be marrying. I confirmed that yes, this was a big problem in Britain and yet surely it was expected. I mean, you move to the West, you have kids, they get educated locally it is an inevitability that they are going to have broader outlooks and expectations on life as their peer group is going to be far more diverse, not only from a religious perspective but also in general life experiences . Surely parents have to accept this fact?

I realised at a certain stage in the conversation I had gone too far, however, when I mentioned relationships with women. I have experimented as have a lot of girls my age, but knew by the reactions of the girls it was time for me to stop blabbing. Ayesha had also warned me about revealing too much as the 'desi aunties' constantly reported back little snippets of what I had said to Dad and although he was powerless to act I knew the information he had on what I got up to was freaking him out. It was time, I realised, for me to take a grip and learn more about their lives which is exactly what I did.

The first thing that shocked me was the wearing of the hijab. This to me had always represented male oppression and masculine demands in that a woman should only be exposing herself to her husband and male folk in the home. She was effectively their possession and nothing more. How wrong I was: far from it. It came as complete news to me that Pakistan is not monolith, in other words it isn't mandatory to wear this item of clothing. Why the hell had I been so misinformed? Some of my relations were wearing niqaabs, covered up from head to toe in public. However, once in the home the amazing outfits underneath came out – all designer and unbelievably glamorous. The shoes – my God, their shoes – they were truly to die for. What had I been missing all this time? These women were not subjugated victims, they were so much more savvy, independent and educated than I ever imagined. Suddenly I saw the uses it served; no more lecherous, vile men like Frank looking you up and down with no resistance or boundaries whatsoever. How heavenly it all seemed.

Plus, for those that choose to wear a hijab, no more bad hair days; if they can't be bothered to wash their hair so be it, just whack one of those on and the problem is solved. A simplistic approach and yet even after I had attended a rally on the pros and cons of religious dress for women I found myself supporting the arguments despite Ayesha's opinion that they were ridiculously dated and scarily oppressive views. Of course, I agreed that women and men are equal in all walks of life and that they should share the same rights and obligations. Why would I also not agree with the fact that taking the veil is a means of protection for women as Muslims truly believe that when women display their beauty to everyone they degrade themselves by becoming objects of sexual desire and become vulnerable to men who look at them as sexual objects? The hijab to them solves the problem of unwanted sexual harassment and unwanted sexual advances, which are so demeaning for women, with men getting mixed signals believing incorrectly that the women want their advances by the way they reveal their bodies. It almost made me want to return to England dressed in the full gear.

All I know is when it finally came to the end of my sojourn in Pakistan I never in a million years believed I would be sitting in a house with all my female relations playing Scrabble, drinking Alphonso mango juice with a little splash of vodka, dancing, singing and celebrating the fact that part of my heritage was from such a fascinating, beautiful and amazingly dynamic culture. I also knew, however, that I had had enough of being celibate and couldn't wait to find myself in the arms of my dearly beloved Boris. I just hoped and prayed to God and Allah that the feeling was mutual.

35

BORIS

Oh my God, the tension that has been spreading through me in the last two weeks has been unbearable. I had absolutely convinced myself that the love of my life was going to be whisked away by her father to Pakistan where she was going to be forced into marriage. Anyway, it hasn't happened and my babe arrived home last week looking as sexy and gorgeous as always, if not more so; must be all the samosas and curries she's been consuming. She thinks it's the distinct lack of alcohol, but whatever it is, she looks gorgeous. Her hair is shimmering – seriously, it looks so glossy she looks like she's been shooting a hair product advert. Coupled with that gorgeous olive skin I am the luckiest man in the world. I haven't laughed as much as since she arrived home. God, it feels so good.

She missed Frank, the twat, coming into the kennels to get his 'precious girls' (his words, not mine). It was bloody insulting to my intelligence having to blow-dry and cover the runts' fur in pink ribbons ready for their live appearance on television. How did he wangle that one? I tell you, he is a real master of self-promotion. I took a leaf out of his book agreeing that if I scratched his back by taking his last-minute booking he would scratch mine by advertising the kennels. So funny, the twat's head blocked our acrostic pledge and all that could be seen was the word TWAT behind him.

Trust in us
We will
Adore and pamper
The ones you love

Frank, of course, was totally oblivious to the background and just kept on blabbing. It was one of life's precious moments and fortuitously I had the hindsight to record it. Zuleikha and I had such a laugh playing it whilst downing a few beers weeks later. Needless to say he is now known as 'Twat'.

Joking apart, I couldn't be happier. Zuleikha is cool; we are pretty in tune with one another. Ramina's also chilled and pretty laid-back. The only one who is a bit of a pain is Kasim; he is a real spiv in some ways. Doesn't he know it isn't cool to race cars pissed and stoned out of his head? Problem is he pulls the wool over Ramina's eyes. And even worse, his dad is aware but just sees it as a phase and a rite of bloody passage – yeah, right, until he kills some unsuspecting person trying to cross the road.

It's easy to excuse it all saying he's had it tough over the years and it's not his problem but then again, he needs to bloody well grow up and get a grip. Guess he's gone against the grain and chosen to live a life completely removed from that of his dad's. There's a weirdo; I just don't get Tariq one iota. I really can't stand him. In my opinion he is an absolute shit. I just don't get how Zuleikha seems to worship the ground he walks on. It's not as though he's been around. Poor Ramina has had to bring them up single-handedly and yet Tariq seems to be gaining all the benefits.

When Zuleikha announced she was going to a wedding in Pakistan, I was convinced she wouldn't be coming back and that Tariq was going to get her married off to some randy, old, rich bastard. Thankfully, I was wrong; I guess he's met his match in his daughter; no one will walk over her. Nevertheless, it was such a relief when she returned to England; I reckon Tariq's master plan failed. I know one thing, he isn't keen on me – long hair and piercings are not his cup of tea. I definitely get the vibe: 'Hard luck, mate, I'm here to stay'.

Louisa, my mum, is really fond of Zuleikha, thank God. I know some of my girls were not the types she wanted me to get hooked up with. Zul's definitely the first girl she's waxed lyrical about. Poor thing, she's definitely had it tough. When I think back to how she must have been and how she must have felt when my dad, big Boris, came into her life. A shy, awkward, overweight American girl (who landed a job through my grandfather's contacts, no interview needed), she wound up working as an au pair for one of the richest men in the banking world in Chelsea, London. There's no way she would have been offered it otherwise. For a start she had no younger siblings and absolutely no idea about working with young children whatsoever. Secondly, she had terrible mood swings and was virtually socio-phobic.

I wonder what they made of her when she first arrived. I mean, come on, she had major weight issues, eating for her was a means of filling the void and that is all she did. The sweeter the better was her motto. I remember her recalling the delight she felt on discovering a larder and fridge full of all the American treats she loved that were banned by her parents. She had literally died and gone to heaven, spending all night stuffing her face to what she thought was her heart's content. That was until the family friends finally issued an ultimatum that, like home, the fridge was now out of bounds for her. They were no longer prepared to endure the heart-wrenching sobs from their children when faced with marmite sandwiches for breakfast as all the tubs of peanut butter and jelly had been consumed.

The family also made it quite clear that they were not paying her to watch TV 24/7 and that she was expected to interact and play with the two children. It was relatively embarrassing when they asked her purely out of interest if she knew the names of her charges and she was unable to answer. Louisa was also told that the cleaner was not responsible for cleaning her room and leaving skid-marked underwear on the landing and bathroom was also unacceptable. They also had the nerve to tell her she needed to wear deodorant and to wash more regularly and that perhaps taking some exercise may make her more energetic. After this humiliating dressing down she decided she was going to leave and started contacting other agencies. Bearing in mind she'd only been au pairing for a month it didn't take long for her to realise she wasn't going anywhere.

It was a chance meeting with Svetla, another au pair she met in the playground, that, to coin a phrase, changed the course of history for her. God, if only she knew then that this bitch would ultimately end up as her sister-in-law from hell. Suddenly, Mum actually started taking care over her appearance and getting on with the family she was au pairing for. Why? Because she had fallen in love with none other than Boris, my father-to-be.

It was such a shame she hadn't realised at the time that the only reason my father had any interest in her all came down to the fact that he discovered she was working for one of the most successful Americans in London. He often reiterates this story claiming he was the first person ever to invent networking. Hello! Hasn't this strategy existed since the days of the caveman? Anyway, in his own words if he had to "shag this ugly, smelly, overweight, socially inept mate of his sister's to meet the guy who would maybe offer him a job in his empire, so be it". What he didn't get the measure of, however, was the fact that the family she was au pairing for had actually become very fond of Mum and felt a degree of responsibility for her welfare. It was for that very reason that John, the successful American, felt it was his duty to have a pep talk with Dad about respect, honour and integrity as Mum was a vulnerable young girl with issues and the last thing she needed was to be unfairly treated by him.

Well, this to Dad was an opportunity he had to seize; it was a perfect way to impress so what did he do? He confessed his undying love for her and said he was desperate for them to marry her but due to financial instability stemming from job uncertainty he didn't feel he could. At that, the long-coveted position he had dared to dream about in John's company became reality. John had risked putting his reputation on the line by agreeing verbally with Dad that if he did the honourable thing (Were they that desperate for Mum to move on?) then there would be a guaranteed job within the company. Everything had gone swimmingly for Dad; the only thing that was not part of his fantasies, however, occurred the following year when he found himself standing at the altar next to his bride with her questionable hairstyle and noticeably very pregnant gait.

My mother was elated; the love of her life, her Russian hero – my dad – had not only made her feel special, but had also elevated her in the eyes of all the bitches at her high school who in the school magazine had labelled her the girl least likely to marry. What's more she had not only been the first to tie the knot, but had also bagged the best-looking guy in the universe; tall, blonde, Boris the Russian.

It didn't take long for my dad to realise his fatal mistake not only when he saw John's wedding present – an horrific, cheap, tacky vase, but also when it dawned on him that he was never going to be promoted from his current position in the company which still involved making coffees for everyone.

I soon arrived, followed swiftly by my brother and poor Mum didn't only suffer from postnatal depression, she also piled on weight and with that her self-esteem fell to an all-time low. Things between her and Dad were dire – they barely communicated, all of which was exacerbated when he moved my grandparents and auntie Svetla into the family home. Their friendship was definitely a thing of the past. Mum saw her as a complete, manipulative bitch. We boys, however, loved her.

Dad had insisted he spoke to us only in Russian at home which was particularly difficult for Mum, as she really didn't understand the language. Her linguistic skills which were never good weren't helped by severe dyslexia. After eight months of an intensive evening class every Monday night she decided to stop fooling herself and realised she had made absolutely no progress whatsoever and as a result she left.

We loved having the extended family in the home as there was always someone to converse or play with. School was also great as we were the only Russian kids who attended. We didn't ever give Mum a single thought. Looking back now I realise what a struggle it must have been for her. She became totally distanced and disconnected from the family and at the time I couldn't understand why.

The final nail in the coffin was the infamous family holiday that was to be the last one ever. To this day I can recall how excited we were; it was just going to be the four of us as Mum kept reiterating. Determined to get a bikini body I remember the sound of the treadmill echoing through the house as well as all the diet food in the fridge. I also remember auntie Svetla making fun of poor Mum and me feeling bad that they were being so mean.

Things went from bad to worse. The hotel wasn't up to scratch and there were hundreds of Russians which meant loads of carousing in the evenings with copious amounts of vodka. Dad seemed to be glued to his phone and Mum in her books. We were all in a pokey room as there had been an issue with the booking. Relaxing it was not – Mum was often in tears and Dad oblivious. It didn't help that we were constantly fighting. Dad would disappear for hours on end scuba diving so we would just be on the beach all day in the blistering sun. My brother then got severe sunstroke so it was the three of us (no idea where Dad was), stuck in a stiflingly hot room with a totally ineffectual fan, watching video after video, willing the evening to progress whilst the sun blisters healed.

One day we ventured out to buy ice creams along with a very memorable Russian woman; she was the most beautiful human being I had ever seen. I just remember swallowing hard and found it difficult to stop myself staring. A true embodiment of all the fairy stories I recalled reading as a child, she represented the evil figurehead who was deceptively beautiful. She was all eyes and lips with a mass of blonde hair. Matchstick thin and very elegant she made me feel very on edge in a negative way.

Queuing behind her it was hard to miss the conversation that followed. "I want banana milkshake," were her words in faltering English to which the vendor replied, "Sorry, madam, we have no banana milkshakes." She then replied, "What you mean you have no banana milkshake? I drink yesterday, why not today?" "Madam, we don't have today, sorry." Well, it soon became obvious this woman was not going to give up easily. "Okay, you have bananas?" to which the vendor replied, "Oh yes, madam, we have bananas." She then replied, "Okay, you have milk?" The vendor looked like he had lost the will to live at this stage. "Yes, madam, we have milk." "Okay," she then shouted, "as I have just said I would like a banana milkshake, you have banana and you have milk, this to most normal people is called a banana milkshake." The vendor's response was, "No, madam, this is banana milk, we don't have banana milkshake." In response to this the woman breathed in deeply and then announced, "Get me a regular coffee." The vendor continued as though wanting to continue the outrageous discourse by asking, "Madam, would you like hot milk in your coffee?" The woman, obviously assuming he was being ironic, guffawed realising it was better to placate him rather than to piss him off at the risk of him spitting in her coffee. She then responded with, "No, thank you, please can you just add a splash of cold milk?" The look on her face in reaction to his words, "Ahhh, madam, I am afraid we only have fresh hot milk, no cold milk," was utterly priceless. "What do you mean you have no cold milk? If it is fresh it will be cold then you make it hot. Milk does not come out hot. I would like cold milk."

The poor vendor looked gutted. "Ah, but, madam, when the milk goes into the coffee does it matter whether it is hot or cold as the water in the coffee is hot?"

With that the woman put her wallet back into her bag, asked the vendor if he was for real and then flounced out of the café.

Mum was incredulous. "What a rude, awful woman," was all she could say. "I think she is well known; a famous actress perhaps. I recognise her, she is obviously used to her own way, but why talk like that? Boys, take heed, always be polite to people. See how awful she sounded? How arrogant and unkind." I was also pretty shocked; I had never heard such aggression particularly from someone who was so magically beautiful. I did also secretly agree with her dilemma but thought it better to keep that opinion to myself. I also kept something else to myself. A few days later when out with Mum I spotted Dad on a sunlounger kissing the woman from the ice cream shop.

A few weeks later, however, the shit hit the fan. Mum and Dad happened to be at a dinner party back in Britain with their English friends when a discussion about things getting lost in translation ensued. Dad then started regurgitating the entire conversation we had overheard at the ice cream parlour referring to the lady in question as being his secretary. Erring on the side of caution Mum did not immediately launch into accusations but did some detective work. Devastated, she did discover that the woman in the front of the queue was indeed Dad's secretary. Wasting no time she confronted him and as if relieved that he could now reveal his secret there was no stopping him. Yes, she had taken a holiday at the same time as us and as if to rub salt deeply into the wound she was indeed staying in our hotel, literally four rooms along from ours. Dad (surprise, surprise) had bankrolled her and what's more they had managed to touch base many times during the trip. The thought that all that time we were stuck in the room with my brother suffering from sunburn, whilst dad and his fancy woman were literally a few rooms down.

The relationship went far deeper than Mum had assumed. She wasn't just his secretary; it also transpired that she had been Svetla's best friend in Russia and his childhood sweetheart. They had rekindled their love when Mum was pregnant with me and he had travelled back to Russia supposedly on business and had met her there. Both families knew each other well and really as he said to Mum he should have followed his heart which pointed to love and happiness, not to his head which pointed to Mum and her connections. Dad then confessed that Anna was his life, and that he couldn't bear to be parted from her. Now the secret was out at least he could end the double life that was becoming increasingly difficult to endure.

That was such a tough time for my mother; my brother and I went to live with her. I think my father finally relented as for a start the bitch really didn't want two boys living with her and her lover; we cramped her style too much. She never wanted children let alone boys that weren't hers. It didn't end there because not long afterwards my grandparents and Aunt Svetla were ousted from the house and her parents moved in.

We loved being with our mum. She was great and very laid-back. Yeah, we still went to my grandparents for lunch and it was still a traditionally Russian affair despite the fact that they were now living with Aunt Svetla in her boyfriend's house. Being Polish he didn't quite share their passion for all things Russian. Things had therefore been toned down considerably.

Fortuitously for us due to the change in circumstances Dad appreciated that it was easier for him to visit us at home. Luckily Mum being the tolerant person she was had never let their personal situation become embroiled in our relationship with Dad. Far from it she actively encouraged him to join us for dinner as much as possible and rarely if ever referred to his domestic situation with Anna and her parents. Consequently Dad played a much more significant part in our life throughout our teenage years and became the father we had always longed for him to be. At times it was deceptive and I would often convince myself we were a happy family of four with no extenuating circumstances. Friday meals were becoming a ritual occurrence and Vladimir and I would look forward to them each week, particularly as we would often go out bowling or would do something fun before eating.

That all changed, however, the day Vladimir finally told Dad he was gay. Mum and I were already in the know. In fact, we had met Mark, one of the guys he was seeing. Both of us had accepted the situation without any questions. It had literally been a case of Mum saying "Vladimir, are you gay?". Vladimir's confirmation, "Yes", meant that there was nothing more to say on the subject. I had to slip in my affirmation of, "Cool", thereby conveying my response and that was basically it.

Vladimir had, however, raised the issue that he felt Dad needed to be told by him in a more controlled manner. It was his idea to visit both our grandparents, Aunt Svetla as well as Dad and to tell them collectively on his own. Mum and I did not give any further thoughts on the matter. That was until the day Vladimir arrived home in a terrible state. It transpired that his attempt at explaining his sexuality in Russian got lost in translation (or so he thought) and Boris started advising him on seeing a shrink and taking antidepressants to combat his illness. Switching to English he attempted again. Relieved to see Dad smiling Vladimir assumed he had finally broken through. He was soon to realise, however, that this was in fact not the case. The smile was in fact a grimace and following on from this all hell broke loose.

With no hesitation Dad thumped Vladimir in the face; the things that came out of his mouth were despicable and inexcusable. He was a "child of Satan", a "fucking faggot", and "an insult to the Russian people and a fucking disgrace to his family". Trying to calm him down Aunt Svetla and my grandparents' words had no effect, and further enraged him. He began pummelling his son whilst simultaneously unleashing a torrent of verbal abuse screaming in his right ear. Vladimir remained mute and motionless at the head of the table, his head in his hands. When his father finally stormed out of the room, Vladimir pulled himself up and then tear-stained and shaken he left the house with no further comment to anyone. When he arrived home his face was the picture of absolute misery. It was heartbreaking and we could do nothing to placate him.

From that day onwards Vladimir never referred or spoke to my father again. My father in the clear light of day realised his outburst had been unforgivable and inexcusable. However, his subsequent imploring to be forgiven by Vladimir had no effect whatsoever. He had struck a nerve and the damage was permanent. Letters were returned unopened and the phone was not picked up. When Dad came to the door begging for Vladimir to answer him he was met with a steely, unresponsive stare.

Vladimir himself changed over the next few months and sadly, although it was noted, Mum and I assumed he would eventually snap out of it. He would sit downstairs just staring into space not focusing but looking as though he was in a trance. In an attempt to engage him I would start my bantering in different accents. He had always responded either telling me they were basically crap or sometimes he would congratulate me on actually sounding convincing. Not this time, however; he barely seemed to register I was addressing him. What could we do? Mum and I knew he was depressed but had no idea to what degree. He spoke about being incredibly lonely and that his life was hopeless with no future. Still, however, we underestimated the extent to which he had gone under. He would say things like, "You'd be better off without me", "There's nothing you can do to make it better", "Nobody understands me – nobody feels the way I do", and "I just can't deal with everything – life's too hard". He would wander around the house at all hours, sleeping during the day. We knew he really was suffering when he no longer waxed lyrical about the delicious food Mum would spend hours concocting. But what could we do? In retrospect this was something new, no one in the family had ever suffered with mental illness and it was beyond anything that we had ever had to deal with before.

In time, however, things did start improving all thanks to Vladimir's boyfriend, Mark, who started visiting the house. I have no idea how they met, he just turned up one day and it was such a relief for Mum and me to see animation back in my little brother's face.

Mark was such a great, easy-going guy. He became part of the family and things started looking up. Not, however, as far as my father was concerned. Vladimir had cut all ties and the idea of any reconciliation looked more doubtful as time progressed.

We were in the house one Saturday, Vladimir had invited Mark for dinner and Mum was cooking her signature dish – beef wellington with all the trimmings. I popped out to buy some wine and Vladimir was sorting his room. He had been the most positive I had seen him in ages and the fact that he was having a huge sort out of his room that morning had really buoyed Mum and me up; it was as though he really was moving on and rejuvenating. I was a little shocked when he handed over what had always been his prized possession, his coin collection, but didn't give it much thought. Hugging Mum and telling her how much he loved her I felt a wave of emotion that he was back to his positive self. Mum and I locked eyes and I could tell she was feeling my vibe. Life was good again.

Returning from the supermarket armed with champagne as well as wine I had a feeling the night was going to be a good one. Something inexplicable hit me as I entered the hall. To this day I still can't explain it. It was a feeling I desperately hope I never experience again, one of foreboding and doom. Walking up the stairs I knew as soon as I saw the note on the door in Vladimir's writing saying, *Do not enter. Please call the police*, that my darling brother, my partner in crime, was hanging lifeless and swollen behind the door as I forced entry. I don't remember much more apart from Abba blasting out in the kitchen and then Mum's distraught face as I told her about my horrific discovery. Seeing her legging it up the stairs and hearing her devastated crying will be something that will never leave me. A mother should never have to go through what my poor mother did desperately trying to revive her youngest son at the same time knowing there was no hope whatsoever.

There was no note, just a pile of vinyl records with my name on them, a pile of books for Mum and two pairs of jeans and a photo album with Mark's name on them. His room for once was spotless and we realised why he had the huge sort out of his room. It just didn't add up; things seemed to be so much more positive for him. Why did he feel the need to end it all? Surely, he knew he was loved. It was all so inexplicable. I have learnt now that is the whole thing around suicide; there is no logical explanation. It is just one of those terrible things that happen. The guilt, however, never leaves you. Even to this day I wrack my brains on what Mum and I could have done to prevent the situation. Dad, of course, has always blamed himself and I understand why he does and in no way can I excuse his irrational and utterly unacceptable reaction to Vladimir's news about his sexuality. However, I also see his pain and guilt and I feel sorry for him. His inner turmoil is visible for all to see, he has aged beyond all recognition and although a lot more humane than he ever was before, my brother's suicide will be the huge rift that will never really facilitate a truly close father and son relationship between us ever.

During this awful, turbulent time I was unable to work. Luckily Alice had been an absolute star and actually suggested I took time off to support both myself and Mum in coming to terms with our devastating situation. I didn't stay away for long, however, as the pull of Zuleikha was too tempting. Furthermore, I knew work would be a positive move for me and would be the ideal place for me to channel all my pent-up emotions into something more positive. Vladimir would have wanted this and it was a further reason why I turned up earlier than had been discussed and agreed.

There was an unspoken spark between Zuleikha and me, but for the record it had not been acknowledged. Admittedly it was something I had been working on before Vladimir's untimely death and as I stepped foot back into the kennels I had promised myself I was going to throw caution to the wind and decided once and for all that I would invite her for dinner. I had not vouched, however, for emotions getting the better of me and the minute I heard her kind words of sympathy about my terrible loss I literally collapsed in her arms overcome with emotion. It was with reluctance and regret, however, that I finally had to extricate my head from the top of her glossy, wonderful smelling hair as my neck was aching like hell. The rest is history; she literally barely let me out of her sight for the entire day she was that worried about my mental state. At one stage I looked up to the sky and although it sounds corny now I actually raised my fist and heard myself saying, "Thanks, bro." That evening we went for dinner and in all the doom and gloom that had been part of my life, that night will go down in history as one of the most amazing ever and marks the day I fell in love.

36

FRANK

Well, things had definitely been looking up for a while and life was manic. I had even been referred to as a local hero on one radio station which has increased my self-esteem no end. Due to popular request I even graced my presence at Mum's nursing home so widespread was my fame and Mum being Mum, who is quick to exploit anything that gives her some recognition, begged me to come directly after being on air. Despite announcing who I was with most of them nodding in what appeared to be general acknowledgement, I don't actually think they had a clue. One in fact called me Tom Jones, no joke, and for one hideous moment I thought she was going to throw her knickers at me. The others seemed to think I was the goddamn bell-ringing teacher. I've been called some things in my life but that takes the biscuit. Mum, bless her, looked like the cat that had got the cream. I know she loved showing me off to her number one sworn enemy, Ivy, who lives across the corridor. Smug was an understatement as she clung to my arm simultaneously eyeballing Ivy who didn't take her fish eye off us throughout the time I was there.

Admittedly I was slightly disappointed that no one asked me to switch on the city Christmas lights but at least I was asked to read out the winners of our local pub quiz and then gave them their prizes. The standing ovation I received on walking in quite overwhelmed me,

I must say. It felt so good. Mind you, Jackie said my white shirt looked grey with beer stains down it which was bloody embarrassing; typical of her to put a dampener on it. I swear she washes things then sends them off to be ironed and they come back dirtier than they were in the first place. I caught a glimpse of the guy that collects it all. He, his car, his missus and the bloody great big dog with a massive lolling tongue all look like they need environmental health warnings slapped on them. Lazy cow, my missus, is all I can say: why can't she bloody well iron it herself?

Anyway, the celebrity thing has been good but the only problem is there is barely any money coming in and I keep borrowing more and more for the private detective agency I'm setting up. I've had to sort out office space, office equipment and of course the ubiquitous girl Friday who also happens to be bloody gorgeous. Coincidentally, she is Siobhan's friend's daughter and was the one who was interviewed by the press when Siobhan went down. It was her who reiterated how shocking the events were and how never in a million years would she have held Siobhan responsible for such a heinous crime.

That's the thing though in my line of work; it's often the ones who seem most unlikely that are most likely to have committed the crime. Anyway, I've done a few minor cases over recent months – lots of disputes between neighbours involving sabotaging another one's possessions as well as trespassing on private land. I got a fantastic array of misdemeanours recorded on the very subtle CCTV camera I had hidden up a tree as the man blatantly scratched all down the side of the car with a penknife. I knew we had nailed him. Bloody dumb idiot missed the flickering red light up a tree, for goodness' sake, even though he appeared to be staring blatantly into it. My portfolio is looking good. I've just been creating a website on all the services I run with a view to perhaps branching into France and Germany – who knows, I could be a tax exile if things progress as well as they are.

37

MARGOT

Life is one big holiday for me at present. Returning from my blissful sojourn in the Maldives, I agreed with my doctor that I need at least another month off bearing in mind the terrible trauma I have been through. He has duly obliged and now having sent all the documentation off along with the approval of the main board, I am again footloose and fancy-free although still obviously in mourning over the shocking events of late. I have decided to utilise my time sensibly and as a result have decided that both Patsy and Matthew deserve, after all they have been through, to do something nice.

I am thinking either a safari in Africa, or a repeat trip to the Maldives. I know that Maurizio will pull out all the stops. I think he had a rather nice, unexpected shock when I treated him to a quickie behind a palm tree on our last night. Thought it would be nice to give him a little taster. Or perhaps America again, but this time California. Perhaps a road trip along Route 66 will appeal. I am seeing them at the weekend so will discuss it then. I am pretty excited about all these forthcoming events. Just need to see if it is worth Carlos coming on the next trip or whether I may stick to my casual encounters which are so much fun.

38

JOHN

I haven't a clue whether I am coming or going at present. Thank God for Alice is all I can say. She has been an absolute godsend helping to support the kids. Luckily Matthew has got really involved in looking after the dogs. It transpired that Zuleikha who works in reception knows all about our family situation; her mum has some distant connection with Margot. Anyway, she and her boyfriend, Boris, have been amazing. Matthew actually gets up in the morning with a smile on his face and races off to feed, walk and groom the dogs.

Patsy is the worry; she is so bloody thin. I just can't get why she is doing this to herself. There was a stage when she was actually beginning to look normal again, but she confided in Alice saying that at least when she was thin people recognised that she was ill. Once she looked normal again people had no idea of the mental anguish she was feeling. I get that, I really do. But what the hell am I, as her parent, her dad at that, meant to do to support and bring her back to health?

We have been in to see Siobhan a couple of times in the mental health unit; that is bloody depressing. It's like being an extra in *One Flew Over the Cuckoo's Nest*. She looks dreadful and you can barely get a logical word out of her. At the same time, whenever the kids go they get so upset we are literally back to square one again. Margot keeps hassling me about taking the kids on holiday. I know she means well, it's just trying to accommodate and placate everyone that is stressing me out. I'm so relieved Alice has agreed that it's much better Matthew stays here now he's in a routine helping with the dogs. Boris is giving him some hot tips on dog grooming this week which should be fun for him. It was her suggestion that Margot and Patsy go off on their own which thinking about it could be a great idea.

39

MARGOT

I've just returned from John's place. What a great little number he's got there. He has shacked up well and it's a dog's paradise. They must be making an absolute fortune. Funny, both John and Alice are morphing into dog-like images; cute looking but they are so not bothered about self-grooming. I'm surprised he hasn't had a word with her about her long grey hair. Guess he likes them natural – all to their own.

Anyway, he really needs to get a grip on things. He told me Patsy was looking great and is coming together. Who the hell is he kidding? She looked diabolical, so thin and pasty looking, I swear she is wasting away in front of our eyes. The problem is he sees her every day and has become used to the way she looks. I haven't seen her for a few months hence the shock.

Like hell she is being weighed every day at the clinic or if she is I bet she is knocking back gallons of water beforehand. I wonder if they are wise to these things; anorexics will stoop to anything to delude people into a false sense of security thinking they are on the road to recovery. Anyway, we have concluded that Matthew will stay home and I will take him away some other time. For the time being I will focus on Patsy and what I can do to support her in some form of recovery. I have the address of a clinic in Beverley Hills that advocates cognitive behavioural therapy in reference to eating disorders, and it is residential. There are activities every day all geared towards recovery as well as developing interests and hobbies that may never have appealed to Patsy, but might be worth pursuing.

She will be in residence for a week. I will be staying *in situ* and will accompany her to the various activities. The stipulation, however, is that the patients eat with the staff and fellow patients, but not with family and friends. If they keep up their eating regimes and don't vomit, take laxatives or try and hide the food, their reward is seeing their family/friends the following day. I so hope this works. I'm really hoping it will bond us together and that she will confide in me and that going forward we could perhaps form a mother-daughter relationship now poor Siobhan is out of the picture.

It's been tough at work as well as the terrible shock of Clarissa's death and of course the revelation after all these years. Perhaps we will be able to put it behind us and look forward to the future once Patsy has done her residential course and all is hopefully going in the right direction. I have then rented a house on the beach in Santa Monica where we will decamp to. I'm envisaging barbecues on the beach, ogling the gorgeous, young, muscle-bound lifeguards, walks on the beach with our resident dog (I've agreed to babysit a friend's dog as I know Patsy loves them) and swimming in the ocean alongside tireless surfers. I've also got a friend who is a hypnotist and she has seen three teenagers she vows are no longer suffering from issues with food so it may be worth getting her to meet Patsy too.

If all goes according to plan and Patsy is well, I'm planning to take a road trip to venture inland where we will stay in the most amazing guest house near to some incredible gorges (Carlos took me there a couple of years ago). Once there we will relax in the beautiful thermal springs surrounded by glossy palms, and as it is all situated in a bird sanctuary you are treated constantly to the mellifluous sounds of hundreds of birds singing. Whilst there we will also have some spa treatments and generally pamper ourselves. This will then be followed by a spot of retail therapy on Rodeo Drive as well as driving through Beverley Hills checking out all the magnificent mansions. I've arranged to hire a very special car for that and I know Patsy is going to love it. I am so excited about this trip and just can't wait to explain it in full to dear Patsy.

Another positive thing is I happened to mention in passing to a particularly irritating, lascivious, sycophantic, greasy estate agent that I was thinking about putting my house on the market (like hell, and if I was I wouldn't be handing the privilege to him). What I needed, however, were some tickets to a concert in Malibu that were like gold dust and were proving impossible to get hold of. (I had done my homework and knew his wife hailed from California.) Sure enough the letch couldn't do enough to help and a week later two tickets landed on my desk at work. That would be another treat to be added to the list for Patsy.

40

PATSY

I've just come off the phone to Margot and I am so excited. She is such an incredible auntie I can't believe what she has arranged for me. We are going to California. I just can't wait. It is so kind of her; hopefully I will get sorted and my life will be back to normal. I hate this existence. I hate being so obsessed with what I've eaten every single waking day of my life. It totally dominates everything.

It will be so nice if the clinic works out, to then rent a house in Santa Monica; what an amazing thing to do. I love America, not just for their sitcoms, movies and food. I also love the American people, they seem so much more chilled than the British. Oh my God, imagine if I met a Californian surfer dude. That would shut my friends up. They would be absolutely gobsmacked. I am literally counting down the days to my departure, I seriously can't wait.

I haven't told Mum yet. I can't bear to. I still can't believe all this shit. It really is unbelievable. I keep thinking I am in a surreal nightmare. I just cannot wait to escape.

41

FRANK

Jesus wept; real life detective stories can't match this one. It has actually done my head in. I've decided to leave the life of crime once and for all. I would say I will leave it to the professionals, but obviously that is not true. So what happened? There I was preparing my notes for a case from an estranged wife and mother who was trying to trace her son who she believed has been abducted to Egypt by her ex-sister-in-law, when I noticed some copies of the photo of Scarlett and Siobhan in Browns restaurant. Since the case a couple more photos from the guy whose first photo caused all the furore have trickled in and been filed accordingly. Something suddenly caught my eye. I felt as though all the blood in my body had seeped out; it caught me full on – I was absolutely staggered. Pulling out my old reading glasses I looked again. Jesus Christ, there it was staring me in the face. Shit, it had been there all along and I hadn't clocked it, what the hell! It hit home immediately – this meant Siobhan had been telling the truth all along – it bloody well wasn't her.

The ring ensconced on her finger was the same as the one I had always worn on my little finger. It was a solid gold signet ring that had belonged to my mother's father. It was distinctive; the family crest for DuPont is a flag etched on the front of the ring in 18-carat gold with white gold on the outside. I had reluctantly given it to Margot and you would have thought I'd given her the world; I knew she was wearing the ring the night Scarlett died because she had caught her finger in the door at my place. I recall blood coming from a cut and how dramatically her finger started swelling around the ring. She was adamant all was fine and thwarted any attempt on my part in easing it off, claiming that she could deal with it. When it really did stop her blood flow she claimed I had permission to saw her finger off. We had for some reason started laughing hysterically at this farcical situation.

Looking again at the photo I just didn't get it; how could it possibly be Margot? She had peroxide hair when I'd been seeing her and I had never once seen her looking like this. Gothic was Siobhan's trademark; she would never go out without a starkly white-powdered face coupled with liberal, and I mean liberal, amounts of heavy Kohl under her eyes, coupled with the black dyed hair. She had this whole panda crossed with Wicked Witch of the South going on. Yet it wasn't Siobhan, it was Margot and the ring gave it all away.

Something else was nagging away at me and I couldn't quite deduce what. I could feel it staring me blindly in the face and yet I couldn't work out what the hell it was. Working through the events again on that fateful day it suddenly clicked. It was toothpaste – I remember searching high and low in the bathroom, feeling really pissed off at pulling out a load of dried out bits of cotton wool covered in black and cursing Jackie for stuffing her rubbish on my side. There was toothpaste everywhere covering this strange black residue. Christ, I recall now glancing down at the bath in the kids' room and it was there too. Assuming it was body fat because that's what I'd been told the black scum was at our local swimming pool, I made a mental note to nag my poxy teenagers about cleaning up after themselves.

That bloody black stuff must have been the crap Margot had used to camouflage herself as Siobhan. It was everywhere. I must have been at work totally oblivious to the fact that the bitch was in my house taking all that crap off her evil, ugly face, ensuring by the time I returned later that evening, food and sex were the order of the day.

Jesus, how could I have been so bloody stupid? What the hell was I on, for God's sake? I can recall the seductive smell of aromatic curry that night and thanking God it was going to be a cheap night in terms of not having to go out for dinner.

Jesus, that was another thing, I had been her bloody alibi. I had lost my job, self-worth, reputation and almost my marriage over her. It had been absolutely devastating. My cover had not only been blown but I had also committed one of the biggest errors of all time. Having not looked closely at timings I had missed something so significant, it was all down to my complete self-obsession and introspection and all about being pissed off at being rumbled because of my overactive dick. If only I had looked at things more closely I would have seen the discrepancies and realised that this cold-hearted bitch was a complete low-life liar. She had obviously fabricated timings and had lied to all and sundry including me that she had been there all day.

Jesus, I didn't get in until late that night, I know that, as I had been working a late shift at work. Sex had been endless; Jesus, maybe she drugged me – I felt as though I was hammered. Mind you, I was also on cloud nine knowing the kids and Jackie were gone. No wonder I was confused about timings.

That was another thing; the cardigan she had on, I remember thinking it looked grubby – some of the face make-up had obviously rubbed off on it. That must have been the cardigan that Clarissa observed as being Siobhan's and they had all fallen for the image that Margot was trying to pull off. No wonder the cardigan when I first saw the photo in the magazine rang a vague bell.

Why the hell had Siobhan not been more adamant it wasn't her instead of being so compliant and acting as though she was relieved she no longer had to carry the burden of her heinous crime? All this time she has been incarcerated; it just doesn't make sense. Perhaps her mother's denial had so affected her it was almost as though she had nothing more to live for. What the hell had made Margot do something so fucking awful? Where the hell had it all gone so wrong?

Now what? How am I going to prove Margot had lied after all these years? Now I think back to what she was like when Scarlett's body was discovered – Jesus, she deserved an Oscar for the act she put on. You could feel her pain. All that crap about how she had lost her sister – Jesus, what a load of bollocks. It was all so terrible.

Mind you, what I did was not much better. What the hell was I thinking of? Jeez, she wasn't much older than Jess. Why didn't I see through it all? Christ, she probably targeted me intentionally knowing one day I would be an invaluable alibi. I had studied all the dogma – all the dos and don'ts of etiquette in my position – so why did I lose the plot along the way? All for a shag and that was it. End of story.

Looking at it from her perspective she had a dysfunctional family and an old git preying on her emotions making her feel she was special. It wasn't her fault she was so fucked up – genetics and upbringing had caused it. Perhaps she didn't know what she was doing. Jesus, I really don't know. Perhaps I have scarred her?

What now? Should I just let things go and say nothing? Siobhan on paper has nothing to live for, her family is dead, she's estranged from her children, and has no friends, no future. She would probably be locked up forever now. Margot, on the other hand, now has a life and I know she is involved with Siobhan's kids and is supporting the daughter through a pretty severe health issue as well as seeing a lot of the son. Amazing what snippets of gossip you can glean through your wife. One of her mates just happens to be a cleaner at Siobhan's ex-husband John's house. Mind you, sounds like he's spending more time at his fancy lady's place which just happens to be the bloody dog kennels Sugar and Spice stay at. What a small world!

Margot is a woman now, but had been a young girl at the time of the murder so may have repented by now. I owe it her. Maybe I can make amends for exploiting her vulnerability and instead destroy the evidence and forget it ever happened. Professionally it is also going to look bad; I will be a laughing stock and will be likened to Mr Clouseau; I won't be the local hero, I will be the bumbling idiot.

42

PATSY

Oh my God, I can't believe this, it's like something out of a film. Here I am surrounded by bloody psychotic nutters. First, it's my mum who I discover not only had a false identity at university, but also became so obsessed with some poor fellow fresher she stalked him and he was forced to leave college. Then she's a suspect in the murder of her older sister, then my granny drops dead and then it turns out the sister who has orchestrated an adoption within the family murders the girl that she was really close to. Then when Aunt (bitch) Margot knows the game is up she gets the murdered daughter's mother to implicate her other daughter in the murder through a photo where she is disguised to look like her. Then, thank God, justice prevails because the flawless plan was not actually foolproof and what goes around has come around and now she is locked away for good.

Looking back now I can see how divisive Margot was. She was always putting Mum down and laughing behind her back. I feel sad, as I would laugh too and say what a cow and a pain my mother was.

I know my mum felt bad thinking she had caused my anorexia, but looking back now it was obviously down to me because I felt it was the only thing I could control. I was pissed off with the way Mum and Dad were constantly arguing. I felt they were trying to control my life deciding what I should do. I was adamant I didn't want to go to university and yet they wouldn't hear of an alternative. I remember being so resentful then Margot was whispering in my ear telling me to live my life and to follow my dreams. She called my mother a bitch and said how controlling she was. It definitely coloured my impression.

Margot to me was so edgy with her tattoos and piercings and the fact she was such a successful businesswoman. Looking back now I realise she is a ruthless, cold-hearted murderer and I couldn't have been further from the truth. She has wrecked everything in life she has touched. If only Aunt Scarlett had not been so kind to her on that fateful day they first met.

I'm so relieved I didn't get to California after all with Margot on what sounded such an amazing trip. Imagine how tainted my memories would have been? That's my goal; I would absolutely love to take Mum there in the future and to spend some bonding time with her. I want to get better so that I can and it will be on my terms. I will organise the entire thing; we won't be going to a clinic to support me. We will be going as a normal mother and daughter to have a bloody good time. I know if I have a chat to lovely Alice she will support me in all of this. Dad will too but I just feel it will be easier to talk to her about it. She is so lovely, kind and supportive. The thing I really like about her is that she has never said anything bad about Mum and has always insisted me and Matthew visited her whether we liked it or not. Strange too, how she was right all along. I will never forget what she said the night we arrived home from school after the awful event with Mum and Clarissa.

"John, it just doesn't make any sense whatsoever. Why on earth would Siobhan want Scarlett dead? She saved her life in the first place all those years ago. It was her sister, for goodness' sake, and by all accounts they were always really close. Siobhan was so protective of her, you yourself said that. Why on earth would she have wanted her dead?"

43

RAGI

Well, I think I have met the one woman I want to spend the rest of my life with. I feel sad I didn't meet her earlier but, in her words, I think then I would have been too boring for her. I was so overwhelmed arriving at Cambridge I just threw myself completely into my studies rather than socialising and drinking. Then when the time came for me to chill a little, it ended in disaster.

Meeting Siobhan in the library I had no idea how needy and damaged she was. Now I know about her situation it all makes sense. She was basically someone that needed love and support. Her sister had died and it sounds like no one thought about how she must be grieving and feeling. Everyone in her family was dealing with the grief themselves and assumed she would deal with it likewise. She was just a child really and it was my misfortune she fell in love with me. Perhaps if I had known her struggles I wouldn't have judged her so harshly at the end; regrettably, however, I didn't.

I had never really had much to do with people outside my social circle in London at school. I was such a grafter because my mother had instilled into me that it was imperative I got qualifications and a career. She was the same with my sister, probably more so; she would constantly reiterate how lucky we were to have access to an education, something my mother never had as it was denied to her when growing up.

Mum met my father through an arranged marriage. Living in Kenya at the time having fled the civil war in Somalia it was her father who encountered her future husband at the mosque. Residing in England Ragi senior was in Kenya rescuing members of his family who had become stranded by the civil war in Somalia. He was also on the lookout for a young bride and knew if he struck lucky and could find one that hailed from the same tribe as him it would be an ideal opportunity to marry. Never one to miss a bargain, Ragi senior knew that due to the war, brides' parents no longer expected exorbitant dowries as had been the case. When he learnt about the extremely well-connected family she hailed from he could not possibly 'look a gift horse in the mouth'. It was made even more attractive, it might be added, when the dowry was waived all together.

The main reason he wanted a local girl was because he felt that the Somali girls in London were far too westernised. He felt they dressed indecently, disobeyed their husbands and mixed freely with men. My mother had enjoyed a pretty liberal upbringing with her parents and siblings and up until then this whole new life that was beckoning was a terrifying prospect. She had no choice but to acquiesce so at the age of nineteen she found herself a wife of a man she barely knew, in a foreign country where she could not speak a word of English and living in London. For three years she basically lived in a cramped flat with her in-laws and various other relatives of her husband.

She had my sister and me in close succession and as we grew up this is when issues arose between her and my father. Firstly, she would not allow my sister to undergo genital mutilation which caused huge arguments. Further issues arose to the point that my mother knew she could no longer continue the relationship. Luckily it was not an acrimonious separation – my father had contacts with many other families who were desperate to marry their children off. He just let my mother go and made it very clear, however, that he would not be supporting her financially.

Knowing the sacrifices and risks she had made I was determined to make something of myself. Luckily the amazing headmaster from my school in Tower Hamlets mentored me. When he suggested I tried for Cambridge I really thought he was jollying me along. I can remember the goose pimples on my back when I first visited the beautiful city for my interview. Seeing the backs of Kings and Trinity it immediately conjured up scenes from *Brideshead Revisited* although I was reliably informed by some smug know-it-all fellow interviewee after voicing my impression, that I was in fact mistaken and there was no correlation as Waugh's setting was actually Oxford and that the two cities had very distinctive differences. Trudi happened to be at the meeting and she immediately won me over with her response.

"Yes, but I get exactly what you mean. You are talking about the whole thing that surrounds the Oxbridge phenomenon; two highly iconic, equally brilliant, very traditional British establishments which from first impressions in terms of content, architecture and history and even names, appear to be very similar." That was it, I was smitten. An intelligent, articulate, attractive girl who wasn't afraid to speak her mind; who wouldn't be seduced by such a thing?

Imagine my surprise when months later having unpacked my bags in my college room there was a knock at the door with a request to borrow a teabag. Surely it was fate that had obviously brought us together as there stood Trudi on the threshold. It transpired by sheer coincidence (I learnt much later on that she had actually swapped rooms with a fellow student once she learnt where I was staying) she was in the room next door to me. That was it really, we did not leave one another's sides for a considerable amount of time after this. I was in seventh heaven; who else wouldn't be with this pretty, intelligent, uninhibited girl who found it intriguing that I was still a virgin?

It was only as time went on, however, that I realised she obviously had issues. It was in short becoming very obvious she was obsessed with me. If she so much as saw me talking to another female she would confront me in the room. When I denied it she would stalk me. I would suddenly become aware that she was always there on campus watching and following me.

On one occasion I was really pissed off as one of my friends mentioned that she had been interrogating him about where I had been the previous afternoon. She obviously hadn't believed I had gone to supervision as I had told her. He said to me, "What she is doing to you is not bloody normal; she is like your shadow. Does she ever go to her own lectures, as it seems to be wherever you go she is always a few yards behind you?" The fact that other people were beginning to notice really bothered me.

That afternoon I confronted her about it in the nicest way I could. The last thing I expected was her reaction. She literally smacked me across the face and bit my arm almost through to the bone. She threatened suicide; it was terrifying. I had never had such a confrontation in my life. My mother, sister and I would have disagreements, naturally, just as I did with my few school friends, but I had never suffered any physical violence in my life and it was shocking. I immediately apologised. I can't believe I was so bloody stupid. Looking back now, I realise that I spent my entire time trying to placate her, trying to please and make her happy, absolutely terrified that I had driven her to the point of suicide. If only I had realised help would have been available for me and things could have perhaps been pre-empted before they got to the point that they did where I was no longer able to stay at Cambridge.

After the incident I became much less sociable for fear of another outburst; it was such a shame as up until then I had met some fantastic people. A couple of girls carried on trying to chat and to invite me to things, but gave up after they realised it all seemed pretty futile. Trudi was obviously delighted that it was just the two of us for a while.

Towards exam week, however, things took on a significant change. Although I didn't realise it at the time, I was becoming increasingly exasperated at Trudi, who despite my assurances was shadowing me around the campus wherever I went. Not only that, she had virtually decamped to my room and the situation was becoming intolerable.

The bedder for our corridor, who I would chat to now and again about Kenya (transpired she had grown up there), actually commented to me one morning about Trudi. "Don't you ever stay the night in her room? It's unfair she comes in here, trashes it and goes back to her lovely clean room with all her books neatly organised on the table. It would drive me mad." Feeling my blood rising and resisting the urge to scream and shout about how much I loathed the situation, self-control set in and my reaction was pathetically mild. Not wanting to rock the boat there and then as exams were looming I vowed to myself that the situation could no longer continue. Once they were over I was going to start exerting myself and vowed to end the futile relationship.

Unbeknown to me, however, things were about to change. It was after one of the final lectures before the exams that two other students, Clara the beret girl being one of them, approached me and asked if I wanted to join them in group revision to add a different perspective on all the notes we needed to revise. This had been at the instigation of our supervisor who emphasised how it was good to go through different medical theories on various subjects and how it was good to hear different views on certain topics. I was all for this and as a result we ended up working all night with meritorious determination to cover everything.

In the early hours of the morning Trudi was sitting at my desk going through my papers with no embarrassment at all. When I asked her what she was doing she became rebarbative and very prickly telling me to mind my own business. I was then stunned by her response, "Who were the sluts you were with?"

I honestly had no idea what she was talking about until she mentioned the revision sessions. My only response was, "What are you talking about? Let me tell you now the best way to defend yourself against calumny is by ignoring the false convictions of others. I'm telling you now it's not true. Nothing happened. Hand on heart. It was revision and nothing more." How she heard of our planned exam revision sessions I still to this day have no idea. It was her next sentence that changed everything for me.

"I wonder if you will rape them, too."

"What are you talking about?" was my retort.

Trudi then said, "You heard what I said, do you think you will rape the two of them now you have finished raping me?"

I looked at her aghast. I felt sick and powerless so I just ran. I ran and ran and ended up somewhere near a place called Fen Ditton. I was absolutely beside myself. I felt mortified. My main concern was the shame I would bring on my family. I sat on the riverbank and wept like a baby for what seemed like hours. I did not go back to my room. I couldn't bear to face the music. I had no idea what Trudi had in store for me next.

The morning after my night traipsing around Cambridge I decided to go and see my supervisor immediately. The minute I saw her kind, understanding face, that was it, I literally broke down there and then in her office telling her everything. I was amazed at how kind she was; she had always totally intimidated me as she was such a brilliant, efficient lecturer and I had no idea she would be so empathetic. She said certain things had been noted about Trudi's relationship and mine, but she didn't elaborate. There was also a brief reference to emotional issues that again she didn't go into. If I had known it was the fact that Trudi's sister had died in mysterious circumstances I would not have judged her so harshly. Actually, on reflection it is probably better I didn't as I would have been terrified about upsetting her the entire time and God knows what the outcome may have been.

I think the bedder must have vouched for my innocence. I am also glad I addressed the situation with my college as nothing more came of it. I knew, however, in lieu of the false accusations that I could no longer continue at Cambridge and would with immediate effect have to leave. There was a suggestion that Trudi would receive a disciplinary warning. I urged the college not to push this, however, as I felt she needed emotional support instead. My director of studies urged that the college really did not want to lose me. I was an exemplary student destined for high places. Much as I was tempted, my decision was made.

With that I left Cambridge and did not see Trudi again. The bedder very kindly packed all of my things that I collected from my supervisor. I left my postal details with Clara; she was someone I hoped I would see again and I also wanted to have the chance to explain why I had become such a hermit. I was lucky in that I managed to get a transfer to do medicine at UCL, which was brilliant. It was strange being home again, but good to feel I had my sanity back. My mother and sister had no idea about the ordeal I had encountered at Cambridge. I was too ashamed to tell them. In fact, the only one I confided in after the supervisor was Clara who I discovered knew a lot more than I had realised.

When I think back now to how we were living in a high-rise flat on an estate, living literally a hand-to-mouth existence with my mother working as a cleaner and supermarket packer and how far I have come since, I have to pinch myself. My sister works in human resources in a big international company and I'm now a surgeon in a huge teaching hospital with a vast team; it's like a dream come true.

It hasn't been an easy journey and one of the things that I have come across which didn't ever affect me growing up and being at university has been the attitude to the colour of my skin. I remember when I was working as a houseman in a hospital and went to treat a patient. He started to mimic monkey noises and shouted he didn't want to be treated by a gorilla. I was mortified but ignored his comments choosing to remind him that our blood was the same colour, and if we were organ donors, no one would be able to differentiate whose organs were the black man's and whose were the white man's as they would be the same.

On another occasion someone commented they wanted a doctor that was English and when I started talking to them in my very English accent they looked horrified. I have learnt to hold my head up high and not to let people's ignorance affect me. First and foremost I am a doctor and I am not going to enter into any discourse that will compromise the job in hand. If people really refuse to be treated by me then I accept it. I am no longer surprised when my intentions are misunderstood or misinterpreted, I will just move on to the next patient. I know it is their loss because I am a good doctor.

Mum has obviously suffered prejudice whilst she has been in Britain. I remember as a child traipsing round to various properties that had confirmed vacancies only to be told as soon as we turned up, that the properties were taken. As if punishing herself she would then ring up only to be told the properties were still vacant. It was heartbreaking but there was nothing we could do.

One of the most satisfying, happiest moments in my life was handing over her very own set of keys to a house that we had purchased for her. It was a terraced house on the outskirts of London with a garden very similar to the houses we looked at renting years before. Both my sister and I expressed how amazing and supportive our mother was and how we were totally indebted to her for her unwavering support throughout our lives.

It was Clara who contacted me about the reunion. Once she had assured me Trudi was not on the list I had agreed to attend under her name. I guess my decision was based on nostalgia. It would be fun to meet people I may or may not have recalled from college days. It was also going to be my first social outing for a long time as what with one thing and another socialising had been very low down on my list of priorities.

I am so grateful I turned up. What a wonderful evening; it was so nice to see faces of those I recognised as well as meeting people I hadn't met before. I definitely felt a significant frisson with Jane. It was this amazing feeling, I can't pinpoint it exactly, but looking into her eyes there was so much warmth, but also sadness behind them. Subtly checking out her fingers for rings and seeing nothing adorning them I felt optimistic. Sadly, however, I felt my connection was not reciprocated as next thing I knew she had glanced over my shoulder and announced that she had to leave.

"I'm so sorry I have to go, I've just seen my friend is having a panic attack." All I could think to myself was I have heard some excuses in my life, but that took the biscuit. I hoped it wasn't a message. The good thing was that I managed to get her contact details before she rushed off.

Now many months on I look at Jane and I feel love. She makes me laugh, and she makes me shriek and cry with happiness. She's beautiful, intelligent, understanding, modest, self- deprecating, generous and interesting. She is caring, and the life and soul of wherever she goes. She is a wonderful mother, best friend and partner. I could go on and on. I seriously have never felt so totally in love.

Up until I met her I had always socialised with younger women, nominally nurses as I am normally working in close proximity with them. I've met some lovely girls but the relationships have always felt uneven as in the workplace I am effectively their boss, but meeting Jane we are both on an equal footing. This has got to be the elusive thing called love without a doubt and what's more, I have a feeling she too has the same feeling. I pray I am not being presumptuous.

Our first date was one of many. We visited the National Portrait Gallery wandering around looking at Reynolds, Hogarth, the Pre-Raphaelites, Sargent, and Henry Moore. Then we went to the Tate for a more modern take and various other exhibitions. We wandered around Hyde Park, fed ducks on the Serpentine, took a rowing boat out and got caught in the rain. The next date was a curry with my mum and sister at a great Indian restaurant on Brick Lane. It warmed my heart seeing the three of them getting on like a house on fire.

Jane and I are forever talking. I feel I know so much about her life, her children, Robert, her toy boy, the boob job and the devastating shock she had being diagnosed with breast cancer. I felt bad for her when she told me honestly that having had her mastectomy she felt she was no longer a woman but I felt my reassurances were far too clichéd. "Of course you are a woman, you are a beautiful woman." All I needed was Bob Marley's rendition of 'Woman' in the background to make it even cornier. I know that the best thing was to just let her talk and unload all that she was feeling and this is what I did. I think the fact I work in a hospital environment where I am often the deliverer of devastating news to people I can empathise with the way she was feeling. One minute, life is ticking along with various trivialities that dominate our thoughts, and the next thing the knowledge of being seriously ill with the prospect of death now positioning itself in the not so distant future, changes everything forever. Taking precedence over everything, it is a grim reaper, an omniscient presence reminding us constantly of the tenuous hold on life.

I have a very demanding job in the hospital during the week so it's been lovely coming home to Jane who has become totally immersed in her new hobby, cooking. What's more, it's healthy food which tastes delicious. It's fantastic for me too as I have always either eaten at the hospital canteen or grabbed a takeaway and beer with the television for company. You would think in my fifties I would be bothered about my health, but luckily, I have my mother's high metabolism and being tall can hide a multitude of sins and as a surgeon my job is pretty physical anyway.

Jane's children came to visit one weekend. I would have loved a family, but it just hasn't happened. I'm afraid work has always been my baby; my mother has always called me a workaholic. I would laugh it off but looking objectively I guess she's correct. Aren't all mothers generally? I don't regret it though; it's not as though I have worked myself to an early grave in the process. I have always had an inordinate amount of energy and as a result I am perfectly happy with a few hours' sleep.

This was when I created my other baby, the education charity for women in Africa. In fact Lucy, Jane's daughter, who is training to be a teacher, gained real experience during the time she travelled with me to visit the various schools I had raised sponsorship for. It has given us a connection which has been a great relief as I know combining families can be somewhat tricky. I am very aware I don't want to become another father figure in Lucy's and Jack's lives. Of course I will be supportive but my main prerogative, however, is that ultimately they will want to spend time with me rather than being forced to. At the same time I will also respect the fact that they will want to spend time with Jane alone which also suits me fine.

44

JANE

It has been over a year now that Ragi and I have been together and not a day goes by without the two of us reaffirming our love for one another either in person or verbally by telephone. We are totally in tune, I just feel sad it's taken so long to find the real love of my life. I would love to have known him at eighteen but then again in his own words he would have been too boring and old-fashioned for me. He is adamant his huge Afro and tight trousers that were always far too short for him as well as his crippling shyness, would never have appealed to me. I beg to differ, however; he is a beautiful man both internally and externally. He is so caring and kind. I feel terribly sad that he went through what must have been a terrifying ordeal for him with Siobhan and yet he keeps defending her. Bearing in mind what she has been through he doesn't feel it was her fault she clung onto him; it was the psychological mess that had been going on at home that had led ultimately to her demise. He pointed out how she had tried but failed to make her parents proud of her, finally getting into Cambridge knowing how excited they were about the prospect of Scarlett being a student there. And she had lost her sister. I guess he's right, I just find it amazing he has the empathy. He really is such a kind, good person.

It also makes me sad that by staying with me he is giving up the option to have his own children. He keeps reiterating the fact he has mine, as well as his nieces and nephew, and most importantly of all he has me. We are so compatible in everything; mind and body. I have always thought of myself as being frigid; now, if I am not kissing or holding Ragi's hand I feel incomplete. Never before had I felt so in tune with someone. He is my rock, my anchor, and literally means everything to me. We laugh, we sing, the days unfortunately go far too quickly whenever we are together. I thoroughly love every minute I am with him.

Although almost everything between us is perfect there is, however, so much sexual tension sometimes I feel I have no control and just want to smother him in physical affection. It does not take long, however, to return to Earth and to look at things objectively. Why the hell in heaven would he be interested in a body that has not only gone through the menopause and childbirth but has also survived cancer? I'm a middle-aged woman who has refused reconstructive surgery because she is proud of her scars as they are a constant reminder of what she has been up against, fought and conquered. I felt liberated at the time; now, however, I feel inadequate and incomplete. How can I possibly imagine he would choose my body over the firm, beautiful bodies of the younger nurses he has dated? Realistically I knew that going forward, I was just going to have to be content with fantasies and instead just embrace all the love without the deeper level of intimacy that I know I craved.

45

FRANK

Jackie and I have decided to leave the rat race; well, that's our plan. For the time being we are raising funds and are renting out rooms in our house and hosting foreign students. I'm seriously thinking about doing a TEFL course as there's serious money to be earned once I've done the course. I have been informed by my contacts that it is extremely desirable amongst the cognoscenti particularly because I am a Brit. I am, however, just a little concerned as my spelling and grammar are not great. However, I'm sure I'll be able to wing it. The students spend a fortune on lessons and the beauty is I would be able to do them from home. I mean, all I need to do is stick on a couple of typical English films, ask them questions about it and hey presto, Bob's your uncle – day's work completed.

We've had some nice students: two Italians, a young boy and girl who coincidentally came from the same town but didn't know one another – they certainly do now. In fact, Jackie had to bang on Francesca's (the Italian girl) door in the early hours of the morning saying if Raphael was in her room he needed to leave as the rule was no visitors in bedrooms at all times. (In her room, my arse; he was quite definitely in her bed, and God knows, but judging from the sound effects, it was a good place.) I was hoping it might spur and inspire Jackie on for a bit of nooky, however, if anything it had the opposite effect as she started on about the whole violation of the home larky. The fact, as I kept pointing out to her, that it 'isn't their home', was like water off a duck's back. Her argument was they were 'home from home in a foreign country' and for the 'time being' we were their 'surrogate parents'. Jesus, I certainly didn't have that opinion; they were a tax-free means of income, end of story, nothing more.

Jeez, then what happened? Well, they stayed at our place for the month then left. Imagine our surprise a few months later when a stunning wedding invitation landed on the doormat. There was definitely an air of royalty about it in the handmade paper, stuck onto embossed posh card with hand-painted petals as the border. Written in gold ink calligraphy, we could just about deduce Raphael's and Francesca's names. How lovely; we were both so made up and felt really flattered. *Job well done*, was my immediate thought. Jackie acted as though she was the bloody mother of the bride, she was that excited. Anyway, the long and short of it is we accepted. Problem was even that turned into a huge hassle as the bloody muppets had failed to put an address on the invite so we couldn't RSVP to them. I wasn't a detective chief superintendent for nothing and with my powers of investigation managed to track them down and obtained a phone number. Jackie, good on her, had learnt a line from some language book and recited it over the phone. God, I was cringing though, she sounded so bloody English. "*Buongiorno*, how are you? *Spero che tu stia bene ci piacerebbe venire al matrimonio sei piu gentile gracia* for the invitation." I am guessing she was saying as agreed 'yes please, we would love to come'. Sounding a bit miffed after all her efforts, Jackie was surprised that the news we were coming was not greeted with the euphoric response she had expected. In fact, if anything, Francesca had sounded a little off-hand and unenthusiastic. Putting it down to nerves at the prospect of so many people attending, we had no more thoughts on the matter and began preparing for our exciting weekend away.

And what a weekend it was. It was bloody marvellous from beginning to end. The Italians certainly know how to enjoy themselves and we felt honoured to be there. The lamb and gnocchi were to die for, real melt in the mouth jobs. Then the fresh mozzarella with the ripest, most succulent tomatoes I've ever eaten. The wine was great – copious amounts so that kept me happy. The girls that served it were bloody gorgeous with tits the size of melons: I could barely keep my eyes off them. The mother of the bride was also a bit of a looker and had a soft spot for me. I gather there aren't many bald men in Italy or in that particular village anyway and as a result she kept massaging my head. Jackie was not too happy about that and kept flouncing over giving me the look.

The mother of the groom was the complete opposite, an absolute miserable bitch and the looks she kept giving us – blimey, there was something she really wasn't happy with, it was written all over her face. Only problem, it was in Italian so I was none the wiser. Probably just as well. She looked like she was a proper tough cookie and not someone I would want to cross. Thank God for Sugar and Spice; imagine if we had a Champion the Wonder Horse. I should have listened to Jackie and not watched all *The Godfather* films before our trip. Interestingly there was also a very negative vibe between both families although I had no idea why. My perceptive intuition was spot on I was to learn later.

There were only two other English guests. We sat with them but didn't have much in common. International art dealers from London – Eva and James had bought a huge amount of art on Raphael's family's behalf over the years. They certainly gave me the distinct impression money was no object in all their amazing purchases. I was beginning to see why Francesca's family were so enthusiastic about the wedding along with the now widely acknowledged fact the bride was also with child. Raphael's family, however, considered the entire affair in Eva's words "an unmitigated disaster".

It transpired (according to Eva), the Miossi family were hoping their son who had been educated in one of the best international schools in Switzerland, would meet like-minded people with money and status and fall in love perhaps with a girl from a titled family. What happens, however? He travels to England to attend a language course and falls madly in love with a working-class girl from the village he had grown up in. Apparently, the hostel in which they were both staying in England had no controls whatsoever.

In Eva's words, "They were allowed to fornicate into the early hours. The wardens were appalling. They had no control whatsoever. There was nothing else to do in the hostel, the food was awful, and the house was cold and dirty. They ended up in the bedroom eating food they had bought in town and huddling together to keep warm. And look where they are now; he is trapped. She is expecting his baby and her family were of course delighted. Why wouldn't they be? Let's face it, Raphael's family own most of the village and the surrounding area for miles. They are extremely wealthy. I bet her family just couldn't believe their luck."

My Jackie's face was a picture. "Well, I think it's lovely news and it is a fantastic celebration. It's not often people marry for love these days," was her priceless comment.

Eva then delivered the final *coup de grâce* as far as our little sojourn to Italy had been by her following words: "The Riina family, without conferring with the Miossis, decided to put out the announcement in the two local newspapers so that everyone knew the family she was marrying into. Not only that they also sent announcements to everyone and anyone they have ever encountered throughout their lives. Their names and date of the wedding were set out on handmade paper all done in calligraphy style in gold ink. Honestly, you would think they were royalty; completely over the top. All I can say is, thank God there wasn't an RSVP at the end of them as goodness knows how many people may have got the wrong end of the stick."

There wasn't a lot we could say in response to that. Jackie just coughed profusely and commented on the amazing interior of the building we were in. I put my nose in my wine glass, counted to three, then poured myself another one rapidly. The woman then said, "Who do you know out of the bride and groom and how?" I proceeded to unravel one of the most ridiculous stories I have ever concocted about how I had met Francesca's grandfather in Italy years ago and how I had kept in touch with the family ever since. It all sounded very convincing and I could tell Jackie felt the same as I stopped to catch my breath and enjoy another slurp of the amazing red wine. "So perhaps you can tell me why her father isn't giving her away, could you? We've all been dying to know." For once I was genuinely lost for words.

Other students that followed from these were pretty generic; they were all variations on the same thing apart from the fact that they were from different countries and spoke foreign languages. It was fun for a while hosting them and took the edge off the tension and angst I had been suffering over the past year regarding my decision to go through the correct channels after the whole Margot incident unravelled.

I still for the life of me cannot understand why Margot did what she did. After all the family did for her it just doesn't add up. She was obviously eaten up with that much obsessional jealousy she lost all rationale. It was all about Clarissa recognising her as the 'ideal daughter'. I'm really tempted to contact Siobhan and to make amends with her. I handled it all so badly. What was I thinking of? I actually feel so ill thinking of the events leading up to that calamitous day. It was ultimately me who was instrumental in her incarceration and it doesn't make me feel good. I still have the recording of Clarissa's final words that are going to live with me forever.

46

JACKIE

This has been very strange for me and I am not really sure how I feel. One minute my life is pretty normal, my husband's out of work getting under my feet at home and driving me and the kids up the wall then suddenly he's out there solving his own cases – a proper Sherlock Holmes, my Frank. But it isn't as straightforward as it seems because next thing he's on another level and it's bloody Sherlock and Agatha Christie combined. He may piss me off big time but when it comes to matters of the law my Frank's the man.

We got to go on breakfast telly – that really was something, little old me up there with the stars. Ahhh, bless, if only Mum and Dad were still alive they would have been so proud. It's like it was in the old days when I was the DCS's glamorous wife turning up to various events with my hair all done nice and outfits with handbags to match. Not bad for a Tottenham girl, eh? My mates were all well jealous; I still haven't heard the end of it. I even managed to put in a plug about my latest venture – the home-tanning booth set in a tropical paradise, all thanks to Zigi Stamford. I thought I would give him a plug as he has been so great to Frank and me what with the disastrous flood and all that. Well, you've got to get in there and make the most of golden opportunities such as these. Frank had the nerve to call me tacky. I soon shut him up about being tacky;

shagging a murderer in our bed is what I would call tacky beyond tacky. He's such a twat at times.

The *Tropics in the Home* thing is definitely something I want to get into in time. Frank's fantasy about setting up a private agency just ain't gonna happen; he is too bloody lazy. In the meantime, we're hosting foreign students. I thought it would be a lovely way for our kids to learn a language yet Frank says why should we stress them out when they won't be living anywhere but England. They've both got foreign partners so it will be interesting to see if Frank's opinion is right. Anyway, to make money from this venture Frank's worked out we are only to spend a pound a day on their meals. I mean, for God's sake, a pizza costs around that amount and if he thinks I'm making my own pizza dough he has got another thing bloody well coming.

We've had four students staying and so far, so good. They are Italians, so pretty easy. I just cooked pasta in a butter sauce throughout their time here. It kept them happy and on the nights they didn't want that dish they just went out. Mind you, they did that a lot towards the end. I guess the pasta was a bit boring, but at least it filled the gap, which meant Frank was happy and off my case due to the fact I was keeping costs down. We got on so well with the students, they were lovely. We even spoke to their parents on Skype – bless them. Mind you, it was mainly sign language as I didn't have a clue what the old man was on about. He kept throwing his hands in the air, that's all I do know. God, looking back he was probably insulting us and we wouldn't have had a clue.

I'm afraid I did lose the plot a few nights before they left as Raphael and Francesca obviously became boyfriend and girlfriend. Admittedly they made such a beautiful couple. I was not happy, however, about them being together in the bedroom. It didn't seem right to me. I would have been furious had I known Jess was up to such things when she went on her language exchange to France. I had to constantly bang on their door and ask him to go back to his room. Honestly, they sounded like bloody werewolves. I had a real go at Frank one night when he deliberately turned down the noise on our television so he could hear the commotion going on next door. It didn't sound anything like the sort of noises I would equate with sex. Mind you, Frank's the only man I have ever slept with so maybe I'm missing something. Bless him. Give me a cuppa any day. I only do it because I feel sorry for him; it shuts him up and puts him in a good mood so it's usually worth it. I just wish I could have a TV on the ceiling.

It was certainly a one-off experience at the wedding. *Mamma Mia!* The Italians are so different from us Brits; they are so dramatic and larger than life and I thought I spoke a lot! Blimey, I have never seen people speak so much and so quickly to one another. Mind you, I have no idea what they were on about. Some tried speaking to me in English and that was a trial in itself, I had to really concentrate. Francesca's mum was lovely and not at all hostile. I was terrified she was going to have a go at me for letting them get together at such a young age but no, she just kept saying 'thank you' over and over again reiterating about how happy she and her husband were that they had spent money on the English course. (I'm not so sure about the course; I don't think Francesca learnt much and I don't recall her saying one word in English, not even thank you.) In addition to this they kept repeating how "fantastic it was Francesca had married such a wonderful man who would be able to look after her for the rest of her life".

Frank being Frank now thinks he and Italians share a bond and he's decided he wants to take it one step further and for us to move lock, stock, and barrel to Italy. I tell you, the mind boggles. He doesn't speak a word of the lingo apart from 'yes', 'do', 'please', 'hell', 'goodbye' and 'cheers'. Who the hell in heaven does he think he's kidding? I certainly do not want to move over there. The thought of watching 'Corrie' in Italian does not appeal one little bit. I mean, come on, being in England feels like I'm abroad half the time. Just a shame we couldn't import the weather rather than the foreigners that keep coming in.

47

RAGI

Up until a few weeks ago Jane and I had never spent a night together. I would stay and eat dinner and we would sit on the sofa kissing passionately, chatting or listening to music. Or we would go out for dinner, to the theatre or cinema; it was lovely. I often thought about touching her when we were on the sofa but really didn't want to put her under any pressure. I did decide for her birthday, however, that I would book a weekend away as I knew she was desperate to visit Thorpeness. During our usual mammoth-long phone conversations I did manage to mention at the end whether she would be interested.

"How would you like to go to Thorpeness for your birthday? I would love to take you there as I know you've mentioned wanting to see it." At these words I thought to myself any minute now she will fulminate on all the reasons as to why she cannot possibly make the trip. I was, however, pleasantly amazed by her response.

"Ragi, I would absolutely love to. How thoughtful, you remembered me wanting to go there."

I felt very strongly I did not want to pressurise her in any way so mentioned that we could do it in a day from London. We could go for a nice lunch somewhere then I could bring her back home in the evening.

“No, I would love to stay there for the weekend,” was her response. *First hurdle over* was my initial thought, then I said, “I will book two rooms next door to each other.”

“I really want to spend the night with you,” she replied. For once in my life I was lost for words.

The following Friday that’s where we were heading. The journey from London was pretty horrendous as due to the sudden onset of sun and the fact it was a bank holiday weekend it seemed like the whole of London was heading to East Anglia for the sand and sea. Arriving finally around five o’clock we collected the keys to the house. It was an easy place to spot, thank goodness, as I really didn’t relish the idea of driving down country roads trying to spot a glass-fronted house as knowing my sense of direction it could have been a long night of searching. The house thankfully was beautiful with a stunning glass frontage directly onto a shingle beach with panoramic views of the sea.

The cook had left a rib of beef from a local butchers infused with fresh herbs on the counter along with prepared roasted vegetables and a delicious looking potato dauphinois dish. The plan was to leave it slow-roasting in the oven for a few hours along with some roasted vegetables all cooked in their own succulent juices ready for us to eat when we were ready. Hand in hand we wandered over the pebbly beach skimming stones out to sea seeing whose stone bounced the most across the expanse of water. We sat down on a blanket, the sun shining, and shared a bottle of champagne looking out to sea throwing compliments to one another about how much we loved one another in different accents. Then Jane rested her head on my shoulder and we sat there for a while each engrossed in our own thoughts. It got colder as the sun started to set and noticing the crepuscular creatures running across the sand we decided it was time to wander back to the house. As we entered, the delicious smell of aromatic herbs mixed with the slow-cooking meat assailed us. I lit the fire and we sat on the rug staring at the flames. The next thing I knew the two of us were passionately kissing; never before had I felt so much desire and love for someone.

Asking if I could remove her top, I felt the reticence and embarrassment at her response. "You are going to be horrified. I'm embarrassed, there's literally nothing where there should be and it's just blubber and scars everywhere else."

I started kissing her again and slowly removed her top. We locked eyes with one another and I gently touched her beautiful chest. I then moved slowly down and started kissing the whole area, telling her how beautiful she was, the most beautiful woman in the world, and how I absolutely adored her. I wiped her tears away, held her in my arms and continued kissing and caressing her body. Her hand then rested on my groin and I thought I was going to burst. She started removing my clothes and then her own; all the while our eyes were locked together. Now naked in front of the fire we continued kissing and touching one another all over.

Guiding me towards her we both moaned with absolute pleasure as I entered her. We remained like this for what seemed like an eternity just enjoying such closeness, our bodies bonded together. We both climaxed at the same time and then lay in one another's arms just staring at the flames, sated, satisfied and blissfully happy. At some stage we made it up the stairs and ran a warm bath, I lit the candles and we lay there soaping one another looking into each other's eyes. After out bath we dried and lay on the bed with its beautiful thick Egyptian cotton sheets, and again desire prevailed and our two bodies moved in unison. Afterwards, we lay in one another's arms listening to the waves crashing onto the shore. We were at one with everything, we were in paradise and did not want to ruin the moment.

At two o'clock in the morning we finally sat down to our delicious meal. The meat was succulent and delicious. We were both ravenous and devoured everything on our plates. Supper/breakfast over we staggered up to bed waking up many hours later the following day and literally staying in bed, making love, drinking tea and chatting. By late afternoon we went for a walk on the beach and ate fish and chips in a pub down the road.

Monday morning it was back to reality. I had to leave at a very unearthly hour to attend a conference. I left the love of my life at the kitchen table drinking tea as she was going to catch a train home using the journey to meet a friend en route. She said she had certainly had the best birthday ever. I wanted us to stay there forever; it had all been so perfect. I left knowing that our relationship had moved up to another level and I felt complete, unadulterated euphoria at the thought of it.

48

JANE

When Ragi rang and suggested going away for the weekend to Thorpeness I felt like crying with happiness. When, however, he backtracked and suggested going for the day I wanted to cry. Something inside me then just said, "Go, woman, this is your chance, don't mess it up".

I stopped him mid-track and very nearly unleashed all my inner passion. "Ragi, please just take me. I want you. I want us to have wild, passionate sex. I can't stand this frustration any longer." I didn't, however; my immortal lines were, "What a lovely idea, I personally think it would be better to stay up there, it's such a long way to go, Rag. I think it would be nice to make a weekend of it, don't you?"

"Yes, yes of course. I couldn't agree more. Shall I book two rooms?" Ragi had replied.

"What would you like to do? I'm happy to go along with your choice?" I could barely contain myself and wondered if he had noticed my voice was wavering.

Ragi replied, "I know exactly what I'd love to do but I am too much of a gentleman to suggest it."

I could barely contain myself. "Go on, I dare you, try me."

"Well, it would be my dream to book a place for just the two of us. But that may be completely opposed to what you have in mind.

I feel very awkward actually that I have put you in this embarrassing situation."

That opened the floodgates and I literally could not stop myself. "Ragi, please listen to me. I would absolutely love to spend the weekend with you and the thought of the two of us in a bed together would be heavenly."

That was it, the conversation then ended with him insisting I left everything to him and that he would collect me at four o'clock the following Friday.

Two days later I checked into a beauty spa and had everything waxed, plucked and sorted. Excited was an understatement; I could barely contain myself. I felt like an eighteen-year-old on the brink of life. It was the most wonderful feeling in the world.

Those two nights in Thorpeness were the most amazing nights of my life at the time. Mind you, months on from there it's even better. That night we laughed, we cried – well, I did. I finally lost the plot and told him about how I felt about my body. He was so kind and tender. I felt so awkward when he started kissing my scars and yet something inside me melted. He was so incredibly gentle, sensuous and seductive. I went with the flow, stopped rationalising and worrying about how self-conscious I was and ended up feeling the most beautiful, desired woman in the world. He really was everything rolled into one; passionate, yet incredibly gentle. Talking, touching and exploring one another's bodies I didn't want the night to end.

We spent two heavenly days with one another, taking walks along the beach, eating the most delicious food, talking, laughing and having the most mind-blowing sex ever. Better than all my fantasies. I couldn't believe I had bagged myself such a wonderful human being. He was beautiful not only on the inside but also on the outside. He was simply gorgeous, a complete god. Endless, athletic, muscular legs, toned torso, big broad shoulders, that tight, taut, beautiful backside. The very well-endowed bit was the real icing on the cake. By the end of the weekend I was left in no doubt that we covered most of the positions listed in the *Kama Sutra*. That was definitely the last thing I had expected.

When he kissed me goodbye that Monday morning as he went on to a work conference dressed in his pinstripe suit looking so dashing, smart and gorgeous he reminded me of some matinee idol. In reality, however, there he was running a busy hospital as well as operating on countless people. It was difficult to reconcile such a sensible, serious, responsible adult with the completely athletic, sensual, considerate lover that he was proving to be. I was simply madly and passionately in love with him. Life had never been so good. I was indeed the luckiest woman in the world and I bet Thorpeness had never seen anything like it.

With such love, passion and excitement in my life I haven't forgotten the present and I am constantly having flashbacks to the whole Siobhan situation. I really can't believe it was not her after all that murdered Scarlett. Well, I can believe it as I would never have believed she was capable of murder. The only explanation at the time that I could think of was that it was down to insane jealousy wanting Scarlett annihilated as she could no longer deal with the constant comparisons when growing up. I wonder what went through her mind when she made the decision to come to Cambridge – was it a tribute to her sister or did she want to try and please her parents by showing them she was just as able? Why did she change her name? I still don't get her motives either for organising the reunion. I guess she didn't think Ragi was going and that by reconnecting with old college friends it was her way of reconciling the past with the present.

She is definitely quirky and obsessive but surely that has been exacerbated over what has happened to her in the past. I guess whenever she had someone that meant something to her it was the fear of losing them that made her cling on. Ragi himself has said how their relationship was normal initially, but as things plateaued between them this was when the dysfunctional behaviour set in.

Thankfully I never met Margot. How she has managed to live with herself and her crime for all this time completely astounds me. I don't understand her motives either. That family took her in, did everything they could to support her and look what she did to thank them. That terrible scene at the end with Clarissa thinking Siobhan was the one that had murdered Scarlett. Where does a person go from there? It's a simply heinous, dreadfully sad situation.

It is crazy and inexplicable as to how Ragi and I were drawn to one another with no prior knowledge that Siobhan had played such a huge part in both our lives. All these theoretical questions I constantly go through in my head about her situation and yet I have made no effort to visit her and have them answered. I have a terrible guilty conscience thinking back to how kind she was to me when I was ill and how ungrateful I was. Then again, her behaviour before and after the reunion was both inexcusable and illogical.

I wonder how Siobhan is going to adapt to real life once she is released from the mental care institution. Clarissa has gone, and Patsy and Matthew are no longer living at home. John told Robert they have both chosen to remain living with him and Alice indefinitely. There are also no friends that come to mind although John also told Robert that Alice has struck up a connection with Siobhan which is good.

Financially I am sure she will be okay, as I would imagine Clarissa's will may now work in her favour. I wonder if she will be paid compensation for wrongful incarceration? Something tells me she won't. I also have a hunch that with her ability to slip through systems Margot will manage to manipulate the law somehow and have her conviction either overturned due to time lapse or will argue at the tax payers' expense, of course, that the evidence is not concrete or reliable enough. Who knows, I just think Siobhan will have to be prepared to accept that this may happen.

On the other hand, and I think pretty unlikely, perhaps Margot will go through an epiphany where she suddenly has an insight into her soul and realises it is not a good one, repent of her sins and put everything to rest by admitting her guilt. This entire situation is without a doubt the last thing anyone would have envisaged happening in this predominantly middle-class, middle-aged, suburban home county from where we all hail. Indeed, the local citizens will definitely have something to talk about other than the weather for many years to come.

49

PAT

Jed and I were sitting in the front room eating corn chips and nachos, drinking beer and watching the usual crap that shows on a Friday night TV. We both particularly like the whodunnit true-life murders, sort of modern-day voyeuristic *Columbo*-type things. There are some crazy nutters out there is all I can say. Most of them seem to be American at that. Guess it's because guns are legal so it's easier to shoot people dead and run. Jed always knows who's committed the crime and I'm guessing a major in psychology obviously helps. Being a mathematician I'm not so hot on the inner soul baloney so never seem to get the right guy.

Watching something the other night was pretty scary. It involved a regular guy travelling on his own on a business trip. There he was sitting in bed, watching a movie, eating popcorn and minding his own business, just before he settled for the night. In the room next door a bunch of teenagers were hanging out drinking and eating pizza. One of the guys had a gun and for a laugh pretends to shoot at a buddy, missing him of course, but scaring him enough for them to have a row and the gun goes back down to the car into the glove compartment. End of story, the guys carrying on drinking, get up the next morning, check out and go back to their respective lives. Guy on the bed no longer has the ability however to do this, as the chambermaid discovers; he's in bed as dead as a dodo. The police arrive, but the forensic scientists can find no visible injuries on him and it's assumed he's had a heart attack. The only thing that is slightly inexplicable but not major is a tiny patch of fluid that's emitted from his right testicle where there is a slight laceration. The post-mortem results, however, show major intrusive injuries consistent with a beating. It is suggested that he may have been kicked in the groin and beaten up. Next question was, who by? The guys in the next-door room were questioned but denied any interaction with anyone else in the hotel.

It was only when a private detective was called in and friends of the drinkers in the next room mentioned an altercation and a gun that was fired being the only incident that had occurred. He decided to visit the motel room the guys were in and whilst there noticed a mark on the wall which had been disguised by toothpaste smeared over it. On further investigation he discovered another, albeit smaller, mark in the adjacent room belonging to the lone man on the bed. Once the photos of the autopsy had been looked at in great detail again they realised it was the stray bullet which had gone through the wall and had the terrible misfortune of hitting the man's scrotum from where it tore through his body causing internal damage and the guy bled to death. The jerk that had caused it was then sentenced to ten years in prison because the judge concluded he was basically a klutz for brandishing and pretending to shoot his mate at close range with inadvertent horrific results. I was nowhere near correct and I assumed he'd topped himself. Jed, however, realised almost straight away.

We had knocked back a few more beers due to the tension of the whole thing. Jed was out for the count whereas I had been quaffing back caffeinated Coke in conjunction with the beer so was feeling kinda buoyed up. I started channel surfing and was about to switch off when a face appeared on the TV and I felt myself go cold. It was some retrospective thing about a girl whose mother had supposedly killed her sister. You had a dad and his kid being interviewed and,

Jesus, it was my sister on that screen – that kid looked the goddamn spitting image of my sister, Julia. Jesus, it was uncanny. I was literally about to shake Jed awake to take a look when the next image really did take my breath away. Actually, it wasn't the image as I would never have recognised her in a million years, it was her name – See-oh-bahan O'Brien. That Julia lookalike was her goddamn daughter; Jesus, I just could not believe it. The kid must have been around eighteen and went by the name of Patsy; shit, she had named her after me. She was my first ever one-off summer romance if you can call it that. It had actually started off as a dare and a laugh then I got sort of carried away with her devotion to me. The way, however, she followed me around the camp really freaked me out. It was kinda creepy. It got to the point that wherever I went she turned up.

Jed had no idea, thank God, and still doesn't. I took one more lasting look at the kid on the television and I swore she was mine – it felt kinda weird looking at her; poor thing obviously had issues. She was cute, but way too skinny. What a blast from the past. Wow, this was so surreal; there I was on a weekend away with my partner and on the TV was a girl who was potentially my daughter. Jed has no idea whatsoever and I guess it has to stay that way. He'd be freaked; I swore I stayed celibate at camp; mind you, sleeping with See-oh-bahan made me realise how much I love Jed so good has come out of it. It is all so fricking weird. I need a beer and a cigarette.

50

MARGOT

Well, so my game is up. In some ways I am relieved; it was all getting rather tedious having to comfort and placate everyone left, right and centre. Do I have any regrets? No, not really. I guess going to California with Patsy would have been fun. I was planning to set the cat amongst the pigeons on her last day, playfully suggesting that she may for all she knew be half American. It is definitely something I would like to explore with her one day. It is only fair she knows. I mean, is it just me who has guessed the truth? Doesn't John have any suspicions? Mind you, he is pretty moronic; he probably hasn't given it a moment's thought. Matthew, bless him, will probably be ecstatic knowing that Patsy is not his full sister, after all.

It will be interesting to see how things work out going forward. Of course, I will deny everything; how can anything be proved? All the evidence from a photograph, we will see how legal aid gets around that one. Shame, prior to that everything had gone so smoothly. No doubt Frank is revelling in the fact that for once in his life he has got something right.

There's an eclectic group of people in this place. I've caught the eye of one of the prison officers. He has huge shoulders and biceps – a cover-up for certain inadequacies so I have heard. Time will tell. He is certainly nothing like my normal type but I am game for anything. One thing I do know, with the ridiculously strict regime here it's going to be *No drink, drugs and rock & roll for a while.*

51

SIOBHAN

I've been drowning in a myriad of tears; I cannot believe how powerless I have felt from the start of all this. The evening I spotted the photograph brought everything back to me, all the horrific nightmares that began when Scarlett was reported missing. I had been out the night before, felt like shit the next day and all I wanted to do was sleep. I'd got together with some guy called Dogsbreath who turned out to be a complete weirdo. I mean, who calls themselves by such a name? I was so off my head it could have been Charles; to me there was no difference. Anyway, he was weird, really bloody weird and lived up to his name. I have no idea what we got up to that night but all I know is I woke up the next morning, naked with his arm around me.

I had to get home and that's what I did although I have no recollection of how I did. As soon as I crossed the threshold I ate and then went upstairs and crashed until the afternoon. That was surreal coming downstairs to Mum getting hysterical over Scarlett's whereabouts, then me ringing round to all her friends trying to work out why she hadn't contacted us for twenty-four hours. Margot was home too. I remember looking over at her and wondering which party she had attended as she looked no better than I did. Bearing in mind what I know now, she had not long since murdered my sister; I guess that explains why she looked fucking awful.

Still suffering from my debilitating headache I decided to go and lie down on the sofa in the front room. The noise I woke up to was like a primeval scream and I hope never to hear a noise like it again. Mum was lying on the floor screaming and just adjacent to her were two very young-looking policemen. They didn't have to say a word; I just knew.

That night was horrific. Poor Dad had to go and identify Scarlett's body while the rest of us stayed at home holding a vigil. I was convinced it was mistaken identity and that she was going to walk through the door at any moment. I recall seeing Margot's grief-stricken tear-stained face and feeling empathy and a connection with her. We had both lost the most important person in our lives. If only I knew then what I know now.

Discovering that Margot had impersonated me was so devastating; worse still was the fact that my dear mother actually believed it was me. Why the hell did she take the side of Margot? My counsellor did offer an explanation and I can half believe it about Mum's sight having deteriorated and how she probably didn't realise the connotations once she had supposedly identified me in the photo. I cannot believe that I didn't notice the earrings that obviously weren't mine. I didn't even have pierced ears, for God's sake. Why the hell I didn't pick up on that is beyond me. Why didn't my mum notice it? I suppose she didn't see them, God only knows. Thank God Frank recognised the ring; if he hadn't been as observant as he was I would have been incarcerated for good. I mean, how was I going to provide an alibi who went by the name of Dogsbreath? I still to this day have no idea who he was, and what the hell I got up to that night.

The one good thing from all of this is that I am much more aware of my issues and my obvious problems at maintaining relationships. My counsellor has highlighted the fact that I develop obsessions with people I am involved with to the point that their lives must become an intrinsic part of mine. I infiltrate everything they do and feel rejected and terribly hurt if I am not included. Obviously this has stemmed from losing Scarlett; her passing has left behind huge insecurities. I am terrified this could happen to subsequent loved ones and feel a need to control the situation.

There are, of course, other issues that the counsellor has raised stemming from low self-esteem, and always feeling that Scarlett was so much better than me and that consequently my parents loved her more. I am learning about cognitive strategies to overcome my destructive thoughts which of late have been a constant presence.

I still don't know why I pushed the reunion; I think I was in total denial. The repercussions with regard to me being under a different name just didn't cross my mind. I'm in total shock that Ragi thought I was stalking him. I thought we were in a relationship so how could that be? Over time, however, I have begun to see things from his perspective and realise how I did indeed become too possessive and overbearing. I do not, however, recall the rape accusation; it was obviously shouted in a blind, illogical rage. At least now I am working through things trying to make sense of my behaviour at that time.

I can't believe I am out having been a victim of the justice system. Knowing I was innocent all along and yet being treated like a complete criminal, it was so terrifying. No one believed my story, and my friends have slipped by the wayside. John surprisingly has remained very supportive. Alice, and I can't believe I am saying this, is an absolute brick, real salt of the earth. Her support has been faultless, not only to me but also to Patsy and Matthew. The lovely thing about her is, she doesn't want to be their mother and never wants to take my place. She will, however, always be there for them no matter what. It still hurts that my children don't want to live with me but it is something I have to accept. Looking at it from a different perspective perhaps I should see it as a liberating factor now I just have to be accountable to myself and no one else. It is now all about 'me'.

It is softly, softly in my relationship with Patsy. I have been told to keep my distance whilst she is going through treatment. I can't wait for when she is well enough to take a trip to California and chill at her request. We've made some plans and the positive thing is each day she adds something else that she would like to do. Once I have been away with her I am then going to take Matthew to Kenya to witness the great wildebeest migration in the Masai Mara. He is also adding lots of things that he wants to include on our itinerary so hopefully it will turn into a trip of a lifetime for both of us.

I had one more mission left and that was to settle things between Jane and Ragi. The number of times I have reached for the phone with my rehearsed speech asking to meet up with them both. I was then going to just say 'sorry' and highlight the fact that I was totally aware my attitude and behaviour towards them have been nothing but diabolical and inexcusable. I wanted to stress my wish to put things behind us and to go forward. I would also love to say, "I think you make a wonderful couple" and to wish them both all the happiness in the world. The last bit I realise is as totally unrealistic as hell because deep down I'm as jealous as hell.

The day I was released from the mental institution, the only thing that was waiting for me on the other side was my good old car (courtesy of John), with a full tank of petrol. It made me realise how lonely my life had become. At least, however, I had the freedom now to go wherever I wanted to. The only problem was my satnav needed updating and I decided I didn't want to risk ending up in the middle of nowhere on my first night of freedom.

Waiting at the traffic lights something made me glance to the left and I couldn't believe what I saw. There, walking arm in arm, were none other than Ragi and Jane. They made a strikingly handsome, happy couple and of all the people for me to spot minutes after being released from the institution, it was crazy. They were heading towards a restaurant that had recently opened; I remembered reading about it in the local news the year before.

Perhaps this could be my chance: this was all meant to be. Parking my car I decided I would eat at the restaurant and at some stage would wander over to their table and ask for their forgiveness. Now or never I knew if I didn't seize this opportunity there would never be another one.

Thankfully I had made the effort on leaving the institution to look good and had decided to wear the outfit I'd worn to the infamous reunion. It felt so much better than the bog-standard overalls I had been wearing day in, day out. The four plastic bags would be ruining my image, but I couldn't remember which bag had my wallet and book in, so decided to take them with me.

The restaurant was one of these trendy avant-garde kind of places full of beautiful, high-profile people. I was beginning to regret my rash action, but decided to see things through. The last thing I wanted to create was more regret in my life, now I had returned to life outside. Spotting a cosy table by the window I headed towards it. Once there I realised I was literally facing Ragi and Jane. They were, however, right on the other side so there was a safe distance between us. Fortuitously they were so engrossed in conversation my presence went unnoticed. I appreciated the luxury of being able to spy on them unawares but at the same time felt a wave of envy seeing how happy and in tune they were with one another. It was all very disconcerting as I knew I would never experience such passion again. At that point I ordered a large glass of wine. If the worst came to the worst I would take a taxi home.

Quaffing my wine back more rapidly than I had intended I went through all the things I planned to say. I kept remonstrating with myself, one minute saying, "I can't do it, no I can't" then contradicting myself with, "yes, yes, I can. Let's go". With that I turned ready to stand up and face my demons. Something made me look to the right, however, and it was then I locked eyes with Jane's. The anger and hostility in her eyes were unavoidable. Knowing she was marching over with one sole reason, this being to interrogate me, I knew I had to get away. I just did not have the emotional capacity to cope with any more confrontation.

Jane had paused at this point. I stood rooted to the spot, downed my wine in a matter of seconds and felt anxiety and fear forming at the same time. Crushing the wine glass in my hand I held on to the shards whilst letting the rest fall to the ground. For what seemed like hours I felt all eyes upon me. I had to leave as quickly as possible. Grabbing my bags, aware, but totally unperturbed by the fact that I hadn't settled the bill and thinking to myself, *let me be incarcerated again, there is no way I'm remaining here*, I ran for my life through the restaurant into the outside world.

52

JANE

One afternoon Ragi and I were enjoying an al fresco dinner in a newly opened French brasserie in the centre of town, one that served the usual delicacies only associated with Gallic food, all laden with abundant amounts of garlic and seasoning, when I suddenly spotted Siobhan heading towards a table by the window to sit down. Age had not been at all kind to her and she looked dreadful. For a start her hair needed a damn good wash, it was lank, grey and screaming out for highlights. Her skin was incredibly lined and her eyes looked swollen. She really did epitomise someone who was incredibly stressed and deeply unhappy.

The four plastic bags she was carrying did nothing at all to enhance her image. In fact, they merely exacerbated her image of an old bag lady of no fixed abode. The only thing that did look incongruous was her totally inappropriate outfit for she was wearing the highest heels ever, along with an incredibly tight dress which accentuated the sort of curves that are far better left hidden.

As she walked in I mentioned to Ragi it was now or never. It was time to make amends. I wanted to put negative things behind us and reconcile our differences. Hoping she would feel the same I rose from our table and started approaching her. Aware I was taking a gamble I became more reticent the nearer I got. What if she started making accusations at me, or started crying hysterically? She certainly looked very self-conscious rubbing her hands and constantly flicking her hair almost aware she was being watched. Her demeanour slipped into a more relaxed mode when the waiter appeared at her table with a glass of wine. I continued approaching constantly ruminating on the fact that I may come to regret my impulsive act. It was at that moment a sixth sense seemed to kick in on both our parts and suddenly our eyes locked. I smiled then hesitated slightly as I noticed she had become very pale. At the same time I saw the remnants of the wine glass scattered onto the tiled floor. I was motionless, literally frozen to the spot. Grabbing her bags, Siobhan legged it out of the restaurant as quick as a flash.

I was absolutely astounded; I could not believe the way she had behaved. In some ways though I was relieved. What would I say to her after all this time? So much water had gone under the bridge it would have been very awkward. Where do you start with someone that has gone through as much as she has? I felt bad that I'd been such an appalling friend. We shared so much yet now I see her as a complete stranger. If only she had confided in me when she first saw the photo. I just can't understand why she let herself be victimised – it's all so tragic.

53

SIOBHAN

After what she had witnessed a sense of doom had permeated every pore of Siobhan's body and she had just wanted to disappear. How she made it out of the room in front of all those people including the one she had once regarded as the love of her life was beyond her. The simultaneous shattering of the glass clasped in her hand along with vertiginous heels sliding in all directions over the spilled drink hadn't helped the situation. The only assumptions people were bound to have made was that she was as pissed as a newt. Hyperventilating and retching consecutively, once in the multistorey car park, she had time to ponder the irony of the entire spectacle – for the first time in a very long time she had never felt so sober after a night out.

Fumbling for her keys Siobhan finally reached the inner sanctuary of her car, her only source of comfort being that she was now free to curl up into a totally undignified embryonic position. Ripping her glamorous and tight Ghost dress in the process she found herself rocking to and fro on the hard, plastic seats of her utterly impractical Mini. Jolted from the transitory escape she suddenly remembered her parking ticket had not been paid for. Rather than waste the time accruing more expense she unthinkingly stumbled out of the car, narrowly avoiding being hit by a departing vehicle, and staggered across the car park to the ticket machine. Given her current state of mind it was something she almost desired; obliteration from her current situation would be a welcome release.